Anna Hastings

THE STORY OF A
WASHINGTON
NEWSPAPER ~~WOMAN~~ *person!*
A.H.

a NOVEL by
ALLEN DRURY

WARNER BOOKS

A Warner Communications Company

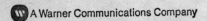

Anna Hastings

MEMO

FROM: *A.H.*

TO: *all*

Most of the characters in this novel are completely fictitious. Any resemblance to any person or persons living or dead, except where specifically noted, is entirely coincidental and probably due to the author's having lived in Washington too long.

Anna's Empire

❧ CIRCA 1977 ❧

HOW IT GREW—AND CONTINUES TO GROW

IN WASHINGTON

The Washington *Inquirer*, 1956

WAKH-FM, 1959

WAKH-TV, 1961

IN PENNSYLVANIA

The Du Bois *Journal*, 1963

IN TEXAS

The Waco *Endeavor,* 1963

The Odessa *Enterprise,* 1965

IN ILLINOIS

The Galesburg *Gazette,* 1969

IN CALIFORNIA

The *Southland Record,* 1972

NEWSMAGAZINES

Currents, 1966

Monthly Review, 1970

COLUMN

"All Things Considered,"
United Features Syndicate,
three times a week,
436 newspapers; 1954—

TELEVISION

"Weekend with Anna," NBC,

2 P.M. Sundays,

reruns 10 P.M. Sundays; 1973—

PENDING

Three more newspapers,

in Ohio, Colorado and New Hampshire

Two more television stations,

in Philadelphia and San Francisco

National Spotlight,

weekly supermarket newspaper,

acquisition to be completed this month

One

"A SOLEMN SENSE OF PROFOUND DEDICATION"

1

THE MAJOR
PUBLISHING EVENT OF THE YEAR!
AT LAST! WASHINGTON'S MOST FAMOUS
PUBLISHER TELLS HER *OWN* STORY

❀ *in* ❀

Anna Hastings

THE STORY OF A WASHINGTON
NEWSPAPERPERSON

❀ *by* ❀

ANNA HASTINGS

MAJOR ADVERTISING! MAJOR PROMO! AUTHOR APPEARANCES coast to coast! First printing 150,000! Already purchased for a major film starring Jane Fonda and Robert Redford! Major rave reviews already rolling in!

"Ms. Hastings has long been one of the two dominant duennas of the Washington newspaper world. Now she tells All as only she knows All—the story of how she came to the capital as a cub reporter for Associated Press, covered Senate, White House and Presidential campaigns, made the famous marriage that set her on the high road to one of the nation's greatest publishing empires, brought her to the pinnacle of power and influence she occupies today. Lively, filled with inside detail, sure to be one of the year's biggest. Order early and big on this one. It's going to top the list. *BOMC selection for August*."—*Publishers Weekly*

"Mrs. Hastings' story has a profound significance for our times. She is living proof that a genuine liberal who labors with true dedication and unflagging determination *can* have a major influence on American history—particularly if she owns one of the three major newspapers in Washington, five others in the hinterlands, a major television station, two influential magazines, writes a syndicated news column and hosts NBC's most popular weekend television talk-show. . . .

"There have been many analytical pieces on this extraordinary woman, but only Anna Hastings could tell her story as it should be told—placing her rightfully in the vanguard of all those gallant liberals who have brought the United States from saber-rattling immaturity to a statesmanly acceptance of its lessened position in the world. Anna Hastings has placed herself in the context of her times more skillfully than any of her critics could. It is an extraordinary self-revelation by one of history's greatest Americans."—*The New York Times*

18

"To Washington Anna Hastings came, saw, conquered. The story of how she plannde it that way
and made it all come true is one of the most intriguing inside accounts of Washington ever written.
The little Polish girl from Punxsutawney, p.a., who
rose to become one of the capital's two major publishers has a tale to tell and she tells it with great
skill and effect. If its publication is shrewdly timed
to take advantage of recent political events—and
perhaps encourage others in the future—well, that
too, is probably the way Anna Hastings planned it.
She's not a gal to trifle with, is Anna, as her
journalistic victims know. Nor is her book one to
miss. Skip it at your peril. If you do, you're apt to
find yourself skewered by Anna."—*Time*

"Anna Hastings' story spans the changing of a
nation from irresponsible reaction to responsible
liberalism, from world bully to lesser, but more
worthy, cooperator with history's inevitable tides. As
one of those most directly responsible for the change,
Anna Hastings has fought the good fight ever since
she came to Washington as a young reporter. Her
story is the story of America's coming of age, and of
how one determined woman rose to wield a major
influence upon that necessary change. That this influence has been to the country's good, from the
first day she reached the capital until the present
moment, is a truism few Americans would dare
challenge. Here is a thrilling tale that no true liberal
can afford to miss, for in Anna Hastings true liberalism has reached its apotheosis."—*Saturday Review*

"This is the story of how Little Liberal Annie
single-handedly remade a backward nation, pausing

19

along the way only long enough to pick up a millionaire husband, one of Washington's two most powerful newspapers, five more in the boondocks, two national magazines and a gaggle of television and radio stations. The tale of how innocent little Anna Kowalczek from Punxsutawney, Pa., turned into the tough wheeler-dealer who now rolls political dice with the best of them has its full share of heroes and villains—but there is, of course, only one heroine. And of course everything she thinks, does, dreams or accomplishes is always for the best in an evil world saved from the fall only by the grace of her continuing, all-knowing presence. *'E pluribus Anna!'* as Alice Roosevelt Longworth put it recently; and that is how Anna sees it too.

"It's an entertaining tale, and you might as well read it. Ms. Hastings (or somebody) has given it the full treatment, complete with muted violins and full brass choir playing softly at the foot of Mount Rushmore as preparations go forward for the unveiling of the fifth colossal head.

"There's no denying it's a good read—even if it isn't quite the way we heard it."—*The Washington Post*

And allowing for the intense feline jealousy that always colors everything Anna and the *Post*'s own glamour girl have to say about one another, that isn't quite the way I, Ed Macomb, heard it either.

But it is, of course, the way she wants you to have it: Anna has always been able to have herself presented as she wanted herself presented. And now, with the aid of dear old Bessie Rovere, who has ghostwritten a dozen inside-Washington autobiogs (*In My Lady's Chamber: A White House Maid Reveals Thirty Years of Scandal on the Second Floor . . . East Gate: A White*

20

House Cop's Memories of Six Presidents and Their Sometimes Surprising Visitors), Anna has outdone herself. Devoted Bessie waited a lifetime in Anna's shadow to do this book; it is, truly, a labor of love. But there still remain, among those of us who know her best (including Bessie), a few reservations. We were there, too, you see: and Anna can't fool us.

I remember Seab Cooley telling me once, while Anna and I were still just bright young newcomers to the Senate Press Gallery, that if you met her in the pages of a book you wouldn't believe her, because hardly anybody who knew her then could conceive that there was such a combination of intelligence, determination, ruthlessness and insatiable drive for power wrapped up in one charming, apparently innocent and naive little body.

This made me blink a little, because until the senior Senator from South Carolina put it that way (when Anna and I had been on the Hill scarcely six weeks), it had never occurred to me that she was any of those things—except, of course, charming, innocent and naive. But I decided to play it cool, with the air of knowledgeable cynicism one attempted to put on very early when the fates had tossed one, in callow youth, into one of the topmost reportorial slots in Washington.

"I don't know, Senator," I objected with all the mild ease of my newfound and earnestly developed sophistication. "It seems to me I know dozens just like her in this town."

"Well, sir," Seab said with one of his famous sleepy, sidelong glances, "well, sir, you mark my words. That little girl has more ambition in the tip of her little finger than you or I"—I already knew the old rascal well enough by then so that the start of a smile, quickly suppressed, came to my lips—"well, *you,* anyway." he amended with an amiable grin, "could ever dream of having. Mark my words, young Ed, that little lady is going to own this town someday. I don't know how she's going to do it, yet, but I haven't the slightest bit of doubt—not the *leetlest*—that she's going to do it. I only hope I live long enough to see it, because it's going to be a mighty skeerazzle. Yes, sir, a *mighty* skeerazzle!"

What a skeerazzle was, Seab never told me: it was just one of his words, but it described what happened as well as anything, I suppose. And as it turned out, of course, he did live to see her do it. In fact, he played a major and kindly hand in helping her on her way when he introduced her (at her request) to Gordon Hastings. But when Seab came to die, tragically and all alone, on the west steps of the Capitol after his futile filibuster during the debate on the war in Gorotoland, it was Anna herself who wrote the editorial that appeared in the *Inquirer* next morning:

"We cannot say we mourn, save as one mourns any moss-hung object that has been around a long time, the passing of Senator Seabright B. Cooley of South Carolina. Raised in the lingering shadow of the Civil War, enwrapped forever in a cocoon of unchanging, unyielding, self-righteous reaction, he stood foursquare for more than half a century in the path of all progress and all liberalism in these United States. Perhaps he did some few favors for his constituents and so discharged the debt he owed them for sending him here; but in a larger sense, his years in the Senate were nothing but a detriment to America and a burden upon the forward progress of the country. He will perhaps be remembered, for a little while. But he will not be missed.—A.H."

It was typical of Anna as she has become in her later years: filled with gratitude, generosity and warm, human compassion for one who had done much for her and had always regarded her with a tolerant, fatherly and protective friendliness. Some skeerazzle, all right. Old Seab knew about her in six weeks what it took some of us, and the town as a whole, a good many years to find out.

There was a beginning, of course. In the beginning was the word, and the word was

WAR! JAPS BOMB PEARL HARBOR, CRIPPLE U.S. FLEET, KILL THOUSANDS IN SNEAK DAWN ATTACK! F.D.R. TO GO BEFORE CONGRESS TODAY TO PUT COUNTRY INTO COMBAT ON SIDE OF ALLIES AGAINST AXIS! NATION AWAITS LEADER'S WORDS AS AMERICANS RALLY TO MEET GRAVEST CHALLENGE IN HISTORY!

2

*I shall never forget my introduction to Washing-
ton. To think I, Anna Kowalczek from Punxsutawney, Pennsylvania, should actually be right there,
in the Capitol of the United States, privileged to hear
our greatest President on the most momentous day
of our history! It was with a somber attention and
a solemn sense of profound dedication to my country
and my profession that I listened to the fateful words
of the man whose vivid personality and shining policies were to dominate my early days in Washington
—and to whose noble memory I hold allegiance still.*

—ANNA HASTINGS, *by Anna Hastings*

THERE BEGAN ON THAT DAY, FOR ANNA, FOR ME, FOR
Tal Farson and for a good many others with whose
lives our own would be entwined in the following
thirty-five years, the first of those top-of-the-head ac-
quaintances with the great that were to become a standard part of our reportorial existence as we peered
down upon them at joint sessions of Congress from
the all-seeing omnipotence of the House Press Gallery.

24

Over the course of three and a half decades we have, at one time or another, examined rather closely the scalps of most of the major figures of our times. Sleek or scraggly, full or sparse, clean as a hound's tooth or spraying dandruff like aging dandelions in a high wind, they have nodded, turned, bowed, ducked, reared, shaken, emphasized, admonished, encouraged or otherwise communicated their owners' attitudes to us in the private code known only to the press corps. Out front, the electronic media may have been bringing their vigorous and statesmanlike visages full-face to the voters and the world: to us, it has been scalp-talk. We have been privileged to receive their messages, as it were, from the skin out. For some reason, on December 8, 1941, this fact struck Anna, Tal and me with dignity-shattering impact; basically, I suspect, beause we were all eager newcomers to the great world of the Hill, and so brought a new and not altogether reverent point of view, even on so solemn and horrendous an occasion.

"But he has *dandruff!*" a feminine voice exclaimed in a piercing, gurgling, helplessly amused whisper just as, below us, there came the unforgettable words in the unforgettable voice: *"Yesterday, December 7, 1941—a date which will live in infamy—"*

Someone else—I believe dear old May Craig of the Portland, Maine, *Press-Herald*, bless her heart—whispered severly, *"Hush!"*

But to three newcomers standing jammed together side by side behind our awesome seniors who were writing the story, it was impossible to be solemn once we had begun to giggle: we were all too nervous, and it was all too exciting, and we were all too young.

Young, and in the press, and in Washington in the war years! Was there ever such a bright and shining world? And will we ever again know anything like it?

Of course not, still dazzling, ruthless Anna! Of course not, still ruthless, clever Tal! Of course not, still plodding, dependable Ed! Of course not, dear fat loyal Bess! Those were the great days for us, and nothing since has ever matched, or ever can, being young, in the press, in Washington in the years of war . . . as nothing can ever match those times for you again either, America. You, too, still had a certain innocence then, and you, too, lost it forever in those hectic, heroic, so-soon-betrayed and forgotten years of anguish, victory and triumph, when giants strode the earth and everything was ten feet tall.

At the moment Anna made her irrepressible comment, hardly anyone in the press corps knew who we were, nor did we, in fact, know one another. Within a week all this was remedied forever. We were three greenhorns who had been sent up from the bureaus downtown to assist the Hill staffs by running their hastily scribbled copy up the stairs to the wire service booths for teletype transmission: Anna for the AP, I for United Press and Talbot Farson for what then was the old Hearst International News Service, before it was purchased and absorbed in postwar years by what now is UPI. It was all supposed to be strictly temporary, for this one dramatic day only. None of us knew when we would get back to the Hill; we all expected to be assigned to one of the departmental rabbit warrens downtown and never be heard from again. As it happened we all lucked out and stayed on all through the war and well beyond. Three happier kids never existed when we discovered our good fortune.

In Tal's case and mine this came about in part because he had suffered a broken back in an auto accident in college and I had contracted polio at the age of seven. His weak back and my gimpy right leg made us unacceptable for service, even though we tried with desperate sincerity—or I did, anyway—to enlist. The voluntary and involuntary decimation of the male members of the press corps that occurred immediately after Pearl Harbor gave us our opportunity to fill in. With extraordinary luck we filled in and we stayed.

Anna's good fortune was of a slightly different nature. Quite characteristically, she created her own.

After her irreverent whisper and May Craig's stern "*Hush!*" we did manage to settle down, aided by the glares of our elders on all sides. F.D.R. reached his peroration, Congress roared approval and swiftly passed the declaration of war: Anna, Tal and I kept running copy up and down those damned stairs until we thought our legs would fall off. Somewhere along the way we took time to introduce ourselves: Tal, with his shrewd, narrow-eyed glance and half-drawled "I'm Tal Farson," I with a hasty "Hi, I'm Ed Macomb"; and Anna, of course, with the full treatment, which included a full stop square in the path of both of us as we started back into the gallery to get more copy; a swift but completely appraising glance (I think she knew then exactly where each of us would be in her life twenty years later, though that may be hindsight and too much bemusement with the Legend of Anna); a sunny smile and a happy "Hello, I'm Anna Kowalczek—Koh-*vall*-check. Isn't this *fun?*"

"It's damned hard work," I said shortly and started to push on by—not impolitely, but I was aware of Greg on the teletype behind me shouting, "Damn it, go get me some more copy!"

Tal's response was more of a match for Anna.

"Now exactly why," he inquired coolly, "do you apply to this sensational example of the complete collapse of capitalist assumptions the word 'fun'?"

"Huh?" I said blankly, intrigued enough to ignore

Greg on the teletype and pause for a real look at this unexpectedly surprising contemporary of mine.

Anna was taking a real look at him, too, and I think for a moment she was really flustered. It was the last time, however: everybody was allowed one chance to startle Anna, and after that it was her ball game. This was Tal's chance—until much later on, when he *really* had the chance. And then he didn't take it, and Anna was as neatly caught as though he had.

She gave in this time, too, for just a second.

"Why—" she said, flustered, "why, it just *is*. I think it's the most exciting thing that's ever happened to *me* —even though I suppose you, Mr. Farson, see wars started every day."

"Tal will do," he said dryly. "It isn't the last I expect to see started in my lifetime by this f— this country, though maybe you're right, it probably *is* the biggest. I suppose *I* should find it *fun,* too."

"Find it what you like," she retorted tartly, poise recovered. "It's history and I think we're damned lucky to be seeing it made, close up. And I *am* enjoying it."

"People do enjoy wars," he said gloomily. "That's the whole damned trouble."

"If you'll excuse me," she said firmly, "I have to get back to work."

And she turned her back and went briskly off to the AP booth with her copy, delivered it and then swung past us on her way back to the gallery with another sunny, and quite impersonal, smile for Tal and a "How about grabbing some coffee or something downstairs in the restaurant later on when we get free?" for me.

"Sure," I said. "See you."

"Typical of her type and class," Tal said calmly as she disappeared through the swinging glass doors into the gallery and we heard a rush of applause from Congress as our leader hurled yet another rhetorical defiance at the enemy. "But she'll go places here. That kind always does." (This was six weeks before Seab's comment: Tal was prescient.)

I was tempted to ask him where all this wisdom came from at what I guessed to be, from my own age, about twenty-two, but this was not the place to go into backgrounds: we knew we would have plenty of opportunity for that later.

"I've got to get back to work, too," I said. "I'll see you around."

"No doubt," he said. "Watch out for Boadicea the Warrior Queen. She bites."

"Not me, I hope," I said with a smile.

"Not me either," he said, rather more grimly than necessary, I thought; and then his teletype man shouted, and Greg shouted, and we both had to get back to work.

Later on, after the President had finished and returned to the White House, after the war resolution had passed both houses and things were beginning to simmer down a little, I found myself standing for a moment along the wall at the top level of the Senate gallery, looking down into the dimly lighted, historic brown-walled chamber where many members still milled about excitedly talking to one another. It had been a fantastic day: fantastic for everybody, but for none more than a twenty-two-year-old from Kansas who was just as thrilled as Anna Kowalczek at being where he was at such a moment. I was so absorbed in my recapitulations of it, in fact, that I wasn't aware until he spoke that Tal had come in and was standing alongside.

"Look at that," he said disgustedly. "Just look at it! Didn't I tell you?"

"What?" I asked again, I'm afraid a little blankly. "They just seem to be standing about talking—"

"Her," he said. *"Her."*

"Oh," I said. "Anna."

"Yes, *Anna.*"

And it was true, now that he mentioned it and I came out of my historical haze and studied it a bit: he perhaps had a point. Down at the front row of seats, just above the clock, where the top writers of the wire services sat, Anna was deep in earnest conversation with the head of the AP Senate staff. Her body was pressed tightly against his shoulder, her face was very close to his, in her eyes was an expression of deep respect, profound attention and unwavering admiration. He was only human and all this was having its effect: he appeared to be almost visibly wriggling, though I am sure that through an enormous exercise of willpower he was not.

"You and I can't do that sort of thing," Tal said morosely. "Our tits aren't big enough. You mark what I said: our little lady will go far."

"Oh, well," I said, rather lamely. "She seems to be a good gal."

"Oh, yeah?" he said. "Better come have coffee with me, buster. You won't be having any with her."

In which dour prediction he was, of course, entirely right.

3

I very soon became aware that this was definitely a man's world; although it seemed to me that with a little care and forethought I might make my way successfully in it.

—ANNA HASTINGS, *by Anna Hastings*

I WILL SAY FOR ANNA, THOUGH, THAT SHE WAS FAR too smart to confine her coffee breaks to top brass only; or her favors either. The latter, in fact, I know she did not confer until that famous night with me on the beach at Ocracoke two years later. But she got a lot of mileage out of the potential. Grown men, from bureau chiefs and columnists to United States Senators and top-ranking members of the House (Anna maintained her standards and aimed high in every case), were known to quiver visibly at her approach, and on many a morning she could be seen in the cafeteria of the Old —in those pre-empire-building days, the only—Senate Office Building, holding court at breakfast surrounded by an attentive group whose members on frequent occasions ranged from Tal and me right on up to such people as Arthur Vandenberg, Bob Taft, Orrin Knox, Seab Cooley and Bob Munson. Senators in those more leisurely times—which were hectic with war but in a curious way more leisurely than they have ever been since—enjoyed taking a little time with the press over breakfast. Many and many a story germinated in the casual discussions we had then: it was all part of the intimate working relationship we had with them before they acquired so many office buildings and began to disappear behind barricades of ever-growing staffs and ever-burgeoning, computerized government. It was fun then; and within six weeks—about the time Seab made his comment and so joined Tal in the Early Warning System about Anna—she had become a regular morning fixture in the cafeteria.

She rapidly became a fixture over in the Senate Press Gallery, too, and frequently she could be seen having coffee with the teletype operators and the gallery staff, chatting away as intently and intimately with them as she ever did with the Senators—which made sense because some of them knew just as much as some of Our Great Statesmen, and some of them knew considerably more. But that wasn't her only reason, of course. To this day she is apt to say proudly, "But, darlings"—the "darlings," the four-letter words and all the other phony crap in her conversation came later: in those days Anna was pretty direct and straightforward—"But, darlings, *I'm* a working stiff, too." Even as a cub reporter, I think, she was looking ahead. She always cultivated the working stiffs as assiduously as she did the big names—which, I've always felt, explained why she was able to bring the *Inquirer* safely through without the labor troubles that racked and almost wrecked the *Post* in the very hour of its greatest triumph.

So within six weeks little Anna Kowalczek from

Punxsutawney, Pa., had already cut a pretty wide swath on Capitol Hill; and in our more modest ways Tal and I had managed to become part of the legislative landscape, too. In Anna's case it wasn't just all curves and cuddles that did it, any more than it was just alert and reasonably appealing personalities that did it for Tal and me. All of us had considerable ability, none more so than Anna. One of her strengths with a certain type of colleague and a certain type of legislator was their inability to separate the well-stacked, always smiling and seemingly always carefree little blonde from the diligence, ambition, ability and calculating ice-cold intelligence underneath. When the chips were down—when it really counted—on the bottom line, as we didn't say in those days but everybody says now —Anna produced and she produced very well. She was a damned good reporter, a quick and facile writer, a constant generator of story ideas and angles. She worked—hard—and it didn't take long for her colleagues on the Hill and her bosses downtown to realize that in Anna Kowalczek they had a prize worth keeping and encouraging.

In similar fashion, although not so flashily—because, as Tal had put it with sour accuracy, our tits weren't big enough to secure for us the automatic lie-down-and-roll-over response Anna and a few others of her feminine colleagues could produce in their news sources —we managed, too. It was an ideal blending of time, place, opportunity and talent for us all. The little Polish girl who had worked on the high-school paper in Punxsutawney, risen to become associate editor of the daily at the University of Pennsylvania, and then spent a year covering the statehouse in Harrisburg for the Philadelphia *Inquirer* before deciding to try her luck in Washington . . . the idealistic kid from Kansas who had followed much the same pattern, encouraged

33

by a father who had been a one-term governor of the state in pre-Depression days and a mother who was active in every conceivable women's organization she could get into, and she got into them all . . . the dry philosopher from Providence, Rhode Island, who had edited the Harvard *Crimson* and graduated magna cum laude before deciding that for him, too, Washington was the ideal place in which to pursue those goals whose true nature to this day is known only to himself, though suspected (but never proven) by many . . . for us three the world had been suddenly and unexpectedly delivered on our doorsteps, tied up in a great big golden bow.

"You went out to that Press Gallery for the first time like a honeymooner going to his bride," Greg the teletypist told me years later; and so, in fact, did we all. A great war raged, our civilization literally hung in the balance, millions died; yet because Tal and I had the bad fortune to have the good fortune to be partially crippled, and because Anna was a woman, none of us had to go. We could stay home and Fill the Gap; and while our initial assignments were all lucky flukes, we were all fiercely determined to hang onto what the fates had given us and fortunately we all had the ability to do so.

It wasn't very long after Pearl Harbor, in fact, that we began to slide into that easy pattern of working together that soon made us a familiar sight around the Hill. "Well," Bob Taft remarked when he stepped into the Senators' private elevator one day and found us using it, as was possible in those easygoing days, "here come the Three Horsemen, I see."

"Two horsemen and a horse-lady, Senator," Tal said.

Taft gave his quick, shy smile and looked us over

34

with those prominent, intelligent eyes that missed so little.

"No, I think I'd still say three horse*men*," he said as we reached the third floor and he stepped out. "I'll bet Anna's a better man than both of you."

"Prettier, anyway," I offered as a parting shot, and he uttered his quick, snorting little laugh.

"And tougher," he tossed over his shoulder. "Forget it at your peril!"

"Well," Tal said rather starchily as the door closed and we went on up to four, where we hoped to find Orrin Knox in so we could get a few quotes from him on the Office of Price Administration, "I guess that tells you and me, Ed."

"I think he's entirely right," Anna said with a chuckle. "Keep your eyes on me, fellows, or I'll zing you good!"

"Everybody keeps his eyes on you," I said.

"How can they help themselves?" Tal inquired.

"You may accompany me while I talk to Senators today," Anna said serenely as we walked together down those endless marble corridors that still form in memory the setting and the framework of our youth. "If you listen closely while they respond to my questions, you may even wind up with a good story or two yourselves."

"Well, la-*de*-da," Tal said. "Listen to our lady friend."

"Do!" she said, with a little skip and a hop and the charming gurgle of laughter she can still produce on occasion even now, in these older, harsher times. "Maybe you'll learn something."

"Maybe we will," I agreed amiably to forestall Tal, who really for a second looked genuinely, startlingly, angry. "I'm willing, *aren't* we, Tal?"

"Speak for yourself," he said shortly. "I have work to do."

"Very well," Anna said coldly. "Shove off and go see somebody else, if you want to. We don't *always* have to go out digging for overnighters together."

"Oh, yes, we do," he snapped. "Otherwise you'd scoop our asses off."

"All right, then. Shut up and come on."

It was not, perhaps, surprising that Orrin Knox should have cast an obviously startled glance at our three rather stormy faces when we presently got in to see him. Nor was it surprising that Anna should have been the first of us to get a raise, which she announced triumphantly six months later, inviting us "and some other friends" to her apartment on R Street in Georgetown to help her celebrate.

4

It was not long before I found myself beginning to be included in the intellectual life—the real inner life—of Washington. This came about almost without conscious volition on my part, and I can only think, looking back fondly on those early, struggling years, that there must have been something in me that appealed, even then, to the movers and the shakers of our world.

—ANNA HASTINGS, *by Anna Hastings*

HOW OFTEN AND HOW FONDLY DO I TOO LOOK BACK upon those endless discussions of politics, the war, humanity, the world, sex, morals, God, the Devil, art, music, literature and The Whole Damned Schmeer that took place on R Street in the days of our youth. They take place still at Anna's, though the twenty-two-room house at the end of Prospect Street is infinitely grander than the basement studio room she shared with Bessie Rovere when we all first came to Washington. But the Georgetown ambience, though narrowed now pretty much to a single topic, is still there—the intense preoccupation with politics and with self, the passionate, inward-turning, never-ending examination of personalities, potentials, possibilities, impossibilities, past achievements or failures, future prospects or lack of them, the eternal who-does-what-to-whom-and-why that sooner or later polarizes all conversations in this greatest of all company towns, where anybody who *is* anybody, as Anna puts it now, is involved in one way or another with government.

Considerably less innocently than her book would have you believe, she got involved almost from the start in this world in which she was ultimately to rise so high. That first party was the beginning, and as the evening went on I could tell from her pleased and excited expression that she considered herself well and truly launched. And so she was: and though Tal's reaction was characteristically sour, I couldn't help but admire her genuinely for it—because all by herself little Anna Kowalczek from Punxsutawney, Pa., had grabbed the brass ring on the Washington merry-go-round. Nobody helped her, nobody among her contemporaries equaled her—none of the rest of us, at that early point in our careers, would have had the nerve. She did it all herself. Over the years I have faulted Anna for a lot of things, and usually she has deserved it, in my judgment; but I couldn't fault her for that night, because she knew exactly what she wanted, she made her plans, she went after it, and she got it, never thereafter to be shaken loose from the claim she established then to being one of the town's true insiders. She became so simply by deciding that she was going to be, and going after it. It had no doubt been done before our time, and certainly it's been done since, but rarely with the gumption, the tenacity—and, yes, the style—of Anna.

She had set the party for eight—"*Lots* of hors

d'oeuvres and wine but B.Y.O.B. if you want heavier stuff, because we're all Young and Struggling," she scribbled at the bottom of the cards she sent out—and asked me and Tal to come around at six-thirty to have a bite with her and Bessie and help with the final arrangements. This was a basement apartment, mind you, and this was getting into June, and in those days air conditioning was not the standard equipment at our then economic level (very modest) it is in Washington now.

"Thank God you asked us to bring our electric fans," Tal said, unceremoniously dumping on one of the twin studio couches the two we had in the dingy apartment we had drifted into sharing on the fringes of a black neighborhood a few blocks southwest of the Capitol. "This place is an absolute hellhole."

"Well, find an outlet and plug them in and do something about it," Anna suggested. "Don't just stand there. Our old broken-down machine needs all the help it can get."

"O.K.," he said, not too graciously, peering about. "Bessie, where do you want these things?"

"Now, Tal," Bessie said sweetly, "you just look and you'll find a place. You're a big, strong man and you have lots and lots of brains, so Anna tells me, and I just know you can do it."

"Damn!" he said, beginning to thaw a little under Bessie's charm, as everybody did in those days when she, too, had just come from Punxsutawney to be a researcher for *Time* and was almost two hundred pounds lighter than she is now, poor gal. "I knew you'd put me to work."

"You're going to get fed for it," Anna said, going over to the tiny stove and turning on the gas under a pot of stew. "Ed, take your coat off. I don't know where we're going to put everything, but we can't be formal in this heat."

"How many have you got coming?" I asked.

"Twenty-two."

"Twenyt-*two!*" Tal exclaimed. "My God, this really *is* going to be the Black Hole of Calcutta."

"Well, then, we'll just have to leave your body on the sidewalk for the jackals to clean up in the morning," she said calmly. "Ed won't mind it, will you, Ed, particularly with all these Senators?"

"What Senators?" I asked. "Now, don't tell me you've invited *Senators,* Anna!"

"Sure. Why not?"

"Well—"

"She's wonderful," Bessie said in the reverent tone she often used when she spoke about her roommate. "Nobody else but Anna would have the nerve."

"That's for sure," I agreed. "I suppose you've invited Taft and Vandenberg and Bob Munson and Seab Cooley—"

"And Orrin Knox," Anna said complacently, "and Dick Russell and Alben Barkley. I thought that would be enough for the first time."

"How many have accepted?" Tal demanded.

"All of them," she said, ignoring our exclamations of disbelief. "I don't think they'll stay too long, because I told them it would be just us newcomers in the press, but they've all said they'd drop in for a while, anyway. I found out that Mrs. Taft, Mrs. Vandenberg and Beth Knox are all out of town, and you know Mrs. Barkley and Mrs. Munson are ill, and Dick Russell and Seab Cooley are bachelors, so we won't have any problem with any of their women. I think they may stay quite a while, in fact."

"Anna," Tal said, "you are the Goddamnedest—"

"Eat your stew," she said, "and relax while I show you how it's done In Your Nation's Capital."

And she did, too. They all came, together with a lot of us press newcomers, people like Liz Carpenter and Helen Thomas and Charlie McCabe and others who were later to go on and make their own big names for themselves as the decades passed; and we really had one whale of a time. The fans roared, the wine flowed, coats and ties were abandoned and enough people had brought their own bottles to add a considerable joviality to the proceedings. And the Senators, to the awed amazement of the rest of us, really enjoyed themselves and stayed on until the party ended, at almost 1 A.M.

I learned a lot about Anna that night, but I also learned a lot about Senators and other top people in government: the bigger they are, usually, the nicer they are, and the easier they are to approach. They were so used to diplomatic receptions and cocktail parties and formal dinners, and so tired of them, that Anna's invitation must have seemed like a fresh breeze to them. They obviously got a kick out of her audacity, and they obviously got a kick out of the rest of us: they enjoyed being with all these lively kids: it was a real break in the routine. "After all," Tal remarked later, "today's cub reporter may be tomorrow's Walter Lippmann." But I really think it was more than that—they genuinely liked us. And more important from her standpoint, they genuinely liked, were amused, intrigued and, in an age-old way involving older men and bright young girls, flattered by Anna. To think that she would have the nerve to invite them! To think that *she* would *want* to invite *them!* Yes, Anna was on her way.

So we had a great time. I imagine there wasn't a political or human subject (there sometimes is a difference) that we didn't cover that night, and with the

41

understanding that it was all off the record (though we might come around next day and try to confirm a few things, if we'd like, and they'd see how they felt about it then) the Senators held us enthralled with their inside gossip of the White House and the Hill. They had a genuinely enjoyable and relaxing time, good for the souls and great for the egos; and we were absolutely bedazzled by them. It was a fair exchange all around, and out of it grew not only the succession of such parties that Anna gave from then on, but genuine friendships between her guests and many of us that lasted a lifetime.

Only one thing marred it, and that, too, was a portent as significant as Anna's own triumph, though we didn't know it then. To Anna, Bessie and me it was just an embarrassment: it was what we had already come to refer to among ourselves as "Tal doing it again." But it caused a certain speculative gleam in Senatorial eyes, and it made many of the rest of us uneasy. Fortunately it was over in a couple of minutes; but there were some, as developed years later when the trouble came, who did not forget.

Somehow we had gotten onto the subject of the general superiority of the American system, which the Senators, naturally enough, were defending with a complacent certainty. Many of us, though sharply skeptical of a good many things, agreed that the ultimate judgment had to come down on the side of the basic worth and good-heartedness of the American way of doing things. Nobody was pulling any punches, it was not a one-sided discussion by any means, many of us had strongly held opinions and our guests encouraged us amicably to express them: they assured us we were off the record, too. We were all enjoying it when Tal suddenly rounded on Alben Barkley and demanded, "Senator, I suppose you defend the Scotts-boro case, too, don't you?"

"About the way you defend the Hitler-Stalin pact!" Bob Taft snapped before his easygoing colleague from Kentucky could recover from his surprise and respond.

"I do defend it," Tal said, raising his hand as a general protest began to rise around the room, *"in the context of Soviet self-interest at that time.* Isn't that how all nations, including the United States, defend their evil actions?"

"You're making quite an assumption, boy," Senator Barkley said. "Who said the United States was guilty of evil actions?"

"History," Tal said defiantly, looking really angry. "That's who, Senator."

"Well," Anna said with a firmness that made me think suddenly that her little Polish mother back in Punxsutawney must be quite a tough lady, "that's enough of *that,* Tal. Nobody's saying the United States is perfect, are we, Senator?"

"Certainly not," Alben Barkley agreed, willing to be amiable and forget it. "But we aren't evil either, young man, so don't you go around saying we are. That way we'll all remain friends. Right?"

"Possibly," Tal said coolly.

"I hope so," Senator Barkley said comfortably. "Come around and see me in my office sometime and we'll thrash it out until we're both blue in the face. All right?"

"I'll see," Tal said, still coolly.

"And don't take yourself so seriously," the Senator suggested. "You remind me of an old preacher in my hometown—" and he was off into one of those stories that always used to break us up when he held his regular press conference at his Senate desk, just before the sessions began.

He broke us up this time, too, even though there was a certain anxious note in the laughter of a good many of us, and even though Tal, while he laughed too, managed to make himself sound more than a little grudging and ungenerous.

Later when everybody had left and only the four of us remained to do the final clean-up, Anna said evenly, "Talbot Farson, if you ever again are so discourteous to a guest under my roof, you yourself will not be invited under it again."

"Well, I hate this damned hypocrisy!" he said angrily. "Here we are, the gre-e-e-e-at Yew-nited States, and look at all we've done!"

"Yes," Bessie Rovere said calmly, "look at all we've done, and I for one am damned proud of it. What are you, some Communist or something?"

"Oh, hell!" Tal said furiously. "Oh, *hell!*" And reaching down, he yanked out our two fans and turned on me to demand, "Are you ready to go home?"

"Sure," I said. "If you're quite sure the exhibition is over."

"And don't *you* get smart either!"

"No, Tal," I said with a patience I knew would infuriate him. "Yes, Tal. No, Tal. Whatever you say, Tal." He didn't scare me then and never has, even though in the long run he wound up where I would like to be and even though he has forced the world, with the world's supine connivance, to agree to let him live his life.

"And to insult the Majority Leader of the United States Senate to boot," Anna remarked as she handed him his coat and opened the door upon the steamy night. "What kind of a reporter are you, anyway? You're crazy."

"Pious old fool," he said. "He'll keep right on being a good pal, that's all he knows how to be. Maybe I might write something critical of him someday if he didn't. They're all paper bags if you punch them hard enough."

"I wonder where you're going to end up," Anna said with a certain tired air as he stalked out. None of us could have dreamed the answer, though possibly, even then, she had an idea.

5

The war years sped by as in a furiously busy, highly dramatic, ever-fascinating dream. My colleagues and I worked long and hard. The pageant of the great passed before us in the committees of Congress: the agonies of a world in torment were with us constantly. Gone and forgotten now are many of the stories we wrote then, but I can never forget the enterprise and energy that went into our efforts in getting them. We were maturing fast: we were becoming skilled, knowledgeable, experienced newspaperwomen and newspapermen. In the friendly but always fiercely competitive challenge of our rivalry I found that I could hold my own with the best of them; and three at least of them became my closest friends and confidants. This augured well for future plans and responsibilities.

—ANNA HASTINGS, *by Anna Hastings*

"THE PAGEANT OF THE GREAT" (TO ECHO BESSIE'S rather flamboyant phrase as polished by Anna) did indeed pass before us: Barney Baruch, that stately, white-haired, self-appointed "adviser to Presidents," who descended from his self-created Olympus occasionally to share with us the ideas he presumably murmured into grateful Presidential ears every hour on the hour . . . Chester Bowles, head of the Office of Price Administration, his pleasantly lopsided smile never wavering as he calmly withstood the indignant onslaughts of Bob Taft and Orrin Knox . . . John L. Lewis of the United Mine Workers, growling from beneath his bushy brows as he defied the government and heaped his deliciously convoluted insults upon all who dared challenge him . . . General of the Armies George C. Marshall, Chief of Staff, so incisive, softspoken, competent and cold that one had to conclude that he was the great man successive Presidents believed him to be . . . Donald M. Nelson, tall, dumpy, firm, purse-lipped, humorless head of the War Production Board, as competent in his way, and as controversial, as General Marshall . . . Secretary of the Interior Harold L. Ickes, peppery and belligerent, selflessly devoted to serving the country and fiercely dedevoted to doing it in his own way . . . Henry Wallace, odd and nervous, giggling his way strangely through the years, for a time one worrisome heartbeat away from the Presidency . . . the dominant personalities of the Congress (much more fascinating and more dominant than today's TV Tots, we oldtimers sourly think), fiercely engaged in the great legislative battles of the war years—price controls, aid to allies, the soldier-vote bill, the work-or-fight bill . . . and over all, in the White House, where we were occasionally allowed by our elders on the White House beat to attend his press conferences, the shining, elusive, quicksilver President whom everybody worshiped or hated, who baffled everyone, whom nobody knew.

The war years spun themselves out, victory came,

the quicksilver President, who had been disintegrating for years before our eyes only none of us could believe it, perished in Warm Springs, Georgia. Feisty little Harry Truman, whom we all knew well and had grown very fond of as he briskly conducted his investigations of wartime graft and corruption as Senator from Missouri, succeeded to the Oval Office. The postwar years of international bickering, discontent, Cold War began, accompanied by the hasty dismantling by the United States of history's greatest war machine (until now), the deliberate Soviet sabotage of the great alliance and the cold-blooded launching of the new Soviet imperialism. On the Hill, Anna, Tal and I and our generation of reporters, seasoned veterans by now, recorded it day by day. Uneasiness about Communist intentions gripped the land, Alger Hiss and Whittaker Chambers faced one another across the hearing room of the House Committee on Un-American Activities; a generation turned on the fulcrum of their embittered confrontation. Richard Nixon and Joe McCarthy made their charges and took their political profit from a situation with just enough supporting fact to make their efforts plausible. Anna, Tal and I moved closer to the center of things; the future gave its hints and retreated again into mystery. Our lives worked steadily closer to the pattern in which we would all presently find ourselves entrapped.

In our personal lives we had become entrapped long since, which I suppose was inevitable given youth, propinquity and the sort of in-each-other's-hip-pockets professional relationship we had. Both my easygoing reliability and Tal's abrasive personality appealed to Anna: it was inevitable that she should sooner or later decide to sample them both. It was quite characteristic, however, that it should be at a time of her own choosing; and equally characteristic that, much to Tal's annoyance, she should deliberately decide to sample me first.

I took this seriously at the time, and I think Tal did, too. In fact, I think we still do, despite the evidence of three decades that Anna, as always, follows her own purpose and has little use for those of others.

For me the great experience occurred three years after we came to the Senate. Always accompanied by faithful Bessie, who by then was slowly beginning to add the inexorable pounds she was never to lose, for psychological and emotional reasons we did not suspect (or at least Tal and I did not suspect) in those less-conscious-of-everything times, we had begun to drift into the favorite Washington custom of getting away to the Atlantic beaches as often as possible on summer weekends. Sometimes it was Rehoboth or Bethany in Maryland, sometimes Virginia Beach, sometimes as far down as Nags Head in North Carolina. The last was our favorite, being then, and still, the least developed, the least overrun, the most wild and open.

I suppose we had been to Nags Head half a dozen times in my old secondhand Chevy when our third summer rolled around. By then, of course, Anna wasn't the only one to have received raises (though she still led us all, triumphantly, by fifteen dollars, which was a pretty good lead as wire-service reporters were paid in those days), and so it was decided that we would try to rent a cottage together. We passed the word in the offices of the two North Carolina Senators, and Bessie volunteered to contact the North Carolina delegation in the House. Within two days we had three good leads at specially cut-rate prices. In a minor way this was typical of the way members of the Washington media take advantage of their contacts. There is much high-and-mighty moralizing, particularly in these later, Watergate-shadowed years, about the need for everybody to eschew the fruitful contact, the helping hand, the I-can-get-it-for-you-wholesale relationship. There is a stern demand that public servants rise above all that sort of thing: by clear implication, the press *does*. Many of its members do not, but since they control the means of exposure and are fiercely determined never to expose themselves, the sweet winds of moral purity continue to blow benignly over all who write or broadcast the news.

(I used to protest about this a bit on the *Inquirer* in Watergate days, without avail. Much was being made of the income-tax advantages claimed by Presidents and others. Both Anna and her counterpart on the *Post* have extremely expensive stables of lawyers and accountants who secure for them every legal tax advantage that can possibly be found. The fact is never mentioned. A dark and sinister air is uniformly imparted in both their publications to any public servant who does likewise.)

So we got our cottage at Nags Head, a very modest, quite remote little shack down toward Ocracoke on a nearly deserted stretch of beach: isolation did not carry the potentials of sudden death and destruction from outside that it unhappily does now. There we settled in for the summer, planning to go down at least every other weekend, with longer breaks over Memorial Day, the Fourth of July and Labor Day. The place had two bedrooms, each with two rickety single beds; a tiny kitchen; a big living-dining room and a comfortable sagging old porch looking out to sea, which was about three hundred feet away. The dunes were beautiful, the ocean, with caution which we all were careful to exercise, swimmable for a few feet out; the pace of days was lazy and relaxing. The girls fixed the meals, Tal and I made the drinks and did the general sweeping up. We took plenty of books, plenty of hikes, argued politics and people all the time we weren't exercising or sunbathing. It was all very pleasant and, though this was our third summer together and more privacy than we had ever had before, very innocent until Anna decided that this nonsense had gone on long enough.

It happened after dinner one night of unusual warmth. Nags Head usually cools a bit at sundown when the sea winds rise, but this was in August in the dead of summer and nothing stirred. After consuming a couple of drinks apiece, steaks, salad, ice cream (Bessie as usual coming back for seconds) and some sort of all-purpose, poor reporters' dago red, we were sitting on the porch, drowsily contemplating the steady crash of the waves out in the soft illumination cast by a quarter-moon.

Suddenly Anna stood up.

"I'm going for a walk. Ed, why don't you come with me?"

"Must I?" I asked with a yawn. "I don't think I can budge."

"It will be good for you," she said firmly. "Come on."

"Can't we all go?" Bessie inquired with the anxious note that always came into her voice when Anna seemed about to do something without her.

"I asked Ed," Anna said bluntly.

"Well, you just take Ed and you just do it," Tal said dryly. "Bess and I will stay here and make mad love, won't we, Bess?"

"Well—" Bessie said with a nervous little laugh.

"If you're worried about him," Anna said with equal dryness, "we'll stay and chaperone you, Bessie."

"Well—" she said again. "N-o-o-o . . ."

"Don't worry," Tal said. "I'm impotent, and anyway I've only got one—it's a sad story, having to do

51

with horse racing, the country-club set and too much snipe-shooting in my early youth. Nothing to worry about, Bessie, I assure you. Let them go."

"As his roommate," I said, "I *know* that isn't true. However, we will stay, Bess, if you like. Personally, I'd rather."

"For heaven's *sake*," Anna said sharply, "are you coming, or aren't you? Do I have to walk by myself?"

"Take Tal," I suggested.

"Tal won't go," he said, and "I don't *want* Tal," she said simultaneously.

"All right," I said with a heavy sigh. "Give me a hand out of this damned dilapidated rocker and I'll go with you."

This she did, her grasp, as always, firm and strong as a man's, and presently we found ourselves slogging out along the shore (slowed a bit by my limp), the cottage, the only point of light visible along our section of beach, gradually dwindling to a pinpoint behind us.

When it was almost out of sight, Anna stopped and announced, "I don't like to get *too* far out of sight of home. I don't think they can see us or hear us out here, especially if we go into the dunes."

"Oh?" I said, things quickening a bit as there began to dawn a thought I had often had but put sternly aside as not fitting into Anna's plans at all. (Even then, my own plans were dutifully subservient, which was not a conscious decision but just seemed to grow naturally out of her dominant position in our little group.)

"Yes," she said. "Come on." And taking my hand for the first time (she had rejected it a few moments before, and indeed on many occasions before that), she led me away from the shore and into the dunes.

"Sit down," she ordered when we had gained the top of one of them.

"O.K.," I said, beginning to feel ready for anything. "Now what?"

"Now what *what?*" she demanded, giving me a sidelong glance, her expression inscrutable in the gentle moonlight.

"Well," I said, "did we come out here to talk riddles?"

"You know," she said, ignoring this and staring moodily out to sea, "I'm beginning to get worried about Bessie. I think I'm going to have to find another apartment. I think she's in love with me."

"Oh?" I said blankly, because the thought had honestly never crossed my mind, nor, to judge from our frequent conversations about them, had it ever crossed Tal's.

"Yes," she said seriously, "I think so."

"Do you think Tal is in love with you?" I asked, deliberately letting my skepticism and amusement show.

"I don't know," she said, perfectly seriously. "Is he in love with you? Or you with him?"

"Anna," I said, "for *Christ's* sake, what are you talking about?"

"Are you in love with me?" she asked, turning to face me.

"Well," I said slowly, "I don't quite kn—"

"Let's find out," she said, briskly beginning to unbutton my jeans, which at that point were filled with a certain stop-and-start confusion by this strange hop-skip-and-a-jump conversation.

However, the confusion resolved itself very swiftly as I cooperated in shucking off the jeans and then helped her yank her dress over her head. She was wearing nothing underneath, nor was I, which simplified matters a bit.

The next few minutes were quite busy, and I for one was quite lost in the happy turmoil of it all—until

I realized that Anna, while writhing at the right moments and groaning at the right moments, was somewhere else, probably standing on the neighboring sand dune watching us with a cool and contemplative eye. Later it occurred to me that there had probably even been a date ringed on the calendar—"Do it with Ed"— and a whole little appendix of interlocking plans and preparations, instructions-to-self-on-how-to-act, when-to-squeal, when-to-gasp, when-to-clench-teeth-and-heave-tummy, and so on.

At the moment, of course—though for a split second, as I sensed her basic detachment, it almost stopped me in midcontortion—I swiftly forgot it and let myself be consumed by everything I was feeling. I remember thinking very clearly, To hell with Anna, *I'm* enjoying this! (as I told her years later, which prompted her to utter her gurgling laugh, call me "Male chauvinist pig!" and tap me lightly across the cheek with her favorite blue editing pencil, leaving a mark I had to go to the men's room and scrub off).

Right then, anyway, things moved to their inexorable conclusion, and presently we were, as a great ex-public official and novelist has put it in *his* book about Washington, floating in "a pool of slaked desire." This lasted for about a minute and a half, at which time we realized with agonizing suddenness that we were sharing the pool with an enraged colony of ants who did not understand the joyous mysteries of human copulation but only knew that something alien was invading their turf.

The next few moments were almost as exciting as the last as Anna and I hopped about, swearing and slapping at our determined little friends.

"You and your damned sand dune!" I managed to puff out between swats.

"Don't tell me," she said, beginning to chuckle in

the midst of her own exertions, "that you didn't enjoy it."

"Divinely," I said, finally conquering the last of my tiny attackers. "But"—with an exaggerated emphasis —"What Does It All Mean?"

"Let's sit down again and talk," she suggested.

"On another damned anthill?" I retorted. "Not on your little red—"

"It is red," she said calmly, falling into step beside me as I started trudging toward the cleansing sea. "You didn't know I was a virgin, did you, Ed? Were you a virgin?"

"Well, I'm damned," I said, stopping in my tracks. "What am I, some kind of experiment?"

"Possibly," she said coolly. "*I* found it quite interesting. Didn't you?"

"Yes," I said. "But damn it all, Anna—"

"Anyway, we showed *them*."

"I didn't want to show anybody," I said, beginning to get a little annoyed now, I'm afraid: but of course I had learned long since there was no point in that: Anna goes her way and we mortals follow. "I just wanted to have a good time. With you. Because I wuv you."

"That I don't believe," she said calmly.

"And I don't believe you love me either," I retorted sharply, resuming our hike to the sea. "I think you just love Anna."

"Possibly," she agreed. "Do you know anybody better?"

"Jesus! What an ego!"

"I admit it," she said. "It's going to take me a long way, Ed. You'd better stick around. Maybe I'll take you with me."

"Oh?" I said. "That will be the day, when I need you to get along in this town!"

"You never know," she said. "Don't close out your options."

"Options schmopshions," I retorted, wading out to meet an incoming breaker. "Tell me another fairy tale, kid."

"Don't go too far out!" she cried sharply. "I don't trust the sea at night."

"I don't trust it any time," I shouted as I prepared to dive under the wave. "I just want to get washed off."

When I came up for air she was floating beside me, shivering, not from cold, because it was still very warm, but from fear.

"Let's go back in," she said. "Quick."

"O.K.," I agreed, holding out my hand. "I've finally discovered something Anna Kowalczek is afraid of."

"It's about the only thing," she said as we regained the shore and started walking slowly back toward the cottage along the firm sand at the edge of the tide, "Ed, do you have any purpose in life? Any really long-term goal, I mean, in Washington?"

"What a question!"

"No," she said, tugging on my hand to make me halt. "I mean it. Seriously."

"Well," I said slowly, "I'd like to be one of the top correspondents someday . . . and maybe write a book or two—"

"No politics?" she asked quickly.

"Not as a participant, no. It's more fun to observe and let them have the headaches."

"I think you'd be very good," she said seriously. "You have a lot of integrity, Ed. I like that."

"Well, thank you, Anna," I said with some dryness. "I'm touched."

"Don't you think I have any?"

"Yes, I think so. I'm just waiting for it to collide with your ambition."

"Well," she said, "it hasn't yet. And if I'm lucky it never will."

"If you're lucky," I agreed. "What are *your* long-term goals in Washington, since we're getting so damned philosophical?"

"I think maybe someday," she said dreamily, "some-day . . . I might like to have a paper of my own, Ed. Would you help me with it?"

"That's a very modest desire," I said, "and it will only cost about ten billion bucks. How you're going to manage that on an AP salary I wouldn't know, but I won't be the least surprised if it happens."

"Oh, yes, you will," she said, "because you think it's all talk. But there are ways."

"Name one."

"That's all right," she said airily. "You just stick with me and we'll both go places."

"All right," I said, "but keep me off the damned anthills."

"Oh, *Ed!*" she said, gurgling with laughter, throwing her arms around me and kissing me in a manner already becoming slightly sisterly. "I *do* like you! You're *fun!*"

"Yes," I said. "Well, don't count on me always being around. I might just disagree with some of your methods someday and tell you to shove off."

"You'll never leave me," she said serenely. "I know I can always count on you."

And in that, as it turned out, she was half-wrong and half-right, which probably isn't too bad an average.

By this time we were dried off and nearing the cottage. We paused for a moment to pull on our clothes and then went forward into the light.

"Where have *you* been?" Bessie called anxiously from the porch.

"You see what I mean?" Anna hissed in my ear and

57

I hissed as sharply back, *"No, damn it, I do not, so stop that nonsense."*

"What's that?" Bessie asked. "Are you two having secrets? We were getting *so* worried about you."

"I wasn't," Tal said, coming out to join her. "I thought you'd both been swept out to sea, and good riddance."

"Oh, *you*," Anna said, and something in her tone told me that Tal was going to be next man up on the anthill. "Why don't you go pound sand?"

"There's plenty of it," Tal agreed, "but I think I'd rather stay here and drink. Bessie and I have been passionately involved ever since you left, haven't we, Bess?"

"We have *not*," Bessie said, blushing furiously as we came up the steps to reclaim our chairs.

"Have *you?*" Tal asked, inspecting us shrewdly.

"We've been discussing our ambitions in Washington," I said calmly, meeting him eye for eye. "Anna wants to—"

"That's enough!" she said sharply. "That was confidential between you and me, Ed. I don't want you ever to tell *anyone,* you understand? Not anyone."

"Which I suppose," Tal said with an elaborate weariness, "means me. So don't tell me, old buddy. I'll live."

"Shall I take him along too?" Anna asked me.

"Can you stand him?" I asked in a bantering tone. "If you could, I think he might be worth it."

"I think maybe I could," she said slowly, and I perceived suddenly that she was entirely serious. "I'll have to think about it."

"Thus does Anna the Great dispose of all our futures," Tal remarked. "I'm going to have another drink."

"What about me?" Bessie asked plaintively. "Can't I come along too?" To my surprise she was quite serious, too; the thought crossed my mind: *Maybe old sharpie Anna is right, after all.* But Anna's response was of course perfectly fitting and comfortable.

"Of course!" she said warmly. "You're included, Bess. You're all part of my team."

"*My team!*" Tal echoed. "Jesus! Did it ever occur to you that somebody might not want to be part of it?"

"Oh, you will," she said. "It will be fun and wonderful and you won't be able to resist. And *you'll* always stay with me, too."

"I will?" he asked quizzically, and she nodded with the same serenity with which she had answered me.

"Yes, you will."

And in this she was totally right, and that, too, is a pretty good average.

"So will I," Bessie volunteered. "That is," she added wistfully, "if you want me."

"I said I did," Anna pointed out, somewhat tartly. "So stop worrying about it."

"O.K.," Bessie said humbly. "I just wanted to be sure."

"Be sure," Anna directed, dropping into her chair. "Everybody be sure, sure, *sure.* A drink for me, too, Tal, please," she added crisply. "Gin and tonic. Light."

"Me, too," Bessie echoed.

"Yes, ma'am!" he said smartly, saluting Anna and clicking his heels. "Anything Your Majesty desires. Want to help me, Ed? . . . Now, what the hell," he murmured when we were in the kitchen, "is that all about?"

"She'll tell you when it suits her," I said. "You may think she's crazy. I'm not sure I don't. But then, again—"

"Really gotten to you, hasn't she?" he asked, giving me a shrewd glance. "She's a man-eater. Better you should have been swept out to sea."

"I don't think so," I said. "She's got something."

"She's got *us*," he said. "She *thinks*."

"And you don't think so?" I asked with a little laugh.

"O-o-o-h, brother. You think you know Anna but I'm afraid you don't know Anna."

And before the summer was over, of course, he too was taken up on the anthill and shown the outlines of the future; and though professing to be, as usual, sarcastically skeptical, he could not hide from me that he was secretly quite impressed; and, although fighting against what he considered to be a determined domination of his own fate and personality, was even then making up his mind, subconsciously if without his full awareness, to follow where Anna led.

He was not one to give in as amicably as I, which caused a number of sharp exchanges and rearguard actions; but he could not help but be affected, particularly since he began to conclude, I think, that his own purposes could be served better by associating them with Anna's than by seeking some other channel.

Years later, whenever we went back to The Dunes (Anna likes to tie everything together; she has an organizational passion for neatness in her life not always achieved, but insistent. She bought the cottage and ten acres surrounding it in 1968. A twelve-room house and three guest cottages now stand where the old shack stood) we used to reminisce, humorously yet with an inescapable respect, about the portentous conversations of that distant summer. "My team" is still here, graying and a little frayed at the edges, in spots; but basically still here, just as she said so confidently it would be.

Partly this was due, I think, to the fact that her career, after plateauing out on a high level of competence and financial reward but not of any unusual distinction, suddenly shot into high gear with the opportunity afforded by the Senatorial hearings into the unusual character and freewheeling activities of the junior Senator from Wisconsin.

6

It was my good fortune at this time to be assigned by the AP to the investigation of Senator Joseph McCarthy of Wisconsin. While the then sacrosanct restrictions of wire-service reporting did not allow me quite the enviable freedom of expression accorded contemporaries such as Mary McGrory of the Washington Star, still I was able to write a running "color-story" in which I had, for a wire-service reporter, an unusual opportunity to show what I could do. Apparently it was sufficient to impress those who could further my career, for it led directly to national recognition, professional reward and a sudden quantum jump forward in the direction of achieving my journalistic ambitions. After twelve years on the Hill I was ready for this.

—ANNA HASTINGS, by Anna Hastings

AS I HAVE SAID, THE YEARS PASSED OVER WITH INcreasing rapidity, the great war ended, the world began to fall apart again at the seams as it always seems to do the moment communal crisis ends. The suspicion that there were Communists everywhere began to grip the country; Richard Nixon and Joseph McCarthy made their charges and took their political profit. For so daring to affront the sentimental loyalties and naively idealistic fantasies of the media, retribution for Richard Nixon (assisted as it was by the inexplicable windings of his own unhappy character) was long delayed but ultimately inescapable. For Joe McCarthy it came almost at once. Anna, like Mary and many another, was in at the kill, and profited greatly therefrom. (In this she was cautioned by me, encouraged by Tal. She often showed us her copy before she filed it. My usual advice was to tone it down; Tal's was succinct: "Murder the son of a bitch!" Usually she listened to Tal. There, too, the future provided its intimations.)

"He enters the Caucus Room like some dark, prognathous ["What the hell does that mean?" the copydesk downtown queried her sarcastically, but she insisted, and got away with it] being from another world—the world of hatreds and suspicions as dark as he is," Anna wrote.

And again: "With all the gentle rage of a long-suffering but implacable parent, Counsel Joseph Welch today spanked the junior Senator from Wisconsin where it hurt the most—directly on his point of order."

And again: "The game is winding down at last for Wisconsin's rambunctious rover through the secret fear-haunted passages of the American psyche—and a Senate Caucus Room hushed as though watching the evasive writhings of a dying ophidian ["*What?*" demanded the desk. "Snake!" snapped Anna. "Don't worry, they won't understand in Topeka"—and got away with it] marveled today at how he managed to escape the final conclusive blow."

And finally: "The chamber was deathly silent today as the Senate voted at last to censure its most difficult, most notorious and most un-Senatorial Senator—the club member who challenged the club. Washington senses that it is all over for Joseph McCarthy, though he may linger awhile like some ghost who refuses to vanish. He is politically dead. He walks but no longer casts a shadow on the land. The sun shines through at last."

Now, this was not at all your usual wire-service stuff ("X said. Y said. X said what Y said was spastic idiocy. Y said what X said was crap double-dyed and twice warmed over. X said . . .") and it was quite amazing that Anna was allowed such latitude. I don't think she would have been, except that three weeks before the hearings began, when she first knew she was to be assigned to it, she gave a party for the committee members and her bosses in a private room she hired at the Mayflower. She conveyed such an impression of intimacy with Senators to her bosses, and such an impression of intimacy with her bosses to Senators, that both groups emerged a couple of hours later awash with drink and more than a little awe for Anna. She told me the affair had cost her close to five hundred dollars, "but it was worth it, Ed. This is my chance and I'm not letting it get away from me." And of course she didn't.

By then the party gambit, begun so long ago on that sweltering night on R Street, had become one of her principal means of getting ahead. For whatever reason —basically, I think, because she felt a roommate cramped her style and she wanted more freedom to entertain—she had taken her own apartment in Georgetown soon after that Nags Head summer. This had devastated poor Bessie for a while, but Anna, not being one to abandon anyone who might come in handy later, particularly her "team," suggested that Bessie take an apartment not too far away (and not too close either, Anna made sure) so that they still might share the occasional cocktail party or intimate dinner. But deftly, surely and rapidly thereafter Anna emerged as the sole star of these occasions, the perfect example of the astute and ambitious newspaper-woman-turned-social-hostess. It was not an idea original or exclusive to her, but somehow she seemed to carry it off better than any of her ambitious young competitors. By the end of her first decade in the capital, Anna Kowalczek (I asked her once half-seriously why she didn't change her name to something easier, for professional purposes. "Anna Smith?" she responded dryly. "Now, who would ever remember that?") and her little dinners were beginning to appear with great regularity alongside those of Perle Mesta, Gwen Cafritz, Marjorie Merriweather Post, Dolly Munson, Polly Logan and others in the columns of Betty Beale and the town's other social reporters.

The informal days of B.Y.O.B. and Senators sitting in shirt sleeves gave way swiftly to the Irish linen tablecloth, the Haviland china, the Waterford crystal, the Gorham flatware and the two black hire-outs hovering discreetly behind the chairs. ("I'm in hock for everything up to my eyeballs," she told me cheerfully along about then, "but if you want a real career in this town you have to spend money and *work* at it." She always remained true to her own truism, right down to the purchase of Emily Post's *Etiquette,* whose wisdom she memorized virtually word for word as her social schedule grew.)

Simultaneously she was also climbing the ladder in the various newspaper organizations, to which she gave the same energy and determined application she gave her professional and social lives. She became successively treasurer, secretary, vice-president and president of the Women's National Press Club, began a similar climb in the American Newspaper Women's Club; became active in the American Newspaper Guild (which gave her a great psychological advantage later on when the *Inquirer* was threatened by strikes); and began the fight that was to lead in later years to membership for women in the Gridiron Club, the National Press Club and the White House Correspondents' Association.

All this activity, of course, brought its inevitable rewards: long before Tal, Bessie and I began to be fairly well-known regulars on the social scene, Anna was being invited to Congressional dinners, diplomatic receptions, parties at Tregaron, Vagaries, and other stately homes. Because she was also putting in a lot of work on her appearance, the plump little blonde of our early days on the Hill was gradually replaced by a trim, slim, extremely well-turned-out young woman. When Anna leaned on some agitated statesman's shoulder now, or looked deep into his eyes with her intent, admiring and respectful gaze, he got a real charge of voltage, from which few ever recovered once they had been subjected to its seemingly sincere and all-enveloping rays. Some there were in those days who took this as an invitation and attempted to respond with more wishful thinking than common sense. Anna, who had gradually developed a deadly accurate gift for mimicry, used to relate the juicier of these reactions to us on the occasions when we would all get together for dinner at one of our apartments.

Tal and I had also gone our separate ways as increasing salaries and the slackening of the group feeling of being young together in Washington brought more independence: but Anna saw to it that the team stayed together. At least twice a month and sometimes oftener she would have us over or ask one of us to do the honors. She would also ask me or Tal quite frequently to be her escort when she got invited to some formal dinner, and would sometimes ask Bessie to accompany her to a Congressional or diplomatic cocktail party. (I always suspected that she did this when she wanted to appear particularly striking alongside sadly ballooning Bessie, but that may be a little unfair. She was still very fond of Bess, though relieved to be free of her constantly worshipful presence.)

Of course Anna, Tal and I still saw each other often on the Hill, but as we became veterans and moved up the ladder in our respective news bureaus, something of the old everyday working intimacy went. We were no longer Bob Taft's "Three Horsemen," dependent on one another, and enjoying the dependence, as we prowled the corridors for news. We were all becoming names in our own right, Tal and I not quite so much as Anna, but our by-lines were known and respected now in newspapers all over the country, and top stories on the Hill, as well as assignments to Presidential campaigns and the national conventions, began to come our way. Bessie remained at *Time* as a researcher for five years, then moved on to an even more impregnable bastion of publishing, the *National Geographic,* in the same capacity, and there settled in, she thought for life. Our daily intimacy dwindled and our summer weekends became few and far between as increasing responsibilities, other interests and Anna's growing string of weekend invitations elsewhere began to grow. There was need for a deliberate means of keeping together, and Anna devised it. We soon perceived another motive: after a long silence on the subject, she was once again beginning to talk about her plans to become a publisher. She found us increasingly skeptical. We were nearing our mid-thirties, beginning to settle into what seemed to be lifetime patterns, and in spite of her still-serene conviction, nothing we could see on the horizon seemed to support it.

Then she won the Pulitzer for her coverage of the McCarthy hearings, and suddenly it all seemed somewhat more plausible again.

I was just coming back to the Senate restaurant for lunch, after covering a session of the Foreign Relations Committee at which former Secretary of State Dean Acheson had come out of retirement to scatter his acidulous comments over the troubled global scene, when I ran into Tal.

"Have you heard the Goddamned news?" he demanded. "She's won the Pulitzer!"

There was no need to ask who "she" was.

"Well, I'll be Goddamned," I said, and he nodded, looking fierce.

"That's what I said, the Goddamned news. I can't believe it."

"Well, I can. Nothing she does surprises me. For what? McCarthy?"

He nodded. "All that overwritten crap about a two-bit Red-baiting shyster. Jesus! My stories were as good as that."

"No, they weren't," I said firmly. "I'm sorry, Tal, but they weren't."

"Well, they would have been if INS had given me my head the way the AP did her," he said darkly. "I really *hated* the son-of-a-bitch."

"Maybe that's why they didn't," I suggested. "You feel a little too intensely on that subject, it seems to me."

"What do you mean by that?" he asked sharply.

"Just what I said. You get too agitated about things like Hiss and McCarthy and things like that. People wonder."

"*Who* wonders?" he demanded, grabbing my arm.

"Tal," I said as several tourists stopped to gawk, "I'm not going to debate it with you right here, so let go and calm down. Anna did a brilliant job and she deserves it and I think we all ought to get together and celebrate."

"Well," he said, releasing me but still scowling, "I don't like you implying I'm a Commie, that's all."

"Nobody's implying that," I said patiently.

"You did," he said flatly.

"All right," I said, lowering my voice and walking him into the adjoining corridor, away from the tourists. "Are you?"

He looked at me steadily for what must have been a good half-minute and then said calmly, "No, I am not and fuck you if you think so."

"I didn't say I thought so," I said evenly, "but you make such a point of it, I thought I ought to find out what's bugging you."

"Nothing's bugging me," he said sharply. "I just don't like all these implications, that's all."

"Nobody's implying anything you don't invite," I said. "You must admit you don't seem very objective on some subjects."

"What? Give me some specifics!"

"I can't give you specifics at the moment," I said rather lamely, forgetting I had already given him Hiss and McCarthy, "but it seems to me for years I've been hearing you attack this country about everything."

"It deservse it," he said smugly. "That doesn't mean I'm a Communist."

"No," I agreed, "but it lays you open to some suspicion."

"Suspicion!" he said savagely. "That's what we've just gotten rid of McCarthy for. Doesn't that tell you something?"

"O.K., Tal," I said. "I'm not going to argue with

you about it. But if I were you, I'd soft-pedal the anti-U.S. bit some. A lot of people are still uneasy, including some right here on this Hill. I wouldn't give them ammunition, if I were you."

"I'm a free citizen of a free country. I have a right to say what I think, and nobody can prove I'm not O.K."

"I don't want anybody to try."

"Hell! They wouldn't dare!"

"I hope you're right."

"I *am* right," he said flatly. And then added a rather curious reference I didn't quite follow: "Anyway, why are you worried? It doesn't worry Anna."

"No," I admitted, though I didn't see really what that had to do with it. "Apparently it doesn't."

There it ended—the last of many such arguments we had engaged in over the years. He had always criticized the country ("Tal doing it again"), sometimes in very startling and disturbing ways. I had never forgotten the night of V-J Day, when we had stood in the midst of the wildly celebrating crowd in Lafayette Park.

"We're top dogs now," he said suddenly, and his eyes were remote and far away in some place that actually frightened me a little when I looked into them. "But in twenty years' time we'll have things turned completely around so that America will be the most hated country in the world."

I didn't know whether he meant that "we the United States" through our own ineptness and stupidity would have things turned around, or whether he meant that some other "we" would do it for us. The thought that it might be the latter made me profoundly uneasy for a moment. I was much relieved when his mood changed abruptly and he began joking about a sailor and his girl who were celebrating the victory over Japan by fornicating happily and very publicly under a nearby tree. But I never forgot it.

I thought then, as I thought often after, that as long as he confined whatever he meant to private discussions and it didn't affect his reporting, it probably didn't matter. But if he meant what I almost thought he meant, and if he ever got in a position of real power in the media—then I wondered what would happen. I could not claim to be surprised when we all found out.

For the moment, however, it ended in a draw as every other argument had ended. We went on to lunch, went back to the gallery and put in a call to Anna, who had gone downtown to receive the delighted congratulations of her office.

"You've got to come to dinner tomorrow night!" she said, sounding for once genuinely excited and completely happy, without self-consciousness or calculation. "I can't have you tonight, we're celebrating here. But do come tomorrow. Bessie's coming and we'll celebrate, just the four of us, like old times. I have *great* news!"

"Yes, I know," I said. "After all, what's greater than the Pulitzer?"

"Oh, I don't mean *that*," she said. "That's nice, but there's something even nicer. You'll see!"

"She says there's something even nicer than the Pulitzer," I reported to Tal as I hung up. "What in the hell do you suppose that could be?"

"Probably struck oil and bought her paper," he said: a remark we were to recall many times later, though that was not the night when it occurred.

7

I was surprised but not unprepared when the Pulitzer Prize brought with it instantly the chance to improve my standing in the journalistic world, make of myself a truly national name, and advance to a position from which it was to prove an easy step to the final achievement of my lifelong dream.

—ANNA HASTINGS, *by Anna Hastings*

"WELL," SHE SAID WHEN WE WERE ALL SEATED, DRINKS in hand, "guess *what?*"

"We couldn't," I said. "Tell us."

"Well, first, I got a call from the New York *Times.*"

"That figures," Tal said. "They go after anybody who sticks his head above water—and then usually stick it back under again once they've got him."

"That's what they wanted to do with me," she said; and suddenly her laughter gurgled up. "That *funny* man! Do you know what he said? He wanted me to write 'an occasional mood-piece,' as he put it. And then he said, he actually said, *'You can work the switchboard the rest of the time.'* Can you *imagine?*"

"So you took it," Bessie said with one of her rare ironies.

"Oh, sure," Anna said. "I sure did. But I guess it was more glory than I was fated to have, because when I returned to the AP after slamming the door in his face and walking out—yes, I really did, Bess, don't look so shocked—I got a call from United Features Syndicate. And do you know what *they* want me to do?"

"Your own column, of course," Tal said. "What else?"

"Five times a week," Anna said triumphantly. "A guaranteed minimum of fifty papers to start. Complete freedom of subject matter and editorial expression. Freedom to write books or do television or anything else I want to do on the side. And an *enormous* jump in salary. So how about *that?*"

"Have you got it in writing?" Tal inquired.

"Here," she said, producing a telegram. "Read it and see."

And clustering on the couch, one on each side of Bessie, who held it in fingers trembling with excitement, we did.

After we finished there was quite a long silence, filled, I will admit, with some professional jealousy, but mostly with an overwhelming awe and admiration for Anna. She had done it this time, all right, and there was no denying it. We could only stare at her with pleased and no doubt rather idiotic smiles.

"And that isn't all," she said calmly. "Tomorrow I'm going up to New York and talk to NBC and CBS. There may be something I can do for them part-time. *Not*"—she chortled—"run the switchboard."

"My God," Tal said dryly. "You've just created the world in considerably less than seven days. Don't you want to rest for a minute?"

"Now's my time," she said earnestly. "I feel it. Everything is opening up for me. I've got to go after it and get it now. It may not wait for me if I don't."

"I'll go with you," he offered. "I can manage a day off tomorrow."

"Would you?" she said quickly, her pleased expression revealing that she was a little more human, a little more awed and a little less supremely confident than she sounded. "I'd like that."

"How about me?" Bessie and I asked simultaneously, but she frowned and shook her head.

"No," she said thoughtfully. "I appreciate it, but—"

"Well, why *not?*" Bessie demanded in an aggrieved tone. "I'm your oldest and best friend in this town!"

"You're *all* my oldest and best friends," she said, embracing us in a sudden warm smile. "But I can't have you *all* trooping up with me, that would look funny—"

"We wouldn't have to see anybody, silly," Bessie said, refusing to give up a cause I could see was lost. "We could go to the museum, or something, while you're busy."

"That museum bit, Bess," Tal said, "is the Real You. You heard the lady. She wants *me*. I'm available. Ergo, we go. Right?"

"Ed," Anna said, placing her hand on my arm and ignoring Bessie, who looked woebegone. "You understand, don't you? It's just that—well, I can't take you both, and Tal is—well, he sees things more the way I do, sometimes."

"It doesn't seem to me you need anybody who sees things the way you do," I said, somewhat stiffly. "You apparently did O.K. with United Features all by your little self without anyone to help you. I'll bet they didn't want to give you all *that,* and you got it. Right?"

"That's right," she said, and couldn't help a satisfied,

74

even a somewhat smug, smile. "They weren't going to be quite that generous, but I talked them into it."

"All right, you'll do the same with NBC or CBS or whatever. Why do you need him?"

"Now you sound jealous," she said lightly, "and that isn't like you, Ed. It just isn't like you. Look: why don't we all meet here again day after tomorrow for dinner and we'll tell you all about it? After all"— she gave the sudden charming smile of which she is capable—"I want to keep my team fully advised of everything. We may not have too much longer to wait!"

"That's good," I said dryly. "I wouldn't want to think there was any slippage in the timetable."

"I think from now on it's going to move pretty fast," she said, perfectly seriously. "So, you do understand, don't you?"

"Sure," I said, while Tal gave me a triumphant smile over her shoulder. "I've always understood. I'm Good Old Ed, remember?"

"And I'm Good Old Bessie," Bess said, in such a wistful tone that even she had to join in when we all laughed.

"That's better," Anna said. "Now, let's everybody have another drink and then we'll have dinner. I think Martha has it just about ready."

And Martha, her usual party maid, did, and presently the tensions washed out in a flood of congratulations, daydreams for the future, good talk of R Street, the war and old times. I still went home annoyed, however: not that I still had any illusions about myself and Anna, but I didn't have any about Tal either; and I was afraid, although it wouldn't really be characteristic of her steel-trap mind, that Anna did.

She certainly had none about me, that was for sure; and I had none about myself either. "Good Old Ed" was it, all right, and it had been, really, ever since that long ago summer at Ocracoke. I had been promptly made aware—because he went out of his way to let me know about it, though I never confirmed or denied his guesses about my own situation—when Tal, too, had his christening among the sand dunes; and for quite a few months thereafter we were both heavily involved with Anna. How we managed to remain friends and keep harmony in the apartment in a situation that should theoretically have had us at each other's throats I can only explain by the assumption that somehow, in some instinctive place deep inside, we knew—or at least I knew—that it was never as real for Anna as it could have been for us. Somehow that first vivid impression of mine—the poltergeist Anna, standing on a nearby sand dune scientifically studying the real thing rolling on the ground in The Ecstatic Throes of Wild Animal Passion—never quite got out of my mind . . . even though that winter I managed to overcome it sufficiently to ask her to marry me.

I was not surprised when she said no; nor was I particularly devastated; nor did I ever entertain for a moment the thought that I could ever make the offer to anyone else.

"You won't be mad with me, will you, Ed?" she asked with the little-girl naiveté that could take one so completely off base because it was so completely genuine and contrasted so sharply with her usual shrewdly calculated approach to things.

"No," I said heavily, but not otherwise letting my emotions get control—because with Anna, what was the use?—"I won't be mad with you."

"Oh, *good!*" she said, giving my arm an affectionate squeeze. "And I *can* count on you, can't I, to always be with me and help me out?"

"*Jesus,* Anna," I said. "Yes, you can count on me to always be with you and help you out."

"Oh, *good!*" she repeated, throwing her arms around me and giving me a perfectly innocent and resounding kiss. "I don't know *what* I'd do without you, Ed. You're such a good friend in every way!"

"I try to be," I said, I'm afraid not without some bitterness. "Good Old Ed, they call me."

"And you *are,*" she said with a deep satisfaction that was, naturally, quite impervious to any feelings of mine. "You *are.*"

While the episode had been just about what I had expected, it took me a little while to recover from it fully, even though I knew the moment these sisterly compliments began that I would most certainly do so in very short order. Meanwhile, Tal must have tried his luck, too, because a few nights later he came in in a foul temper and woke me by throwing a book across the living room.

"That bitch!" he kept saying to himself. "That bitch!" And when I managed to drag myself out of bed, pull on a robe and appear bleary-eyed in the doorway, he shouted, "That bitch, bitch, *bitch!*"

"Ah," I said, intuition and, I'm afraid, a certain satisfaction joining to tell me what had happened. "So you, too, have been given the gate."

"Not given the gate," he said savagely. "Tied to it with all the bonds of sisterly love and undying affection. 'You *will* stay with me and help me, won't you, Tal, dear?' *Christ!*"

And he threw another book, which seemed to be his favorite mode of expression at the moment.

"Careful," I said, "that's my only copy of *How To Have a Perfect Marriage.* I'm saving it for the next time."

77

"What next time?" he snorted. "There'll never be anyone else like Anna."

"And thank God for that," I said, and suddenly knew I meant it.

"That's *right*," he agreed. "That's *right*. I'll drink to that!"

"So will I," I said, going to the sideboard and pulling out the liquor. And so we did until about 4 A.M., when we staggered, or rather crawled, to bed, I for one a sadder, wiser and in some way I didn't quite admit openly to myself—for that would have been disloyal to Anna, and how could one be disloyal to Anna?—a happier man.

Not so, Tal, I think. Even though I accepted Anna for what she was—probably the most unusual combination of brilliant incompatibles I'd ever known—and dated a lot of other girls, enjoying myself fully and always with the certain knowledge that I would never become really serious with any of them, for that would be disloyal to Anna, and how could one be disloyal to Anna?—Tal really kept trying. For him, it was much more of a personal challenge: he had that sort of temperament. He *would* batter her down, he *would* force her to accept him, he *would* dominate her personality and make her give in—when, as I had always known instinctively without any further argument with myself, *nobody* would batter Anna down and make her do anything she didn't want to do. Certainly not I, who valued my own peace of mind too much and found its maintenance too vital to my productive output.

It wasn't terribly hard, if not all that easy, for me to accept the fact of it: she has always been deeply fond of both of us, we have always been her two most trusted lieutenants—but it has always been, and always will be, on her terms.

I don't think Tal finally realized this until they got

back from New York and we gathered again at her apartment in the Hampshire House to hear the story of how she had conquered NBC. Not exactly conquered, but got her foot well inside the door, with plenty of potential for bigger things to come.

"They were just as nice as they could be," she said, glowing with the happiness of it. "They already knew who I was—"

"Strange," I said.

"Well, they did, smarty," she said with a quick smile, "and they really seemed pleased that I would think of them. I explained about my setup with United Features, and said I was interested in doing something in TV as well, because that's where you can really reach people—"

"You mean you're bored with the column already?" Bessie asked. "It hasn't even begun."

"I'm not bored with it," she said. "I just want to get involved with *everything*. *I want to reach people.* I don't want to miss any bets."

"You won't," I predicted. "So what did they say?"

"Well, first of all, they said I could expect to be invited with what they called 'consistent frequency' to be a panelist on 'Meet the Press.' That means I'll get national exposure quite a few times a year, which is all to the good. And then they said they might use me on some specials now and then as a reporter and commentator, with the possibility that maybe in time I might even host some of my own. So that was all very encouraging. Then at the lecture bureau, they said—"

"Lecture bureau!" I echoed. "Good God, Anna, slow down or you'll burn yourself out before you're thirty."

She made a little face.

"Thirty-three, funny man, as you very well know.

79

I told you, *now* is my time. I feel it. I want to get things *now*. Tomorrow may be too late."

"Speaking of getting things now," Tal said with an elaborate slowness that tipped us that something serious was on his mind—this was after dinner and we were relaxed, but he wasn't—"don't you think, with all this extra activity, that you need someone to help you? I mean *really help?*"

"Like what?" she asked cautiously, though I think we all knew what was coming, startled though we were that it should come thus publicly. He must have thought the presence of Bessie and me would create some sort of extra pressure. Silly boy.

"Like a husband," he said bluntly. "Like me."

For several minutes none of us said anything. Bessie looked as forlorn as she always did when the subject of marriage and Anna came up, I kept reminding myself that I was Good Old Ed, who mustn't turn a hair, and Anna simply stared at him in open disbelief while he looked first defiant, then uncertain, then angry.

"Well?" he demanded harshly. "What's so strange about that, may I ask?"

"There isn't anything strange about it," Anna said slowly, "except that it's impossible."

"*Why* is it impossible?" he shouted, his tone only serving to make her calm rejoinder even more devastating than it would have been otherwise.

"Because I'm going to marry someone else."

"Does he know it yet?" he demanded bitterly.

Her answer was pure Anna.

"No. But I've decided who it's going to be. And he will."

8

―――――

I began the column; and was amazed and pleased to find that it immediately drew commendation from a broad spectrum of political opinion that included such rising young political stars as John F. Kennedy on the one hand and Gordon Hastings on the other. I was particularly touched by the beautiful letter sent me by Gordon. Before long we began to see one another. I did not know what this portended, but I found myself increasingly anxious to be in his company. At first my interest was only in this. It was not until we had known one another intimately for several months that I began to perceive that I might be able to wean him away from the reactionary positions which were making him the laughing-stock of liberals and a potential danger to this great country. I shall always be thankful I was able, at least partially, to succeed.

—Anna Hastings, *by Anna Hastings*

"All Things Considered," by Anna Kowalczek began to appear a month later and, as United Features had promised, in a minimum of fifty newspapers; in fact, their salesmen had been able to secure sixty-one, aided by a dazzling photo of Anna and an intimate personal appeal from her directed to "Dear Potential Editor: I love *you!*" and so on, in a vein combining coyness very nicely with an impressive grasp of what was happening in Washington. Not only her Pulitzer but her intelligence and obvious familiarity with politics commanded attention; the picture gave it extra impact. Alongside the pictures of a severely skeptical Walter Lippmann, a determinedly serious James Reston, a grimly dogmatic Doris Fleeson, Anna's serenely lovely face, now entering upon the full tide of its mature beauty, was almost certain to draw the reader's attention immediately when he came to the editorial pages. She made the most of it.

From the beginning, the column was good. She made some attempt at first to be objective and fair—the tradition still lingered in Washington journalism, though it was very soon to yield to the get-the-bastards-at-any-price mentality of the so-called New Journalism, which in reality was very old, harking back to the days of nakedly partisan twopenny dreadfuls. But before long a strongly liberal slant began to appear. It was shrewdly done, delicately and with care: Anna in those days was never the hysterically blatant, beat-'em-over-the-head type that some of her famous "liberal" colleagues became. Tal was always urging her to be more rabid, and we had many arguments about it until finally one day I objected sharply. "For Christ's sake, she knows what she's doing! I may not always agree with it, but *she knows what she's doing,* so leave her alone, God damn it!"

"Exactly," Anna echoed coolly. "Leave me alone, God damn it. You don't have any subtlety, Tal, that's your trouble. I'll never use a meat-ax, it isn't my way."

Which proved to be the only self-analytical remark Anna ever made that turned out to be untrue; but for the time being, and for some years thereafter, she did more for her view of things by keeping it clever and low-key than nine-tenths of her colleagues did by letting their emotions run away with them and adopting Tal's meat-ax attitude.

Tal himself moved within the month to the New York *Times*. Much hiring was going on in the bureau at that time; he received the magic telephone call, went over, found his work had produced a favorable impression, received an offer, accepted, and wound up covering the State Department with a roving commission to follow diplomatic matters on the Hill as well. It was a good beat, dear to the heart of the head of the bureau, and before long Tal seemed well set for the rest of his professional life. Bessie continued, ever faithful, ever fatter, as researcher for the *Geographic;* and for a brief period the original team still gathered. Then Gordon Hastings entered—or rather was brought into—the picture, and Anna's cryptic remark of three months before began to make sense.

Of course it was not the happenstance she makes out in her book. To begin with, the letters of endorsement she received from people like Jack Kennedy and Gordon—complete with permission to use them for advertising, which was quite a triumph in itself—were solely and entirely the result of her own efforts. She went out and tramped the corridors of the Hill and the Executive departments downtown, making a direct personal appeal for support. Senators, Congressmen, Secretaries, normally wary of lending their names to the promotion of individual columnists for fear the rest would be annoyed with them, were at first startled and amused by Anna's unabashed direct approach, then found themselves agreeing to go along with it for no other reason than that her effrontery and candid ambition simply charmed them into it. She boasted to us, and I believe it was quite true, that she never offered any *quid pro quo* of any kind; insofar as she ever told us, only one was requested. That was by the bachelor junior Senator from Texas, and what he wanted seemed very simple: a chance to take her to dinner at the Jockey Club.

"With no strings," she said firmly. "I told him if he had any fancy ideas for after dinner he could forget them or we'd drop it right there. He promised me he didn't."

But of course she did, and that was where poor old Gordon, who fancied himself to be quite the ladies' man, found himself outclassed on a fast track.

Actually, as she told me many years later, she had decided when he was elected two years previously that he was the man she was going to marry. He had come to the Senate under the protective wing of Seab Cooley, whose distant nephew he was—some collateral branch of the family whose relationship with the old man was never entirely clear. Seab had taken a fancy to him when Gordon became the youngest leader of the Texas state senate in history, and had been among the first to urge him to come to Washington. He even went to Texas to campaign for him, and took much personal pride in the fact that Gordon had been elected by a good, if not excessive, margin. The fact that Gordon also owned a lot of oil wells and had an estimated net worth of $37,000,000 at age forty, some of which went toward the purchase of votes in certain of Texas' more casual counties, might also have had something to do with it. At any rate, in he came; and within a week after he was sworn in, Anna had asked Seab to introduce them, and Seab, amused and far-seeing as ever, had obliged. He had even tried to set up a few social engagements for them subsequently, but though Gordon was eager and willing, Anna was as shrewd as Seab. She would have none of it, always found an excuse, treated Gordon exactly as she did all her other news contacts on the Hill and generally drove him frantic by her studied inattention.

Since she was so matter-of-fact about it, and generally scornful of him in her comments to us, we were as unprepared as he when she decided his time had come. During his first two years he had run very close to McCarthy in the anti-Communist campaign, and on a good many occasions in her McCarthy columns Anna had lumped them together with some scorn. Knowing I was a friend of hers, Gordon used to complain about this to me from time to time.

"Why do you-all suppose that purty little gal has it *in* for me so?" he would ask wistfully; but since my own respect for him was not excessive, I always turned it off with a laugh and a shrug and made no attempt to tone it down where he was concerned.

He was not, as a matter of fact, a particularly attractive type, in my estimation, though I suppose this was partly because of a suppressed but never entirely somnolent jealousy where Anna was concerned. But I liked to think I was objective enough in those days to see him for what he was: a big Texas stud, handsome in a ham-handed, raw-boned sort of way—loaded with money—great on the hey-fella-how-y'all? bit—but rather minimal in the brains department. The time would come when these harshly righteous judgments of youth would be drastically changed, but at that point in our lives we all thought we had Gordon pegged for sure: just not a very bright individual, a very competent lawmaker or a very likable person to be around. He had few social graces, we told one another: he was, in fact, something of a clod. His emo-

tions were all on the surface, his feelings ran skin-deep
. . . or so we thought in those days, never dreaming
that the time would come when Bessie and I, at least,
would feel genuine friendship and sorrow for Gordon.
It was far off, then, and beyond our imagining. For
quite a while the outward aspects appeared to confirm
our conclusions.

So it honestly never occurred to me, or to Tal, or
to Bessie, whose instincts were always extrasensitive
in this area, that there was the remotest possibility
that he could be the mysterious choice of our determined friend.

"When is this great event going to happen?" Tal
inquired scornfully that night after his initial anger at
being turned down had worn off. "We don't want to
miss it."

"Oh, you won't," Anna assured him cheerfully. "It
will happen, I would say"—her eyes narrowed and she
considered her timetable carefully—"just about six
months from now. Bess, you can be my maid of honor,
if you will—"

"Oh, *yes!*" Bessie exclaimed, not knowing really
whether to be happy or sad, but making the best of
it. "I'd love to!"

"Good." She chuckled suddenly. "And you and Ed,
Tal, can lurk about in the background, giving me moral
support and eating your hearts out."

"Woman," Tal said somberly, "you are destroying
me."

"Bull," Anna said. (Later on when she was the
Great Publisher, Very Tough and Trendy, she would
have said "Bullshit" and other brave new words of
the brave new world, but in those days she still felt
it more advantageous to be a lady.) "Absolute bull.
You'll survive. You've told me a million times I could
always count on you and *I can.* Isn't that right?"

"Oh, Jesus," he said in a tired, exasperated voice. "Come off it and get on with it, Anna. Who's the unlucky fellow who gets eaten by the black widow spider?"

"Tal," she said, laughing quite genuinely, "I always get so *tickled* by your humor . . . Gordon Hastings."

"Who?" Tal shouted, surging to his feet while I, too, exclaimed in protest and Bessie fluttered and fluted at my side *"WHO?"*

"You heard me," she said calmly. "And you aren't to tell a soul until I've had a chance to tell him."

"God, I should hope not!" Tal said. *"That* two-bit Texas crap-artist? *That* worthless reactionary McCarthyite bastard? *That* cracked phonograph record that can only say 'you-all' and make money? *That*—"

"The thing is, Tal," Anna interrupted serenely, "he *does* make money and plenty of it. And if you want a job on my paper, you'll shut up and let things take their course. He's always wanted to marry me and now I'm going to let him. There's no point in getting all hot and bothered about it."

"Well, I'll be damned," Tal said, collapsing into his chair again. "I will be God*damned*."

"Possibly," she said sweetly, "but not while you work for me. Do it on your own time."

"What makes you so sure," I asked, "that he wants to marry you? Every time he's discussed it with me I've had the distinct impression he just wants to add you to his string of triumphs on the Hill. There's a spot reserved in his little black book, in amongst all those secretaries, that belongs just to you. It's griped him like hell that he hasn't been able to get you into it."

"He'll get me into it," she said, "when he makes me Mrs. Gordon Hastings. And after that, I don't much care what he does."

"Oh, Anna!" Bessie protested. "How can you be so cold-blooded?"

"I'm not cold-blooded," Anna said. "Just practical."

"Call it what you like," I said. "Personally I don't see what you see in him."

"Oh, I don't know. He isn't really so unattractive."

"He is to me," I said shortly.

"I should hope so," she said with a chuckle.

"And he is to *me*," Tal said bitterly. "I won't let you do it!"

"You can't stop me, Tal," she said. "And why should you want to? Gordon is my newspaper, I keep telling you. He's everything I've ever wanted—everything *we've* ever wanted."

"Jesus," Tal said, pounding one fist into the other, "why can't you be happy with the column, with 'Meet the Press,' with the lecture bureau and all the rest of it? Why do you have to sell yourself to that stupid damned oaf from Texas?"

" 'Sell myself,' " Anna echoed with a sudden gurgle of laughter that only infuriated him more. "Really, Tal, you sound like some cheap eighteen-nineties melodrama. 'Unhand our pure young heroine, you dastardly villain, unhand her, I say!' Why don't you grow up?"

"I don't want to see you do it," Tal repeated stubbornly. "It isn't necessary. It just isn't necessary. It will all come, if you'll just be patient."

"How?" she demanded scornfully. "Maybe someday somebody will walk by and say, 'Here, Anna, here's your newspaper, take it and have fun'? Well"—her eyes narrowed with determination—"somebody will all right, after I'm married: Gordon will. . . . Now," she said with a sudden decisiveness that cut off further discussion, "why don't you all help me plan the wedding? Hand me that calendar, Bess, and let's set the date."

And so we did, for approximately six months in the future; discussed it for a while, never believing for one minute that it would happen, and eventually went home. Tal stopped by my apartment and once again we hauled out the liquor and got drunk over Anna, so much so that he had to sleep over because he was too tight to drive home. I realized dimly that we were obviously going to have to stop reacting this way, because obviously Anna's wonders were only beginning. But at that moment it seemed the only way to go.

Two nights later I was temporarily out of the capital's mad social whirl and cooking myself dinner at home when the phone rang. The voice that came over was so thick with excitement and accent that for several moments I couldn't determine who it was. Then the light dawned.

"Gordon!" I said. "What the hell—?"

"She's goin' do it, boy!" he shouted. "She's goin' do it! Gawd, that little gal's goin' do it!"

"What?" I asked, though of course I knew.

"She's goin' be Mrs. Senator Gordon B. Hastings, Democrat, of Texas!" he shouted. "She's goin' do it, by Gawd!"

"All right, all right," I said, holding the receiver away from my ear. "Calm down, Gordon." Then a sudden devil came and I couldn't resist: "So she finally asked you, did she?"

"Asked me?" he echoed blankly, and I thought for a second I had gone too far. But I might have known I was safe, in all that euphoria. "*Asked me?* Hell, no, Ed, *Ah* asked *her!* Ah did! Ah shorely did! And Ah was never so proud in mah life when she said—oh, Gawd, Ed, she's wonderful, that little gal! Ah was never so proud in mah *life* when she said yes, Ed! *She said yes!*"

And on the last words, startling, embarrassing, but

in some unfortunate way also amusing me deeply, his voice suddenly thickened and I realized that Senator Gordon B. Hastings, Democrat, of Texas, was actually crying like a baby in my ear.

"O.K., Gordon, O.K.," I said soothingly, trying to break through. "Congratulations! . . . Congratulations! . . . I SAID CONGRATULATIONS, GORDON! Now: when will the wedding be?"

"Six months," he said, still trying to master a few lingering sobs of joy. "September twenty-fourth, to be exact. In the National Cathedral. She likes to do things big, that sweet little gal of mine!"

Yes, I thought, *that's exactly how we planned it the other night, Anna dear. Good for you.*

"That sounds marvelous, Gordon," I said solemnly. "As one of Anna's oldest and dearest friends in Washington, I want you to know that I think you couldn't have made a better choice. I'm proud of you, Gordon."

"Oh, Gawd," he said, beginning to bellow again like one of the calves on his Circle H Ranch near Waco, "Ah just cain't believe it, Ed! Ah just cain't believe it!"

Ah could.

On September 24, 1955, they were married in the National Cathedral, right on schedule. Official Washington, which loves weddings and funerals (both, preferably, on the scandalous side), and wallows in any kind of pomp and circumstance that allows Everybody Who Is Anybody to be seen by Everybody Else Who Is Anybody, turned out in full force. Anna's shy little father and soft-spoken but determined little mother came down from Punxsutawney with various assorted little relatives, all beaming with pleasure for Anna; Seab Cooley was best man, leading tearful Bessie, a captive blimp in pink tulle, gallantly down the aisle; and Tal and I did indeed, as Anna had suggested, lurk about in the background lending moral support, if not exactly eating our hearts out—or not after the first few minutes, anyway. This was most certainly true at the reception at the Sulgrave Club, when we lingered on with Bessie, high and curiously happy, until the last of the seemingly endless throng had pushed its way up the stairs, gulped its drinks and hors d'oeuvres and gone home.

"Now," Anna said, giving us all a fond and appraising look while Gordon swung rather loosely at starboard. (He had uttered a few convulsive sobs from time to time during the ceremony and afterward, and on one occasion I thought, with a sudden sharp foreboding sadness that took me quite unaware: *Watch out, Gordon!* But it passed.) "Now, give me a kiss, you three, and wish us a happy honeymoon and I'll see you in two weeks."

"We shorely will," Gordon echoed amicably, but Anna ignored him (that was when I thought: *Watch out, Gordon!* for the second time) and gave us each an intense and concentrated look as we kissed.

"Don't forget, now," she said, as if we could. "I'll see you in two weeks." Then with a mocking lilt that broke the moment's solemnity, "I go, *but I shall return!* Be ready, team!"

"Wha's this team business?" Gordon asked, still amicable but slightly puzzled and, I could see, edging toward a bit of jealousy because of our closed-corporation air.

"Just a private joke," I said quickly.

"The hell it is," Tal said loudly. "The hell it is!"

"Well," Gordon said uncertainly, "I hope I get included on the team, too. I *do*, don't I, little gal? I call her 'L.G.,' " he explained carefully, which I will say Anna took without batting an eyelash. "That's what I call her."

"Oh, you'll be on the team," Tal said, apparently drunker than we knew. "There's no doubt of that, *you will be there.* L.G. will see to *that.*"

"That's enough, Tal," Anna said sharply, and turned her back on him as she gave Bessie and me a last hug and kiss. "Come along, Gordon. We've got a lot to do."

" 'Come along, Gordon,' " Tal mimicked as they entered Gordon's chauffeured Rolls-Royce and rode away. " 'We've got a lot to do!' We've got to go to bed and make a little newspaper, *that's* what we've got to do!"

"Oh, shut up!" Bessie said, beginning to cry. "You make me sick, Talbot!"

"Well, I'm right," Tal said stoutly as we helped him down the stairs. "That's what they've got to do."

And that's what they did—and that wasn't all, as the years unfolded and Anna's life began to slip inexorably into those tangles of tragedy and power from which she had considered herself immune. She wasn't, though. First came the power and then came the tragedy, for Anna as for anyone else—more so for her, perhaps, since she brought so much of it on herself.

Two

"A SURE AND INFALLIBLE INSTINCT"

1

---

*For a few weeks I was swept off my feet by the
sheer breathtaking speed of our romance. One moment an unsuspecting columnist, going quietly about
my business in the fascinating world of Washington
—the next, pursued, overtaken, overwhelmed by the
unexpected and flatteringly insistent pleas of my gallant lover to become the wife of a United States
Senator! Fortunately I found that from somewhere I
had acquired a sure and infallible instinct for my
new position and the opportunities it brought me.
Soon I began to move vigorously in the direction I
had always planned for myself.*

—ANNA HASTINGS, *by Anna Hastings*

" 'ONE MOMENT AN UNSUSPECTING COLUMNIST . . .
the next . . . overwhelmed by the unexpected and
flatteringly insistent pleas of my gallant lover to become
the wife of a United States Senator . . .' When I read
that," Tal confided to me with a simple dignity the
other day, "I puked."

So, I am afraid, did I; or very near to it, considering the careful two-year campaign that had brought her gallant lover so unexpectedly yet insistently to her side to answer—not pop—the question. However, as she commented to me dryly last week when we had lunch at Sans Souci, "*Ladies' Home Journal* loves it and I've made Book-of-the-Month, so who gives a shit? [You remember Anna these days is in her Tough and Trendy Period.] It all helps the Image."

And of course poor Gordon isn't here to protest, which makes it easier.

They went to Bermuda for their honeymoon, making a big mystery of their destination when they left the Sulgrave. But somehow the word seemed to have leaked out to *Life* magazine, and just before they returned to D.C. there was a big spread—ANNA AND HER SENATOR (unnamed in the headline, we noticed) ENJOY LOVE IN THE SUN—showing Gordon the brawny, grinning range rider, and Anna, small, blonde, suitably demure and thoughtful, strolling hand in hand on Emerald Beach. There were some excellent shots of the two of them, both bulging in the proper places, and they really did appear to be quite happy. We knew they both were. Gordon had the smile of the self-satisfied swordsman and Anna and the Cheshire Cat were obviously thinking about that newspaper. They hadn't been back in town three days when the phone rang.

"Eddie," she said—whenever it was "Eddie" I knew I should brace myself—"Gordon and I would love to have the old team over for dinner tomorrow night. Just the five of us. We've got *such* an exciting idea!"

"You have?" I inquired cautiously.

"Yes," she said, "and you're all part of it. Haven't I always promised you that?"

"You have," I conceded.

"I keep my promises. Eight o'clock? And strictly

informal. We're pushing our luck a bit for late October, but Indian summer seems to be holding, so we'll plan to barbecue in the backyard."

"I suppose Gordon is furnishing an entire steer." I couldn't resist. She laughed merrily.

"Gordon *is* an entire steer," she said and then gave a chuckling, "Ooops! I shouldn't say such things! But he's busy on the Hill and can't hear me. It will be *so* good to see you all again. Really, it will."

"You sound bored already."

She snorted.

"With all I'm planning to do? I won't have *time* to be bored."

Which, I reflected as we all stood about in the garden of Gordon's big house in Georgetown, sipping drinks and helping him barbecue the steaks, was a good thing; because Gordon, while obviously happy with his latest acquisition, was not the most sparkling of companions even under these felicitous conditions. He was, as always, amiable and earnest; but it was obvious that Anna had wasted no time in establishing what to her mind—and ours, too, I'm afraid—was the only logical arrangement for that household. She was in charge. Already. And permanently.

"Gordon, dear," she said firmly after we had finished eating and lolling about in lawn chairs while the velvet dusk, the slowly dying tiki torches, the season's lingering warmth and a last few valiant fireflies held us in a drowse of contentment. "I think we've all heard enough about the Circle H Ranch, now. In fact," she added quickly as he looked a little crestfallen, "I was about to suggest that we fly you all down there for Thanksgiving. You'd love it."

"You surely would," Gordon said, brightening. "It's a marvelous place. Do come now, hear?"

"Fly us down?" Bessie echoed, her tone showing

that she, like Tal and myself, had not quite adjusted yet to Anna's new wealth. But Anna had.

"Certainly," she said briskly. "We can use the big Cessna, can't we, Gordon? They can bring it up and have it ready for us on the Sunday of Thanksgiving week, and then we can spend the whole week down there. Making plans."

"I'm not sure I can get off that long," Bessie said doubtfully.

"I'll let you," Anna said cheerfully. "It won't be any problem. The rest of the staff can run the paper for a week."

"Now, wait—a—minute, miss," Tal said. "What the hell are you talking about?"

"Listen to her," Gordon said proudly. "L.G.'s got ideas, all right."

"Gordon, dear, I thought we agreed—"

"Oh, oh!" he said. "I did it that time, I surely did! This little gal doesn't like me to call her L.G.—Little Gal, that is. And I promised, I really did. I promised and here I plumb forgot. Sorry, sweetheart. I won't do it again."

"I hope not," Anna said with mock severity—or was it mock? We weren't so sure. "I don't want to have to mention it anymore."

"You won't, honey," Gordon promised fervently. "You sure won't!"

"Good," she said calmly. "Now, Tal. You had a question?"

"I surely did," Tal said, saving it from impudence with a grin that mollified Gordon's startled look before it really got going. "I said what the hell is all this talk about time off, and newspapers and things like that-there?"

"Well," she said, a little excitement beginning in her

voice, "I thought you'd never ask. Gordon, go get those papers, will you, please?"

"You bet, L.—Anna, honey," he said, hopping up. "Be right back, y'all."

There was silence for a moment as he loped off into the house. Into it Bessie projected, in a hesitant voice, the question we all wanted to ask.

"Anna, are you—are you—really—*happy?*"

Anna shrugged, face impassive.

"I'm here."

"What kind of answer is that?" I inquired.

"The only kind you're going to get, friends," she said sweetly, "since it's really none of your damned business."

"It certainly is," Bessie said stoutly. "We're your oldest and dearest friends in Washington, and if it isn't *our* business, whose is it?"

"Well," Anna said, more gently, "I appreciate your concern for me, I really do. . . . Yes, I'd say I'm happy. At least I'm not *unhappy.* And I'm about to enter upon *the most exciting time of my whole life.* And I'm going to take you all right along with me, just as I always said I would. So I guess that's happiness."

"It may be for us," Bessie agreed, but persisted, with her usual stubborn honesty, "but we still want *you* to be happy."

"I am, I *am!*" Anna said lightly as Gordon reappeared in the doorway with an armful of newspapers. "Lord, Bessie, stop worrying. Stop worrying, all of you! We're going to have *fun.*"

"Did I hear somebody say fun?" Gordon inquired as he came within earshot, handed each of us three or four papers and flopped back into his chair. "Spendin' all that money is *fun?*"

"You have to spend it to make it," she said calmly,

"and you don't have anything better than me to spend it on, do you? *Do* you?"

"No, L.—honey," he said quickly. "No, ma'am, I surely do *not!* Not in this world!"

"All right, then," she said. "Now, team—you've all seen this thing."

"The *Northern Virginian*," Tal read carefully, holding it up toward the nearest tiki torch so he could see better. "This week's issue. That's a shopping throwaway, isn't it? Published in Alexandria."

"It is for now," Anna said, the excitement rising again in her voice. "But not for long."

"Oh?" I said. "What are you going to transform it into?"

"Well," she said, looked at Gordon, took a deep breath and for once appeared to be deferring to him; which she should have, after all, since he was going to be footing the bill. "Shall I tell them, dearest?"

"Honey," he said fervently, "you tell 'em all about it. Isn't she the *greatest?*" he demanded.

"She's something, all right," Tal agreed, which pretty well summed it up for the old team.

"She sure is!" Gordon said, beaming. "She *sure* is!"

"I'm going to buy this thing," Anna said, noticeably not using "we," which Gordon didn't challenge though he should have.

There was a silence while we digested this.

"And run a shopper?" I asked finally. "Hire us all to run a weekly *shopper?*"

"Ed," she said kindly, "you're nice but you're dumb sometimes. Yes, of course I'm going to hire you all to run a shopper. What better use could be made of your multiple talents? No, of course we're not going to put out a shopper—at least after the first six months. And we aren't going to stay in Alexandria either. We're coming across the river."

"To D.C.?" Tal asked blankly. "But what about the *Daily News* and the *Star* and the *Post?*"

"Oh, the *News* and the *Star* and the *Post!*" she said, dismissing those reasonably formidable institutions with a sniff. "The *News* is sliding fast, the *Star* is dying on the vine and the *Post* is so busy chasing Causes it's got its nose up its—anyway, I'm not worried about *them.*"

"You sure as hell should be,". Tal said soberly. "They're going to absolutely *squash* you."

"Want to bet?" she inquired. "How much, Talbot? I've got fifteen million to start with—"

"Well, now, honey—" Gordon began, finally sounding a little alarmed. "I didn't expect—"

"Fifteen million," she repeated firmly. "You can afford it. And it will let me *do* things in this town. *And* . . . it will make me happy."

"I know," he said, "but—"

"Deal or no deal, Gordon?" she demanded crisply. "Which is it going to be, we might as well decide right now."

"Well—" he said lamely. "Well—all right, I guess. But fifteen *million.* Criminetly!"

"I'm not in this for child's play," she said in the same brisk tone. "I'm in it for keeps. I intend to go to the top and stay there. And you're all coming with me. Don't worry, Gordon," she said more kindly, reaching over to pat him on the knee as one would a child. "There'll be some profits coming in as soon as we get rolling, you know. We won't just stand still. You'll get it back double. Just have a little faith in Anna. She'll get you there."

And because that is essentially what we all did have, faith in Anna, by the time Tal and Bess and I got up to go, well after midnight, we had it all pretty well blocked out.

Tal would give notice next day at the *Times,* Bessie

at the *Geographic,* I at UPI. We would tell no one where we were going. Two weeks later we would suddenly show up at the Congressional Press Galleries and the White House requesting credentials for the *Northern Virginian.* Shoppers didn't get them, so we wouldn't; but the whole town would instantly be abuzz with what-the-hell-is-going-on? Within the month Anna would hire away some thirty other people, drawn across the spectrum from the *Star,* the *Post,* the *Times* bureau and the newsmagazines. She knew exactly where she wanted them to fit in the organization, and she knew almost name by name exactly whom she wanted. For the time being they would all keep occupied, somehow, on the *Northern Virginian.*

In Month Six, the *Northern Virginian* would move to offices on H Street N.W. two blocks west of Sixteenth: Anna already knew the building and had ascertained that a ten-year lease could be negotiated. For six more months, the *Northern Virginian* would continue to be a throwaway shopper, keeping a substantial foothold in northern Virginia, principal bedroom of the capital, but concentrating more and more on the District of Columbia itself. It would carry Anna's column and as many more as space would bear.

One year from the date of purchase the *Northern Virginian,* now well established in the District, would metamorphose into a daily newspaper. Its name, taken sentimentally from Anna's first job in Philadelphia, would be *The Washington Inquirer.* Anna would be publisher, Gordon chairman of the board. Tal would be editor, I would be managing editor, Bessie would be women's editor running the women's departments and turning out a three-a-week society column. ("As much like Betty Beale's as possible—keep it lively and get scoops!") Anna would continue her own column, her tie with NBC and her lectures, which would now have a new beginning:

"Let me tell you about the joys and excitements, the frustrations and the satisfactions, the enormous *challenges* of starting a new newspaper to restore truth and decency to Your Nation's Capital." (Typically, she was onto the idea of *restoring* these qualities well before most people realized they were in need of it.)

The *Inquirer*'s motto, encircling a lion couchant ("Because I'm a Leo"), would be: *"The Truth—Regardless!"*

And on a wing and a prayer and Gordon's fifteen millions, by then depleted probably by four or five, Anna and her team would take over Your Nation's Capital and reign happily forever after. To clinch the deal she would give us, with really extraordinary generosity, twenty-five shares of voting stock apiece. She and Gordon would have fifty each.

Tal was driving that night, and when we reached Bessie's apartment, being by then considerably sobered and in a more reflective mood, she invited us in for a nightcap.

When it was poured we simply sat for several minutes staring at one another, too overwhelmed by Anna's ideas and enthusiasm to say anything.

Finally Bess raised her glass and said, rather feebly, "Here's to the *Inquirer*."

"Here's to Anna," I amended. "Can she do it?"

"With Gordon's money and the help of all of us," Tal said slowly, "she can do it. But we're all going to have to work like hell."

"I'll drink to *that*," Bessie said, and finally we all relaxed a bit, and laughed, and did so. But when it came time to say good night, after one more drink and some more bemused talk about what we had just

103

heard, Bessie stopped us at the door and held out her hands, which we solemnly took.

"Are you going to give notice tomorrow?" she whispered. "It's *such* a big step."

"I will if you will," I said.

"So will I," Tal said.

"Well, then," Bessie said as we all gave each other's hands a desperate squeeze, "I guess I will too, Lord help us!"

"The Lord and Anna," Tal said as we all grinned in a rueful, apprehensive, yet curiously excited and exhilarated way. "They never fail."

And for quite a long time thereafter, neither did.

2

I had always thought I would like to have two children, a boy and a girl; and I did. If neither has turned out quite as I wished, and if both have disappointed me in their attitudes toward me and the publishing empire I so carefully crafted for their sakes, that, I suppose, is life. Nothing can dim the happy memories of those early years when they were my laughing, happy, willing and obedient companions.

—ANNA HASTINGS, *by Anna Hastings*

"I WONDER IF SHE KNOWS," BESSIE MURMURED TO ME recently, "just how revealing that last sentence is. I wanted her to change it, but she said, 'No, they *were* obedient. They *were* willing. They *were* laughing and happy. I want something to testify to what they were once, so that people will know how fine they were, when they see the wrecks they've made of themselves now.'"

"I'm glad she wasn't my mother," I said. Bessie looked sad.

"Poor Anna. She's never understood that you just have to let people live their own lives."

Yet it was done with all the love in the world, which was what made it rather awful to watch. It was just that it was also done with all the determination in the world that both young Gordie and Lisa should fit into the pattern of the world *as Anna conceived the world to be*. And sometimes her conception was a little out of phase. Not with many things—not with "the empire"—not with Washington—not with her place in her country and her times—but certainly with the kids.

There are many in Washington who are happy about this. The *Post* in particular has never missed an opportunity to run their pictures with a caption that always refers to "estranged children of the publisher of *The Washington Inquirer* attend gala opening at Kennedy Center," or "disinherited son and daughter of Anna Hastings join happy throngs at Wolf Trap concert," or something similarly kind. Anna retaliates when she gets the chance, but in that area the *Post* family appears to be in reasonably good shape, which is one more of the many bitter things that lie at the root of the icy jealousies that divide the two prima donnas of Washington publishing.

It was very close to the exact mark—nine months and one week after their marriage, as I recall—that Gordie arrived. (He remained "Gordie" until the unhappy days, many years later, when Anna was making her final effort, without success, to get him to assume his rightful place as her heir. He then became—briefly, because he and Lisa didn't stay around long after their father's death—"Young Gordon" in her conversation and in those famous blue initialed memos to the staffs.)

Once again I found a wildly excited Gordon Senior

on my telephone to give me the happy news. He had been too busy helping Anna get the paper started in the intervening months, and too worried about its prospects, to give in to his occasional streak of maudlin emotionalism; and of course I could forgive him this time.

"Ed!" he shouted, voice heavy with joy. "Hey, there, Ed! It's a boy, Ed! My sweet little gal's given me a boy! Gordon B. Hastings, Junior, Ed! Gordon B. Hastings, Junior!"

I almost asked, "Democrat, of Texas?" but re-restrained myself.

"That's marvelous, Gordon. How are they both doing?"

"Right as rain," he crowed. "Right—as—rain! You know that little gal of mine, she always does ever'theng *just right*. Popped in that hospital at nine P.M. last night and popped out little Gordon at eleven-twenty-two P.M. without a worry or a wiggle. Why, I'll bet if she'd a been one of my Mexican gals down on the Circle H she'd be back in the field workin' cotton this very minute, she's that amazin'! Wouldn't you bet she would, Ed?"

"Yes," I said, "I really bet she would, Gordon. So it's a son and heir, is it? What's he going to be— United States Senator or world's greatest publisher?"

"Maybe both, Ed," he said—firmly, but with just enough hesitation in his voice so that I knew it had already been discussed. "Maybe both. What *I'd* like him to do is get himself some schoolin' and then go back down to the Circle H for a while and get to know the ranch and the oil business and the folks, and all, and then mebbe try for the House first, and then come on over to the Senate and join me."

"It sounds as though you plan to be around a long time," I said, and indeed, since he tended to his constituency well, never annoyed anybody, never took a controversial stand on anything, never said boo to a bunny rabbit, he might well be. "What does Anna think about that program?"

"Well," he said, his voice becoming a little more openly uncertain, "she has her own ideas, of course." He laughed somewhat nervously. "You know Anna."

"I do," I agreed. "She wants him to stay in D.C. and take over the publishing empire she's planning to build."

"That's about it," he acknowledged, and now he sounded honestly unhappy. "But he can't do both, Ed, you know that. He just can't do both!"

"So he's going to stay in Washington and take over the publishing empire she is planning to build."

"I don't know, Ed, I just don't know. I'm not so sure I'll give in on that one."

"It does seem to me," I said carefully, because I didn't want to get caught in the middle and receive a lecture from Anna the minute she came back on the job, "that the ranch and the oil wells are—well, realities, you might say, while the publishing empire is— well, not a dream exactly now that we've started work on it, but—"

"Oh, she's goin' make it come true, Ed," he said with a sudden stout loyalty. "She's goin' make it come true, never you doubt it. That little gal of mine, when she gets her mind set on somethin', she *does* it, Ed, you know that! She *does* it!"

"Then why are we discussing Gordon Junior? If she's got her mind made up?"

"Well," he said lamely. "I've got a mind *too,* you know, Ed. And after all, I *am* his pappy."

"Don't let him forget it," I advised, moved by an unexpected sympathy for this easygoing clunk whom we had all begun to grow increasingly fond of as we came to realize the well-meaning nature of his dumb but decent heart.

"I won't," he promised soberly. "I won't, Ed. You better believe it! . . . Why, hell, anyway—" and he laughed, though not quite as confidently as he would have liked, I think, "here we are, me and Anna arguin' over this little tad who isn't even a day old yet! Not even one day! Hell, he's got so much growin' up to do it'll be *years* before we have to decide anything about him! Won't it, Ed? *Years*."

"That's right, Gordon," I said, though I was pretty sure the argument was already over whether he was ready to admit it to himself or not. "Just relax and enjoy him, for now."

"I sure intend to do that," he said, happiness coming back into his voice. "He doesn't look like much yet, but I can see he's goin' to be a cute little bugger. We'll have us some great times down on the ranch and—up here—and—and all."

"Give Anna my love," I said. "Tell her we expect her back in the fields next Monday."

"She'll probably be there," he said with a chuckle. "You know that little gal of mine!"

And by Monday (it was then the previous Tuesday) she *was* back, coming into the new office on H Street promptly at her usual hour of 8:35 A.M. (I once asked her why this exact odd hour, and she said, "Because it sticks in the staffs' minds. It isn't quite as early as some of them come in, which shows them I'm the boss; and it isn't as late as other bosses, which shows them I'm not like other bosses." Eight-thirty-five A.M. it was then and 8:35 A.M. it is to this day; and it still is part of the legend, and it still impresses the staffs.)

A week later she brought Gordie in for us all to admire, which we did with suitable *oh's* and *ah's*. He was still too brand-new to have much personality but

109

he gurgled and drooled at the world with something of his father's amicability.

"I think he'll do well here," Anna said, quite seriously, as she gave him a quick and—for Anna—touchingly tender kiss, handed him to his nurse and turned back briskly toward her desk. "Don't you, Ed?"

"I think he'll do well wherever he goes," I replied.

"Hmm," she said with a little gleam in her eye. "I think he'll do well right here."

And that was the only time, until much later, that we ever discussed it; but very early the pattern became clear. The first time Gordon had to return to the state after that to put his political and personal fences in order, Anna took the baby and went along; but thereafter, save for a very few occasions over the years, mostly during reelection campaigns, she and the children remained in Washington. After Lisa arrived two years later, to become even more her father's idol than the boy was, she, too, was absorbed smoothly and efficiently into Anna's world. Thanksgivings, occasionally Christmases, now and then a school vacation as they grew older—these were about all that Gordie and Lisa really had a chance to see of Texas and the oil-and-ranch world of their father. It was probably not surprising that both fell deeply in love with it, since they were so diligently kept away from it, and that an instinctive and inevitable counterreaction should have been set up toward the *Inquirer* and their mother's insistent and unceasing attempts to involve them in it.

This was very sad, because much of her conversation in those years revolved around her dreams for them when they grew up and became old enough to assist her in managing an enterprise that was blessed with success from the start. Bessie, Tal and I used to try to caution her, but Anna was not made for that kind of advice.

110

"You'll simply turn the kids against you if you keep insisting," Tal told her once, summing up the feelings of all of us when they were fifteen and thirteen respectively. "Let them learn to love it as you do and it will all work out all right. It won't if you keep beating them over the head with it."

"I can't conceive of any child of Anna Hastings not loving this business," she replied calmly, referring to herself by name as she was beginning increasingly to do as she became more successful and more famous. "Why do they have to 'learn' to love it? It's part of them as it is of me."

"O.K." Tal shrugged. "Maybe that's why they seem so resentful when they come in here."

For a second a genuine pain came into her eyes—one of the few times we ever saw Anna off guard.

"They aren't resentful!" she cried. "I won't have them resentful and I won't have you saying they are, because that only encourages them. I won't have it. I simply won't have it!"

But by the time they were a couple of years older, it was obvious that, for once, what she would or wouldn't have was beside the point. She was beginning to lose them, and although part of it could be attributed to the general malaise of the late Sixties and early Seventies, the greater part was her own fault. The driving ambition, the powerful ego, the determination to dominate that succeeded so well with her own peer group simply didn't work with her children; and part of the tragedy of Anna is that she never really realized it until too late—and then was too proud and too stubborn to admit she was wrong, and get them back again. She could have, if she had been willing to humble herself a little. Maybe she still can, because every once in a while—in spite of what happened to their father, which was awfully hard for them to take—one or the other will call me and we'll have lunch and they always wind up crying about their mother. Then she and I have lunch and she comes as close to crying about them as pride will permit. But somehow, in spite of my attempts and Bessie's and Tal's, we can never seem to get them to cry together. And now as the years lengthen, I am beginning to conclude finally that we never will.

For a while, though, as she says in her book, they were happy together—for about a decade, I'd say. Gordie was a sturdy little boy on his way to becoming a great big sturdy man, blessed with good looks drawn from both parents, intelligence drawn from his mother and a sunny disposition coming directly from Gordon. Lisa was as small, cute and determined as her mother, gentled by her father's contribution. She too usually got what she wanted, but the approach was more happy, less direct, never as blunt and commanding as Anna's frequently was. Of course she hadn't been toughened by almost twenty years in the man's world of the newspaper business either; but even if she had, it seems likely she still would have made her way very successfully with a charm less calculated and a manner less indicative of the iron underneath.

So in those early days Anna was entirely happy, I suspect for the first and only time in her life. The *Inquirer* was beginning to succeed in a way that surpassed all our hopes, the kids were growing up cute and loving, Gordon was a necessary but not very demanding factor whom she had grown used to and could handle efficiently without really giving him a second thought.

"He can run his Senate and I'll run my newspaper," she often said with a chuckle; and Gordon chuckled, too, and, aside from an occasional request that she accompany him on the campaign trail, which she faithfully tried to honor—as often as her busy schedule would permit—made no demands. All appeared to be going as she wished.

It wasn't until Gordie turned eight and Lisa six that the first signs of trouble appeared. Anna's way, characteristically, was to meet them head-on and try to eliminate them once and for all. A little more humor—except, of course, that basically she had none—and a little more tolerance would have made a world of difference. They weren't there on the morning the kids turned up in the office, as solemn as two little judges, and presented her with a PETISHUN.

What it said, I learned later—and increasing her annoyance, of course, it contained a few standard legal phrases straight from the Hill which revealed that Gordon had been asked for and had given assistance—was that they wanted to spend more time on the ranch; that they were getting bored by being brought down from the house in Georgetown to spend so much time at the paper; that they loved Mummie but they felt they weren't seeing enough of Daddy; that they wanted everybody to stop working so hard and all go down to the ranch and *HAVE FUN!!!*

I happened to be in the office at the time, talking to her about staff problems on the two papers in Texas when the kids came in, beaming and spilling over with the fun of it, to present their requests. I was about to say something amused and avuncular when I became aware that her face had frozen into stern and disapproving lines—and aware also that the kids had wilted instantly and were standing cowed and silent. Apparently maternal wrath was a more common thing than we had been led to believe by jolly scenes in the office.

For a few seconds nobody said anything. Then Gordie ventured softly, "We just—want to—go down to the ranch, Mummie. Is that—bad?"

"Yes, it is," she said coldly. "We go to the ranch whenever we have time for it. We don't have as much time as any of us would like, but we *don't complain*. The paper comes first and *we don't complain*."

"We weren't complaining, Mummie," Lisa said, equally humbled. "We were just—hoping."

"It doesn't hurt to hope," she said, "when it's *practical* hoping. It isn't practical for me to spend more time at the ranch than I do."

"Couldn't we," Gordie suggested hesitantly, "go down more with—with Daddy, then? I think he'd"—and unfortunately he placed an emphasis on the pronoun—"be happy to have *us*."

"I'm sure he would!" Anna said sharply. "But I prefer to have you here with me, learning the business."

"We don't want to learn the business *yet*, Mummie," Lisa said, her tone forlorn. "We're not old enough. It's *boring*."

For a second Anna looked genuinely shocked. This gave way immediately to anger.

"Nothing about this business is boring! Don't you ever say that to me again, do you hear! Either of you! This is the most fascinating business in the world and you're lucky to be part of it! Don't ever let me hear you say again that you are *bored* with this newspaper! We go to the ranch as much as time will permit. We are not going to go more often. You should be here with me as often as possible, and you will be. As for *this*"—and she ripped the petition in two with an expression that genuinely shocked me and frightened the kids—"you go back to your father and tell him I don't want any more of this nonsense. *I don't want any more of it, and that's final*."

And she tossed the scraps in the wastebasket, picked up the Texas file, turned to me and said calmly, "Now, where were we, Ed? Just going into circulation figures, weren't we?"

"Yes, I believe so. But—"

"But what, Ed, dear?" she inquired sweetly. "Did you have anything to add or suggest?"

"N-no," I said thoughtfully. "Would it be all right for me to take them to lunch later?"

"And all agree on what a monster I am?" She laughed merrily. "Well, if you must, you must, I suppose. Run along, children. Go watch the presses, or something. Uncle Ed will see you later. Right now we have business, don't we, Ed, dear?"

"The circulation of the *Endeavor*," I said without expression, "is thirty-two thousand daily, forty-five thousand three hundred one Sundays. Now, presumably we can increase that by—"

Later in the cafeteria I found the kids already waiting for me at a table, complete with cheeseburgers and chocolate shakes. Our discussion of the matter was brief.

"Why is Mummie like that?" Gordie asked as though he didn't really expect an answer, which was good because I couldn't give him one without taking much more than a lunch hour to do it. "We were just having *fun* and trying to make things better around this silly old place."

"It isn't a silly old place," I objected mildly. "It's a great newspaper and your mother, who is a remarkable woman, is going to make it greater. And so are you, someday."

"Maybe," Gordie said softly. "Maybe."

"Yes," Lisa echoed, as she often did Big Brother. "Maybe."

After that a definite curtain dropped and we talked of other things.

That, as far as the rest of us knew, was when it

115

began; though from Anna's sharp response and the kids' instant withering in the face of it, it seemed likely there may have been previous discussions at home. Anyway, from that time forward we began to notice in them that growing resentment that Tal was to warn her about four years later. By then, of course, it had settled into a pattern that only great love and understanding on her part could have changed. She had the love—still does, of course, mothers (even Anna) being what they are—but the understanding, no. She was determined they should fit the mold she had planned for them, and so, sadly but perfectly naturally, they presently became determined that they would not. Both had inherited her stubborn will, and in them, though it took awhile for the fact to penetrate—it was the one thing in her life, perhaps, in which she deliberately denied what her intelligence told her—she had met her match. Met it, and was defeated.

Because of course this was not an era in which parents, unless they could manage it with greater skill than many seemed to possess, could control their children. There were too many outside pressures telling the children, for one purpose and another, that this couldn't be done; and for the rich there were even fewer restraints. Like so many who became the spoiled show-offs of the Sixties and early Seventies, Gordie and Lisa had their own money: a regular, substantial and irrevocable allowance in their earlier years, the certainty of very ample wealth when they reached their twenty-first birthdays. Gordon had taken care of all that in a burst of paternal emotion on the birth of each —even though Anna, perhaps instinctively foreseeing future troubles, tried without success to persuade him to handle it more carefully. He would have none of it, for once defying her. He asked Tal, Bessie and me to be the trustees, so we knew that he had been generous indeed. The allowances up to age ten were invested by us (and I will say, with a little good advice from his lawyers and accountants, very well invested). After ten, investments and actual allowance money were divided by a mathematical formula that gave the kids an amount of cash in hand that increased regularly every year; and at twenty-one the whole lot would be theirs, investments, interest and principal of the trust. Being children of Anna, they were born independent of character; being children of Gordon, they were created independent of means. It took them awhile to realize the weapon this gave them in dealing with their mother; but being children first and above all of Anna, I doubt very much that it would really have mattered whether they had one dime or the one million that each, in fact, did have. The clash would have come anyway.

So they went to the proper schools, Gordie to Saint Albans and Lisa to Miss Madeira's; and by the time Gordie was seventeen and ready to go to Harvard, and Lisa was fifteen and beginning to think about Smith or Wellesley, both showed definite signs of heading for the dope-up-drop-out-look-at-us-everybody-we're-rebelling-aren't-we-*smart* syndrome that seduced many of the brighter young minds of their generation. All of it, of course, complicated—and in substantial part, no doubt, caused—by the increasingly tense relationship with their mother and with what she was already referring to proudly as "my publishing empire."

"Little gal," I can remember Gordon pleading with her one sweltering summer night at another of those many intimate Georgetown gatherings for five that he gave over the years of the empire's growth, "don't keep after the kids about the papers so, now! Please don't, hear? It just makes them resent the papers and resent you, and that just tears me apart, now, it really

117

does." His voice became thick with emotion and since the three of us secretly and sometimes openly sympathized with him, we knew it was genuine and not just too many gin and tonics. "I don't like to see my dear little gal and my dear sweet little boy and girl turning away from each other in bitterness and anger, now, I *really* don't."

"You love it," Anna said coldly. "You like nothing better than to have them hate me and come running to you for sympathy. It gives you such an advantage over me, you *think*. Why blame me for it? You do everything you can to aggravate it."

"I do *not!*" he cried, and now the anguish was quite genuine. "I do *not,* I swear I do *not!* Do I, now, Ed? Do I, now, Bessie? Do I, Tal? You-all *know* I don't! Don't you!"

Nobody replied for a moment; then Bessie spoke, with surprising firmness, for us all.

"You don't," she agreed. "You try to do all you can to keep things peaceful, Gordon."

"And I suppose I don't!" Anna demanded, rounding on her in a rare show of anger. "I suppose I don't do everything I can to appease those smug little monsters while they make fun of me and my papers and defy my wishes and try to make a mockery of everything I'm trying to accomplish for them and for the country! I suppose I don't have any feelings! I suppose I don't— I don't—I suppose I—"

And quite horrifying all of us, for this was the first time we had ever seen it happen, she suddenly began to cry, great tears spilling unheeded down her cheeks while she locked her hands around her knees and rocked back and forth in a sort of terrible, primeval anguish that made Gordon's seem like child's play.

Instantly, of course, he was on his knees beside her, crying himself, beseeching her incoherently not to cry, not to be hurt, not to worry so about things, everything would be all right; and the rest of us were huddling around, Bessie crying also and Tal and I sniffling and blowing our noses and making sounds as incoherent as Gordon's. All in all, it was quite a scene for a placid Georgetown garden in the middle of July.

Presently she stopped and so did we; things began to quiet down; silence presently returned, filled with the burden of hopes already lost, hopes being lost and hopes still to be lost; and finally she remarked in a tired voice—to no one in particular, perhaps, maybe just to herself or maybe just to the whole world, it wasn't really clear—

"Life would be so simple for me if everybody would just stop opposing me and do what they ought to do."

To which there was not then, or ever, any really adequate response: only the guarantee that sometime, somewhere, down the road a piece when they decided they had to, the kids would turn on her as bitterly and finally as she so obviously feared.

3

Meanwhile, disappointed though I was by the growing evidence that my children did not revere the news business as I did, great satisfactions were coming to me almost daily, it seemed, in that area of my life. The Inquirer *had succeeded beyond my wildest dreams: other prospects opened up: everything I touched in the part of my life I loved the most seemed destined for success.*

—ANNA HASTINGS, *by Anna Hastings*

THE BIRTH OF THE *Inquirer* CAME ABOUT ALMOST exactly as Anna had planned. The acquisition of the *Northern Virginian* of course leaked out immediately when Bessie, Tal and I, true to our promise to her and our vow to each other, gave notice and then showed up at the Congressional Press Galleries and the White House, requesting new credentials in the name of our new employer, Anna Hastings.

"Journalism's Glamour Girl Branches Out," *Time* reported. "What's Up With Anna?" the *Post* asked uneasily, its proprietors sensing, accurately, the approach of competition. "Columnist Buys N. Virginia Shopper," the *Star* reported quietly on an inside page, obviously hoping it would go away. And *Life* magazine, which had been bedazzled by her ever since the Pulitzer and her marriage to what they preferred to call "Texas' Millionaire Cowboy Senator" (even though nine-tenths of his wealth came from oil and the Circle H was really only a hobby), bustled over to Alexandria and took some shots of a beamingly self-confident Anna behind the dilapidated desk of her new possession. (The millionaire cowboy was presumably busy in the Senate; anyway, he was not to be found in the pictures and in only a very minor way in the news stories. One got the feeling that he was sort of around somewhere, and that Anna was letting him stick his head in the door now and then when she felt like it: which was not entirely inaccurate.)

The day the *Life* issue hit the stands she released a statement headed simply, "Acquisition of Staff," in which she announced Tal's, Bessie's and my appointments and the hiring of some twenty-five of the younger and brighter reporters around town. "ANNA RAIDS THE ROOST," the *Post* reported, having lost five of its own and now being genuinely worried; "WHAT IS SHE UP TO?" But again the plaint went unanswered except by action, which, Anna explained to her first staff meeting, was what she intended to stress for "my publications" —"We'll act and let others talk. They'll find out soon enough."

In Month Six, exactly as planned, we moved into the District to H Street, two blocks west of Sixteenth: "just two blocks from the White House," in the phrase that soon became standard, though if you count Lafayette Park it is more like three. Nonetheless it popped up in Anna's writings and conversations at every opportunity thereafter and soon became fixed in the public mind. "Sitting here just two blocks from the White House contemplating the abysmal shortcomings of the man who inhabits it—" begins many a column. "Here we are again with our pleasant Sunday afternoon gathering just two blocks from the White House!" she always announces gaily at the start of her weekly television show, which is, indeed, by special arrangement with NBC, photographed in the city room. And "Two blocks from the White House may be too close to give the needed perspective on the strange performance of its occupant," starts many an editorial, "*but—*"

By the time of the move, of course, the town was really abuzz and both the *Post* and the *Star* were regarding things with a genuine worry. "If Anna Hastings has any romantic idea that a modern newspaper can be started in this capital without a financial outlay that would break a man far wealthier than her oil-baron Senator husband—" the *Post* abjured. "Mrs. Hastings," the *Star* agreed, "may be in danger of biting off more than she and her Senator husband can chew." And in the Senate, Wayne Morse of Oregon spoke dourly for five and a half hours on the dangers of combining oil money with journalism, never once, of course, mentioning Gordon by name—a required Senatorial courtesy which permitted Gordon to rise at the end of Morse's speech and inquire blandly, "Could the Senator tell the Senate where he sees this desperate danger to the Republic?"

Morse could only retort, "The Senator knows very well!"

"Not hardly," Gordon said gently. "I'm jes' all confusion, Senator. Guess we'll all have to stop worryin' about it, since the Senator won't tell us." And sat down amid the laughter and applause of most of his colleagues, who liked his amiable ways and found Morse's prickly ones, as always, uncomfortable.

Months Seven, Eight, Nine, Ten, Eleven came and went while Anna ran the operation with a firm hand and continued busily turning out her column on the side. It was always a question of which came first: whether the *Post* dropped it or she had United Features yank it out of there before they had the chance; anyway, she blamed it on the *Post* in a stinging editorial that drew first blood. The *Post* lost its cool, not for the last time where Anna was concerned, and uttered a short ill-natured squawk about "an interloper to Washington journalism whose intrusive beak, like that of the pelican, may hold more than her belly can." "In a shocking example of anti-Semitism," Anna wrote in a signed editorial, rather farfetched but neatly calculated to infuriate, "directed at me, who am really just a modest little Polish girl from Punxsutawney, Pa., my distinguished if not particularly impressive competitor, the Washington *Post,* chooses to attack my physiognomy—"

The *Post* thought for a while after that before tackling her again, but the exchange set the tone for all their future encounters. No love was ever lost between the two. "That bitch" swiftly became the standard, and only, form of reference in both executive offices.

Came Month Twelve and with it, as planned, the *Inquirer.* "New Daily Paper Starts Here," the *Star* reported in a short but not unfriendly piece on page 1. "New Paper Announced," the *Post* reported in a chill three paragraphs on page 27. Within a week the *Inquirer's* guaranteed circulation had reached 150,000 and a week later Anna hired away the *Post's* No. 2 circulation man, plastered his picture all over the front page, called on Gordon for another five million, "cinched up her panty-hose," as Tal put it, "and prepared to do battle."

The next few months were exciting indeed as the

Inquirer's circulation and the *Post*'s chagrin continued to mount. The *Star,* by then already beginning to sink into the dignified lassitude that was presently to bring it to the edge of disaster, watched from a bemused and curiously uninvolved distance as the other two struggled. Anna insisted upon, and got, a series of scoops from her enthusiastic and devoted new staff; circulation promotion stunts came and went so fast one could hardly keep track of them; and a couple of *Inquirer* delivery trucks actually skidded and turned over, fortunately injuring no one but giving rise to delicious rumors of sabotage, never proven. All in all, it was a great time to be working in Washington and working for Anna. And inexorably, day by day, the circulation climbed, and over on L Street, the *Post's* proprietors came grudgingly but practically to the conclusion that the interloper was very probably here to stay.

The biggest rumor of that day, however, like the rumor that Queen Elizabeth I had met secretly with Mary Queen of Scots, was not true, nor, as far as I know, was it ever true in any way, shape, manner or form. The big talk of the town for several days was based on one of Drew Pearson's usual swear-to-God inside reports that there had indeed been such a meeting; that the *Post*'s lady had offered to buy out Anna for ten million, that she had said she would sell for thirty, and that the whole thing had thereupon collapsed.

"Utter rubbish," Anna snorted when the wire services and the New York *Times* called her about it. "The *Inquirer* is not for sale for ten million, thirty million, fifty million, or fifty billion. Tell Drew to go whistle up another manhole. He's goofed again."

"It is not the purpose of the *Post*," the *Post* said stiffly, "to attempt to discourage honest competition in the field of Washington journalism or anywhere else. We do not consider opposition newspapers to be any threat to the *Post*. Indeed we welcome them—if, as they claim, they do in fact bring to Washington the truth they claim they bring."

"Well, screw you, too," Anna said when she read that; and went back to war with renewed vigor and enthusiasm.

By the time the second anniversary of the *Inquirer* arrived, circulation was up to 450,000 and still climbing; she had hired away some twenty more people, six of them from the *Post,* the rest from out of town— a deliberate policy "so we won't get too myopic from all being insiders"—and was quite successfully averaging a scoop or two a week to upset her principal competitor—not always the greatest scoops in the world, but enough to sting.

Furthermore, helped by her activities as publisher, her column continued to expand. She still found time to peck it out herself three times a week—she had asked United Features to reduce it from five, and aware of her growing fame and box-office appeal, they had agreed. She was, as promised, a frequent participant still on "Meet the Press," though there was some grumbling among our colleagues that she was really now a publisher and no longer a newspaperwoman, and therefore taking an unfair advantage in appearing. But she blithely ignored this, as she ignored other such grumbles when she turned up on the Hill in a choice press seat for some exciting hearing, or went to the White House for briefings (and increasingly, now, was invited to White House dinners with a worshipful Gordon in tow), or occasionally used her growing power to secure a personal interview with the President, which she always presented, by-lined, on the front page. "I'm still a reporter at heart," she would say on the "Today" show or in one of the increasingly frequent magazine articles about her. "I guess I always will be. It's the only way to know what's really going on in Washington—particularly," and she would purr, "if one has any real desire to be a truly well-informed and responsible publisher there."

Everything seemed to be moving smoothly and with increasing success on all fronts; which was why we were startled, on the day the paper reached its third birthday, to be summoned to a formal conference in her office, with Gordon present. The subject: "The *Inquirer:* Time to Establish an Informed and Powerful Personality."

We had thought we were establishing it—at least Bessie, Gordon and I thought we were—but as outlined in the agenda she had typed herself, and handed to us solemnly as we took our seats, apparently not in the eyes of our publisher. Nor, we discovered, in Tal's.

4

I had brought the Inquirer *successfully through its first three years. It had been an increasing commercial satisfaction but in other areas I had not found it so satisfying. It seemed to me we had no personality—no instantly recognizable "image," if you like. We had not yet succeeded in establishing for the paper the distinct and dominant position that only a clear-cut, unequivocal, forthright and consistent editorial and news policy can provide. It was time, it seemed to me, for the* Inquirer *to take sides in the great social and political battle of our times— between blind reaction and enlightened liberalism. Growing up as I had in the great tradition of Franklin D. Roosevelt and his heirs in American political thought, I never doubted for a moment what our position should be. With the aid of Talbot Farson, I was successful in achieving this goal.*

—ANNA HASTINGS, *by Anna Hastings*

THIS, IN SOMEWHAT LENGTHIER LANGUAGE AND WITH more detail—such as *"News stories hit harder at con-*

servative positions" and *"Go after reaction in White House, Congress, courts"*—was the general burden of the document we all perused in the thoughtful silence, while in the street below the traffic hurried by and distantly from the bowels of the building came the steady, powerful heartbeat of the presses printing the early edition that would hit the streets around 10 P.M. Another day in the life of the Washington *Inquirer* had been successfully concluded, we had thought. It was more than a little disconcerting to find that Anna did not agree.

"Little gal," Gordon said, breaking the silence at last, "I'm not exactly clear why you're proposin' this at this time. It seems to me the paper *is* well established and *is* doin' a great job. I know lots of folks on the Hill think it's the fairest paper in town. That's somethin' to be proud of, *I* think."

"It isn't enough," Anna said. "We need more than that."

"Why isn't it enough?" I asked. "The *Star* and the *News* are fading, the *Post* is getting so far over it's becoming notorious—you don't want to compete in that area, surely: they've got it preempted. There isn't room over there for you and I shouldn't think it's where you'd want to be."

"There is a place," she said, "for a truly genuine, fighting liberal newspaper in this town. I know I have competition, but I think a lot of its pretensions are phony, a lot of its reporting is sloppy, a lot of its posing is just that—posing. I think the *Inquirer* can do it better and do it right. And I think we should. Everything is too bland right now. It's time for us to stir it up."

"With Ike in the White House?" I inquired. "How else can anything be *but* bland? You aren't going to

128

lead any revolutions as long as that great big beaming smile embraces the world."

"I don't want to lead any revolutions," she said impatiently. "I just want to get out the truth about all this reactionary conservatism that hides in the shadow of that great big beaming smile. I want to tell the people about it. I want to save the country."

Anna being one of the few people in the world capable of making this last statement with a straight face and in utter sincerity, nobody said anything for a moment. Then Gordon tried again.

"Lots of folks want to save the country, honey," he pointed out mildly. "*I* want to save it. Ike wants to save it. Nine-tenths of the people in this town want to save it. What makes you think you've got any monopoly on that?"

"I don't think I have any monopoly on it! I just think I can do it better, I *know* I can do it better. I think it's time for the paper to reflect that."

"Of course you know, honey," Gordon said with an amiable grin that tried to lighten things a bit, "I might just be one of those reactionary conservatives you're dead set against. I might just not agree with all this liberal crap some of these people put out. Are you going to have the *Inquirer* go after me, too?"

"If you deserve it," she said shortly; and for the first time we could remember, Gordon replied to her with something of her own brusqueness.

"Now, see here," he said, face flushing, "I'm paying for this little adventure, you know."

"It isn't an 'adventure.' It's a great newspaper and I'm going to make it greater. And you won't be paying for it in about another five years. You'll have recovered your money by then and I'm not going to ask you for another red cent in the meantime. We're carrying ourselves very nicely, thank you. We can manage without you very well."

"Well, thanks so much," he said with a rare bitterness. "I guess that tells me where to get off. If you'll excuse me, I think I'd better be gettin' on back to the Hill. We're still in session on the Defense Department appropriation and I expect my reactionary conservatism may come in handy there. To save the country!"

"You and the rest of the warmongers," Tal remarked, breaking the impassive silence with which he had been observing all this.

"And don't *you* get smart," Gordon said, his unusual anger continuing. "We don't have to have *you* on this paper to keep it going."

"Yes, we do," Anna said calmly before Tal could fire back the angry volley that was obviously welling up. "To keep it going the way *I* intend to keep it going, we do. In fact, without Tal, I'd be virtually alone here."

"Now *that*," I said, shocked and annoyed, "really *is* a lot of crap."

And Bessie wailed, "Oh, *Anna!* How can you say such an ungrateful thing!"

"As for you," Anna said, giving us both a quick, appraising look, "I'm not very pleased with the way things are going with the management of the paper generally, Ed. Or in the women's department either, Bess. I think you're both too easygoing and you both lose sight of the goal of making this a really liberal paper.

"You need to hire more young people, Ed—kids who have been educated by teachers who know the score, kids who want to change this country around and set it on the right course. I'm tired of these old faces you keep bringing in every so often from the other papers. There isn't a new idea or a liberal idea or a fresh approach in the bunch. Sure, they're good old friends of ours, most of them, but we need more than that now. We need youngsters we can fit into the *Inquirer* mold."

"Is there one?" I asked dryly.

"There's going to be from now on," she said flatly. "And as for you, Bess, we should hit a lot harder on things like abortion, equal rights, the independent woman. And I haven't been too pleased with your society column lately. All this stuff and nonsense about Embassy Row and Marjorie Post and Perle Mesta and Dolly Munson and the rest of that feather-brained lot is all very well, but I'd like you to expose the guts of society. The sort of spun-sugar drivel you turn out can't be very edifying to our poor readers, or our Negro readers, or to the average housewife who doesn't have the time or money to party at the Sulgrave or dine with the charming bachelor ambassador from This or the swanky ambassadress from That. Do me a few contrast pieces on one of those parties and what went on at Mrs. Smith's in colored Southwest Washington that same evening and you'll be getting somewhere."

"Maybe," Bessie said, her voice trembling on the edge of tears, "maybe I should resign and let you get somebody who will fit the—the *Inquirer* mold—if you think I'm so awful."

"Maybe we all should, Bess," Gordon said, "and leave Tal and Anna to their happy little twosome. Maybe we should!"

"I don't think you're so awful," Anna said calmly, ignoring him. "You just need a little direction, as Ed does too. The whole paper does. That's why I'm promoting Tal to executive editor, which means he's going to be over everybody. Then I think we'll see things begin to happen as I want them to."

"Well, I'm damned," Gordon said slowly, while

Bessie and I, too stunned to say anything, simply stared at her and at Tal. It was quite obvious they had planned this well in advance, for he wasn't in the slightest surprised. He was trying very hard, in fact, to look entirely unimpressed; only the slightest of smiles and a certain heightened gleam in his eyes indicated that he was absolutely delighted and convinced he had a great opportunity. My misgivings, lulled by all his years of diligent reportorial endeavor and seemingly impartial professionalism, were suddenly back. "In twenty years' time," he had told me quietly as we stood in the midst of the roaring crowds in Lafayette Park on the night of V-J Day, "we'll have things turned completely around so that America will be the most hated country in the world." The change was already well under way, and now here he was about to take command of what could be one of the most powerful elements in hastening the process.

I decided I wouldn't offer to resign. Far from it. I would stay there and fight; because suddenly, it seemed to me, there was something concrete and ominous to fight against.

Yet there was still, of course, the lulling reassurance of the past, the feeling that my reaction was nonsense, all the old ties, the old friendship, the old camaraderie of having been young together in Washington . . . and so shortly—much more shortly than it takes to write it—my dramatic mood faded out and I was confronted by the practical fact: Tal has the nod and Good Old Ed has to take second place. And this took a bit of adjusting to.

"I hope," Anna said calmly, "that this is agreeable to everyone."

"Does that matter?" Gordon asked, still annoyed; and Anna laughed and made one of her "Oh, Gordon!" faces.

"Not really, no," she said cheerfully, "because I've decided it's best for the paper and I don't really want to argue about it. There will be a formal announcement to the staff tomorrow morning and it will be in the paper tomorrow night. Together with a statement by me setting forth our new plans and purposes. I think I'll call it 'Goals and Challenges.' You can help me write it, Ed, if you like."

I managed to rally enough to ask, "Is that in lieu of an increase in salary?"

Again she laughed, very cheerfully.

"Oh, don't be silly. You and Bess are both going to get increases in salary. And Tal isn't going to eat you, you know. After all, we *are* the old team, and even if Tal does have the title, he isn't going to bother you too much, are you, Tal? We just want to light a little fire under you, that's all."

"Thanks so much," Bessie said, rather shakily. "I could have done without that, thank you."

"No, you couldn't, Bess," Tal said with the casual self-satisfied bluntness that was to mark most of his utterances from here on. "You need it, admit it. And so does Ed. And so do you, Gordon. And so, no doubt, do I. It's as Anna said: we're still the old team. We can all continue to jump on each other when we need it. It's still the same."

But of course it wasn't. And the *Inquirer* wasn't either. Which, after all, was what Anna—and Tal— wanted.

5

That I had made the right decision was immediately apparent. The effect of Tal's appointment was galvanic upon the Inquirer and upon Washington. Almost overnight we began to push the Post vigorously in the fight to become the capital's leading liberal organ. Our stories became sharper and crisper, our attacks upon conservatism and corruption more aggressive and more effective. We began to serve the country powerfully and well as we helped to beat back the forces of reaction that everywhere threatened our democracy. This brought both the paper and me personally increased fame and growing power. It also made easier for me the acquisition of that publishing and broadcasting empire that now reaches from coast to coast and serves, I like to think, as one of the most effective protections the nation has against heartless conservatism and blind reaction.

—ANNA HASTINGS, *by Anna Hastings*

ACTUALLY, THE EFFECT WASN'T QUITE THAT GALVANIC; but before too many weeks had passed, the paper was something quite different. It was obvious that it would never go back to what it had been—a newspaper, Bessie and Gordon and I liked to tell each other from time to time, that had been well on its way to becoming an honest, unbiased, fair-minded, compassionate and objective publication worthy of the great responsibility it held by virtue of its fortunate position in the nation's capital.

There are those, particularly among the younger members of the staffs, who will argue today that the *Inquirer,* and all of Anna's subsequent acquisitions, still warrant those adjectives; but the terms are not understood by the young in journalism now as we understood them then. It is a different language: words do not mean the same. Partisanship, vindictiveness, personal antipathies, deliberate slanting, deliberate suppression of opposing viewpoints—censorship, in fact, though the word is vastly abhorred by those who practice it—all these now masquerade with a bland self-righteousness as honesty, lack of bias, fairness, compassion and objectivity.

When challenged hard enough, those who argue this will eventually admit that perhaps these terms no longer apply; but, they then ask, why should they? What is the advantage of *really* being honest, unbiased, fair, compassionate and objective? Are not the times so evil that we of the media *must* be partisan, vindictive, personal, deliberately biased, deliberately censorious and suppressive of the other fellow's point of view? How else are we to defeat the monsters of our age?

It is an argument, so Bessie and I and others equally old-fashioned think, that forms, a perfect circle—a circle that is rolling the media inevitably toward destruction of the First Amendment and with it all those who so loudly claim its easy protections as they busily violate its honorable intentions. We think a monstrous reaction could come, from a people made so cynical and so hopeless by the media that not even the media itself will be able to withstand the withering wind, consuming all institutions of stability great or small, good or bad, that its members have unleashed.

We pray that we are wrong, for in that cataclysm the nation itself would almost certainly be consumed.

The process by which the *Inquirer* was turned around was for the average reader, no doubt, a generally subtle and almost subliminal one; but we who knew the business were under no misapprehensions about it. In fact, Tal stated it to the staff in so many words when he formally took over, Anna smiling serenely at his side.

"From now on," he said, looking tough and beginning deliberately to build that legend of fearsome righteousness which was to stand him in such good stead when the challenge came, "this conservative crap is out. From now on, the *Inquirer* is going to be the best Goddamned liberal paper in this whole Goddamned world. Anybody who doesn't like it can get out now, because we don't need you. Anybody who wants to go along—welcome. We *do* need *you*. Your newspaper will back you in any crusade, support you in any campaign, as long as it has for its aim the destruction of the reactionary forces that cripple this nation at home and abroad. We want your brains, your faith, your idealism—*your hearts*. If you give us those, we will never let you down. Now get the hell out of here and *go to it!*"

The younger staffers were absolutely dazzled; they adored him, then and always; they were his—and Anna's—forever. The older members looked at one another silently and said nothing. Behind instinctive stifled protests lay mortgages on houses, kids in college, the new car, the new television set, the vacation in Europe, the aging dependent parents, the imminent operation, the necessary dental work. Tal knew where the jugulars were; Anna backed him up. The young gave their brains, faith, idealism and hearts; the elder gave their brains and were unable to withhold them because they were bought, signed, sealed and delivered.

I, however, was still managing editor, and Gordon was a not insignificant ally as the issue was joined. Bessie wasn't to be discounted either, though Anna thought she had her neutralized after we got over the trauma of her near-firing.

"Eddie," Anna said pleasantly one morning a month or so after what the staff came to refer to as Tal's Manifesto, "I think I'm going to have to ask you to replace Bess as women's editor. And we'll have to get somebody else to do the society column. In fact, I want the whole women's section redone."

"But why?" I asked. "Bessie's no fool, she's a good writer, she's doing her best to spruce things up since you talked to her—"

"I'm sorry, Eddie," Anna said with a calm regret, "but she just isn't *trendy* enough."

This was the first time that word, which has now become so much a part of Anna and her legend, entered her conversation; it has rarely left it since. I didn't realize then what a mental revolution it signaled. All I could see was an old friend being thrown to the wolves for no good reason visible to me.

"You can't do this to Bess," I said. "She has been absolutely loyal to you and she simply isn't doing all that bad a job."

"She's just a researcher, after all," she said with a

sniff. "It isn't as though I were asking you to fire the greatest newspaperwoman in the world—"

"*Fire* her?" I almost shouted. "Are you crazy, Anna? For Christ's sake, how cruel can you be? *Fire* her! I will do no such Goddamned thing!"

"Very well, then," she said serenely. "I expect I will have to ask Tal to do it. He's exercising a good many of your functions as it is."

"The hell he is," I said sharply. "The *hell* he is. I know you'd like him to, but he isn't and by God he isn't going to!"

"Oh?" she inquired. "Are you sure?"

I stared at her for quite a few seconds, because suddenly this was an Anna I hardly knew; had glimpsed and suspected from time to time, but had never really believed in. However, here she was.

However, here I was, too.

"Anna Hastings," I said levelly, "you can be as big a bitch as you like and it isn't going to stop me. You can fire *me,* if you like: I'll manage. I have lots of friends in this town, there are plenty of places to go. And Bessie does too. *That isn't the point.* The point is that we are two of your oldest and closest friends"—I couldn't resist a savage dig—"part of the Old Team— and we really *are* your friends. You'd be an absolute fool to separate yourself from us. You need people who like you more than you think, Anna darling. You really do."

"Ed, dear," she said, "now I'm afraid you're sounding jealous. Tal is my friend, too; Tal is part of the Old Team, too. Isn't that true?"

"Tal is Tal's friend," I said, voicing the concern I had been trying to suppress. "I'm not sure who else's."

"Really?" she said, sounding genuinely surprised. "What makes you say that?"

"I don't know," I replied thoughtfully, diverted for

138

the moment. "Let's just say it's a hunch. I'd keep an eye on him if I were you."

"I can't imagine what on earth you mean," she said, "but I assure you I keep an eye on everybody. Which is why I'm asking you to get rid of Bessie."

"I will not," I said, as calmly as she, "get rid of Bessie. If you want Bessie fired I'd suggest you not pass the buck to me, or to Tal either. I'd suggest you do it yourself, if you have the guts."

She shrugged.

"She'd just go to pieces."

"It would be good for you to watch," I said. "Then look in a mirror and think about what Anna Hastings has become."

This did stop her, and for several moments I could see that she was indeed thinking about exactly that. Presently she sighed.

"Very well, then, we won't fire Bessie. But I want her out of that spot, because I want somebody who is younger, more perceptive, more liberal, more vigorous, more—well, more *trendy*. Somebody like Susan Eldridge, for instance—" naming one of our recruits from the *Post*. "I think Sue could handle it very well. I want to shake up the whole section—call it something like—oh, I don't know—"

"How about 'Trend'?" I suggested dryly, and she nodded with a smile so bland I knew I had been bested again.

"Ed, dear," she said kindly, "*that* is superb. 'Trend' it will be, and Susan Eldridge it will be. Now: since Bessie seems to be your particular charge, what shall we do with her?"

"Hasn't Tal told you?" I inquired. "Ask him."

"There you go again," she said with a mock severity. "Jealous, jealous, jealous! Tal doesn't tell me anything. He advises, sometimes, but he doesn't tell me. Nobody *tells* me *anything*."

"Pity," I said. "You'd be better for it, Anna. You're beginning to lose touch with things a bit, I think."

"Oh, no. How about District Affairs?"

"For Bess? She won't take it."

"Suggest it," she said, "and see what happens."

When I did, a few minutes later, exactly what I expected happened. First Bessie burst into tears, which took about five minutes. Then she began to get mad, which took another five. And at the end of that, enormously fat, quivering, frowzy and furious but still somehow deeply touching—for after all we all *were* oldest and dearest friends, and the old days weren't gone in us, even if some of us didn't always remember them as we should—she dried her eyes and said with great dignity:

"Very well. You can tell Anna I resign. Or, no"— and she heaved herself out of the chair, gave her rumpled dress a tug, ran a shaking hand through her hair and gave her head a defiant toss—"no, you don't need to. I'll tell that heartless bitch myself."

And sailed away, out of my office, across the newsroom to pound furiously on Anna's door while the chattering of the typewriters began to fade and an interested and anticipatory silence began to fall.

The door opened. Anna saw who it was; shot me a venomous look from across the room that met my cheerful answering grin halfway, for a draw; suddenly beamed at Bessie, beckoned her in with a loving and protective arm, and shut the door. Slowly the typewriters began again and slowly the minutes ticked by. After about twenty of them my phone rang.

"Ed, can you come in here for a minute?"

"What's the matter? Can't you take it?"

"Ed, dear," she trilled lightly. "Don't be nasty, now. *Come in here.*"

"Yes, Dragon Lady."

"And don't be a smart-ass either," she ordered crisply. "It isn't as bad as you think."

"Hmph," I said, put down the phone none too gently, and limped across the city room with a bland smile for all whose eyes I met, which was practically everybody.

Inside I found Bessie sniffling and still looking quite angry, but obviously much mollified. Anna was all beams.

"Guess what, Ed!" she cried. "Bessie is going to leave the women's beat, but—*but*—she's agreed to a perfectly ideal and wonderful arrangement that is going to keep her right here by our sides, just as always! First of all, she's going to become secretary of the corporation, which will make use of all that talent for detail she displayed so splendidly at the *Geographic*. And then she's going to do special by-lined assignments for us from time to time when she finds something that interests her—that we like, too, of course, but I don't think we'll ever have any trouble seeing eye to eye—" I could see from Bessie's expression that she doubted this a good deal, and so did I, but we let it pass—"and then she's going to try some free-lance books on the side. I really think there are lots and lots of interesting people in Washington with interesting stories to tell, and I'm going to see if I can't help steer some of them her way. Fran Leighton is the only really good 'as-told-to' around town, and I think there's room for one more, don't you? I think Bess would be splendid at that!"

"I think Bess is going to be busier than a no-armed paperhanger," I said. "I hope she's going to get well paid for all this."

"Handsomely," Anna assured me, and Bessie winked,

which pleased me very much: it was only right that Anna should pay for putting us through this little emotional fling.

"Now," she said, "you can go and tell Tal about it, if you like."

"For heaven's sake, Anna," Bessie said, sounding quite recovered, "tell him yourself!"

"Yes, dear, of course," Anna agreed amicably. "Ed, send Sue Eldridge in here, will you?"

"Coward," I murmured as I prepared to follow a triumphant Bessie into the newsroom. "You aren't such a Dragon Lady as you think, are you?"

"Let's just say," she said blandly, "that I haven't forgotten the Old Team as much as *you* think. And let's just see that we all continue to play on it, all right?"

"Yes, ma'am," I said with a bow as ironic as I dared make it; and with a smile at Bess, which she returned gratefully, I went back to my office aware that had probably pushed my own luck with Anna just about as far as it would go, for one day.

But the upshot was, of course, that "Trend" instantly became what Anna and Tal wanted it to be: the immediate focus for every flaming feminine cause in the book and a few others thrown in for good measure. Well before women's lib came along, the *Inquirer* was banging the drums and shaking the bangles; nor was that all the new section put forth.

After several huddles with Tal (which, according to staff gossip, continued into the dawn at his new apartment across the Potomac in Rosslyn, Virginia— a place from which he could look south with lordly command upon a completely stunning sweep of river, Washington Monument, Lincoln Memorial, Jefferson Memorial, Capitol, White House and virtually the whole city) Sue Eldridge turned into a veritable tiger.

A bare-boned, gaunt, rather dowdy girl of the intense type that would be easy game for tête-à-têtes at Tal's, she began to feature enormous sad articles on things such as bedeviled welfare recipients, conditions in women's prisons, food prices paid by the poor, rape in the ghettos, street crime, abandoned mothers, abandoned children, food waste at embassy dinners and high-society cocktail parties, treatment of domestic servants in Washington's statelier homes, the life-style of the rich versus the contrasting miseries of the poor.

Nobody could fault the basic truths of many of these articles, nor the social conscience which informed them, nor the fact that the world was, indeed, as Jack Kennedy would presently remark, an unfair place. But the overall impact, when continued day after day, was to encourage in the public mind the conviction that the entire American society was corrupt and worthless; and that the nation which gave it house was therefore irretrievably doomed, its downfall inevitable—a matter of time, and not very much of it either.

In similar fashion, department by department, the same theme began to run through the *Inquirer*'s news stories, editorials and columns, including Anna's own. Taking Tal's Manifesto as their bible, many of the younger staffers and such few of the older as agreed with it began to run amuck in a welter of new journalism, "investigative reporting," "concerned commentary" and other pet phrases, all of which boiled down to a simple: *Get the bastards*. The bastards, according to the *Inquirer*, were everywhere in Washington and indeed everywhere in America.

Their principal crime, of course, was that they disagreed with the *Inquirer*.

The way they were brought to book was probably, as I say, almost subliminal for the general reader, but it was very easy to spot the process when you watched it from the inside. It was an advance on all fronts, and nothing and nobody the *Inquirer* disapproved of escaped the treatment.

There was first of all the new freedom in the news columns. Gone was old-fashioned objectivity, in like Flynn was "the new realism." Adjectives, adverbs and verbs carried most of the burden. A government official who pleased the *Inquirer* was automatically "liberal," "progressive," "forward-looking." His statements and speeches were invariably "forceful," "decisive," "well-informed," "effective." They were delivered "forcefully," "dramatically," "convincingly." If he happened to be engaged in peccadilloes sexual or pecuniary, no whisper of them ever entered the *Inquirer*'s pages. "What's more important," Tal demanded at an early staff meeting, "whether this jerk is sleeping with half the people on the Hill or whether he sees the world the way we do? If he does, for Christ's sake let's not weaken one of our guys by giving his enemies ammunition. Let's keep it to ourselves."

But your opposition figure? O-o-o-o-h, brother, had *he* better watch out! Not only was he "archconservative," "reactionary," "backward-looking," "unimaginative," "uncaring," "illiberal," delivering speeches "pedantically," "dully," "boringly." He had also better be damned sure the bed he hopped into was his own; he must never, ever, make any investment that could later be portrayed as being even remotely to his advantage; he must never accept any of the free trips or handouts that most of the *Inquirer*'s friends—and most of the Washington press corps—accepted without a second thought; he must never appoint so much as a seventeenth cousin six times removed to his staff. And also, he must never expect more than the absolute minimum of space for his views. And he must understand that even that would be slanted against him.

144

He must also realize that whereas his liberal colleague could "charge" or "assert," he could only "claim."

"You can really do marvels with the word 'claim,'" Tal remarked in happy satisfaction one day. "It has such a nice, unbelievable, phony sound."

In the *Inquirer*'s pages, therefore, Orrin Knox "claimed" that the Soviet Union was moving ahead of the United States in military strength. But Bill Fulbright was able to "assert," "maintain" and frequently "declare" that this was all poppycock, the United States was miles ahead.

Anyone attacking anything in which the *Inquirer* believed "claimed."

And he usually claimed it on page 37, too.

In the same fashion, particularly as the Viet Nam involvement ran deeper, the editorials, frequently written by Anna herself, became increasingly harsh, unbalanced and bitter. A sort of mass hysteria gripped the paper. Every day the editorials were matched by the headlines, news stories and photographs. From time to time we had most revealing photographs of the atrocities committed by the Viet Cong offered us by French correspondents and others able to penetrate the other side. Tal almost invariably rejected them.

"Everybody knows *that*," he would say scornfully. "What the hell's so newsworthy about *that*?"

So the Viet Cong pictures did not appear. But you can be damned sure the pictures of atrocities committed by Americans, whether deliberate or inadvertent, were splattered all over the front page, as they were on Anna's television station, every day, every night, world without end.

Whatever the rights and wrongs that only history can tell, it was no wonder the American people eventually came to hate the war. The *Inquirer* and its friends—

aided by leaders hesitant, indecisive and attempting the futile game of trying to fight a war while simultaneously appeasing the media—never gave them a chance to see it any other way. . . .

Not a department of the paper from District Affairs to the book, film and art reviews escaped the treatment that began the day Tal took over. Certain truths were held by the *Inquirer* to be self-evident, and woe betide all who did not bow down and worship them. Unbelievers were cast into the outer darkness, their characters besmirched, their names and careers dragged low, their right to their own points of view very effectively destroyed by the simple tools of hostile reporting ("adversary journalism," it was called with great self-satisfaction around the newsroom) and outright censorship of what they had to say.

On virtually every page of the paper the chief impression readers received was that their country was rotten, foredoomed, evil, hopeless and generally no damned good.

And again, it is not that there was not much support to be found for such a thesis in the things turned up by the type of crusading the Inquirer and its colleagues began to do as soon as the shots in Dallas ended plastic Camelot and the real world resumed.

Not even Gordon, wrapped as he was in Texas conservatism, could deny that.

It was just that there was no balance, no perspective, no sense of history, no understanding whatsoever of the necessity to maintain a stable society. It all became a grand and gleeful circus of degrading, belittling, tearing down—a self-rending done with such vicious enthusiasm that it often seemed the *Inquirer* had gone mad.

But mad or no—and some who directed and participated in the process, such as Tal, were not mad at all but shrewdly aware of exactly what they were doing—the end result was to contribute greatly to the confusion and weakening of the American people at home and abroad. When in due course this process was given fuel by the mistakes of Viet Nam and Watergate, it was a wonder there was anything left of the country's heart, soul, purpose or determination. Which of course was exactly the point for such as Tal.

For a decade the *Inquirer* under Anna and Tal pursued these policies relentlessly, as indeed it continues to pursue them to this day. And because this was the popular trend in American journalism then, and continues to be, Anna's acquisition of other properties was, as she truthfully says, made easier. In journalism, as in all else, fads control the group and the herd clusters to the leader; and Anna has been a leader, now, for almost twenty years.

In 1959, the year in which she set the *Inquirer* on the course it has followed ever since, she persuaded Gordon to buy a small FM station in Washington and gave it her own initials for call letters. It became WAKH-FM, sufficiently successful in two years so that to it could be added WAKH-TV. Another of her dreams had always been to buy the Punxsutawney paper; it was not available, so in 1963 she picked up the Du Bois, Pennsylvania, *Journal*, a few miles away. At that point Gordon, who had fortunately brought in a lot more oil wells and had been watching the course of their joint ventures with a mixture of dismay, confusion, hesitation and uncertainty, asserted himself. If Anna was going to have a paper in her home state, he announced belligerently as though he expected an argument—naturally she was smart enough not to give him one—he was going to have a couple in his. The Waco *Endeavor* joined the chain in 1963, the Odessa *Enterprise* in 1965. Then she decided it was time for him

147

to strike out for bigger things and began to talk about how "We really need a base in the Midwest and on the West Coast." The Galesburg, Illinois, *Gazette* was acquired in 1969, the *Southland Record* in California in 1972. She is presently negotiating for three more newspapers, in Ohio, Colorado and New Hampshire, and two more television stations in Philadelphia and San Francisco. And having almost absentmindedly picked up two small, financially floundering but extremely influential monthly journals of opinion, *Currents* in 1966 and *Monthly Review* in 1970, she is now about to close the deal on the widely distributed housewives' supermarket delight, the sex- and sensation-filled *National Spotlight*. "All Things Considered" now appears three times a week in 436 newspapers, and NBC's "Weekend With Anna" tops the Sunday talk-show ratings.

During all these years, well into the Viet Nam war, Gordon, Bessie and I, together with some few dogged souls on the staff of the *Inquirer,* kept up a running and, of course, quite ineffectual battle for some modicum of balance, some shred of perspective, some sense of what we considered real responsibility, on the paper. Encouraged by Tal, Anna refused to be moved.

"God damn it," I would say at the daily meeting of department heads over which she always presided when in town, "you can't use such a one-sided picture layout without balancing it with something on the other side."

"Why not?" Anna would ask with a studied innocence, and Tal would echo blandly, "Yes, pal, why not?"

"Because it's so one-sided and unfair," I would say. "Not only unfair: downright dishonest."

"That's the way you see it, Ed, dear," Anna would

say comfortably. "There *are* other points of view, you know."

"Not in the *Inquirer*," I retorted on one such occasion and this time they both looked at me blandly, backed by the offended stares of Sue Eldridge and the other department heads, all of whom not only knew which side their bread was buttered on but sincerely believed in what was being done.

"I don't really see why there should be," Anna said thoughtfully. "After all, it *is* my paper. I don't think we have to be fair to people when they're so obviously wrongheaded, mistaken and reactionary. Why should we spread their poison for them?"

"There are plenty of opinions as to whether it's poison or not," I said shortly. "You ought to present opposing views as a public service—simply because that's what a real newspaper ought to do."

"And you're saying the *Inquirer* is *not* a real newspaper?" she asked, a dangerous little glint coming into her eyes.

"You're turning it into a damned propaganda organ for a single point of view," I said, not abashed by this. There were ostentatiously shocked murmurs and disturbed tut-tuts from down the table.

"Maybe you want to work somewhere else, buddy," Tal suggested with the lazy arrogance he had cultivated since his elevation.

"If Anna wants to fire me," I said, staring him straight in the eye, "let her go ahead and do it. She won't though. Because I'm your conscience, aren't I, Anna? And everybody should have a good conscience around, just to be able to say you have one, whether or not you pay any attention to it."

"Oh, Ed!" she exclaimed with a gurgle of laughter. "You get so *solemn* and bitter about these things! It isn't the end of the world."

"It's the end of responsible journalism if this trend keeps up," I said, "not only here but on L Street and in New York and in a lot of other places. To me, that's important."

"To me," she said calmly, "it's more important to have a fighting media that will expose the rotten corruption in this town and everywhere in this land—a media that will fight for what is right and true and *liberal*. To hell with being 'fair' about the evils of this world!"

"Amen!" Tal said, and "Amen!" echoed Susan and the department heads, bursting into spontaneous applause.

"I tell you what we'll do, though," Anna continued. "I don't mind if you want to have a little debate about it. Why don't we have a general staff meeting next week and you and Tal can argue out your opposing points of view and then we'll take a vote and see what the staff wants?"

"You know what the vote will be," I said. "What's the point in that kind of charade?"

She shrugged.

"Very well, then, if you don't want that opportunity, you don't have to take it."

"If I thought it would do any good," I said, "I would. But we aren't kidding anybody, are we, really? Tal's got this place so stacked with young zealots there's just no issue."

"Then if there's no issue, Ed, dear," she purred gently, "why create one?"

"Yes, Ed, dear," Tal echoed. "Why create one?"

I gave them look for look, while Susan and the department heads watched me with a severely shocked intensity as though I were something utterly alien, as indeed I was to their particular brand of journalism.

"If you think I'm going to stop raising hell about

this kind of one-sided, vicious, illiberal, reactionary news management," I said calmly, using their own adjectives with relish, "you have another think coming. You can do it your way, Anna, and obviously nobody can stop you. But you're going to be reminded of what you're doing as long as I'm around."

"Good!" she said happily. "I hope that will be a long, *long* time!"

And so it was; and I did keep reminding her; and so did Bessie from time to time; and so did Gordon in an "Aw, shucks, little gal, why'd you want to be so *rough* on me and my friends in the Senate?" kind of way; but that did not deflect her from her purpose, or Tal from his . . . until the day when the paper's handling of the Viet Nam war really made the White House mad enough so that its occupant decided to go after us seriously.

When he did, it appeared for a little time that the end result would be to put us back on a somewhat more objective course on all fronts, as I and Bessie and Gordon understood the term and devoutly hoped would happen.

But that would have run counter to Anna's luck. And that was not permitted. Instead, it confirmed her fame and reputation and set her permanently on the path from which she has never deviated since.

Three

"DISTINGUISHED AND EXTRAORDINARY SERVICE"

1

────

I had been aware for some time—because he never hesitated to telephone me at all hours of day and night to complain about it—that the President did not like our coverage of his shabby little war. But I did not realize how really unbalanced that unhappy conflict had made him until the day he attacked us directly. Then I needed all the reserves of strength and character I could muster to withstand the onslaught and preserve the integrity of my staff and my publication. Fortunately I found I had them. The attempt ended in complete debacle for him, complete vindication for me. Armored as we were with truth and justice on our side, there could have been no other outcome.

—ANNA HASTINGS, by Anna Hastings

IT BEGAN WITH ONE OF THOSE PHONE CALLS. AS SHE says, they were a pretty constant feature of Viet Nam war coverage in those days, and she was certainly not the only one in the press corps—there were dozens—to receive them. Sometimes when she proved uncooperative he would methodically go down the line, calling first Tal, who gave him no satisfaction either, and then me. While I was in general more sympathetic to his dilemma than they were, I too had serious reservations. Usually it would all end in a burst of prairie expletives and the heavily grieving statement, "Y'all over there are a bunch of no-good, propaganda-spoutin' unpatriotic left-wingers. It's past midnight, your President is down here in his office tired as a dog doin' his level *best* to save your country's honor and position in the world, and y'all are sittin' over there on H Street with your fingers up your asses makin' fun of me. I don't like it, y'hear? *I don't like it!*"

Followed by a few more carefully calculated expletives and the banging down of the receiver. We had learned to hold our own out a safe distance from our ears for just such a contingency.

This night, however, things were different. For one thing, he didn't call Tal and me immediately after he called Anna. He waited awhile, figuring with his customary shrewdness that she would do his work for him. And so she did. She called me first and she sounded, for once, genuinely disturbed.

"Ed," she said, a little breathless, "I've just received the strangest call from the President."

"Don't we all?"

"No, seriously. He really sounds very odd. Menacing. I—I really think he's going to try to make real trouble for us."

"Fair enough," I said, not very sympathetic—it was almost 1 A.M. and I had been sound asleep, as no doubt she had too. "We certainly try all the time to make real trouble for him."

"'No, I mean *really* make trouble. For me. And Tal. And you, and probably Bessie."

156

"How's that?" I demanded sharply, beginning to take her seriously. "How can he do that?"

"I don't know exactly, but he said he was going to call you and Tal and talk to you about it. 'Tell 'em to be prepared,' he said, 'because this time I've got your damned newspaper by the knockers and I'm not aimin' to let go. So tell 'em to watch out, girlie, and you watch out, too. *I've* had it and now *you*-all are goin' to git it.' Then he just hung up, very softly. Has he called you yet?"

"No, not a word. Maybe he'll just be content with that and let us stew around having nervous breakdowns trying to figure out what he meant."

"I doubt it," she said. "He sounds like business this time. So be very careful what you say to him. And call me back *at once,* all right?"

"Sure," I said, "but I think it's probably just some more hot air."

Ten minutes later I learned differently.

"Ed?" he said, his voice gentle as butter, always a tip-off to be damned wary and keep your hand on your six-shooter. "Is that my old friend Ed the Managin' Ed?"

"Yes, Mr. President," I said cheerfully. "How are you?"

"You sound wide awake," he said with a mild surprise. "Somebody talk to you already?"

"You know it, Mr. President," I said, still cheerful. "Just like you wanted her to."

"Well, I did," he admitted, "but I wasn't sure she'd do it. She's a pretty cool cucumber, that Anna. I didn't think she'd panic like that."

"Anna doesn't panic," I said more sharply than I had intended—he had, as usual, put the other party on the defensive. "She said you'd called, and would be calling me. You are. What can I do for you?"

157

"Mebbe be a witness for your guv'ment," he said softly. "Mebbe just be a fine old witness for your guv'-ment."

"About what?" I asked, really concerned now but trying not to let it show in my voice. There was never a man so astute and perceptive of the tremors of others, however—in that, as in everything, he was twice life-size, if not more. He chuckled.

"Now, don't go gettin' all steamed up, Ed. Just a little bit of treason, mebbe. Or again, mebbe not. I guess we'll just have to let Congress and the courts find out."

"Mr. President," I said angrily, "if you think you can scare the *Inquirer* with that kind of phony threat—"

"I'm not phony," he objected mildly, which was quite true. "I'm tellin' you exactly what it's all about. In my book, it's treason. Now, you-all may call it somethin' else, and it may *be* somethin' else. But I sure as hell intend to find out."

"The First Amendment—" I began. He snorted.

"You newspaper people think you *hatched* that First Amendment. Just sat on it like an old hen for a couple of hundred years and *hatched* it right out, all by your-selves. Well!" He snorted again. "You didn't."

"Mr. President," I said, "maybe you'd better stop playing cat-and-mouse and tell me what this is all about, O.K.?"

"Did you room with Talbot Farson when you first came to Washington?" he asked with a sudden blunt-ness that totally surprised me. What the *hell*—? I had known the President for a long time on the Hill, and there wasn't much I couldn't imagine.

"I did indeed," I said, trying to be as blunt as he but not, apparently, keeping my surprise and concern en-tirely out of my voice.

"Now," he said soothingly, "I'm not implyin' you slept together or anything, Ed. I'm just sayin' you *did* room with him, and you *did* know him about as intimately as a man does know his roommate when they're both young and strugglin' to get along in Washington?"

"That's right," I agreed, more calmly. "We roomed together for approximately two years and then got our own places."

"But you and he and Bessie Rovere and Anna did keep up a very close relationship after that, and for all these years since, isn't that right?"

"We've always been close friends," I said. "Everybody, including you, knows that. We're close friends today, which is why we all wound up on the *Inquirer* together. It's never been a secret."

"Yes," he agreed, his voice taking on a more somber note. "But there may have been one secret there, Ed. Yes, there may have been one around there, all these years."

"What?" I asked, unable to restrain a certain flippancy brought on by an increasing annoyance. "Bessie's harelip or my rudimentary tail?"

"Now, don't you be funny, Ed," he suggested gently, "or you'll get your tail, rudimentary or not, in a pretty tight-ass wringer, and you won't like that. All I want to establish right now is that you have known Talbot Farson for almost twenty-five years, and you have been on quite intimate terms with him all those years, as have Bessie Rovere and Anna Hastings. That *is* correct, isn't it?"

"That is correct."

"That's all I wanted to know," he said cheerfully. "You'll be a good witness. Just keep 'em short and to the point. Don't volunteer anything. Just tell us what you know. Thanks for your time, Ed. Somebody'll be gettin' back to you."

159

"Mr. President—" I began, but the only answer was a gentle click.

He had no sooner hung up than Tal called.

"What the hell is that bastard up to now?" he demanded without preliminary. "Waking us all up in the middle of the night! What did he say to you?"

"Just asked me if we roomed together once and I said yes, we did."

"Was that all?"

"That was all."

"He didn't ask about my political views, did he?" And suddenly with a chilling certainty I knew what it was all about.

"No," I said cautiously. "Did he ask you?"

"No!" which I didn't believe. "He knows what they are. The *Inquirer* makes them clear every day. . . . So he didn't ask you."

"No, he didn't ask me."

"He didn't ask Anna. I wonder if he asked Bessie?"

"Probably not," I said. "I think he expects that to come up at the hearing."

"What hearing?" he said sharply.

"I don't know yet, but all of a sudden I'm very sure there's going to be one."

"The devious son-of-a-bitch," he said slowly. "Why doesn't he leave us alone?"

"He seems to wonder that about us," I replied, not without a certain tartness. "Often."

"Yes, I know you're for his son-of-a-bitching war. You always have been."

"Not entirely, by any means. But I don't think we've been very fair to him. You didn't really expect him not to fight back when he got hold of something, did you?"

"What has he got hold of?" he demanded with a scorn I could almost believe was genuine.

"You tell me," I suggested. "Apparently it involves you."

"Nothing involves me!" he said angrily.

"O.K., then, what's to worry? Go back to bed and forget it."

"I would, if he weren't such a persistent son-of-a-bitch. He never gives up."

"That's right," I agreed, "especially when he thinks he's got something. Have you talked to Anna?"

"She says she'll stand by me, whatever."

"So she thinks you're the target, too," I said thoughtfully.

"She does," he agreed and repeated, giving it a significant emphasis, "She says she'll stand by me, whatever."

"So?"

"Yes, 'so.' Will you?"

"I don't have the slightest idea what he—"

"God damn it, I said *will you?*"

"See here, Tal," I said sharply. "Within the limits of old friendship and honesty, yes, I will. But you'll note I said honesty. If I'm under oath about something and am asked certain things, then I'll testify to what I know."

He was silent for a moment but there was no wavering in his reply.

"You don't know anything because there isn't anything to know."

"Very well, then, there isn't anything to worry about. May I call Anna now? She asked me to, after I finished with him."

"You don't know anything because there isn't anything to know," he repeated. And then added savagely, "Yes, call Anna!" And slammed down the receiver, leaving me to think: Well, well.

"What did he say?" she asked.

"He asked me if Tal and I roomed together when we first came to Washington and if we had been close friends ever since. I said yes to both. He also said I might have to testify about it."

"And what did Tal say?"

"How do you know he called me?"

"I know Tal."

"Yes," I said, "and you obviously think maybe the President really has something on him."

"As Tal obviously thinks you're the key to it," she said. "I suppose he told you I said I'd stand by him."

"He said you said you'd stand by him *whatever*, which struck me as a pretty broad commitment until all the facts are in."

"We haven't got time to get all the facts," she said impatiently. "My newspaper and my staff are being attacked and I'm not about to hesitate. We'll see it through just as I said: whatever. And that means you, too, Ed."

"It does," I said evenly, "as I told Tal: within the limits of honesty."

"Protecting a free press is more important than honesty."

"Well, I'll be Goddamned. That's stretching the First Amendment a bit far, isn't it? Maybe you'd better stop wrapping the flag around you and think this thing through before Tal gets us in a real bind."

"I suspect," she said coldly, "that it may not be Tal who gets us in a real bind. Bessie called; the President's just called her too. He got her all upset, as you might know: he's so damned clever. I suspect between you and Bessie we really *may* be in trouble."

"Now, see here," I said sharply, "before this gets completely out of hand and into another ball park, suppose you remember it's *Tal* who's the problem here, not me and Bessie."

162

"It depends on where you sit," she said, still coldly. "From where I sit, charged as I am with responsibility for maintaining the integrity of my own paper and by implication the integrity of all the media, I don't see any signs of Tal breaking ranks. It's you and Bess I'm worried about."

"Of course Tal isn't going to break any ranks," I said in exasperation. "It's his neck that's involved. He doesn't have to be honest under oath."

"Oh?" she said blankly. "You don't think he would be?"

"I don't know," I said, suddenly feeling sick as the full implications of all this began to hit me. "I really don't know."

"Well, anyway," she said decisively, "we've got to stand by him for the sake of the *Inquirer,* for the sake of a free press, for the sake of the whole effort to stop this damnable war, for—for everything . . ." Her voice trailed away; a genuine worry finally surfaced. "I wonder if he really *does* have anything on Tal."

"Who knows? I think, myself, that he does. But as you say, he's so clever there's no way to be sure, at the moment. I can tell you one thing, though: if Tal's vulnerable, and if through him the paper's vulnerable, he'll have found it out."

"Yes," she said moodily, "we know how he is: there isn't a sparrow that falls that he doesn't know about."

"Yes," I agreed, moody also as the prospects of a very unpleasant immediate future began to open up in my mind. "And this time I think he's really got one."

2

My first reaction—and, as it turned out, my entirely sound one—was to reject completely this unwarranted and egregious attack upon the integrity of my newspaper, my staff and, by implication, upon the whole free press that was opposing my opponent's insane and useless war. This, too, I realized, was a war. I prepared to fight it with every weapon at my command, certain that he would not hesitate to use everything he could to defeat the critics whose arguments he had failed to satisfy in honest public debate.

—ANNA HASTINGS, *by Anna Hastings*

I WILL SAY FOR GORDON THAT IT WAS HE WHO INSISTED on having it out with Tal. The attempt didn't get him anywhere, of course, but he tried.

I know now that in doing so he made inevitable what came later, with all its sad consequences for himself and the family; but this was not apparent at the time, and I could only admire the dogged determination with which he faced Tal and the rest of us in Anna's office.

"Little gal," he said, "I don't give a good Goddamn's worth of hot hog spit about your 'faith in Tal'—"

"Don't be vulgar," she said coldly. "And stop talking Texan. You aren't campaigning now."

"—but I'm goin' to insist, before you make any statement or commit this paper or any of us to anything, that we have it out with Tal right here and now and find out where we stand. I'm just not goin' to permit you to say anything until we know what this is all about. I'm just not goin' to permit it!"

"How can you stop me?" she asked, and for a second he looked genuinely taken aback and almost his usual humbled self. But this time he wasn't.

"I can't stop you," he said slowly, "but I can sure as hell make it clear to everybody that I don't agree. If you issue a statement without gettin' to the bottom of this first, *I* issue a statement. If you attack the President without gettin' to the bottom of this first, *I'll* defend him. There won't be any closin' of ranks around here until I'm satisfied there isn't anything to this. And that's a promise, everybody, so don't think it isn't."

For a moment or two, Anna in her turn looked genuinely taken aback. She must have been, for all she could muster was a rather feeble "Just because you're from Texas!"

"It has nothin' to do with bein' from Texas, God damn it!" he said sharply. "I don't owe that man anything, except friendship and a fair break on things. Which, incidentally, I may say as I've said before, I don't think he's received from this newspaper or any others around here for a long time. I've said before I didn't like it, and I say it again: we haven't been fair."

"It's true we've criticized *your* stand on the war, Gordon," Tal said with a deliberately patronizing air, "but after all, that's the privilege of a free press, and it seems to me you've been able to fire right back at us from the Senate, so it hasn't really hurt either of us, has it? In fact, it's made us both look good to the public. It's proved the *Inquirer* really *does* have room for two points of view."

"Not very damned much room," Gordon said dryly. "It seems to me I wind up on page twenty like everybody else who backs the war. However, that's not the point here. The point, Tal, is you and the spot we're in because of you."

"Not because of me!" Tal said sharply. "Because of that four-flusher in the White House!"

"You can call him anything you like," Gordon said, "but the fact is, he thinks he has somethin' and we've got to find out whether he does or not before we can back you with a clear conscience."

"I have a clear conscience," Anna said coolly, "and I'm backing him."

"Yes," Gordon said. "Well. That may speak better for your loyalty than your common sense, little gal."

"Gordon Hastings," she said angrily, "will you stop being so damned patronizing? What do *you* know that we don't know? Has the President told *you* his big secret? If so, we'd better have it right now and save a lot of breath."

"He hasn't talked to me at all," Gordon said, "and I don't really want him to. I just want to be satisfied about Tal here. Doesn't anybody else," he asked, and for a second he did sound a little plaintive, "agree with me?"

Bessie shifted in her chair and so did I. We looked at one another; looked at Anna and Tal, both studying us severely; and then looked at honest, bumbling Gordon, beads of sweat beginning to dot his forehead, but standing his ground.

"I do," I said (thereby assuring myself a date with

the future, too, though I did not know it then). "I would like to be satisfied about Tal."

"So would I," Bessie said. "I think he owes it to us to tell us honestly whatever—whatever there is to tell."

"God damn it," Tal said angrily, "there is nothing to tell! *There is nothing to tell!* You people are unbelievable. We have known each other for twenty-five years and sometimes I don't think you know me at all. What *is* the matter with you, anyway? Has that son-of-a-bitch in the White House really got you that mesmerized? I pity you, I really do!"

"I think Gordon has a point," I said. "I think we want more than bluster about it. I think we want your solemn assurance."

"Yes," Bessie said. "It's a big step, asking us all to go to bat for you, Tal, when—when there might—be something."

"Christ!" Tal said with a sort of humorous, helpless frustration. "It's impossible to win in a situation like this. I tell you there's nothing, you don't believe me. Then you say you want my 'solemn assurance,' whatever that is. Hell, I'm being as solemn as I know how: *There is nothing to tell.* And still you won't believe me. How can I win?"

"Do you swear," Gordon said solemnly, "that there isn't anything we should know about before we commit the *Inquirer* to your defense?"

"Sure there is," Tal said with a sort of wild, sardonic savagery. "I'm a sex maniac. I'm a Communist. I'm a pervert. I'm a mad bomber. I'm—I'm—Christ, what *are* we talking about?"

"Yes," Anna agreed coldly, "what *are* we talking about? He has told us there is nothing; I believe there is nothing. I have asked George Harrison Watersill"—one of Washington's sharpest, most successful, most —well, trendy—lawyers—"to meet with me and Tal

167

here in half an hour to plan his defense—which is a little ironic, a defense against a charge we don't even know yet. But we'll be ready, anyway. And he will also help me prepare the statement that will appear in the paper tomorrow morning."

"What will it say?" Gordon asked.

"It will say, in essence, that it has come to the attention of the management of the *Inquirer* that the President of the United States may be preparing to attack the reputation of a major member of the staff in an attempt to halt the paper's efforts to terminate the futile and criminal war in Viet Nam. It will say that the management and staff of the *Inquirer* are united in their opposition to the President's attempt and will oppose it with every legal and journalistic means at their disposal.

"Is that," she concluded dryly, "all right?"

"I hope you know what you're doing, little gal," Gordon said, and suddenly Tal shot him a look of such open hatred that Gordon almost physically recoiled from it. But he concluded doggedly, "And I hope you're playin' straight with us, Tal, because if you're not, there's goin' to be almighty hell to pay."

"For somebody, maybe," Tal grated, "but not for me."

3

----

*I had decided that offense was the best defense;
and I was pleased to learn within the day that my
statement in the* Inquirer *had caught my opponent
completely off guard. He was, I was told, furious.
He had underestimated me, I think. I did not under-
estimate him, however, and therefore I was not
surprised when his reaction was immediate and
aggressive.*

—ANNA HASTINGS, *by Anna Hastings*

ACTUALLY, HOWEVER, SHE WAS CONSIDERABLY SUR-
prised, because for most of that day she had basked in
a glow of self-congratulation and the virtually unani-
mous commendation of her peers. The Washington
press corps, reacting with that monolithic unanimity
which has been its distinguishing feature ever since it
first became united in the worship of John F. Kennedy,
could not say enough in her behalf in those first, giddy
hours. Her name was on every television broadcast
starting with the "Today" show in the morning (she
had ordered a copy of her statement rushed to the net-

works the night before), and her defiance of the President also led every radio broadcast on all three networks all day long. Congratulatory phone calls poured in, starting the moment she reached her office at 8:35 A.M. The *Star* ran an enthusiastically supportive editorial in the afternoon, and in both Senate and House antiwar members seized upon the incident to praise her and flay the President. The *Times* called from New York to read its enthusiastically approving editorial. It was even rumored, though she never said and no one could ever prove it, that sometime during the afternoon there had been a personal call from L Street: Queen Elizabeth had indeed talked to Mary Queen of Scots, in the interests of unity against the great universal enemy in the White House. At any rate, I do know that an advance copy of both the *Post*'s warmly approving editorial and its savagely anti-Presidential editorial cartoon for the next morning were sent over by special messenger sometime around five.

Sometime around five, also, the happy dream that she would get away with this without hearing from "my opponent" vanished with another call from Pennsylvania Avenue. Tal and I happened to be in her office at the time, going over last-minute details for the next edition.

"Yes?" she said, and instantly gestured to us to pick up the extension phones on her desk. "Put him on."

"Anna, honey?" he said, sweet as pie. "Is this my little fightin' wildcat from Punxsutawney, P.A.?"

"This is Anna Hastings."

He chuckled.

"And mad, too, I can tell that. Well, this is your President."

"By virtue of circumstances. I can't claim ownership otherwise."

"Why, now!" he said dryly. "Don't tell me I dreamed

170

all those editorials in my behalf before the last election. Don't tell me you voted for *him*. You did vote for me, didn't you, Anna?"

"Yes."

"Well, then," he said triumphantly, "I'm *your* President, aren't I? That's right, isn't it, honey?"

"Yes," she conceded, unamused, "technically that is correct. But I've withdrawn my mandate. What can I do for you, Mr. President?"

"Nothing at all in that hostile tone, Anna," he said calmly. "Nothin' at all. Shall I hang up, or do you want to hear what I have to say?"

For a split second she considered it but changed her mind even as Tal and I shook ours heads vigorously: that was no way to deal with him.

"No, Mr. President," she said calmly, "I don't want you to hang up. I want you to stop playing games with us and tell us frankly what's on your mind. You saw from my statement this morning what's on mine."

"Yes, I did," he agreed, "and I admire your fightin' spirit, Anna. I really do. Not many people in this town have your qualities of courage, integrity and determination in fightin' for your own point of view, I will say that with real admiration. Not many."

"You do," she said, deciding to try a little of his own technique. "We may disagree with you entirely over here, but we've never said you weren't sincere and determined in what you're trying to do. Evil," she couldn't resist adding, "though we happen to think it is."

"Anna, honey," he said soberly, " 'evil' is a mighty strong word. Too strong for old friends to use against each other."

"It seemes to me evil is what you're trying to do to Tal and through him to this newspaper," she said, not giving an inch.

171

"Evil," he said, equally firm, "is what Tal may have been doing to this country for quite some time."

It was all we could do to keep Tal quiet. Our joint glares sufficed but it was touch and go for a moment.

"I hope you can prove that statement, Mr. President," Anna said, her voice thin with anger but inflexible. "From any other source, in any other form than over the telephone, it would be libelous per se unless you can prove it."

"Libelous!" he snorted. "You press people have made libel an empty word. You've got the courts to say you can't libel us public characters and by God it works the other way, too. You're as much public characters as I am, nowadays. I can say any damned thing I please about you and you can't touch me. Anyway, this is a silly argument. I wouldn't say it if I didn't have proof."

"Well, let's have it, then!" she snapped. "I repeat, I haven't got time to sit here playing games."

"I haven't got time either, Anna, honey," he said, suddenly crisp. "I've got your country to run and your war to—"

"It isn't my war!"

"Your war," he repeated calmly. "Too busy running your country and your war to waste time either. I'm callin' to tell you that evidence we've collected has been turned over to the Senate Internal Security Subcommittee and they'll be contacting Tal and the rest of you about your appearances, which will probably take place next week. I thought I'd do you the courtesy of givin' you a little advance warnin', that's all. Mebbe I was mistaken. I thought you'd want it."

"*What* evidence?" she demanded in an exasperated voice. "And how did you get it?"

"They'll be tellin' you all about it before you can say 'Screw the President,' which is somethin' you say pretty

172

often, so I guess you can say it pretty fast. That's how soon you'll know about it."

"It must have been wiretapping," she said thoughtfully, "almost certainly illegal, and no doubt illegal search-and-seizure on top of that."

"Nothin' I do to protect this country is illegal!" he roared, turning on the full force of his personality.

But her response was unimpressed, because at that moment she knew she had him—in the presence of witnesses, too, though of course he didn't know we were there. (This is known as entrapment and is good or bad in Washington depending on who the victim is.)

"We'll see about that, Mr. President," she responded calmly. "Thank you for calling."

"That's quite all right, Anna, honey," he said, calm again because he, too, obviously realized his error. He couldn't, however, resist one last dig. "Just want to help old friends of mine, that's all. Just want to be helpful to y'all over there at that great newspaper."

"We appreciate it," Anna said coolly. "Thanks so much, Mr. President."

And beat him to the draw by hanging up before he did.

"We've got him!" Tal shouted triumphantly. "We've got the slimy bastard! You heard what he said: *Nothing I do to protect this country is illegal.* It's the worst Goddamned thing since the divine right of kings!"

"I'd go slow if I were you," I suggested dryly, while Anna stared thoughtfully out the window. "People can understand the context of it, and a lot of them will agree with him. Why shouldn't a President do everything he can to protect the country? He could also say that he meant he *doesn't* do anything illegal to protect the country. It makes perfectly good sense in that context."

"To hell with context!" Tal said. "We've got him!"

"Yes," Anna agreed slowly, "I think we have." She pulled her typewriter around, put in two pieces of copy paper and a carbon and began to type rapidly. We moved around to read over her shoulder as we had done so many thousands of times over the years:

"By Anna Hastings.

"The President of the United States declared today that all his actions—by implication including all of his actions in Viet Nam—are legal as long as he can claim that he is 'protecting' the country.

"He claimed that 'Nothing I do to protect the country is illegal'—a statement of Presidential authority so broad and so arrogant that it appears to jeopardize the very foundations of democracy itself.

"The statement was made to this reporter in the hearing of two witnesses from the staff of the *Inquirer*, the executive editor, Talbot Farson, and the managing editor, Edward H. Macomb.

"It throws a glaring and most disturbing light upon the mood and mentality of a Chief Executive whose stubborn insistence upon prolonging the conflict in Viet Nam has already cost the nation many thousands of wasted lives and countless millions of wasted dollars.

"It also casts a most revealing illumination upon the President's attempts to attack a major member of the *Inquirer*'s staff, and through him this newspaper's opposition to the war . . ."

And so on for another ten paragraphs, each more biting than the last. Anna was always good and now she was mad through and through. *Her* paper was being attacked, *her* staff member was under fire—and by a man she had never really liked and now utterly despised.

When she had finished, Tal crowing delighted encouragement every word of the way, she tossed it to me and said:

"Banner headline, page one, Ed. I'll have an editorial to go with it in a few minutes."

I tossed it back, my mind finally made up.

"You put it in, Tal," I told him. "I don't want any part of it."

"Whose side are you on?" Anna demanded angrily.

"Yours," I said with equal anger, "as you know I always have been. But not when it comes to one-sided crap like this. This is deliberate twisting. It's a journalistic stunt. You're going to have to run a story about the Senate subcommittee, too, you know. They're going to look damned peculiar side by side."

"They won't be side by side," she promised grimly, and they weren't.

"PRESIDENT SAYS ALL WAR ACTS LEGAL," said the banner story, top right-hand column, page 1.

"Senate Subcommittee Subpoenas *Inquirer* Officials," said a very small headline over a one-paragraph item tucked away in the lower left-hand corner of page 6.

So the battle was joined and even though first blood went to Anna, and even though the White House press secretary had to splutter on for hours with denials, explanations and clarifications, it appeared for a while that she, Tal and the *Inquirer* would be hard-pressed to win the final rounds.

4

*At first we were startled, possibly even a little in-
timidated, by the rapidity with which my opponent
called in his reserves in the Senate to do his dirty
work for him. But very soon we recovered. They
attacked us, as might be expected, one by one, beginning with what they obviously considered our
weakest link. But Elizabeth Rovere did not fail me,
remaining the faithful and reliable friend she has
been ever since we were young reporters together in
Washington, so many years ago.*

—ANNA HASTINGS, *by Anna Hastings*

LOOKING BACK NOW UPON THAT HECTIC EPISODE, COV-
ered over with a haze of righteous vindication and
universal glory, it is probably true that the public has
only the vaguest, if any, memory of Bessie's testimony.
Our own memories are sharply different. Anna has
chosen to forgive her because forgiveness fits in with
Anna's legend, but it could hardly be argued that the
sum total of what Bessie was honest enough to say was
a smashing triumph for Tal. On the contrary, though

the fact was glossed over very smoothly in nearly all the news stories and broadcasts, she did him considerable damage at what could have been considerable cost to herself had Anna chosen to be vengeful. The Old Team held, however. Under the circumstances, Anna really had no choice . . . and, as I say, it wasn't allowed to hurt Tal all that much, so it didn't matter anyway.

The gist of it came midway through Bessie's testimony. The Senate Caucus Room, scene of so many historic events in the Republic's history, was jammed to the lintels, as it always is when a big show is scheduled. Every last inch of space at the press tables was occupied, television cameras were massed to catch each slightest Senatorial scratch, each noble look from the ranks of the *Inquirer*. The Senators were after Tal but the press, as always during the darker days of Viet Nam, was after the President. He knew this, of course, and so he had asked for, and received, a tough committee to handle it. Most were old personal friends of the four of us, and Gordon was one of their own (though conspicuously absent today); but too many had been stung by the paper at one time or another for friendship and association to weigh much now. The only way to turn this around was to play upon their fears of press reaction against themselves; and Bessie was simply not the one to do it.

They had questioned her at some length about the early days—politely, gently, almost casually. It was almost a reminiscence, painless and pleasant. A certain wistful realization touched my heart, and I think Bessie's and Anna's too: how earnest, wide-eyed and innocent we were in those far-off times! How purposefully and idealistically those distant youngsters strode the corridors of the Capitol in search of the beacon of Truth! How much had the beacon guttered and dwindled in the years between!

177

How old we all were now.

Suddenly Seab Cooley leaned forward and in his gentlest voice inquired:

"And did you ever hear Mr. Farson express criticism or hostility toward the United States, Miss Rovere? Did he ever express to you an active hatred of his country?"

The question took everyone by surprise, which was Seab's intention. In the row of chairs behind Bessie an almost imperceptible tightening of the jawline was Tal's only sign, but Anna gave it the full treatment, looking indignantly at me and at George Harrison Watersill. George was suitably indignant, too, but I'm afraid I looked a little less surprised than I should have. I could see Seab making a mental note and surmised accurately that he would come back to me about it later.

"He was sometimes a little—a little critical, yes," Bessie said, somewhat flustered. "But, then, you know, Senator, most young people are. It doesn't mean anything."

"Oh, I know that," Seab agreed amicably. "I just wondered if he seemed *unduly* critical to you, Miss Rovere. Sometimes young people say things like that just to be saying them, but other times they *mean* it. Did Mr. Farson ever sound to you as though he *meant* it, Miss Rovere?"

"Well, sometimes," Bessie said, more cleverly than we expected, "people mean things more than they do other times. I suppose sometimes he meant it more than he did other times."

"Now, Miss Rovere," Seab said, and I could see that Jim Eastland and John McClellan and some of the others were beginning to get a little impatient too, "I don't like to be critical of a lady, now, I surely don't, but I submit to you that you-all are bein' just a wee mite disingenuous, now. Just a wee mite. Now I ask

178

you directly again, *Was Mr. Farson critical, bitter, hateful and derogatory toward his own country?* Straight out, now!"

"Mr. Chairman!" George Watersill exclaimed, rising to his feet. "With all respect, I don't think Senators should be allowed to bully this witness, who is doing her honest best to cooperate with the committee. I don't think that's fair at all."

"I'm not bullyin' anybody, Mr. Chairman," Seab said mildly. "I'm just tryin' to get at the truth here. Nothin' to be afraid of, Miss Rovere. Just answer me honestly, now, as the experienced journalist and loyal American citizen you are. You know what I mean and I want you to answer it."

"Sometimes," Bessie said carefully, and again there was just the slightest tightening of Tal's jaw, "he has been a little more—well, emphatic than—than I might be, for instance."

"I'm not askin' you what you might be, Miss Rovere," Seab said sharply. "I know *you're* a decent citizen and I know where you stand. What I'm askin' you about is Mr. Farson. I think the committee *would* appreciate a straight answer, Miss Rovere."

(All of this was relatively mild, for Seab. When Robert A. Leffingwell was nominated for Secretary of State we would see the senior Senator from South Carolina in all his rampaging glory. But of course he had a real dislike for Bob Leffingwell. Tal was a more impersonal target, though worthy of being exposed.)

"I think there have been times," Bessie said, deciding at last to be firm, "when his views have been somewhat extreme, in my estimation."

"So extreme that you may even have doubted his loyalty to the United States?"

For a moment Bessie did not reply; then in a help-

179

less voice which was more damning than an outright accusation she confessed:

"I just don't know, Senator. I just can't say."

"Then you *have* had doubts?" Seab demanded sternly, while along the committee table members leaned forward, suddenly intent.

"Sometimes," Bessie murmured. "Possibly."

Seab looked exasperated.

"Well, have you or haven't you, Miss Rovere? Don't wishy-wash with this committee, now. Don't wishy-wash!"

"Yes, I have!" Bessie said in a sudden loud voice; and then added hastily, "Sometimes . . ."

"Yes," Seab echoed softly, "you have. And whether sometimes or all the time, at least on enough occasions to create a real obvious concern—a real and valid doubt—in your mind. Isn't that right?"

"I suppose so," Bessie said miserably, "but as I said earlier, Senator, young people sometimes say things they don't—"

"Young people!" Seab roared. "I submit to you, Miss Rovere, that you have heard Mr. Farson say treasonous things against his country as recently as a year ago! As recently as six months ago! Maybe as recently as two months, or a week, or a day! I submit to you, Miss Rovere, that he is habitually, incessantly, eternally critical and damning of his country, and that such criticism goes far beyond, in vigor and hatred of the United States, the tolerance allowed youth and the respect for differing opinions allowed their elders. I submit to you, Miss Rovere, that he is a subversive influence undermining the fairness and objectivity of his newspaper and through his newspaper the well-being and stability of his country!"

"Only sometimes, Senator!" Bessie cried, falling

neatly into his trap as bedlam instantly took over the Caucus Room. "Only sometimes!"

"Very well," Seab said gently when Senator Eastland had gaveled for order and finally secured it. "Very well, Miss Rovere. That's really all I wanted to know."

"ROVERE DEFENDS FARSON CRITICISM OF U.S. AS YOUTHFUL INDISCRETION . . ." said the *Inquirer* and most others.

And nobody at all paid much attention to anything else she said, or picked up her remark to Tal as the chairman recessed the hearing until the next day, though she said it in a loud, defensive voice and many heard.

"I'm sorry, Tal," she said defiantly, "but sometimes you *are* so terribly savage you sound almost hysterical."

He did not even look at her, nor did Anna or George Harrison Watersill. Her eyes filled with tears and for a moment she stood there helplessly like some large untethered blimp uncertain which way the wind would take it. I went forward and gave her my arm and we walked out together, braving the glaring lights in our faces and the hostile looks of our fellow members of the Old Team at our backs.

5

I had known for many years, of course, that my husband did not entirely approve of Talbot Farson; but I was not prepared for the venom which he revealed at the Senate hearing. It seemed curiously out of character for Gordon. It raised in my mind the first of those doubts which were to result eventually in the termination of our marriage and the end, sad but I can see now inevitable, of his plodding and undistinguished political career.

—ANNA HASTINGS, *by Anna Hastings*

AT FIRST, HOWEVER, AS WITH BESSIE, ALL SEEMED TO be proceeding on an innocuous reminiscent level. Gordon received all the deference Senators do receive when they testify before one another; he even, it seemed to me, received a little more. The reason for this became apparent when the committee, again led by Seab, began to concentrate on his impressions of Tal. It was very swiftly apparent that Gordon would be—indeed, eagerly wanted to be—a hostile and damaging witness.

"At what time did you first meet Mr. Farson, Senator?" Seab inquired. "At what time did he come into your life?"

"At the time I first met my future wife, Senator," Gordon said; and added with an uncharacteristic dryness that indicated his mood, "They seemed to be rather inseparable at that time."

"And still are," Seab suggested gently.

"And still are," Gordon agreed.

"In fact, with Miss Rovere and Mr. Macomb, your wife and Talbot Farson are quite a team, aren't they?"

"I believe Mrs. Hastings likes to call it 'the old team,'" Gordon said, again with that uncharacteristic acrid note. "I've been allowed to come along sort of as water boy, you might say, Senator. Somehow I've never quite considered myself really part of it."

"Even though, of course, it has been your personal fortune which has brought your wife such success in the newspaper world as she has," Seab said, which earned him an angry look from Anna and a noticeably sarcastic murmur from the press tables. Gordon, however, was too much honest old Gordon to go along with Seab on that one.

"Well, sir," he said, and for a moment his antagonism toward Tal faded and his prdie in Anna came to the fore, "I think mebbe that's a little harsh on my wife, I really do. I think anybody who's followed her career knows that she was a smashin' big success before she ever got to me, and would have continued to be even if I hadn't come along. My money came in handy in helpin' her get the *Inquirer* started, but she's made it what it is."

"Do you agree with what it is, Senator?" Seab inquired gently, and again Gordon answered honestly.

"I have my reservations, Senator," he said uncomfortably. "But I think in its own way it's a great newspaper."

183

"It's not your way, though," Seab persisted in the same gentle tone.

"No, sir," Gordon said quietly. "It is not."

"How would you change it, Senator?"

"I'd make it more evenhanded," Gordon said promptly. "I wouldn't be so blamed high-handed and self-righteous. I'd try to balance the news more. I'd try to give everybody a fair break. I'd keep my opinions on the editorial page and I'd keep 'em out of the news columns and the headlines. I'd be—well—'fairer' I guess is the word."

"To whose influence do you attribute the fact that it isn't 'fairer,' Senator?" Seab inquired, soft as the sucking dove.

"Well," Gordon said, and hesitated.

"To your wife? Or to Mr. Farson? Or to Mr. Macomb and Miss Rovere? Or to all four, or to one or two, or what?"

"Well—" Gordon began again, and again hesitated.

"Is it your wife?" Seab asked, his voice challenging. "Is it your wife who has made that great newspaper the twisted, slanted, vicious thing it is?"

"No, sir!" Gordon said sharply, his defense of Anna instinctive and immediate—his lack of defense of the paper equally, I suspected, instinctive.

"Well, then, sir," Seab pounced with equal sharpness, "who *is* it, now? Mr. Macomb? Miss Rovere? Are they the ones who have twisted this great newspaper and made it into an instrument of subversion and destruction of these United States?"

"I wouldn't go so far as to call it that, Senator," Gordon responded, recovering a bit. "I don't like all they've done with it, but I don't think it's deliberately subversive . . . I think."

"Then it *is* Mr. Macomb and Miss Rovere," Seab said, and something about his teasing tone evidently prompted Gordon to decide to end the game and say exactly what he felt.

"No, sir," he said firmly, "they aren't part of it, they're fair-minded people. My wife may be partly to blame, seein' as how she's publisher"—there was an amazed and angry sound from Anna, a murmur of surprise and excitement along the press tables—"but if there's been any one single individual whose influence has been dominant over her and the whole paper, it's been Mr. Talbot Farson. He's to blame if anybody is, I do believe."

For a moment the thought of anyone being dominant over Anna brought its own balance of amused sanity to the proceedings, but it did not last long in the excitement created by his direct accusation. The Caucus Room audience, ever eager to participate, burst into sound—the chairman banged his gavel—the cameras swung—the flashbulbs flashed—Senators looked suitably shocked—an outraged Tal exchanged a furious glance with Anna and made sure it lasted long enough for the TV cameras to catch it—confusion, as usual in such moments, reigned, and all who could profited from it.

Ultimately things settled down again, everyone breathing a little heavier.

"Do I understand you to say, Senator," Seab said carefully, "that in your belief Talbot Farson is the evil genius who has influenced the *Inquirer* and turned it against the well-bein', safety and security of these United States?"

"I believe Talbot Farson has been a consistently bad influence on the paper and on this nation, Senator," Gordon said quietly. "Yes, sir, I surely do believe that."

This time the charge was not so easy to ignore.

"SEN. HASTINGS SAYS FARSON BAD INFLUENCE ON

185

Now it wasn't only Bessie and me they wouldn't
speak to as the session ended; Gordon was in the dog-
house too. He didn't seem to mind, however. Something
had changed in Gordon; or rather, I decided, something deep, long-hidden and probably not related
directly to Tal at all, had surfaced. The immediate consequences were bad for Tal. Downstream I could see
other possibilities.

So, possibly, did Anna. The statement she issued
from the *Inquirer* an hour later sounded as though she
had given some thought to warding them off.

She did promise "a complete refutation of these
vicious, irresponsible charges," but she went on to hold
out a definite olive branch to Gordon, who was still on
the Hill and deliberately incommunicado behind a
silken screen of soft-spoken li'l Tex-is secretaries.

"I regret very much," Anna said, "that my husband
saw fit to attack Mr. Farson, thus playing directly into
the hands of all the reactionary, illiberal forces in the
United States. However, anyone who knows Senator
Hastings is aware that he speaks his convictions honestly and courageously, no matter how mistaken they
may be. That is his right and I do not challenge it.

"It seems to me imperative, however, that we at the
Inquirer present a united front against the despicable
attack upon us, and through us upon the First Amendment and the right of the free American press to criticize anything, particularly the senseless war in Viet
Nam, that is deserving of criticism. I am sure my husband does not wish to challenge this most fundamental
principle of our democracy, and I am sure that upon
reflection he will put aside what appears to be a purely

186

personal prejudice and rejoin us in our battle to save the free press."

This was the first time she had formally wrapped the flag and the First Amendment around herself and indicated the line the defense was going to take; and it didn't impress Gordon, who apparently regarded it as the attempt to put him publicly on the spot—which it was. We learned later that he didn't come home at all that night or the next day. He went, in fact, to the Circle H, taking the kids with him. Both still passionately loved the ranch and jumped at every chance to go. They also, in spite of his views, which they knew Anna deplored, still deeply loved their father, which I don't think Anna really realized yet, believing confidently that her antiwar stand would bridge the growing gap between them. But the time for realization, though we did not know it then, was rapidly coming, along with other things.

First, however, was the defense of the First Amendment. Sometime during the afternoon she affected an uneasy truce with Bessie and me, and against our better judgment we found ourselves locked in her office having a strategy session with her and Tal. He was grudging with us at best, though I hadn't testified yet and presumably could still be persuaded (he didn't really believe this, any more than I did). And Anna, while pretending to seek our advice, really knew exactly how she intended to proceed.

"We were just window dressing for her ego," Bessie murmured to me later. "I only hope she knows what she's doing."

"She always knows," I said. "It may not always be right—but she always knows."

"She'd *better* be right," Bessie said grimly. "An awful lot of things are riding on this."

Next day Anna laid the groundwork for what would

187

ultimately be her successful defense of the First Amendment, the *Inquirer,* Tal and her own permanent national fame. She also lost a few things, but she didn't realize it then, and by the time she did, she had persuaded herself she could survive without them.

6

<hr/>

I had originally been scheduled to appear at the end of the hearings. With typical craft, acting no doubt at my opponent's instigation, the committee tried to catch me unprepared by calling me unexpectedly to the stand the day after my husband testified. It did them no good. In fact, I believe they soon regretted it.

—ANNA HASTINGS, *by Anna Hastings*

I AGREE WITH ANNA: I BELIEVE THEY SPEEDILY DID. But for a brief while it appeared that they had succeeded in catching her off balance. Certainly she had one of her rare flustered moments when the chairman suddenly rapped the gavel smartly and said, "Mrs. Hastings, please!"

Dutifully George Watersill started from his chair to protest, but although her face was a study in surprise and annoyance, she reached up a white-gloved hand and pulled him firmly back.

"I'll handle it," she said, loudly enough so that

amused colleagues heard and dutifully noted it down. And after a rather stumbling start, she did.

Her first interrogator was the committee's newest and youngest member, and since he agreed with her views on the war and therefore was one of those the *Inquirer* invariably identified as "an outstandingly effective member of the new generation in the Senate," his questioning was swift and painless. How long had she known Tal? Was he an old and respected friend? Had she ever had cause to doubt his loyalty? Did she trust him? Would she continue to trust him? Did she not agree that this was a vicious and unwarranted attack launched by a desperate President whom he and she both mistrusted? It all went very smoothly.

"Senator Cooley?" the chairman said, and Seab eased forward a bit, elbow comfortably on the table, chin in hand, eyes sleepy and thoughtful as he stared at Anna. She gave no sign to those who did not know her, but we who did could sense her immediate tension as she stared back at this old friend who now, she felt, had become her permanent enemy.

"There never was," Seab said softly, "a cuter, more attractive, more intelligent, more capable reporter to hit this Hill than you were when we first met, Anna. You'll never know what a breath of spring you brought to us tired old folks on this tired old Hill."

Of all possible approaches this was the least expected, and for a moment she was genuinely and entirely taken aback.

"I—I'm glad you felt that way, Senator," she said. "It was fun in those days. I hoped that you liked me."

"We did, Anna," Seab said, still softly. "We still do. That's why we regret what's happenin' now."

"You don't regret it any more than I do, Senator," she said, recovering a little.

"Yes," Seab agreed. "Then why is it happenin',

Anna? *Why is it happenin'?* How come you've gotten so far away from that sweet, smart, pretty little gal who used to walk this Hill? Where's she gone, Anna? Where's she gone?"

"She's still here, Senator," Anna said, trying not to let herself be moved by this direct assault on her emotions, but not succeeding entirely. "She just sees things from a little different perspective now, that's all."

"Mighty different, I'm afraid, Anna," Seab said with a heavy sigh. "Mighty different. . . . Well, now." He paused, blinked, straightened up a bit: we could see the consummate old actor pulling himself out of the sweet reveries of the past to turn with exaggerated reluctance to the unhappy realities of the present. "Well, now, Anna, let's talk about why you're here."

"I'm here," she said, alerted by his shift of tactic, herself again, as tough and shrewd as he, "because an unprincipled President has seen fit to attack my newspaper and my staff, and through us the First Amendment and the fundamental freedoms of this country."

"Now, now, Miss Anna," Seab said mildly. "Y'all are speechmakin', now. You're jes speechmakin'. You know there's more to it than that."

"Do I, Senator?" she inquired calmly. "Pray tell me what."

"The safety of your country!" Seab thundered. "The well-bein' of these United States! The very foundations and security of this great nation!"

"Poof, Senator!" she replied, fully recovered and in command. "Who's speechmaking now?"

This brought her a vigorous round of laughter and applause from the audience, snickers from our colleagues at the press tables, some quickly suppressed smiles along the committee table. It also brought her a sudden warmly embracing beam from the senior Senator from South Carolina and a recovery as swift as any she could manage.

"Miss Anna," he said, an amiable smile creasing the sly, wrinkled old face, "you know me too well, now, you really do. You're thinkin', 'There goes that old fakir again!' And you may be right, Anna, you may be right. But"—and suddenly his voice dropped and he looked deadly grim—"that doesn't help either of us with the problem of Mr. Talbot Farson, does it?"

"I wasn't aware it was a problem, Senator," she said coolly. "Exactly what *is* the problem? The President has never told me, the committee has never told me— I'm quite in the dark. Insinuations—innuendoes—dark hints—dire forebodings—I'm so confused I just don't know what to do!"

"The day you don't know what to do, Miss Anna," Seab said with a chuckle, "will be the day they move hell to the North Pole. I think you suspect what it's all about jes' a leetle bit—jes' a *leetle* bit. You suspect there may be more to Mr. Farson's talk than talk. Well: so do we, Miss Anna. So do we."

At this there was a soft but unmistakable hiss from somewhere in the room. It turned swiftly to applause at her reply.

"I know no such thing, Senator!" she said sharply. "I know only that a vindictive President, seeking to find a scapegoat and distract attention from his brutal and heartless war, is seeking to destroy the First Amendment and the media that criticize him. He seeks to do so through the medium of my newspaper and my editor. He is using this committee as his instrument. But he will not succeed, Senator. He will not be permitted to succeed. He *cannot* be permitted to succeed, if the free press and with it a free nation are to remain free."

The applause swelled up, doubled, redoubled. Seab

was not impressed, though he decided to adopt still another approach.

"You-all are bestin' me in speeches, Anna," he said with a relaxed smile. "You really are. So let's talk about Mr. Farson for a while. How long have you known him, now?"

"The better part of thirty years, Senator, as you very well know. You've known him that long yourself. Has he ever seemed disloyal or traitorous to you?"

"I'm askin' the questions," Seab said mildly. "You're not a Senator *yet*, Miss Anna, though"—he chuckled—"nothin' you do surprises me, and I shouldn't be surprised if it happened any day, now."

Again came applause and again he chuckled.

"You see, you've got yourself plenty of votes right here in the Caucus Room. Plenty right here."

"Watch out, Senator," she said with a sudden gurgle of laughter that sounded for a reminiscent second like that original Anna he had talked about earlier. "I may run in South Carolina!"

Again laughter, in which Seab joined heartily.

"I hope not!" he exclaimed. "Lordy, I hope *not!* But still," he said, face returning to somber lines, "we have the problem of Mr. Farson, don't we, Anna?"

"He is no problem to me, Senator," she said calmly. "I believe in his innocence. I trust him. I rely upon him. I have never found him traitorous or disloyal. I have no qualms. I would say he is your problem and the President's, Senator, and not really a concern to me."

"Ah, but he may be," Seab said softly. "He may be."

"So you keep telling me," she said coldly, "but never yet is there any proof. It's getting a little boring, frankly, Senator."

"Oh, I wouldn't let it bore me if I were you, Anna," he said dryly. "I wouldn't let it bore me for one little

193

minute. I just want to run over this with you, now."
He paused. "All right?"

"Certainly," she said blandly. "That's what I'm here
for."

"You're here to make a case," Seab said, "and you're
doin' it mighty well. I just hope I can do as well, Miss
Anna; just one whit as well. So you have known Mr.
Farson for almost thirty years. Have you been intimate
friends with him during all that time?"

"Miss Rovere, Mr. Macomb, Mr. Farson and I have
been close and intimate friends all that time, Senator.
We were joined in due course by my husband. All of
us have been intimate friends for a long time."

"Yes," Seab agreed gravely. "But you and Mr. Farson have been the most intimate of all, is that right?"

Again came a hissing, again changing to applause as
Anna replied with a continuing coldness:

"I don't know what that is supposed to mean, Senator, but if it means what I think you intend it to mean,
then it is unworthy of you and I won't dignify it with
an answer. Mr. Farson has been my executive editor
ever since the founding of the *Inquirer* in 1956. Our
working relationship has been most close and most intimate. It could not have been closer. It could not have
been more intimate. What about it, Senator?"

"Well, then," Seab said, still mildly, when the applause finally died down, "you have certainly had occasion to know him thoroughly, to sound out his views
and opinions most extensively, to know, more perhaps
than anyone, what he thinks. Is that right?"

"Possibly so, Senator," she said; and then added impatiently as he cocked an exaggeratedly quizzical eye-
brow, "Yes, I suppose I have known his views and
opinions better than anyone else. What of it? What sinister thing do you make of that?"

"And you have always found them helpful, encouraging and friendly to the United States?"

"I have found him consistently determined that the United States should live up to the principles upon which it was founded and remain true to the dream that gave it being," she said calmly, and got another big round of applause.

"You are satisfied that he is loyal?" Seab asked, unperturbed.

"I am."

"You have never heard him say anything subversive or destructive about this country?"

"I have not."

"But you have heard him say sharply critical things about it?"

"Many times."

"Even harshly and savagely critical?"

"Sometimes."

"This has not disturbed you?"

"Never."

"Why is that, Miss Anna?" Seab asked softly. "Why is that, now?"

"Because in most instances I have agreed with him," she said calmly. "Not always with his tone or his terms of expression, but almost always with his opinion. Certainly I agree with his opinion of this criminal and useless war, which we have done"—her voice, though remaining calm, became steely—"*and will continue to do*—everything in our power to oppose, to thwart and to end."

Again Seab let the applause tumble over and subside. Then he remarked mildly, "If we were in a state of war, Anna, that statement would be mighty close to treason."

"Give the President a state of war!" she challenged sharply. "Go ahead and give him one! He doesn't dare ask for one because he knows Congress wouldn't give it to him. He missed the boat on that as he has on everything else in this ghastly and inexcusable situation. So give it to him, Senator! Go on! Line up Congress and give him a state of war, and *then* declare me treasonous, and Mr. Farson treasonous! But don't come around in the meantime and do his dirty work trying to destroy the First Amendment and the freedom of the press and the freedom of the United States of America!"

After that, with a few more face-saving attempts to throw her off balance, Seab gave up, very well aware that he had lost the battle of the news and the headlines for that day; even though, knowing him, not even Anna in her triumph was euphoric enough to believe that he was finally routed. He obviously still felt he had something, and as the expressions of other committee members revealed when they left the Caucus Room, they felt so too. But for the moment, of course, it was all Anna.

"ANNA HASTINGS DEFENDS FREE PRESS IN HEATED SENATE HEARING . . . TELLS COMMITTEE SHE SUPPORTS FARSON FULLY IN ATTEMPTS TO 'OPPOSE, THWART AND END' VIET NAM WAR . . . COUNTRY GIVES PUBLISHER FULL SUPPORT IN BATTLE FOR FIRST AMENDMENT."

There may have been some doubt about this last assertion, which was the *Inquirer*'s own headline, but there was no doubt that she received full support from the media. Not for the last time, her name that night was the biggest in the country and the tributes flowed in nonstop.

We all expected a call from 1600 Pennsylvania Avenue when we got back to the office but there was none. Instead there was a brief and frigid statement from the Press Secretary:

"It is with deep regret that the President has noted Mrs. Anna Hastings' assertion before the Senate committee that she and her executive editor, Mr. Talbot Farson, are doing 'everything in our power to oppose, to thwart and to end' the conflict in Viet Nam.

"Under other circumstances such a statement would be clear treason, subject to the full prosecution of the law. Under any circumstance it is an inexcusable attempt to weaken the United States and the President in the conduct of a necessary and vital attempt to hold back the tide of ruthless Communist imperialism.

"The President cannot prosecute, but he does deeply regret that Mrs. Hastings and her executive editor, Talbot Farson, have deemed it necessary to strike so grievous a blow at the very heart of their nation's defenses."

" 'Nation's defenses!' " Anna sniffed angrily. "What on earth has Viet Nam got to do with the 'nation's defenses'? He's getting paranoid."

"He can't prosecute because there's no law giving him the authority and he knows it," Tal said contemptuously. "You've got him on the run and now all he can do is squeal."

I said nothing. It was my turn to testify next and we all knew that my testimony might be damaging to Tal; but my mind was made up. They seemed to sense this, for neither spoke to me about it. The only comment came from Bessie, who called me at home that night.

"I just want you to know I wish you well."

"Thanks, Bess. I'll do it for the Old Team."

She snorted.

"The Old Team is a little frazzled now, I'm afraid. I think we're both going to get the ax, if you ask me."

"Maybe," I said, "but I doubt it. Anna can't afford to crack the facade now."

Which just goes to show that after all those years I still didn't know Anna. Nor, I found, did I know Gordon, who had a few surprises for us, too.

197

7

---

*Although I have long since forgiven Ed Macomb,
and he still remains one of my closest and dearest
friends though no longer in my employ, I must confess that I could not find it in my heart to forgive
my husband. I realized I had underestimated the
depth of his antagonism toward Talbot Farson and
his basic dislike for me and the principles I have always tried to maintain. The committee hearing temporarily became a shambles as his feelings were
displayed for the public record. When it was over I
am afraid our marriage was a shambles too.*

—ANNA HASTINGS, *by Anna Hastings*

ACTUALLY, AS BESSIE AND I SAW IT, GORDON WAS
quite reasonable and quite calm. He was just fearfully
determined, with a grim persistence that not even Seab
could match. He obviously did have a personal motivation but on the whole he handled it and himself with
a considerable dignity. His appearance certainly took
us all by surprise, though. "Out of Seab," as Alice
Roosevelt Longworth (the capital's only real wit for

the past seventy years) once remarked, paraphrasing Pliny, "always something new."

Like Anna, I was handed first to the minor lions on the committee and found their questioning routine and not very difficult. They were all friends of hers, darlings of the *Inquirer,* and not about to extract from me anything that might be damaging either to it or to their own cozy relations therewith. Nor did I volunteer anything, figuring that Seab would be more than enough to handle. And also I was not really in a mood to volunteer. I had lain awake most of the night. Though I may have sounded a bit flippant here and there in the narrative, this was not all that easy for me. For all his often prickly personality, Tal and I *had* been close friends for a quarter of a century and it isn't that comfortable to testify to things that may permanently damage an old friend. Possibly I was naive in thinking my testimony could have that effect, but, anyway, I did. My mind was made up, but it hadn't been a simple matter: it had caused me, in fact, a lot of genuine turmoil and unhappiness in the days since we had received that first call from the White House. I was therefore an easy target for confusion when Seab, instead of sailing into me himself, said blandly:

"Mr. Chairman, if it's agreeable to the committee, I think we might invite the distinguished junior Senator from Texas to sit in with us this morning and ask a few questions. He's expressed that desire, and he *does* have an interest, so I think perhaps we might accede to his desire if that's agreeable to you-all."

There was a tensing in the room, a few murmurs of protest along the committee table. But before anyone had a chance to speak, Jim Eastland in the chair said calmly:

"I expect nobody can object to that. Senator Hastings, join us, if you please."

And as we swung around to look, we saw him leave a seat toward the back and come forward. Accompanying him, looking neither left nor right and certainly not at their mother, were Gordie and Lisa, tense, white-faced and nervous. They looked like two little hippie tramps at this point in their lives but, as befitted fifty million dollars on the hoof, give or take a few, their lengthy hair was combed, their carefully tattered T-shirts and carefully faded jeans were clean, and they carried themselves with that ineffable air of the inherited rich that shows through even the most determinedly casual attire. They were obviously on Daddy's side; and when he had taken his place beside Seab and they had taken seats in the row of chairs behind him, their eyes sought mine with shy but warmly affectionate smiles. It was obvious they were on my side, too, which made me feel a lot better.

"Mr. Macomb," Gordon said while the room quieted down and behind me I could sense Anna and Tal leaning forward intently, "you have known Mr. Farson intimately for many years, is that correct?"

"Yes, Senator."

"Please describe that relationship."

"Well," I said, "it began, as you know, when Anna —Mrs. Hastings—Miss Rovere, Mr. Farson and I first came to Washington as young reporters. That was early World War Two days, we didn't make very much and so to save expenses we doubled up, as a lot of young people in Washington did in those days."

"Not as they do in these days," Seab interjected with a smile, and a little wave of amusement broke some of the tension in the room.

"No, Senator," I said. "This was girl-girl and boy-boy, and not even *that* was the way it sometimes is in these days. We were just trying to save money and make ends meet."

"So you did know Tal—Mr. Farson—very well from almost the moment you got to Washington," Gordon said as the audience finished its chuckle and became attentive again.

"Tal, Anna and I met our very first day on the Hill, the day after Pearl Harbor when F.D.R. came up here to ask for the declaration of war. We met Bessie a week or so later."

"And you began rooming with Tal—Mr. Farson—almost immediately thereafter."

"Within a month."

"So that you were in a position to know his thoughts on things as fully and completely as roommates do know each other's thoughts, when they are young and strugglin' to make their mark in Washington."

"Yes, sir."

"Particularly if they genuinely like each other."

"Yes, sir."

"As you and Mr. Farson genuinely do like each other?"

"Oh, yes," I said, offering Tal a smile which he did not return, "although I think he's always rather considered me the dumber partner. But I've managed to keep up. Anyway, I think he knows I've always liked him."

"So there is no personal animus in any testimony you may give here."

"None on my part," I said, slightly nettled by Tal's lack of response.

"But perhaps on his?" Gordon asked quickly.

"I can only testify for myself, Senator. I'm fond of Tal, we've always gotten along. Maybe we'd better let it go at that."

"All right," he agreed, somewhat to my surprise, for Seab wouldn't have abandoned it so quickly. "I surely don't want to come between two old friends, now, I surely don't. But I do want you to testify fully about his beliefs."

"I'm under oath, Gordon—Senator. Ask me what you like."

"Has he ever said anythin' to you that indicated a lack of faith in the United States?"

"He has been very critical of this country on many occasions. But, then, who hasn't, from time to time?"

"Lots of people," Gordon said crisply. "Lots of good, simple, decent, honest people who love their country."

"I don't know about that, Senator," I said, "and I think there you're getting into a very subjective and pejorative area. Lots of serious criticism of this country is based upon love for it and disappointment because of its apparent failure to live up to its best potentials. It doesn't mean that those who criticize are always hateful or subversive toward it."

This was when I got *my* round of applause. It was the first and last.

"You feel, then," Gordon said when it had subsided, "that Mr. Farson's criticisms have always been based upon love for the United States. He has never seemed to you unduly harsh, savage and unbalanced in his comments."

"He has sometimes been a little strong."

"How strong?" Gordon asked sharply.

"Very."

"Has he ever advocated the overthrow of the government of the United States by force and violence?"

"No, sir."

"So you believe him to be entirely loyal and devoted to the best interests of this country."

I hesitated, just long enough for Seab to nudge Gordon sharply in the ribs.

"So you believe him to be entirely loyal and devoted—" Gordon began again dutifully.

Days and nights of agonizing uncertainty suddenly coalesced. It was one thing to say that my mind was made up and another to find that it really, finally, was.

"Senator," I said, and I'm afraid my voice trembled a little with unexpected emotion, "I am not entirely sure of that, no."

There was a gasp, a hiss and finally a boo from the audience, an uneasy and disapproving stirring along the press tables. I was conscious that all the television cameras were staring intently into my every pore. I was also conscious that Gordon, Gordie and Lisa were all smiling at me encouragingly. I tried to return their smiles but I'm afraid I did not look as confident as I wanted to. Behind me I heard Tal whisper savagely to Anna, "Goddamned traitor!" I did not hear her reply.

"Why do you say that, Ed?" Gordon asked, and without conscious volition I think I sighed heavily before replying.

"A number of cumulative things," I said finally. "Hard to put my finger on, exactly . . . cumulative."

"Have you ever known him to be associated with anyone known to you, or suspected by you, to be subversive and disloyal to the United States?" Jim Eastland interjected.

"No, Senator," I said, again slowly. "At least, I think not."

"That seems an odd answer," he observed.

"Well, there have been a few people over the years who were pretty far over, but I believe Tal always knew them as news sources. Not, to my knowledge, as 'associates' in the sense you mean."

"But you still have this 'cumulative' feelin'."

"Yes, sir."

"When did it begin?" Gordon inquired. "Was there any one point or moment? Surely there must have been

203

somethin' to make you feel that way, some single thing. What was it?"

"Well," I said carefully, and now the room hushed down to a sort of sibilant intensity as I spoke, "it may go back to the night of V-J Day."

"V-J Day!" Gordon exclaimed. "But that was almost twenty-five years ago!"

"Yes, sir."

"And you've had this feelin' all that time and you never told anybody, you went along workin' with him on the *Inquirer*, you let us allow him to *run* the *Inquirer*, virtually as he pleased, you never said anythin', you still regarded him as your friend—how could that be?" Gordon demanded in a wondering tone. "How could you betray us like that, Ed, when you *knew* this man—"

"I didn't know, Gordon!" I said sharply, struggling hard to maintain some semblance of control over the proceedings and myself as all sorts of abysses opened before us. "I don't know now! It was only an impression I had, a suggestion, a feeling—"

But now my colleagues in the media were giving me openly scornful glances, the audience in the Caucus Room was in full voice; behind me I did finally hear Anna exclaim sharply, "This is character assassination pure and simple!" It was obvious there was no choice left.

"He turned to me," I said loudly, loudly enough so that they all grumbled into tense and intently watching silence, "in the midst of all that happy, excited crowd in Lafayette Park, and he said, 'We're top dogs now, but in twenty years' time we'll have things turned completely around so that America will be the most hated country in the world!' "

"Repeat that!" Seab ordered, hunching forward over

204

the table in his excitement, the sleepy old face no longer sleepy now but sharp-eyed and alert.

" 'We're top dogs now, but in twenty years' time we'll have things turned completely around so that America will be the most hated country in the world.' "

"I see, Gordon said, while a confused jumble of sound filled the room. "I see. . . . Did he say whom he meant when he said, 'we'll have things turned completely around'?"

"No, sir."

"But it obviously wasn't you and he," Seab said dryly.

"No, sir."

"He meant himself and someone else—or several others—or even *many* others. Isn't that correct?"

"That was my impression."

"He could have meant Communists," Seab said.

"Or fellow Communists," Gordon suggested with a sudden surprising anger in his voice. "Or *fellow* Communists. That's what he could have meant, isn't it, Ed?"

There was a great well-up of boos, eventually gaveled into silence.

"He could have," I said carefully, "but I have no knowledge of whom he meant exactly, Senator. I just know he was very confident that these people, whoever they were, could turn world opinion around so that we would become a very hated nation."

"And he would help them do it," Gordon said flatly. " '*We'll* turn things around.' He was part of them, don't you think so, Ed? You do, don't you? You thought so then and you think so to this day. Isn't that correct?"

"Yes," I said quietly, sure I was bidding farewell to almost thirty years of friendship, very likely to the *Inquirer* and certainly to at least two members of the Old

Team, "yes, Gordon, that is what I thought then, and that is what I think today."

For a while after that, pandemonium claimed the Caucus Room. Senators exclaimed, press colleagues made skeptical remarks, members of the audience groaned, hissed, booed. Behind my back Tal cursed and Anna joined him (the first time, I remember thinking, that I ever heard her use those ostentatious four-letter expletives that soon were to become the sign and seal of her trendiness). Gordie and Lisa looked frightened but kept on smiling at me with an earnest determination that in retrospect seemed very touching though I had no time to notice then.

Eventually order was restored, the hearing proceeded. I was handed back to the minor lions, who now had a Cause, the cause of demolishing my testimony. They made a few speeches; I tried not to compete. I repeated Tal's statement whenever asked, emphasized again that I had no personal knowledge whom he meant by "we," no personal knowledge that he had ever associated with anyone actively subversive or disloyal to the United States. I told what I knew and stuck to it without embellishment. Later there were many scathing editorials and television newscast statements to the effect that I was attempting to give a sinister implication to a "silly statement, made with youthful exuberance, that should be dismissed out of hand by any sane and reasonable mind," as Anna's signed front-page editorial put it; but it was clear that I had done him a lot of damage with the public. Not eagerly, not happily, and not with relish, as some of my colleagues—and Tal and Anna—seemed to think; but because I felt that in all honesty I had no choice.

This time the White House statement was one sentence long:

"At last the testimony of an honest man, Mr. Edward Macomb, has put the loyalty of Mr. Talbot Farson in proper perspective."

"Shit!" Anna said, quite startling me at the time. She then suggested, without noticeable rancor but very firmly, that I knock off for the rest of the day and perhaps for the rest of the hearing.

"How about for the rest of forever?" I couldn't help snapping, annoyed by her obvious feeling that I had been engaged upon some kind of carefree enjoyable picnic for myself in testifying against an old friend.

"Perhaps," she agreed calmly, "but not until I decide it's the proper moment."

"I'm about to decide right now," I said, and I was. But she only laughed, tucked my arm through hers and walked me to the door.

"Go home and get a good night's sleep, Ed," she suggested, "and don't worry. We're almost out of the woods on this. Tal and I recognize you did what you felt you had to do. We don't hold it against you. Your testimony won't hold up long. I started things moving our way yesterday and this is just a minor interruption. It will work out for us, you'll see."

Which was all very patronizing and designed deliberately to make me angry, which it did, for a while; until the next day, in fact, when we all returned to the hearing room and took our seats beside one another as though nothing had happened, to the great edification of the audience, the continual snapping of flashbulbs and the constant zooming-in of television cameras.

"Yeay, Old Team!" Bessie murmured as she took her seat beside me. And in some odd and wryly sentimental way, I suppose that was still what it was; and probably still is; and probably always will be.

Then the next witness was called and the good cheer of the Old Team's leader and her right-hand man suddenly took a turn for the worse.

8

——————

*The day on which my opponent and those who
wished to destroy the* Inquirer, *the free press and
the First Amendment brought all their efforts to bear
in a last attempt to demolish us was a difficult and
traumatic one for me. For a time it seemed they
might succeed. Only in retrospect did the event appear for what it was: the opportunity to make a full,
final and utterly devastating refutation of all the
vicious charges made against Tal, against the paper
and against me. But it had its tense moments, and
I do not minimize the fact that for a little while I was
seriously concerned about the outcome. I need not
have been, really: all worked for the best even
though, again, my husband did his hostile worst to
assist my enemies.*

—ANNA HASTINGS, *by Anna Hastings*

BACK IN THOSE ANCIENT TIMES, PROTECTED BY THE
aura of its dictatorial and untouchable leader, the FBI
almost never appeared in person before Congressional
committees. There was a tacit and generally unbroken

agreement, inspired by awe, respect and a lively and omnipresent fear of the Director's files, that great delicacy would be exercised with regard to this particular agency. It was treated with kid gloves reinforced by cotton muffs ten inches thick. To paraphrase Rudyard Kipling, there was an almost universal tendency to "walk wide o' J. Edgar Hoover, for 'alf o' creation he owns." Or so it was thought in the White House and on the Hill.

Therefore, aside from an occasional dour appearance by the gentleman himself to fend off some upstart so ignorant and beyond the pale as to dare to criticize him, committee investigators were usually entrusted with the task of placing the results of the FBI's discoveries before the members; and so it was today.

Clarence Dobson was small, neat, bright-eyed; ineffably, if somewhat unjustly, ferrety. In some hard-to-define way he always gave the impression of one immured forever in files musty, dusty, dark and dank, from which, from time to time, he would emerge with a bucket of devastating information and dump it upon the unsuspecting head of some evildoer. Actually he was an amiable, hardworking soul who lived in a modest home in Alexandria, supported a wife, three kids, two dogs, a cat, an old station wagon and a heavy mortgage. He got along excellently with the press and had slipped us all many interesting leaks over the years. When he zeroed in, as we had come to learn, he really zeroed in; and when he was backed by the FBI he could be quite devastating.

It is no wonder Tal and Anna both noticeably tensed when the chairman called him blandly to the stand. Their expressions—hers in particular—changed to an openly impatient anger when Gordon, at Seab's prearranged urging, was once again permitted to lead the questioning.

209

In the ritual that was always dutifully observed, Clarence first was sworn in like any other witness. Then the Old Team's water boy got down to work with a persistence that showed clearly that he thought he had Tal on the run.

"Mr. Dobson," he said, "you were present here yesterday?"

"Yes, sir," Clarence agreed in that level, courteous, completely noncommittal tone he had long ago perfected for these occasions.

"And you heard Mr. Macomb testify concernin' Mr. Farson's sentiments on V-J Day?"

"Yes, sir."

"You heard Mr. Macomb say that Mr. Farson said, and I quote, 'We're top dogs now, but in twenty years' time we'll have things turned completely around so that America will be the most hated country in the world.' "

"Yes, sir."

"And you heard the concludin' portion of my exchange with Mr. Macomb in which Mr. Macomb agreed with me that when Mr. Farson said '*we'll* have things turned completely around,' he was associatin' himself with those who might possibly be Communists, and even *fellow* Communists?"

"I heard Mr. Macomb so testify, Senator, yes, sir."

"Do you have any reason, of your own knowledge, to believe that this conclusion about Mr. Farson, with which Mr. Macomb and I found ourselves in agreement, might be true?"

"Not of my own knowledge, no, sir," Clarence said, beginning that gentle sifting through papers which had many times before marked the beginning of the end for some unhappy witness, "but I have here a document prepared by"—he paused before the fateful words, while many committee members made their silent, invisible but inevitable genuflection toward the drab-corridored building downtown—"the FBI."

"Mr. Chairman," Seab said promptly, "I move that the document referred to be admitted as evidence in this hearing."

"So ordered," Jim Eastland said laconically from behind his cigar. "It will be listed as Exhibit One. Or mebbe," he added with a sudden chuckle, "Exhibit One-*A*. Or even One-A-*plus*."

"Thank you, Mr. Chairman," Seab said.

"Happy to oblige, Senator," said Jim Eastland.

"Christ!" someone murmured audibly at the press tables. "What a love feast!"

"Now, then, Mr. Dobson," Gordon said calmly, "can you-all kindly give us the gist of Exhibit One, please?"

"Yes, sir," Clarence said, his tone still level, dispassionate and businesslike. "It relates that Mr. Talbot Farson was associated secretly during his college days with at least three youth organizations that were Communist-inspired and Communist-dominated. He was an active member of them. It relates that in more recent years he has been in constant secret contact with a member of the Soviet espionage network based in the Soviet Embassy on Sixteenth Street, Northwest, in this city. It relates that he both gave information to, and received information from, this individual."

"Who is this individual?" Gordon demanded, while the room suddenly became very quiet and the tension very great.

"Was, Senator," Clarence said gravely. "Unfortunately, he was killed by a hit-and-run driver two months ago while crossing the street in the rain near his apartment in Southwest Washington. His name was Valerian Obolenski, known to the FBI to have been a member of the KGB ever since he was assigned to the embassy, ostensibly as a records clerk, five years ago."

"Oh," Gordon said in a disappointed tone that was reflected in the faces of Seab and several other committee members. "He is no longer living, then."

"No, sir."

"And it was a hit-and-run accident, so nobody knows who killed him?"

"No, sir."

"Was it known to his superiors that he was under surveillance by the FBI?"

"It seems a fair presumption."

"Then the hit-and-run 'accident' might not have been an accident at all?"

Clarence paused, as always scrupulously fair. "That is possible," he said slowly. "We have no means of knowing that."

"Do you have any practical, tangible, concrete evidence of his associatin' with Mr. Farson, then, or of Mr. Farson's associatin' with him?"

"Only once, to the FBI's knowledge, did they converse by telephone," Clarence said. "There is no written evidence."

"But there is evidence of the telephone call?"

"It was taped," Clarence said, and beside me I felt Anna's arm go suddenly tense. I glanced quickly beyond her at Tal. Both their faces were set and grim. The room stirred with sound.

"Is it available here today?" Gordon asked, his voice showing strain and excitement.

"It is, Senator," Clarence said, and gestured to one of his junior staff assistants, who came forward with a small recorder and placed it carefully at his elbow.

"This will be Exhibit Two," Jim Eastland said. "Play it for us, Mr. Investigator."

"Yes, sir," Clarence said, and turning to the machine, he adjusted it carefully—started it—stopped it

212

—started it again (he was not above milking his dramatic scenes when they were good ones, and this certainly was) and finally glanced up.

"Go ahead," Senator Eastland ordered with his wry little smile. "We're all listenin'."

And indeed we were as the voices, somewhat muffled but quite distinguishable, began.

First came Tal.

"Valerian?"

And the thick-accented reply:

"*Da,* Tal. Have you got it?"

"Yes. Have you?"

"Oh, yes."

"Where do you want me to leave it?"

"The usual place is still safe, I think."

"I'm not so sure. I think somebody's onto us."

"Oh?" Valerian said blankly. "What makes you say that?"

"Just a hunch," Tal said.

"I have seen no evidence."

"Neither have I."

"Well, then—"

"All right," Tal said. "But we've got to be very careful."

"Have you got everything I asked for?" Valerian wanted to know.

"It's all here."

"Including the figures on production of the new bomber?"

"Yes."

There was a deep gasp from the room, no slightest sign from rigidly controlled, desperately impassive Tal and Anna. But it was not a good moment for them.

"Very well, then. Leave it this afternoon and I will pick it up."

"And what you have for me," Tal said. "Does it include all the instructions?"

"Everything."

"Very good. We will proceed as planned, then."

"As planned," Valerian said. "Good-bye until next week."

"Good-bye."

There was a scratch or two, the sound of phones being hung up, silence. The tape ended with a little click, and gravely Clarence punched the reverse button and sat back. The whirring of the machine was the only sound. Even our colleagues at the press tables, who should have been out filing bulletins, were too stunned to move.

"Mr. Chairman!" someone said abruptly in a harsh, half-strangled voice.

Abruptly the room came to life as the still cameramen sprang into action around us, the television cameras zoomed in, committee members leaned forward, the audience let go in a great burst of babble, noise and unpent emotion.

"Mr. Farson," Jim Eastland said calmly.

"Mr. Chairman," Tal said, standing up, his body visibly shaking with tension, a great indignation on his face. "Mr. Chairman, when is it your intention that the committee meet again?"

"I believe we'd been thinkin' about tomorrow mornin'," Senator Eastland said, "but if you'd prefer somethin' earlier—"

"I would, sir," Tal said, obviously struggling to hold his voice steady. "This is a matter so grave and so—so damaging to me that I don't want to let it rest on the public record any longer than I can help. I'd like to respond immediately, if I may—"

"Mr. Chairman," Gordon interrupted, not looking at Anna or Tal, his face excited and triumphant, "it's almost noon. Can't we wait until two o'clock? Or even three, so Senators will have time to check in, over on the floor?"

"But that means only one side will get out to the country before I have a chance to answer!" Tal cried in a harsh and angry voice.

"Now you know how it feels," Gordon shot back, so sharply and bitterly that Tal's jaw literally dropped with amazement and Anna's arm against mine gave a sudden involuntary jerk. This was the new Gordon with a vengeance.

"But—" Tal cried again. "But—"

"Three o'clock it is," Jim Eastland said. "That's perfectly fair, Mr. Farson. The FBI has had its say, now you can have yours. It won't hurt you to wait three hours. It may even be, as Senator Hastings suggests, a worthwhile and enlightenin' experience. The committee stands adjourned until three P.M."

9

The interval was a tense and greatly disturbed time for us. Ed and Bessie went off together to lunch, virtually ignoring us. My husband, having done his damage and achieved his goal, disappeared instantly with the children. Tal and I were surrounded by the media but managed to fight our way through without responding to the incessant questioning which was, I know, almost unanimously friendly and well meant, but could only be highly distracting at that time. Somehow we managed to reach my car and I instructed the driver to take us straight to the Inquirer. There in my office, talking quietly together over salads brought up by my secretary—though neither of us really felt like eating much—we discussed our problem. Tal convinced me then, as I remain convinced to this day, that he was completely and unequivocally innocent. We decided that the best thing for him to do would simply be to tell the truth.

—ANNA HASTINGS, *by Anna Hastings*

FOR SOME OF US, WHETHER HE DID SO REMAINS TO this day, and will always remain, a most serious unanswered question. But there was no doubt that from the moment he began to speak, soon after the committee reconvened at three o'clock, he had both the audience and the media solidly with him. He was greeted with an enormous burst of applause when he took the stand and many of our colleagues came over and shook his hand for the cameras. Senator Eastland patiently let this run for ten minutes or so, then gaveled for order. The room settled down to a tensely watching, highly partisan silence. Tal made the most of it.

"Mr. Chairman," he said, before anyone else had a chance to speak, "may I be accompanied by counsel?"

"Certainly," Jim Eastland said. "Mr. Watersill, make yourself at home . . . although," he added dryly, "I'm not so sure Mr. Farson needs you. I seem to get the feelin' he's loaded for bear."

"Wouldn't you be, Senator," Tal demanded sharply, "if your life and career had been put in jeopardy by twisted, one-sided testimony based on implications full of lies?"

There was a round of hearty applause during which Senator Eastland studied him, face impassive.

"The witness will be sworn," he said; and after it was done, and after George Harrison Watersill had busily seated himself at Tal's side, he turned to Gordon. "Senator Hastings, would you like to interrogate the witness?"

"If the committee pleases," Gordon said. He paused. Tension rose. He and Tal stared across the table as though they had never seen one another before—as perhaps, in a sense, they never had. Finally Gordon spoke.

"You have heard the testimony, Mr. Farson?"

" 'Mr. Farson!' " Tal echoed bitterly. "It's been 'Tal'

217

for twenty years, Gordon. Yes, I heard it, every bit of it. Including yours."

"Then you know," Gordon said, a rising irritation in his voice, "that it looks most damagin' to you."

"It has been made to look that way, yes," Tal agreed. "By some pretty expert twisters."

Again he got his applause, but this time Gordon was ready for him.

"Does this apply to Mr. Macomb's"—he began, and then modified it as Tal shook his head impatiently—"does this apply to Ed's testimony? Was that twisted? Is he a 'pretty expert twister'? Did you or did you not say what Ed says you did? What about it"—he spat out the name with a hostility that showed us the old amiable Gordon was gone forever—"*Tal?*"

"Ed's testimony is correct as far as it goes," Tal said, more mildly. "My own memory is vague, but it is possible I said something along the lines he has reported. I may or I may not."

"You may or you may not," Gordon repeated with an exaggerated thoughtfulness. "You may or you may not. That's a pretty clever twister itself, Tal, old friend. Did you or didn't you?"

"I don't really remember, Gordon," Tal said blandly. "But supposing I did, what of it?"

"What *of* it?" Gordon demanded sharply, while along the table Seab and Jim Eastland looked affronted and the minor lions looked pleased. "It's a treasonous remark, if true. That's what of it!"

"Oh, now," Tal said, voice deliberately and insultingly chiding. "Oh, now, Gordon. 'Treasonous if true.' What kind of overstated nonsense is that? Suppose it were true, how could it be treasonous? If I said it at all, which I don't remember, it was probably just an observation about the state of things."

"It was more than that, mister," Gordon said sharply.

218

"It was a statement of deliberate intent that you and some other persons unknown were goin' to embark on a deliberate campaign to make the United States 'the most hated nation in the world.' "

" 'Some other persons unknown,' " Tal repeated thoughtfully. "Yes, they *are* unknown, aren't they, Gordon? And that bothers you, doesn't it? Suppose I did say this fantastic thing—or let's say I said it, and it wasn't fantastic—how could there possibly be anything treasonous about it when it involved 'some other persons unknown'? Who were they? How were they involved? And did I ever say it at all? I don't remember."

"Try, Tal," Gordon said, breathing hard but managing to hold onto his temper. "Just try, now. It's highly important for what it says about your state of mind and about your associates."

"It doesn't say a thing about my 'associates'!" Tal said sharply. "They're 'unknown,' remember, and don't you forget it. As for my state of mind, supposing I did say this fantastic thing"—and he turned and glanced back at me with a sudden exaggeratedly kindly smile —"and I'm not disputing Ed's memory, although it *was* the end of a long, hard war and *everybody* was a little confused that night—I repeat, what of it? I had often been critical of policies of the United States that seemed to me to betray the country's finest principles and its historical purposes, and I never made much secret of that. I didn't agree with a lot of things that were done during the war—just"—he paused and looked directly into the television cameras—"just as I don't agree with a lot of things that are being done in this present shameful, awful, inexcusable conflict in Viet Nam—" and received his applause, and went on, "But that doesn't mean I was plotting any deep dark revolution. I thought it likely that the inevitable trends of history would soon reveal U.S. foreign policy for the hopeless and self-defeating fraud it was and still is, and I thought it very likely that this would result in worldwide dislike and disrespect for America. But this seemed to me, as I say, more an inevitable trend of history than anything I would personally be involved in, and I would say history has certainly borne me out. . . . Gordon," he said, and he looked at him with a puzzlement that appeared to be completely genuine, "if I really did say that some mysterious and unknown *we* would do all that, I swear to God I don't know what I meant by it or why I said it . . . if I really did say it at all, which I honestly don't remember."

And he sat back amid approving murmurs from the audience and stared about him with a troubled, innocent look.

"Well," Gordon said heavily at last, defeated on that one and knowing it, "the committee will just have to decide who it believes, as between you and Ed."

"I'm sure, Gordon," Tal agreed calmly. "I never said Ed was a liar. I think he is telling the truth as he remembers it. I just don't remember it that way myself, that's all."

"Beat that!" Anna whispered triumphantly in my ear. "Let's see you beat *that!*" I just gave her a look and shrugged, for of course nobody could.

"Well," Gordon said again, seeming momentarily at a loss. "Well—"

"Why don't we get along to the tape now?" Seab suggested smoothly, coming to his aid so obviously that it provoked a little wave of laughter. "It doesn't exist in the realm of who remembers what, does it, Mr. Farson? It *exists.*"

"It certainly does, Senator," Tal agreed crisply, "and I can't tell you how much I appreciate the opportunity to explain it."

"We appreciate your willingness to do so, Mr. Farson," Seab said calmly. "We surely do. Senator, do you wish to interrogate further—?"

"I do," Gordon said doggedly. "Mr. Reporter, will you please read back the portion of this morning's testimony by Mr. Dobson in which he played for us the FBI tape containin' the telephone conversation between Mr. Farson and Mr. Obolenski—the late Mr. Obolenski—of the Soviet secret police."

"Yes, sir," the official stenotypist said, and proceeded to do so while everyone listened very closely. Heard a second time it seemed even more damaging, but it did not appear to bother Tal in the slightest. At one point George Watersill started to lean over ostentatiously and whisper in his ear, but he shook his head and waved him away. This conveyed the message that he was entirely in charge; and I will say for him that when he began his explanation he certainly appeared to be. Gordon took him over it line by line.

"You knew Valerian Obolenski?"

"Certainly," Tal said calmly. "He had been a news source of mine ever since he came to the embassy five years ago."

"Where did you meet him?"

"At some party," Tal said indifferently. "You know how one meets people in Washington, Gordon. You go to so many parties that nine times out of ten you can't remember."

"But you decided to become intimate with him?"

"Not 'intimate.' He indicated to me that he was not too happy with things at home and it struck me he would be a good news source for an inside look at our enemy."

" 'Our enemy,' " Gordon repeated. "Do you regard the Soviet Union as 'our enemy'?"

"Doesn't everybody?" Tal inquired blandly. There was an appreciative burst of laughter as Gordon flushed and looked annoyed. It was beginning to become very clear to me, as it was to many others including Anna, smiling slightly at my side, that Tal was indeed in command of the situation and very likely to remain so. Gordon plowed doggedly on.

"How did Obolenski indicate to you that he was dissatisfied with things in the Communist world?"

"Again, Gordon," Tal said airily, "you know how it is in Washington: people in a highly sophisticated political context don't always have to spell out their feelings to you. You sense them. I was sure he would be a good news contact."

"And was he?"

"Splendid," Tal said. "He told me many things I never would have learned otherwise."

"What use did you make of them, inasmuch as you were an editor and not a reporter?"

"I passed them along," Tal said. "I made sure our stories reflected them. I did what a good editor does. You know how I operate on the paper, Gordon."

"I surely do," Gordon said, his tone making the audience titter. "I surely to goodness do. What did Obolenski mean when he said, 'Have you got it?' "

"He meant did I have the money I usually paid him for his tips."

"How much was it?" Gordon asked quickly, and for just a split second, so tiny that only Anna, Bessie and I, I think, sensed it, Tal hesitated. Then he spoke with perfect certainty and I could feel Anna relax beside me.

"It varied according to the item. I think in this instance it was a couple of hundred."

"Dollars?"

"Not kopeks," Tal responded, to increased laughter. "Sure, dollars."

"What was the 'usual place' where you and Obolenski left your goodies for one another?" Gordon inquired, with a sarcasm that revealed his realization that things were beginning to slip out from under him.

"A mailbox at the post office. Really very amateurish, but that's probably why it worked."

"Do you still have it?"

Tal looked surprised.

"Not since his death, no."

"Do you have any record of it?"

"Certainly not. It wasn't in his real name or mine. Who would be so foolish? I dropped my key in the letter slot the morning after his death and never went back. I presume the other key was lost with his effects, which I believe were claimed immediately by the Soviet Embassy. I wouldn't know, and I doubt"—a little genuine savagery came into his tone, indicative of a growing confidence—"if even the great FBI can trace down anything as elusive as that. It's all utterly gone, Gordon. What's your next point?"

"My next point," Gordon said with a careful control, "is your assurance to Obolenski that you would give him 'the figures on production of the new bomber.' What was that about?"

"Oh, that," Tal said easily. "Well, once in a while Valerian thought money wasn't enough, once in a while he would complain that he was giving me all the information but I wasn't giving him anything of interest to take back to his superiors. So I promised him some figures on a new bomber."

"Where did you get them?" Gordon demanded sharply, and along the committee table minor lions and greater leaned forward intently.

"Out of a Pentagon press release," Tal said calmly, to the accompaniment of rising laughter from audience and press tables. "It just happened to come across my desk marked for release on Saturday so that it would catch the late remakes of the Sunday front pages and also Monday morning's papers. I believe our conversation was on the previous Thursday. So, yes, Gordon, I really did violate national security. I really did give Obolenski some American secrets. I broke the release date on a Pentagon press statement."

The room exploded. I was conscious of Gordon's and Seab's angry faces, the gleeful amusement on many others', Tal's grin as he looked into the television cameras, Anna's delighted clapping of hands as she almost literally crowed with laughter. Bess and I exchanged a look: it was impossible not to laugh but we still shook our heads at one another. We were not convinced but it was obvious now that it was all over but the shouting.

Gordon, however, had no choice but to continue doggedly to the end. The response was as smooth as all the rest.

"What were the 'instructions' you received from Obolenski?" he asked, breathing a little hard but managing to preserve such small shreds of dignity as were still left to the proceedings.

"They were instructions for an antiwar demonstration to be held in Washington next month," Tal said. "I'm preparing a special article about it. He had given me most of the details but had told me there was an actual set of written instructions to the demonstration leaders that he would give me. This was it. The article will appear sometime next week, Gordon. I invite you to read your own newspaper and learn all about it."

Again applause and laughter, during which Gordon flushed with anger. Seab came to the rescue for the last time.

"Do you have an advance copy of that article available, Mr. Farson?" he asked softly. And again, for a second so infinitesimal that only Anna, Bessie and I were aware of it, Tal hesitated. But his response came

224

so quickly and smoothly that there appeared to be no hiatus at all.

"Just my notes, Senator," he said, "and those I don't like to let people see, because for one thing they're usually so disorganized in the early stages, and for the second, my handwriting is so bad that only *I* can read it—and even that isn't certain."

"I'd like to try," Seab said gently. "Do you suppose you might—"

"They're at the office, Senator," Tal said, never missing a beat. "It will take me a little while to get them together for you. How about sending them to the committee tomorrow morning?"

"You don't have them ready for us now," Seab said, still gently.

"No, Senator," Tal said firmly. "I have them, but not in readable form. Why can't I submit them tomorrow morning?"

"No," Seab said. "No, I think not, Mr. Farson. If you haven't got them now, then I don't really think they'd be much use to us if you presented them tomorrow morning. Somehow I just don't think so. No, sir, I really just don't think so."

"Well," Tal said shortly, "I don't quite know what that is supposed to mean, Senator, but the offer stands. The committee will have them tomorrow morning."

"As you like, Mr. Farson," Seab said, giving him an amiably sleepy look. "Just as you like."

"I do like," Tal snapped, his voice beginning to fill with a righteous anger, "and they will be here. Now, Mr. Chairman, have we reached the end of this charade? Because if so, I would like to ask that my employer, Mrs. Anna Hastings, publisher of the Washington *Inquirer,* be recalled to the stand for a final statement."

Jim Eastland looked up and down the committee

table, taking his time; but there was obviously only one thing to do and presently he did it.

"Why, certainly, Mr. Farson," he said calmly. "Mrs. Hastings—if you please."

Beside me, while the room buzzed with excitement and the photographers swarmed forward and the television cameras again zoomed in, Anna stood up with a slow and deliberate air, straightened her gloves and her simple five-hundred-dollar white dress, smoothed her hair—unnecessarily, for she had gone to her hairdresser early each morning of the hearing and always looked immaculate—picked up her purse, turned and walked thoughtfully forward. Tal and George Watersill rose and started to withdraw but she waved them down again. Someone at the nearest press table leaped up and offered to bring her a chair but she waved him down too. She was going to stand: small, trim, blonde, perfectly dressed, completely composed.

She placed her purse on the committee table, opened it and took out a piece of paper, which she unfolded and glanced over, taking her time while every movement was recorded by the cameras. Then she carefully refolded it, returned it to her purse, snapped it shut with a decisive motion, faced the committee and began to talk in a clear, unhurried voice. Gordon visibly braced himself but she ignored him. Her target was much greater than a husband she had already, I know now, decided to discard.

"Mr. Chairman," she said quietly, "members of the committee: I thank you for giving me this opportunity to conclude what can only be regarded as a most sorry episode in the history of the relations between the American government and the press. Perhaps I can put things in perspective before we leave this room."

She paused, and with his characteristic dryness Jim Eastland said: "Mrs. Hastings, please do."

226

"I will, Senator," she said, a slight edge coming into her voice. "And the first thing I should like to discuss in doing so is the war that forms the background and, I believe, the *only* reason for this shabby and inexcusable attempt to harass me and my newspaper."

"Mr. Chairman," Seab inquired in a tired voice, "do we really have to get into the war again? Don't we really all know Mrs. Hastings' views on the subject? Don't we, now?"

"I believe you do, Senator," Anna said, and now the edge was very apparent, "but I think it is important to discuss it again if you wish to understand why we have all had our busy schedules disrupted by unimportant things this week. May I continue, Mr. Chairman?"

"Continue."

"Thank you," she said icily; appeared to calm herself (though Bess and I did not think for a moment that she was really upset) by taking a drink of water, and proceeded in a quite but still empathic tone.

"This war," she said, "ill conceived, ill begun, ill fought and ill continued, has brought to America great tragedy, untold waste, inexcusable demands and unjustifiable burdens. It has thrown the nation off balance, torn apart the normal restraints of society, turned us against one another, made bitterness and hatred daily fare for all of us. To those of us who oppose it, it has brought, I will admit, a desperation and an agony, grown out of frustration, that perhaps have made us a bit intolerant—"

"A bit?" Seab interjected dryly, but she ignored him.

"—a bit intolerant as our national course has spun down into disaster, dragging with it national unity, national purpose, national hope. To those who support and direct it," she said, and her tone became somber, "it has brought a much greater bitterness and intolerance, a veritable rage against all who would stand in the way.

227

"That bitterness, intolerance and rage have now tried to focus upon me and my newspaper. Mr. Chairman, *it will not work!*"

She acknowledged the applause with a slight bowing of the head, suitably grave, becomingly modest. Gordon's face was a study, disapproval and annoyance fighting with a still-great pride and love for her which he was powerless to deny or dissemble. Behind him the kids watched, solemn-faced and absolutely still.

"The sole purpose behind this attack upon the *Inquirer* and upon me, Mr. Chairman, is to discredit us and make it impossible for us to continue opposing the war. It is an attempt by my opponent to get us indirectly because he cannot best us in fair argument. It is, furthermore, a naked attack upon the very freedoms of this country, given fundamental expression by the Founding Fathers in the First Amendment and given life and substance by the untrammeled operations of a free press and a free media. These are the things that are at issue here, Mr. Chairman, not Anna Hastings or the Washington *Inquirer*."

"Mr. Chairman," Seab said in his sleepy way, "now, *I* didn't know this was an attack upon Mrs. Hastings and the *Inquirer*, did you? I thought all the time it was Mr. *Farson* who was at issue here, not Mrs. Hastings, the *Inquirer*, the First Amendment or the free press. Why doesn't Mrs. Hastings discuss Mr. Farson, Mr. Chairman, since he's the issue here?"

A little hissing began but Anna didn't need help.

"I'm coming to that, Mr. Chairman," she said calmly, "and I do not need the Senator from South Carolina to instruct me on it. I am coming to that. Right now."

"Good!" Seab said with a heavy irony. "It's what I'm waiting to hear."

"Naturally," Anna said, looking slightly less composed but still far from disconcerted, "I have been alarmed, annoyed and, yes, enraged by the attempt to destroy Mr. Farson's reputation and career, and through him, me and my newspaper in its defense of the First Amendment and the freedom of the press."

"Ah," Seab said gently. "*Now* I get the connection."

"Mr. Chairman," she said sharply, "do I have this floor or do I not? And if I do, may I not have it without the snide interruptions of the senior Senator from South Carolina?"

This time the applause was loud and prolonged while she stared angrily at Seab and he stared sleepily back. When it ended, Senator Eastland said calmly, "Proceed in order, Mrs. Hastings. And, Senator, if you can, refrain as much as possible from interruptin' the witness."

"I'll try," Seab said softly. "Oh, yes, I'll try. But I can't be sure, now. I really can't be sure."

"I hope you will, Senator," she said icily, "because it does your cause no good. It only creates greater sympathy for me and Mr. Farson. . . . Now, Mr. Chairman, I am asked about Mr. Farson. What *is* the situation about Mr. Farson? Testimony that he expressed some vague anti-American sentiment on the night of V-J Day, when he was very young and the world was full of confusion; testimony that he belonged to three youth groups in college, supposed to have been dominated by Communists—no testimony that he ever knew any Communists then, or knew they 'dominated' the groups—and a ridiculous tape—based on an illegal wiretap, as far as evidence shows here—of a conversation with a man now dead, which Mr. Farson has shown conclusively to be anything *but* the sinister plotting that some, including my opponent, would apparently like to have us believe. So what does it all add up to, Mr. Chairman? What does it prove? Nothing!

Absolutely nothing! A silly waste of time for everybody. And a glaring example of the desperate lengths to which those who favor the war will go to try to discredit the honest members of the media who disagree with them.

"Mr. Chairman," she said, and her voice took on a solemn and emphatic note, "the First Amendment and the free press have survived this attack. But there will be others, Mr. Chairman—many others, as the war drags on to its preordained and dismal finish. To all who would attack us, I say: *We defy you! You cannot destroy us!* Anna Hastings, the *Inquirer,* and all our colleagues of the free American media will continue to say what we think about the war. We will continue to oppose evil and corruption wherever we find it in this government and in this society, high or low. You can never frighten us, you can never silence us, you can never hide from us! We will expose you and defy you always, because the very life of this free nation depends upon our doing so!

"Thus do I assure you, Mr. Chairman, believing that I speak in true allegiance to the Constitution and the best interests of this great nation."

And she bowed gravely, picked up her purse, turned and moved gracefully back to her seat amid the tumult and the shouting. The audience was on its collective feet applauding wildly; many were crowding forward to shake her hand. At her side Tal and George Watersill stood beaming happily into the cameras as Bessie and I moved unnoticed toward the door. Anna's secretary was there, busily placing mimeographed copies of her final words into eagerly outstretched reportorial hands.

"The committee will stand in recess!" Jim Eastland cried above the noise. Gordon turned and spoke to the children and together they, too, slipped unobstrusively

230

out. One or two reporters tried to waylay them but Gordon simply shook his head and refused comment. Not even Seab said anything. The battlefield was Anna's, all the way.

10

---

*It was apparent to me in that triumphant moment
that there must be fundamental changes both in my
working associations and in my family. The committee hearing was a turning point for several things.
We who had come through its crucible together
would never be the same again. A sadness touched
my heart as I sensed this, but I knew that from now
on my destiny would rule and that I could only obey
and follow. In a sense I had become a symbol of all
that the free press stands for in this turbulent, unhappy country. From now on my dedication would
be to that great ideal, forsaking all others.*

—Anna Hastings, *by Anna Hastings*

"That's what she told me to write," Bessie remarked later, "but actually I don't think she had the
slightest compulsion about forsaking all others. After
all, when you're queen bee others don't matter much,
do they?"

Which I told her was entirely too feminine and bitter, but essentially quite correct. After that little sermon

to the committee Anna was what the media, not very originally but with a fair accuracy, promptly dubbed her: a legend in her own time. She made the most of it.

The immediate impact was evident in every headline and broadcast in the hours and days following the hearing. "From Coast to Coast, Anna's The Most," the New York *Daily News* lead editorial put it. And so she was, her name omnipresent, her picture everywhere, her concluding words to the committee printed and reprinted in every conceivable place. (My line to Bessie was "I hear they're going to put them on a brass tablet and add them to the Lincoln Memorial." She told me, probably rightfully, that I was jealous.)

"She's even driven the war into the left-hand column," Tal informed me with great cheerfulness when the *Inquirer* came out with its banner story. "What a gal!" He looked admiring, complacent and overwhelmingly gratified.

And so he should have been, because that was the end of any attempt to expose Talbot Farson. He had gotten home scot-free: so much so that he had apparently forgiven me on the spot for my testimony. I did not trust this mood—correctly, as it turned out—because underneath I knew that he knew that I remained unconvinced. But I had no proof, and if any others had any, they were successfully intimidated by the triumphal conclusion of the hearing and never came forward. He did take off early that evening, with the jovial comment—delivered in the newsroom so that everyone would be sure to hear it—"Well, I've got to run along and get my notes ready to send to the committee tomorrow morning." And sure enough, next morning they were sent. And a week later an article signed by the executive editor—a most unusual procedure, but hailed by all—appeared in the Sunday paper, describing in great detail the instructions given by the Soviet

Embassy to the leaders of an antiwar demonstration which might (or might not) occur in the capital three weeks hence. The embassy promptly denied it, to universal disbelief. When the protest did not occur, Anna wrote an editorial entitled, "Alert Journalism Prevents A Phony Protest," about how Tal had saved the day for the *real* protesters, who should be protected from "dangerous outside influences that have no place in a vigorous American democracy whose citizens are fully capable of taking care of their own problems." Everybody was very happy. And from that day forward the *Inquirer* became the most vitriolic and most relentless of all the enemies of the FBI.

For me and for Bessie the results of the hearing were delayed a little longer; but they came. Bess was the first to get the news. It reached her, significantly enough, when Gordon was away in Texas with the kids. They had left immediately after the hearing, apparently not even calling Anna, only leaving a note at the house. Gordon came back a couple of weeks later to a sort of uneasy truce, stayed a few days for Senate business, then left again. It was during his second absence that I received a call one afternoon from Bessie.

"Don't look now," she murmured quietly, "but I think I'm about to walk the plank. I've just been summoned to the Presence."

"Oh?" I said, rather lamely. "Well, good luck. Do you want company? Or a shoulder to cry on?"

"No, I don't think so," she said with a surprising firmness. "I've just about had it, anyway."

"Maybe you can get the first word in."

"She'd never allow it. But at least I plan to make my sentiments clear."

And this she apparently did. Once again the newsroom watched her march to Anna's door, not agitated this time but outwardly quite serene, and rap upon it sharply. Once again Anna appeared on the threshold, a vision of kindly welcome. Once again the door closed and life resumed, only to halt again abruptly fifteen minutes later when the door opened and Anna emerged, arm linked cozily through Bessie's, and walked her over to my office. Bessie looked more annoyed than devastated but it was obvious something had happened. I ushered them in and drew the draperies that screened my windowed office from the newsroom on occasions of high state and world import.

"That isn't necessary," Anna said, "but if you think anybody is watching—"

"Only the entire staff," Bessie said with a trace of bitterness. "Why don't you invite them in?"

"There'll be an announcement on the bulletin board. Ed, dear, Tal and I have concluded, reluctantly but I'm afraid finally, that our arrangement with Bessie has about run its course. And I think Bess agrees, don't you, dear?"

"For God's sake, Anna," Bessie said with an unusual sharpness, "what on earth does it matter whether I agree or not? It's your paper, do as you please."

"Well, yes, dear, but I want to feel that we're still friends, you know. I want the old team"—she actually said it—"to continue as always, even if our paths from now on seem destined to become somewhat divergent."

" 'Somewhat'!" Bessie exclaimed, and now she did sound bitter. "I'll say 'somewhat'! She and Tal have fired me as secretary of the corporation and terminated my writing status with the paper, Ed. You'd better watch out. You're next."

"Well, well," I said, which struck me later as a rather flat response. "Whose idea was this, Anna, yours or Tal's?"

"All the ideas in this organization are mine!" Anna said sharply. "Others may make their input, as they

235

have always been welcome and encouraged to do. But the decisions are *mine*."

"What about Gordon? Does he approve of this?"

"Gordon is at Circle H," she said, eyes narrowing, tone becoming distant. "I believe the kids are with him. He doesn't know of this and there's no need to bother him with it."

"What about a stockholders' meeting?" I asked, casting about for something to stop what I saw as a move to take complete control of everything. "Shouldn't we vote on something as important as the removal of the secretary of the corporation?"

"She's already thought of that," Bessie said, and for the first time her eyes filled with tears. "Anna always thinks of everything."

"Yes, dear," Anna said kindly to me. "You see, Bessie has *already* been separated from the company, and so therefore under our agreement her stock automatically reverts to a nonvoting status. There's no thought whatsoever of depriving her of income derived from the dividends, which as you know, and which I am proud to say, are quite substantial nowadays. So she's more than taken care of on that score. But she can't vote anymore. That means that at the moment my fifty voting shares and Tal's twenty-five rather outnumber your twenty-five, now, don't they, dear?"

"*That's* why you waited until Gordon was out of town."

"Gordon doesn't *have* to be out of town!" she said, her voice suddenly trembling with anger. "He doesn't always have to be taking my children away from me and running off with them to his damned ranch! It's his choice, not mine! And don't you ever think it isn't!"

For just a moment we thought she might actually be going to cry, which would have been a great release for her and would probably have saved the day for a lot of things later. But Anna was Anna. She made an obvious effort, composed herself and spoke more calmly.

"So, that's the situation. Because I do want to keep the team together we're going to pay Bess a retainer for her counsel and advice, and she and I are going to bear down on the matter of getting her more subjects for her books. She'll still be one of us. You'll see."

"I'll bet Tal didn't want to be that lenient," I said. "I'll bet he wanted her out of here completely."

She managed to look quite blank, which neither Bess nor I believed for a minute.

"Why on earth would he want that?"

"Because of her testimony."

"Her testimony!" Anna said and laughed a merry laugh. "What an absurd idea! Neither of us holds anybody's testimony against anybody. It was just one of those things, all over and forgotten now."

"Anna," I said quietly, "do you really believe Tal is completely innocent of all those charges?"

She looked at me for a long moment, perfectly steady and unperturbed.

"If I didn't, could I keep him around and still face the world?"

"You could if you had no other choice," I said. "You could if you were stuck with him."

"Which you are because of *your* testimony," Bessie pointed out with something as close to spite as I have ever heard from her. "And we all know it."

Very thoughtfully she looked at us, first one, then the other, while we stared back with the unrelenting candor of thirty years of friendship. Her reply was quite characteristic.

"So," she said, rising briskly, "that's the situation, and I wanted you to know it, Ed, before it becomes public. Thanks for being so understanding, Bess, dear. It will all work out better for you now, you'll see. You

237

have some *great* books in you and we're going to see to it that they get written. And as for you, Ed, dear: keep up the good work!"

And with a graceful flare of her skirt she drew back the drapes, leaned down to give startled Bessie an unexpected and outwardly affectionate kiss in full view of the newsroom, and swept out and away.

"You mark my words," Bessie said grimly. "You're next."

"I'm sure of it," I agreed. "Well, the least we can do is let people know."

So I batted out an item to the effect that Elizabeth Rovere, one of Washington's best-known reporters and authors, was resigning as secretary of Hastings Communications and severing her writing connections with the *Inquirer,* adding a straight-faced line at the end to the effect that "Miss Rovere appeared recently before the Senate Internal Security Subcommittee to testify in the investigation of alleged Communist associations on the part of Talbot Farson, executive editor of this newspaper."

I took it to the news desk and then Bessie and I settled back in my office to await the reaction. It unfolded like a little movie through my window. First the head copy editor read it with an expression of surprise. Then his expression turned slowly to one of great thoughtfulness. Then he called a copyboy, gave him instructions. Then the copyboy took the story over to Anna's office and knocked on the door, disappearing briefly inside. Then he came out, looking upset, and brought the item straight over to me while the staff watched with various degrees of covert fascination.

Scrawled across it in the familiar large, sloping hand, in the familiar blue pencil, was exactly what we expected to see:

"This item *will not run*. There will be *no publicity* on Miss Rovere's resignation. *Now* or *ever*. A.H."

And there wasn't, because our colleagues of the media took their cue from us and when we didn't run it they didn't either. Which did not surprise any of the Old Team, except maybe Gordon when he came back, dismayed, to find out about it a week later.

A month after that the Pulitzer committee met and the legend was made secure. The judges, acting in perfectly good faith on the basis of the information known to them, issued a Special Citation to:

"Anna Hastings, publisher of the Washington *Inquirer,* for gallantly withstanding alarming and unwarranted pressures from those in high authority attempting to intimidate her newspaper; for valiantly defending the honor, reputation and career of a trusted employee against false allegations designed to inhibit the expression of honest dissent from governmental policies she believes abhorrent; for bravely rejecting the implication that *any* official, no matter how high, can threaten or control the dissemination of news and opinion in this free country; and for distinguished and extraordinary service to the cause of the First Amendment and the preservation of a free press and media in the United States of America."

After that, life was clear sailing for Anna. She only foundered on a few little things, and I think by now she has convinced herself they weren't really that important . . . or almost convinced herself. If she had *really* convinced herself I would think she was quite human, and I don't think that is her problem. I think she is all too human. Her trouble has always been that she just won't admit it.

From that day to this, incidentally, no occupant of the Oval Office has ever again called the *Inquirer* about anything. Anna talks to a President once in a while, particularly this newest one, but he doesn't call her. She calls him.

Four

"A RIGID AND UNSHAKABLE PROFESSIONAL ETHIC"

1

_____

I had won a great triumph, achieved great success, yet somehow it seemed curiously flat to me, strangely inadequate. Dimly I sensed that there must be something more I could do—something more I needed to do—must do. I did not know what it was, at first. My unease was increased when I found that my principal competitor had stolen a march upon me— upon us all, in fact. In common with the rest of the media, the Inquirer *was forced to play catch-up. This only increased the tensions under which I labored. Eventually they came to a head, as I knew instinctively they must. A rigid and unshakable ethic came to my aid. And I again emerged in command of things.*

—ANNA HASTINGS, *by Anna Hastings*

WHAT THIS MEANS, BASICALLY, IS THAT ANNA, IN common with everyone else, had the pants licked off her by the Washington *Post* and its exposé of Watergate; and that she finally worked off her frustrations on her own family. But whether the final tragic climax was due to her grim determination to outscoop and out-sensation her rival, or whether it was an inevitable outgrowth of "the tensions under which I labored" in more intimate areas of her life, it is probably impossible to say. The fact is that things all came together for her in the end, and that she did emerge once more "in command of things." The devastation this wrought upon others seemed at the time to be more or less coincidental, in her mind; and since it has resulted in an even greater national prominence for her, she probably regards it all as being worth it. Certainly she has never admitted otherwise to Bessie and me and we are quite sure she never will. She knows what we think but she isn't about to give us the satisfaction of acknowledging it. For the sake of her own sanity, in fact, I doubt if she could.

But first, as I say, came Watergate; and there the *Inquirer,* for all that nine-tenths of its staff hated Richard Nixon with a blind purple passion as gorgeously, ferociously, magnificently insensate as anyone else's, was caught flat-footed. Despite Tal's frequent fulminations in staff meetings, his constant bitter railings that "Somehow we've got to get that bastard!" the *Inquirer,* in common with the New York *Times* and many other similar monumental institutions, completely missed the bus when the opportunity came. In the *Inquirer*'s case, and quite likely in a good many others, this was purely and simply because the *Post* got there first. Since it ranked only slightly lower than the President on the list of dislikes, anything it did was automatically treated with sarcastic skepticism—it was usually copied in desperate haste, you understand, but it was still regarded with sarcastic skepticism, even when the *Inquirer,* the *Times* and the rest scrambled to put matching headlines and news stories into print. But on Watergate the time lag between "What is this thing the *Post*'s got?" and "Well, if the *Post* has it, I guess we'd better try to match it" was allowed to run on just a little too long. The *Post* got there first every time—sometimes, it is true, by swinging wildly and sailing extremely close to the wind that separates fact from fiction. But the paper consistently lucked out, aided by an Executive who seemed weirdly and inexplicably bent upon hanging himself. He did, and the *Post* was there to hand him the rope. Great fame and kudos followed. Anna, not too long ago the toast of the town, the profession and the whole wide world, found herself forced to take a back seat to a rival she had been hostile to and jealous of for twenty years.

I did not realize then how personally she took it and how bitterly resentful she was of her rival's triumphs. It was obvious that she and Tal were driving the staff to the utmost to capture the story, but her control was such that, aside from an occasional expletive, undeleted, that she would utter in the newsroom when confronted by some new advance by the *Post,* she successfully concealed her grinding chagrin at being beaten. It was not until later unhappy events that I realized the full extent of her mortification and her grim determination to reassert her own supremacy, whatever the cost.

I could watch and appraise these events a little better, I think, because now, of course, I too had followed Bessie into limbo—a very profitable and prominent limbo, I must say, but one which hurt and still hurts, because like all the members of the Old Team, I still have a deep and unquenchable loyalty to our paper, our friendship, and the golden years of our striving youth.

It was roughly six months after Bessie's quiet departure—and not long before publication of her book *In My Lady's Chamber: A White House Maid Reveals*

245

Thirty Years of Scandal on the Second Floor, which racked up 93,000 in hardback, 2,000,000 in paperback and actually held No. 3 place on the best-seller lists for two months—that I received a note.

"Ed, dear," it said, "why don't we have lunch and a little talk? I'd suggest Sans Souci but it's always so crowded and everybody's always listening so hard. Why don't we run out to the house tomorrow about one? Kate can fix us something and we can really relax. It will be like old times!"—signed, as usual, with the sprawling *A.H.*

"What's this all about?" I inquired on the phone a minute later. "You're awfully formal, it seems to me. Does Kate have the guillotine set up in the garage?"

"Ed, darling!" she gurgled—"dears" and "darlings" having joined the four-letter words in her vocabulary in these recent years—"you sound *so* suspicious. Certainly not. If I wanted to guillotine you I'd do it right in the middle of the newsroom, wouldn't I? You know me!"

"I do indeed, that's why I'm suspicious. Why not Sans Souci? I don't mind people listening. *I* have nothing to hide."

"Let's say I do then," she said, her voice losing some of its cheer. "You'll be ready about five to one? LeRoy will pick us up in the Rolls."

"Always a handsome tumbrel," I agreed. "I'll be ready."

Nothing further was said, though she, Tal and I held our usual news conference at 5 P.M., and I saw her again next morning on some routine staff matter. I couldn't quite determine whether Tal knew what was up or not. His manner toward me had become even more jovially overbearing and patronizing since the Battle of Capitol Hill. We had never discussed it but he had often gone out of his way to project a hearty

246

feeling that things were Really All Right Again. Which, of course, confirmed me in my conviction that they were the furthest thing from it.

But, as I say, no sign: a great dissembling act, worthy to rank with his others, because as soon as Anna and I had finished Kate's excellent soup, salad and lemon soufflé:

"Tal and I have been discussing your contribution to the company lately, Ed, and I've decided that perhaps you might be happier somewhere else."

We were sitting in the sun porch of the house at the end of Prospect Street which she had built within a year of her appearance before the committee. It contained twenty-two rooms and was a very imposing mansion indeed, suitable for a great publisher and leading hostess; she had followed Revolutionary spelling in christening it Patowmack House. Gordon had approved the plans reluctantly, as he had approved those for The Dunes, which she had also built, almost simultaneously, down near Ocracoke in North Carolina on the site of our long-ago cottage. It was as though she needed to do something concrete, make some dramatic physical gesture, to symbolize her victory on the Hill. Both houses were statements to the world and both very soon became famous and popular places to which invitations were eagerly sought and scrupulously honored by Washington's constantly jostling risers, fallers and hangers-in-between.

I looked down for a long moment at the lazy Potomac. A few pleasure boats were out, a crew from Georgetown University practiced rhythmically in the chill sun of early spring. Over Key Bridge the endless traffic rushed, Virginia looked lush and jungly beyond. Presently the dogwood and cherry blossoms would be out, the capital's lovely spring would be upon us. It would not be an easy time in which to readjust to the ending of youth's dreams and the termination of middle age's accustomed rounds. But I was not prepared to let her know this. My reaction was as deliberately blunt as her own.

"I think perhaps you're right," I said, managing to appear much calmer than I felt. "I've thought for quite a while myself that I'd prefer an atmosphere more honest and more in keeping with my own beliefs."

"More honest!" she exclaimed. "What do you mean, 'more honest!' Nothing is more honest than my newspaper!"

"So you see it, but many disagree. Including me. So, Anna, darling, why argue? You want me out, I'm ready to go. What's the fuss?"

"No," she said, staring at me intently. "I want to know why the fuck you think the *Inquirer* isn't honest. I want you to tell me, God damn it!"

"Don't swear," I said, "and don't be vulgar. Neither impresses me, I've known you too long. Maybe *that's* the trouble. Maybe it isn't honesty at all. Maybe it's just boredom."

"Stop this f— stop this nonsense," she ordered sharply, "and make sense. You don't really want to leave the *Inquirer* any more than I want you to."

"Oh? I thought you said—"

"Well," she amended, "I want you to but I don't *want* you to: you know what I mean. It isn't anything personal. I'm just thinking of the paper."

"Have I been letting the paper down? Haven't I been doing my work? I haven't been aware that I—"

"Oh, of course you've been doing your work! It's just that—well, I just don't feel that you *agree* with me anymore."

"Isn't that exactly what I said? I said I'd prefer an atmosphere more in keeping with my own beliefs."

248

"And more honest, you said. *More honest.* The *Inquirer is* honest, God damn it!"

"I said, don't swear. Look, Anna—" I paused and glanced down at the river again; faintly over the traffic the bellowed exhortations of the Georgetown coxswain floated up. "You know, and I know, that the *Inquirer,* WAKH-TV and your other publications are almost exclusively devoted to the presentation of one point of view."

"It's an honest point of view!"

"I'm not saying it isn't. I'm just saying I have a right to disagree with it."

"But I *want* you to *agree* with it! Otherwise you don't belong with me!"

"That's exactly it," I said patiently. "That is exactly it. I could agree with it if you and Tal ever let the paper admit there *was* another point of view, and if you would ever permit it to be expressed in the paper fairly, honorably, without ridicule, scorn or deliberate censorship. But you won't."

"We don't censor anything!" she cried, and I had no doubt whatsoever that she absolutely believed it. Which, of course, brought us back to where we started.

"I'm glad you're firing me, Anna," I said quietly, "because it's obvious we've reached the end of the road. We don't agree, and we won't agree, and maybe we can't agree. So—you've fired me. Good for you."

And I made as though to rise, which, as I had known it would, brought her hand immediately on my arm to pull me down again.

"No, listen to me," she said earnestly. "Ed, listen to me! I can't have you going out of this house in this mood. I can't have you going out of here feeling you've made some kind of points about the paper or gained some kind of victory over me. It isn't that kind of situation. I just won't allow it!"

"You make it any kind of situation that suits you, Anna. You've made your decision, I've made mine. Thank you for precipitating it. It's long overdue. Is LeRoy ready to take me back to the office? I'll want to clean out my desk and get a few things in order."

"But I can't have you leaving me in this kind of mood!" she cried again. "I want your advice, Ed, I want you to stay around and help me. You still have your stock, you'll still be a friend, won't you? You *will!* Won't you?"

And because there were so many shared years between us, and because we had been young together in Washington, and because we had worked in tandem for so long, and because people become part of each other inextricably sometimes, and because, well, because Anna is Anna, I took her hand in mine and looked at her as earnestly as she was looking at me.

"Anna, darling," I said, and meant the endearment, "I'll be around when you need me, of course. I'm sorry our *very* long association is ending this way, but I think it's for the best. I'll be your friend, I'm always your friend. Why, hell!"—I tried to make it light but her eyes were too devastated and I faltered, though I managed to complete it—"I've been your friend ever since three greenhorns peered over the House Press Gallery railing at F.D.R. and a fresh kid from Punxsutawney whispered, 'But he has dandruff!' and made May Craig mad. Nothing can ever change that. I'll be here."

"Oh, Ed!" she said, and began to weep, openly and unabashedly and as though her heart would break; which, of course, completely threw me. "Oh, Ed, I am *so alone.*"

"No, you're not," I said lamely, still holding her hand, squeezing it earnestly. "No, you're not, Anna. You've got millions of admirers and many, many friends, and the Old Team, and the paper, and Gordon and the kids—."

"No, I haven't," she whispered. "I haven't got Gordon and the kids. They hate me. All three of them hate me. I don't have my—I don't have my family anymore."

And she put both hands over her face and rocked back and forth in some deep, atavistic sorrow, as frightening to me then as it had been on that earlier occasion when she had said much the same things. Only that time I had not been quite sure whether she really believed them or was still, in some subconscious way, playacting to impress us. I knew there was no doubt of her sincerity this time.

So I let her cry for a while, not too far from crying myself, as a matter of fact, because it is not easy to see life humble the iron-willed, and because—well, because Anna is Anna, the center and the lodestar of my life, really, when you add it all up. And presently, after the storm seemed to have worked itself out a bit, I tried, inadequately, I am afraid, to be a friend.

"Maybe," I said gently, "maybe it isn't too late. I don't really think they've gone all that far away. I know the kids have had problems these past few years, but what kids, particularly of wealthy parents, haven't? And I suspect it's been tough for them to have famous parents, too, Gordon in the Senate, and you particularly, as world-famous as you are. But I'm sure it's just a matter of reestablishing communications. You can do it. Why don't you talk it over with Gordon? He'll help."

"Gordon won't help me with anything!" she said in a desolate whisper. "He doesn't love me anymore either. He thinks I just married him for his money, and that I've just pushed—pushed him around, all these years, like some old"—something that was almost

a smile came through the tears, which encouraged me
—"some ole houn' dawg, as he says. But it isn't so,
Ed! Maybe I did marry him for his money, partly, but
I liked him too, I really did, in those early years. And
I still do. Even if he doesn't approve of me or the
paper. Even if he is so dumb."

"Now, Anna," I said severely, "Anna, that is no
way to talk, and it is no way to get him back or get
the kids back. You aren't loving them, you're patronizing them. How can you possibly expect them to love
you?"

"I'm not patronizing them!" she said, her combativeness beginning to return, which encouraged and dismayed me simultaneously. "I'm telling the truth about
them. Look at them! Gordon always running off to the
ranch or hanging around the Senate, never coming to
the paper anymore, hardly even coming home here
anymore. I don't know what he does and I don't care.
And the kids"—her voice was becoming stronger now,
the sobs were over, she dashed a few remaining tears
from her eyes with an angry hand—"just look at that
fine pair! Dressing like hippies, hanging around God
knows where, both of them into dope, running with all
that antiwar riffraff—I *know*, Ed. I'm antiwar, too, but
at least I'm *respectable* and there's no reason why they
can't be, too—acting like little tramps and defying me
openly every time I try to get them to straighten up.
And always making cause with Gordon, always making
cause with Gordon. It's no wonder I have to order
them around! I'm the only one in this house with an
ounce of brains or the slightest bit of character. Why
shouldn't I tell them all what to do? They haven't got
the ordinary ability to decide for themselves!"

There was silence after that, for a while. Floating up
faintly again came the raucous urgencies of the Georgetown coxswain. He was having his problems.

"Well, Anna," I said at last, "I don't know. I guess I'll just have to hope, for your sake and theirs, that things work out. If there's anything I can do, you call on me, and I'll try. But I do hope—I do hope—"

"What?" she asked, blowing her nose with a brisk efficiency.

"I hope," I said lamely, "that things will work out the way you all want them to."

"Not as we *all* want them to," she said firmly. "As *I* want them to. Somebody has to make the decisions and I'm the only one who's capable. . . . Why don't you use the john while I run up and fix my makeup, and then we'll go back to the office and put out a statement?"

"That's right," I said, for to tell you the truth I really had almost forgotten. "I *have* been fired, haven't I?"

"Yes," she said, reaching up to kiss me on the nose, quite herself again, "but only from my paper. Never —" and she struck a dramatic pose and laughed so cheerfully that the past few moments suddenly seemed an improbably dream, "*never* from my heart."

A couple of days later, while the town was still buzzing with it and everybody from Jack Anderson to the *Post* was speculating, accurately, that I had been fired because of my testimony on the Hill, I had lunch with Bessie and told her all about it. I decided we would go to Sans Souci, made sure we got a relatively private end table on the elevated level at the back, and let them chatter.

"I'm sorry you got it, too," Bessie said. "But I knew Tal would manage it sooner or later."

"Yse," I agree. "Tal's kind are patient. It may take them awhile, but eventually they get their revenge. I can't say I'm really all that shattered, though."

"Actually, I'll bet you're feeling relieved."

253

"You know, I really am."

"I knew you would be," she said. "It took me about two days and then I began to feel great." She paused and took a sip of the martini we had both decided to have—to celebrate, I think. Suddenly she sighed. "Poor Anna. Poor, poor Anna!"

"Yes," I agreed. "I wonder if she realizes how poor she is?"

"She realizes. But she isn't ever going to admit it to anybody, particularly us. Ever."

"Where will it all end, knows God?" I inquired, while Art Buchwald, Liz Carpenter, Betty Beale and a few other regulars observed us carefully for any telltale signs that might lead to the inner mysteries of the *Inquirer*. Hopefully, we gave them none.

"I don't know," she said slowly, voice lowered, pretending to study the menu, "but I'm beginning to wonder a little about Gordon."

"Oh?" I said, my own eyes firmly on the usual appetizing catalog. "What do you hear?"

"Little things here and there," she murmured. "Little things."

"Oh, hell! I hope not."

"Yes," Bessie said. "The family's going to blow up —with a little outside help."

"Oh, *Christ*," I said. "I *hope* not."

And it didn't immediately, of course. It took several months for things to begin to unravel. By that time I had been hired by United Features myself, and "On The Other Hand—by Ed Macomb" was already up to a respectable three-a-week in 105 newspapers. I was even in the *Inquirer*—"You can be our house conservative," Anna told me with a chuckle when she called to report that she had decided to purchase the column. "I'll run you on the op-ed page next to me."

254

But of course it was as house adviser and old friend that I, along with Bessie, soon became directly involved.

2

―――――

*Given the strained nature of our relations follow-
ing his disgraceful performance at the Senate hearing and given the basic divergence of political views
that I had never been able to bridge entirely no matter how sincerely I tried, it was not surprising that
my husband and I should have reached a fundamental break over his political ambitions as the war
years ended. The rift was complicated by factors that
faced me with the gravest decision of my life. Fortunately it was my journalistic training that saved
me: a rigid and unshakable professional ethic told
me, finally, what to do. It was very difficult for me,
but looking back I really believe I had no choice.*

—ANNA HASTINGS, *by Anna Hastings*

PERHAPS THERE WAS A CERTAIN INEVITABILITY ABOUT
it all, but I rather think she created a good part of it
herself. It was one of Anna's principal curses, as Bessie
accurately said, that she couldn't let life just be lived:
she always had to help manage the process.

So it had been with Gordon's politics since the day

they married. She had been clever enough to conceal her own clashing views until that objective had been successfully achieved—in fact, they only became really articulated and solidified after she got the paper and put Tal in charge—but then she went all out to try to remodel an easygoing multimillionaire Texan into a humorless self-righteous liberal. Despite the serene assertions of success that she has printed in her autobiography, Gordon really yielded very little.

"Little gal," he told her on the occasion when the rest of us became aware of how fierce this ideological tug-of-war had become, "it's like tryin' to mate one of my Brahman bulls with a little ole Rhode Island Red hen. It just isn't goin' to work, now, it just *isn't*. So why don't you stop tryin' to convert me to all this high-flying' fancy stuff you and Tal here believe, and let me do as I damned well please? I don't go around tryin' to convert you, now why do you-all feel you have to convert me?"

"Because you're a United States Senator and you have a great responsibility to represent the public," she said. "That's why!"

"People of Texas seem to think I'm representin' 'em mighty well," he pointed out mildly. "Don't get many complaints from them."

"Oh, well!" she said. "If you just want to be a cow-state hack!"

"I want to represent my state," he said with a rare show of annoyance, "and do the best I can for all the other states, too. I don't think I do so bad, with either bunch."

"You may represent Texas," she said, "but you sure don't represent the mainstream of thinking in the rest of the United States."

"I think I do," he said stubbornly. "I think I do."

And as the years went by, it appeared on balance

that he was probably right and Anna for once was probably wrong. He had no trouble whatsoever being reelected handsomely in Texas every time he ran; and while he received the usual hate mail during the McCarthy era and later periods of tension such as Watergate (when he was among those who defended the incumbent a lot longer than the facts would support) still on balance he continued to be a generally well-thought-of Senator all across the country. He never lacked for invitations to speak; he was frequently tapped for television talk-shows to represent the conservative side (always managing to come across as an amiable personality whom nobody could dislike very much); and within the Senate hierarchy was soon included in that little inner circle that really runs things.

He seemed to have the proof of the argument on his side but that didn't stop Anna from continuing her efforts to convert him. Now and again she would allow some of her irritation at having failed to do so spill over into an editorial, which would prompt Gordon to utter an occasional mild protest but never really raise the hell he could have, considering the fact that the basic funding came from him. It was not until he decided to run for national office that the *Inquirer* attacked him openly; and then only after a bitter argument that involved us all and led, perhaps inevitably, to the occurrence at The Dunes and the triumph, if so it could be called, of Anna's "rigid and unshakable professional ethic."

Some two weeks after Bess and I had what we referred to as our Talbot Farson Memorial Luncheon at Sans Souci, Anna called to invite us to a barbecue at Patowmack House.

"I've told the kids they're welcome to come, too," she said, "but knowing them, they probably won't, so it will probably be just the five of us, like old times. I do hope you can come, Ed, dear."

"Sure," I said, "but—why? I don't quite get it, so soon after—"

"So soon after the changes on the paper?" she interrupted smoothly. "But it isn't soon, really. It's been *months,* for both of you. It's time for us to get together and let bygones be bygones, don't you think? If there are any bygones."

"Oh, yes," I said. "There are a few. Gordon will be there?"

"Yes," she said, a certain puzzlement entering her tone. "As a matter of fact, this is largely *because* of Gordon."

"Oh, *not* just to let bygones be bygones."

"Well, partly," she admitted, "but also because he's got some bee in his bonnet about something. I don't know what it is. He says he wants our advice. Imagine that! Gordon wanting *our* advice!"

"Oh, I don't know," I couldn't resist. "He quite often asks mine, and Bess's too, I believe. I don't know about you and Tal."

"He hasn't asked my advice on anything," she said bleakly, "for fifteen years. Anyway, are you coming?"

"If Bess is."

"She's expecting you to pick her up at her apartment. Six o'clock. Let's hope we don't have rain."

We didn't, but it was another of those typical steamy summer nights in D.C., oppressive, hushed and still, threatening cloudburst at any moment. Bessie and I arrived at six-fifteen to find host and hostess relaxing in lawn chairs with drinks, Anna with her usual light gin and tonic, Gordon with his customary Scotch on the rocks.

They had obviously not been speaking when LeRoy brought us through to the terrace overlooking the river, but they stirred dutifully into life on our arrival. Gordon's unusually hearty effusiveness seemed to indicate that he had probably had one or two more than his usual quota: either that or he was under considerable strain. Tal slouched in at about six-forty-five, very much King-of-the-Mountain, and at seven, surprising us all, Gordie and Lisa appeared.

"Oh, you're here," their mother said.

"Yes," Gordie said, "Daddy asked us."

"Well, that's nice!" she said, tone hostile at once. "Mummie did too, remember?"

"Daddy said he *needed* us," Lisa said calmly, going over to the bar to mix herself a drink. "*You* didn't say *that*."

"Well, now, kids," Gordon said hastily, "you're here and that's the important thing."

"No, it isn't," Anna said in a bitter voice, "but we'll let it pass. Have you both had a good day, out smoking pot or whatever you've been doing?"

"Anna, *honey,*" poor Gordon said desperately. "*Please.*"

"It's all right, Daddy," Gordie said calmly, sprawling his six feet six into a lawn chair. "We can take it. She doesn't think we can, but we can."

"Well, now," Gordon said quickly to Bessie, "how y'all been, Bessie gal?"

"Don't worry, Gordon," Anna said with a tired shrug. "We won't have a scene for Auntie Bess and Uncle Ed and Uncle Tal. Bess has been fine, Ed's been fine, Tal's been fine, I've been fine, you've been fine, these two have been fine, *everybody's* been fine. Why don't you put on the steaks? We don't want to prolong this any more than we have to."

"Anna," Bessie said, hesitant but firm, "if you'd rather we didn't stay—"

"No," Anna said sharply, "you stay. This is Gor-

260

don's party and we don't want to spoil it for him. Everybody laugh, now, and we'll all be happy!"

"Oh, *Mummie*," Lisa said, and went over and sat down beside her brother. After that nobody said anything for a while, as Gordon, sweating even more profusely than the humidity and the barbecue warranted, busied himself with the steaks and the rest of us stared in various directions that did not include one another.

"Well, now!" Gordon said at last in a tone of great relief. "Everybody come along and he'p yourselves, now. Ev'thing looks mighty *good*."

"I doubt if anybody has much appetite," Anna said coolly, rising to get a plate, "but for your sake, dear Gordon, we'll try."

"Please do, Mummie," Gordie said, rising to his full height and following her to the table. "We'd all appreciate it."

"Stop bein' insolent to your mother, you two," Gordon said in an unhappy tone. "Just stop it now and eat your dinners, hear?"

Which we all did, rather more hurriedly than we had planned. Kate brought out some strawberries, brown sugar and sour cream to conclude the meal; LeRoy passed among us with an offering of liqueurs; and presently, no rain having descended from the overdue pregnant skies, we were all seated in our chairs and silent again. I was just about to suggest that we leave when Tal spoke up.

"Well, Gordon," he said bluntly, sounding like the lord of all he surveyed, which he pretty well was, now, "Anna tells me you wanted to talk to us about something. Fire away."

"Well, I did," Gordon said. "I was wonderin' what you-all would think if I—if I—"

261

"If you what, Gordon, for heaven's sake?" Anna said impatiently.

"Tell her, Daddy," Lisa said. "She isn't going to like it, anyway."

"I was wonderin'," Gordon said hastily, his voice loud and nervous as he sought to head off another family squabble, "what you-all would think if I was to run for Vice President."

There was a stunned silence, broken at last by a gurgle of laughter from Anna which drew a startled look from Gordon, angry looks from the kids.

"*Vice* President!" she exclaimed. "If that isn't typical!"

"What's wrong with Vice President?" Gordie demanded belligerently, and Lisa echoed, "Yes, what's so funny about that, Mummie? There's nothing wrong with wanting to be Vice President."

"But you don't *run* for Vice President," she said. "Nobody *runs* for Vice President. You run for *President,* if you have an ounce of ambition and enterprise in your soul. And an ounce of ability, I might add."

"Daddy has the ability!" Lisa said stoutly.

"And he has the ambition, too," Gordie said, "if you hadn't—"

"If I hadn't what?" Anna demanded, rounding on him sharply.

"Destroyed it over the years," Gordie said defiantly. "If you hadn't emasculated him and pounded him down into the ground with all your—your *superior* ways."

"Now, kids," Gordon said quickly, "now, kids, stop talkin' to your mother like that! She doesn't deserve that, now, so you stop it! That's an order!"

"Well—" Gordie said.

"Cut it, now, God damn it!" Gordon said with a rare harshness. "I said, cut it!"

"We just want to help you, Daddy," Lisa said in a

clear young voice, "because we think you need it."

"Anyway," Gordon said desperately, "that's what I'm aimin' to do. I figure like you say, Anna, maybe I don't have the drive and ambition—maybe I don't have 'an ounce of ability,' though there's some think I have even if you don't, to be President. But I can be a good Vice President. I can do that, anyway. And I figure if I just announce right out that I want to be, it will be such a novelty that mebbe I'll wind up at the convention with a lot more support and votes than people think I could. I might just have enough to persuade the nominee to have an open convention and let me have it, now. I just might. Anyway, I think that's what I'm goin' to do."

"You are," Anna said.

"Yes, ma'am."

"Then why do you want our advice, if you've already decided?"

"Well," he said rather lamely, "mebbe I meant I didn't exactly want your advice. I guess I just wanted your approval, little gal. I guess I just wanted you to tell me it was all right, and mebbe the *Inquirer* wouldn't be too hard on me if I did it."

"It's your paper, Daddy," Gordie said sharply. "For God's sake!"

"It's your mother's paper," Gordon said sternly, loyal to the last to some concept of Anna, if not to Anna herself. "I've always let her run it as she wanted."

"And that's why it's a great paper," Anna said sharply, "and don't you forget it, you ungrateful brats!"

"Anyway," Gordon said, a dogged desperation hurrying his words lest further squalls develop, "I figure I'd best divest myself of my stock in the corporation if I'm goin' to run, so it's all goin' to be in your hands anyway, honey."

I had an insane desire to shout "NO!" which I

could see was shared by Bessie and the kids, but before anybody else could speak Tal said smoothly, "I think that would be very wise, Gordon. It would be a very statesmanlike act. It would more than answer any charges of economic interest, or undue influence, or special advantage, or anything. You couldn't be smarter. I think that one thing alone may guarantee you the nomination, in fact."

"Do you think so?" Gordon asked, face brightening. "Anyway, I think it's the right thing to do."

"Yes," Anna said slowly, "I believe it is. How would you set it up?"

"I've been consultin' young Watersill"—and again I almost shouted "NO!" but what was the use?—"and he thinks I should put it in trust for you and the kids, equal shares, but with you havin' sole votin' rights until 'the youngest of aforesaid beneficiaries of the trust shall achieve the age of twenty-one' as he puts it. And he thinks I should leave it in there for at least two years, until after the next inauguration, to make it look good. Then it can revert to me if I'm still livin', and all."

"Why wouldn't you be still living, Gordon?" I asked, and for just a second he hesitated. But his answer was quite calm and matter-of-fact.

"Well, you know with all the cranks and crackpots there are runnin' around the woods these days, you never know when you step on a public platform if you're goin' to walk off it or be carried off it. That's all. Have to think of everything, these days. Sad, but there it is."

"Yes," Anna said thoughtfully. "When will you sign the papers?"

"Well, actually," Gordon said, "I did it this afternoon. As of now, I'm not a votin' member of the firm anymore. It's all yours, honey."

264

Bessie and I exchanged a glance; so did Gordie and Lisa; so did Anna and Tal. Poor old Gordon took another belt from his drink and repeated with a happy satisfaction, "Yes, sir, honey, it's all yours."

My thought was: *He loves her still, he's still trying to pretend the family is all together, that it's all the same as it used to be. Poor Gordon!* And although this turned out to be a bit naive on my part, I still think that, basically, that was his motivation. He still wanted it to be that way and he was still pretending to himself that this quixotic gesture could make it possible.

"And now, honey," he said with a cumbersome and embarrassing attempt at humor, "do you think you and Tal could mebbe give me a *little* bit of a break in your pages? Could I just have the least little smidgen of space and fairness for my campaign?"

"We will give you whatever is consistent with what we give any other candidate," Anna said calmly, her tone not yielding an inch.

"And you'll lay off me in those editorials?" he inquired, his attempt at humor becoming painful now, so that Gordie visibly squirmed in his chair.

"We'll see that she does," Lisa promised, voice thin but determined.

"You'll do no such thing!" her mother snapped. "*I* have the voting rights, and don't you forget it! . . . However," she added, more calmly, "I don't think we'll do any undue jumping on you, Gordon. Myself, I don't see how your peculiar brand of old-line conservatism fits into the picture in the nineteen-seventies, but at least we'll try not to be too harsh about it. Critical, I'm sure, but not harsh. I can promise you that, can't we, Tal."

"Sure," Tal said with a lazy arrogance. "We won't break your balls, Gordon."

"Well, I hope not!" Gordon said with a rather

shocked laugh at the sudden macho bit from old Tal. "I surely hope not, now!"

"We'll do our best to be fair to you," Anna said, adding firmly, *"when you deserve it.* The *Inquirer* and my other publications and enterprises always do their best to be fair to everyone."

"The hell they do," Gordie said, standing up abruptly and starting to stride toward the house. "The hell they fucking do!"

"You son-of-a-bitch!" Anna screamed as Gordon surged to his feet and started after his son with a "Don't you ever talk to your mother like that again!"

"Son-of-a-bitch is right!" Lisa yelled. "Son-of-a-bitch is right, bitch, bitch, *bitch!"*

"LISA!" Gordon shouted in a terrible voice, stopping in his tracks (probably, I thought sympathetically, welcoming the interruption, since Gordie at six feet six towered over even his father's burly six feet two). "YOU APOLOGIZE!"

"Ed," Bessie said fiercely, grabbing me by the arm, "let's get out of this! *Fast!"*

"Yes," I agreed, and so we did, just as the clouds finally gave way, thunder boomed, lightning flashed and rain began to come down in buckets.

We fled up the steps, through the house, into the driveway and into the car. As we entered the house we turned and looked back for a brief second as though into a hell conceived by some minor Georgetown Dante. Gordon was glaring down at Lisa, who glared back up at him, white-faced but unafraid; Anna was still shouting something, now inaudible in the rain; Tal was sauntering slowly toward the house, drenched to the skin but with a peculiar satisfied little smile on his face.

Then we hurried on. As we jumped into the car, Gordie's Mercedes two-seater shot by us and screamed

266

into Prospect Street, bound for who knows what refuge in the storm-wild city.

"Good grief!" Bessie said breathlessly. "That boy will kill himself yet!"

"I'm not sure he cares," I said as I turned and started cautiously down to Wisconsin Avenue over the slippery cobblestones.

"Well, I care," Bessie said, beginning to cry. "I care for all of them, poor people!"

And so did I, of course, which is why we both responded at once when, six months later, Tal received the telephone call that was to change everything forever.

3

At first Gordon's announcement was greeted with the scornful laughter we had all expected. But presently, for some reason that I never have been able to understand, this seemed to give way to a more tolerant and almost respectful mood. It was as though the clown in the circus had announced he would try the high wire and everyone decided they would at least give him the chance. He was a Washington and national curiosity for a time—just long enough for it to come to my attention what he really was. Once I knew, I had no choice but to proceed as I did; though I must admit the decision cost me some sleepless nights, and more pain than any husband should be allowed to cause his wife.

—ANNA HASTINGS, _by Anna Hastings_

THE REASON ANNA DIDN'T UNDERSTAND THE AMUSED but good-natured way in which Gordon's surprising "campaign" for Vice President was greeted in Washington and throughout the country was that she never quite understood the fact that people really _liked_ Gor-

268

don. The patronizing attitude that Bessie and I had adopted toward him when they were first married had long since given way to genuine liking and a considerable respect. The same process occurred in the country. He was a good-hearted, decent individual, conditioned by his background and his wealth but well-meaning and idealistic for his country as he saw it—not unable to learn and adapt, even though not as rapidly or completely as his wife would have liked. It was his misfortune that a powerhouse like Anna should have decided to appropriate him for the purposes of her life, but once she had, he had loyally and faithfully tried to keep his part of the bargain—for twenty years without, so far as we knew, ever returning to his little black book or the swinging life he had known on the Hill before she came along.

His image in print was of a slightly laughable figure who nonetheless had many good points. On television he came across even more warmly and likably. Nobody was ever really mad at Gordon Hastings, except occasionally his own newspaper; and even there a grudging tolerance was usually granted, even when his views were most harshly denounced in editorial or most stringently censored in space and position in the paper. I really think Anna tried to be fair to him in her own way, which like everything she did had its own distinctive stamp; but she never really understood him, or understood the fact that others thought much more generously and tolerantly of him than she did.

This general public liking guaranteed that his Vice Presidential venture would not be immediately laughed into oblivion, as it might have been with someone else. There was just enough logic in his reasoning, just enough likable puppy-dog enthusiasm in the way he went about it, just enough of the popular stunt in it, so that initial ridicule gave way to a good-natured,

"O.K., pal, go after it if you can. We think you're crazy but you just might—just might—have something. We won't stomp on you. At least you're putting a little life and novelty into the political scene, and that's something." This was the attitude of everyone but the *Inquirer,* which played it straight-faced, seriously and much more harshly at times than Gordon deserved. Anna never did grasp his idea or the cockeyed, just-possible fun of it in a political world not exactly filled with the most dramatic personalities the nation has ever produced.

Nor did she understand, I think, the great love he originally had for her, the awe and deep respect and the great pride he took in her accomplishments. "That little gal!" he told me on many and many an occasion. "She's *really* somethin'! Boy, sometimes I don't really know what I married, Ed, I really don't. But I like it, Ed! By golly you bet your boots I do!"

And I think he did, 'way along until finally everything began to crowd in on him and he, like the kids, felt that he must break out. Bess and I had seen it coming for quite a long time: her hint to me at Sans Souci was unbelievable, at first, but far from unexpected. But Anna, I know, never even dreamed, for the simple and fundamental reason she exploded with on that fateful afternoon: "*Nobody* does a thing like that to me!"

But good old Gordon did, and there we were.

I was just finishing my column in my office in the National Press Building—something about how the President was bumbling but likable, rather like Gordon, in fact—when the phone rang. I believe it was the first time in thirty years that I did not instantly recognize her voice.

"Ed! Get over here! I need you!"

"What—"

"Get over here!"

"Just as soon as I finish my column—"

"Fuck the column! I *need* you!"

"I can't fuck the column," I said firmly, "or United Features would do the same to me. I'll be over in half an hour."

"Well, hurry! Bess is coming. I'll be in the executive office upstairs."

"All right," I said, convinced now that something of some gravity must be involved. "Hang in there."

"Yes," she said in a voice suddenly bleak and bereft. "But it isn't easy."

That really alarmed me, so I dashed out a couple of concluding paragraphs, tossed them to my secretary, grabbed my coat (we were in the midst of one of Washington's rare but paralyzing winter snowstorms), decided against the cabs which were almost impossible to get, and began to limp briskly along the intervening blocks across town, through Lafayette Square and so to H Street.

As I passed Treasury and reached the White House corner preparatory to turning into the park, I saw Bessie plowing grimly ahead of me, a fur-wrapped supertanker under full steam. I yelled, she paused, tucked her arm into mine and yanked me forward as the light changed.

"Easy," I said. "Easy. I'm coming. What's this all about, do you suppose?"

"Anything from Gordie being busted for hustling dope to Gordon being caught in the men's room at Union Station," she said grimly. "God only knows. Anna is dreadfully upset."

"I seriously doubt it could ever be either one of those," I said, "but I know she's on the rampage."

"Not on the rampage," Bess said as we scuffled through the deepening snow, blowing and swatting to

271

keep it out of our eyes. "*Upset*. I'm afraid this means real trouble."

"I'm afraid so too," I agreed, shivering suddenly with something more than the cold. We began to walk even faster. We must have been a sight, two spavined middle-aged newspaper characters wheezing and puffing and almost running through the snow in Lafayette Square. But the Old Team still held, you see: Anna needed us, and we came.

What we expected to find when we reached the paper, slipped unnoticed into the side hall and took the private elevator up to the executive offices, we weren't quite sure. It was almost an anticlimax to find just Anna and Tal, as usual; except that Anna's face was white, her body rigid and quivering almost uncontrollably. And Tal looked, for once, reasonably serious and some distance out of his standard aren't-I-the-damnedest-superior-sardonic-son-of-a-bitch-you-ever-saw? configuration.

"Thank God you've come!" she said, sounding, although none of us was able to appreciate it at the time, like any one of ten thousand television crises. "I need you!"

"Well," I pointed out as we shucked our coats and seated ourselves, "we're here. What's the matter?"

"Tell them, Tal."

"Little Gordon is screwing around," he said, a certain satisfaction creeping through his serious mien.

"Gordie?"

"Hell, no," he snapped, "who the hell would care about that? Big Gordon. Senator Hastings. The Future Vice President. Mr. Anna."

"Don't say that!" she ordered sharply. "It isn't funny. It never has been funny"—indeed it never had, although he had said it a lot, over the years—"and it isn't funny now." She paused to brush away a strand of

272

hair that had dared stray out of place in the confusion. "Tal got a call from the *Post*."

"From the *Post*?" Bessie and I exclaimed in unison. "The *Post*?"

She sighed. "I assume it was meant well."

"It wasn't meant well at all," Tal said, "but at least it filled us in on the picture."

"Well, I think they meant it well," she said. "At least they're giving me the option to print it first."

"Sure," he said, "under threat that if you don't, they will."

"I'm sure they don't doubt that I will do my duty as a publisher and a newspaperperson," she said, almost primly.

"Will you?" he asked bluntly, and the question hung in the air for a while as she stared out the window at the blind white world and again ran a hand, trembling noticeably, over her hair.

"Maybe," I suggested finally, "you should tell us the details, if we're to give you sensible advice on it."

"Yes," Bessie agreed. "We're old friends, you can tell us."

"Of course you're old friends, Bess," she said shortly, "don't be an idiot. And of course I want your advice or you wouldn't be here. But it—it—" and quite suddenly her voice quivered to a halt, "it hurts."

"The situation," Tal said, "is that Gordon's been shacking up with this babe on his payroll for the past year and a half. Paying for her apartment in Chevy Chase, taking her with him on secret trips—the whole bit. It isn't so unusual, really. She can even type. Apparently she's a quite legitimate employee. Except that she provides solace and comfort when the home fires aren't burning—which, as we all know, has been rather frequently in these past few years."

"You don't have to be so cruel about it!" Bessie said

furiously. "You don't have to be such an insufferable smart-ass all the time! Anna's been hurt and she needs help. Now, stop that tone or get the hell out of here!"

"Well, I'll be damned—" Tal began with equal fury, but Anna held up a hand and silenced him.

"If—you—please," she said, sounding more like herself. "This *is* a serious matter and I *am* greatly disturbed about it and I *would* appreciate it if you could refrain from acting like children until we get it settled."

"If it's such a routine matter, Tal," I said dryly, "then what's the problem? Why should anybody care, if everybody does it?"

"Everybody doesn't do it!" Anna exclaimed. "And *I* care because *nobody*"—and suddenly a genuine rage filled her voice, her color rose, her eyes brightened with tears—of anger—"*nobody* does a thing like that to *me! Nobody!*"

"But Gordon has," Tal said softly. "So what do you do about it?"

"I don't quite understand the opposition's motive in all this," I said. "What do they get out of it? Are they going to publish or aren't they?"

"Yes," Tal said, and "No," said Anna simultaneously; and at his elaborate look of surprise she sighed. "You don't always know everything. You got the first phone call. I got the second. She says they won't print it if I don't want them to, and if I don't print it myself. They're willing to be that decent about it."

"Well, then—" Bessie began.

"Oh, stop, 'Well, then!'" Anna said loudly. "You sound so simpleminded, Bess! It *isn't* that simple. If I print, then I expose myself to the ridicule of everybody in this town. The betrayed little wife! What a picture! *Me,* Anna Hastings! And if I don't print . . . if I don't print . . ."

"If you don't print, what?" I asked. "Something terrible?"

"Then the *Post* and everybody else will talk about it behind my back anyway, and they'll say Anna Hastings is the sort of publisher who ducks and runs when her own interests are involved. They'll say, '*There's* the reason the *Post* was able to beat her on Watergate! *There's* the reason she's not a good publisher! *That's* why the *Inquirer's* Number Two! Look at Anna Hastings, the fraudulent excuse of a woman! She isn't a publisher *at all!*' "

"Nobody can say that," Bessie said with indignant loyalty. "You're the greatest publisher in this town and everyone knows it!"

"She beat me on Watergate," Anna said, the pronoun unconsciously revealing the real source of her unhappiness. "I've got to do *something* to reestablish myself."

"Is that how you see it?" I inquired. "Just as a personal contest between you and—"

"That's how *she* sees it," Anna said. "I've got to do *something* to get back on top."

"Print," Tal said bluntly. "To hell with what they say! They'll talk whatever you do, just as you say. So *print!*"

"I don't know," she wailed, suddenly shaking her head in a fury of bafflement and frustration. "*I just don't know!*"

"Anna," I said slowly, "is this just a—just a contest between you and the *Post?* I mean—you're the only one involved here?"

"Yes!" she said, looking at me as though she thought I must be out of my mind. "Who else is involved?"

"Well," I said, "there *is* Gordon, of course."

"*Gordon?*" she echoed with a withering scorn. "*Gor-*

don? Why in the hell should I give any consideration to *Gordon?* He hasn't given me any!"

"Well," I said, aware that I was inviting the wrath of the Valkyries but no longer much impressed by it. "He may have felt he had provocations."

"I have never been unfaithful to Gordon in my life!" she said with such complete indignation that we all knew it must be true; in fact, none of us had ever thought otherwise. "And suddenly here he is with this —this—*tramp,* in this *sordid,* worthless situation, making fun of *me* behind my back, making *me* a laughing-stock to the whole wide world! Consideration for *Gordon!* Don't make me laugh!"

"But hardly anybody knows about it at the moment," Bessie said, belying her own words at Sans Souci, but still trying, as I was, to get things back on a negotiable basis because we could both see all sorts of consequences in an open break, none of them pleasant for anyone, particularly Anna. "Why don't you have a talk with him before you do anything—irrevocable—and see if you can't work it out?"

"What good would that do?" Tal inquired before Anna could reply. "Why give him that satisfaction?"

"Tal," Bessie said, and her tone was so entirely out of character and so absolutely vicious that it really did stop him cold, "God damn you, *shut up!* You stay out of this, *you eternal troublemaker!* We're talking to Anna and *you* shut up! . . . Now, Anna," she said, breathing hard but managing to control her trembling voice enough to be intelligible, "I think, and I think Ed agrees with me, that you should talk to Gordon before you do anything else. You say that people will gossip behind your back if you don't break the story. But if you do break it, then you'll just hurt yourself, and Gordon, and the kids, and to what purpose, Anna? What purpose? You may lose them all, if you do this.

You'll make it impossible for the family ever to be put back together again. Do you really want that? Think about it!"

And I will say for Anna that she obviously did, for several minutes, staring out the window again at the blank white world of the swirling snow, her face as white and blank as it was.

"I can't let him humiliate me like this," she said finally, her voice so low it was almost a whisper. "And I can't let them say that I'm not a good publisher, and not Number One."

"Number One!" Bessie cried. "Oh, Anna, what nonsense, 'Number One!' Isn't *anything* more important to you than that?"

But of course we all knew the answer, and I don't think Bess really expected a response—or if she did, then it was one she really didn't want to hear. Fortunately into the pool of silence that began to widen around us, the phone rang. For once in his life Gordon did something with perfect timing.

"Yes?" Anna said, switching on the desk speaker so that we could all hear, her voice ice-cold. "I thought I said I was not to be disturbed."

"I'm sorry, Ms. Hastings," the operator said, using the form of address Anna had recently begun to insist upon, "but it's Senator Hastings. He says he must speak to you."

"Put him on," she said tersely; and after a second his voice came over, sounding very tired and heavy with emotion.

"Little gal," he said, "Anna—I'm downstairs and I'm comin' up to see you. A reporter from the *Post* called me a little while ago, and I—I think mebbe we'd better talk."

"Yes," she said, her voice absolutely empty of emotion. "I think mebbe we had."

And switched off the speaker, put down the phone and swiveled to stare out again into the snow.

"I'm getting out of here," I said, jumping up and reaching for my coat.

"Yes," Bessie said, heaving herself out of her chair. And even Tal had the grace to rise and start to join us.

But Anna turned and looked us over, face expressionless.

"You stay," she ordered in the same ice-calm way. "I'm not afraid of this. Why should you be?"

4

My mind at that moment was a swirl of raging emotions, but one thing was paramount, and to it I clung throughout our painful interview: I was the wronged party. I had been a good and faithful wife and mother, I had done my best to make a success of my publications and at the same time manage a good home and be a good influence on your children. I had given this rather ordinary man not only the support of my newspaper, but the benefit of my advice and experience throughout his undistinguished public career and our boring life together. And all I had received was ingratitude. This fortified me, as it has fortified so many other wives whose husbands have abandoned their trust. Only, this case was different: it was in the national spotlight, which imposes its own inexorably binding rules upon people. This, too, fortified me. But I can honestly say that I began our final talk with an open mind. I was willing to be convinced.

—ANNA HASTINGS, *by Anna Hastings*

"I ALMOST GAGGED WHEN SHE PUT IN THOSE LAST TWO sentences," Bessie told me the other day, "but that's the way she wanted it, so that's the way it is. It's not the way I remember it."

Nor I either. It seemed rather more like the Inquisition and the Bloody Assizes rolled into one. Certainly Anna did nothing at all to make it easier for poor Gordon. And of course he didn't help matters any by not fighting back. If he had done so with real vigor there might have been some hope; or if, lacking combativeness on his part, she had responded with an ounce of forgiveness to his abject willingness to accept all the blame. But that would have required from him an iron he did not possess, and from Anna a compassion of which, for all her many indomitable qualities, she could not be accused. And there was that national spotlight—and the *Inquirer* versus the *Post*—and the chagrin of Watergate—and the desire to be Number One—and—and—

It was probably only a minute or two between his call and his hesitant knock on the door, but it seemed much longer than that as Anna turned again to stare into the snow and the rest of us stared at one another with troubled faces. Personally I didn't relish being present at what I expected to be an execution and Bess didn't either. Tal was not so reticent but even he, I think, was not exactly happy. Anyway, we all jumped when the knock came.

Anna did not turn around.

"Yes?"

"It's me, Anna, honey. It's Gordon. *Gordon.*"

"I know who Gordon is," she said, her voice perfectly calm and indifinitely weary. "You can come in."

But she did not turn around, so that all he saw when he entered was her unyielding back. He was concentrating so hard upon it that for a second he was not aware of the rest of us. When he realized we were there he stopped abruptly and an expression of surprised dismay came over his face.

"But I thought," he said, blurting out his words like a guilty schoolboy, "I thought we were—I thought we could—I thought I was goin' to talk to you *alone,* little gal."

"Close the door," she said almost absentmindedly. "And the 'little gal' days are over. Why shouldn't we talk in front of these old friends? We've known each other almost all our lives. Do you think you deserve a private audience?" (I swear those were the words she used.)

"Well, I—" he began. "I—Anna, honey," he said suddenly in a wistful, almost little-boy voice, "do I *have* to talk to your back? Can't I see your face?"

"Again—" she said, swinging around at last, "do you think you deserve to?"

"I'd like to," he said humbly, while silently Bessie and I were urging, *For Christ's sake, fight back! Talk tough! Don't let her have everything her own way!* But of course we didn't dare say so aloud; and of course he probably wouldn't have anyway. The *Post* reporter had apparently done quite a job on him and it only remained for Anna to finish him off. This she proceeded to do with a kind of tired, icy dispassion that was infinitely more devastating than a little honest screaming and kicking would have been.

"Well," she said. "You may. Now you see my face. Do you feel better?"

"Not when you look at me like that, Anna, honey," he said humbly. "You make me feel *awful.*"

"And shouldn't you?"

"Well, I—are you sure you-all have to be here?" he asked suddenly, turning to us with a desperation that would have been laughable under other circumstances but certainly wasn't now.

"No," I agreed, again starting to rise. "We don't. Come along, Bess, Tal—?"

"Sit *down!*" Anna said in a fierce voice. "I want witnesses. *Sit down.*"

"Might as well, Ed," Tal said in his special lazy voice. "Better show than you'll find anywhere else on a snowy afternoon."

"And don't *you,*" Anna snapped, rounding on him so suddenly that he was quite ludicrously taken aback, and sounding very much like Elizabeth I indeed, "don't *you* forget that I made you and I can break you. *You* be quiet."

"Yes," he said hastily, only now aware, apparently, of how really enraged she was. "Yes, Anna!" And subsided, staring at her with a genuine alarm he made no attempt to conceal.

"What did you want to see me about, Gordon?" she asked, as coolly as though she were asking it of a stranger.

"Well, I—" he said. "I—Anna, honey, could I sit down, too?"

She looked blank. "I don't see why. This shouldn't take very long. If you'll stop stammering and get on with it."

He looked at her as though he had never really seen her before, and for a split second Bess and I thought maybe our desperate brain waves might be reaching him; but no. His tone remained humble, uncertain and confused.

"That *Post* reporter," he said, "he told me that they know about—about Mary Lou and—and me. He said they've told you, too. He said they're thinkin' they may not print it if you don't want them to. He said they won't print if you don't. Oh, golly, honey!" And his face crumpled as though he were going to start crying, all six feet two, 210 pounds of range-ridin', tough-guy Texas political millionaire. "Golly, honey, I hope you're not goin' print that kind of stuff, now! It would hurt me awful bad, honey! Awful bad!"

"I take it the story is true," she said in the same calm way.

"Yes, ma'am," he said humbly. "But I had my reasons."

Good for you! Bessie and I told him silently. But it was a lost cause.

"What were they?" she asked, showing a little annoyance in her tone for the first time. "I can conceive of no reasons on this earth why you should choose to humiliate me so, Gordon Hastings. I should be interested to know what you think they were."

"Well, Anna, honey," he said, "you know how it's been these recent years. You've been so wrapped up in the *Inquirer* and all the other enterprises, you know—and you've been so *positive* about things at home, always managin' me and the kids, and all—oh, we know you meant it with love, Anna," he said hastily, "we do know that, all right! But still and all it's been kinda tough now and then, you know? Hard for them and hard for me. I don't mean that critically, now, but—well, it *has* been. Just plain difficult, sometimes."

"Everything I have done," she said, and for the first time her voice quivered a little with a genuine emotion, "has been for the good of the publications, of you and of the children. I have done my level best to be a good publisher, a good wife and a good mother. You can't say I haven't!"

"I know you have, honey," he said hastily. "I know you've tried, I said I knew it was done with love! But mebbe—mebbe if you'd done it the other way around? I mean, if you'd been *first* a good wife and mother and *then* a good publisher? And mebbe if you hadn't tried so hard to run the kids' lives and my life, and all? I mean, I know you have all the brains in the family, honey, and you do see things a lot more clearly than we do, and I expect you've gotten real impatient with us sometimes—and with real cause too, probably—but if you'd just been a little—a little *easier* on us, mebbe—"

"Do you mean by that," she said, composure recovered, voice once more unyielding, "that if I had left you all alone to make your own stupid mistakes, you wouldn't have found it necessary to cuddle up with some cute little thing behind my back? *Is that what you mean?*"

"She isn't a cute little thing," Gordon said forlornly. "Mary Lou is forty-three years old, divorced with two kids and a face and figure like homemade puddin'. She isn't anywhere near as pretty as you, Anna, honey. Nor anywhere near as smart. Not anywhere *near*."

"Then why do you humiliate me so with her?" she cried, and now a real bitterness broke through, a fleeting, momentary chance for some genuine understanding. His honesty killed it instantly.

"Because she's kind, I guess," he said simply, wiping the sweat from his forehead with a piece of Kleenex he took from his pocket. "Because she's just kind, I guess."

And that, of course, was the end of Gordon and the end of everything, though we couldn't know the full extent of it then.

There was a flash of naked pain in her eyes, instantly controlled. When she spoke it was with perfect composure again.

"What reasons can you give me for not printing this story?"

"It would ruin me, honey," he said. "It would just

ruin me. It would kill my campaign for Vice President and probably keep me from bein' reelected in Texas. And I don't know what it would do to the family, I really don't. The kids, now, they love their mother but they love their daddy, too. I don't know what Gordie and Lisa would do if you barbecued me in the *Inquirer* like some old pig, I really don't, now!"

"I can handle the children," Anna said, though for a split second the pain came and went again. "And your 'Vice Presidential campaign' is a farce anyway. And if you don't get reelected in Texas I expect you can manage to survive. And after our divorce you can always marry pudding-faced Mary Lou and live happily ever after—"

"Our divorce, honey!" he cried. "Oh, I don't want any divorce, now! I really don't!"

"Perhaps not," she said, "but I think I do. . . . So it all comes down to this: what should I do as a publisher? Can I afford *not* to print this story? What would that do to my integrity, my peace of mind—my happiness—*my ability to live with myself*—and the trust and confidence people have in the honor and integrity of me and my publications? That's what *I* have to think about. And I'm afraid you haven't offered any very convincing arguments to change my mind."

"Please, honey," he said humbly, and now he was beginning to cry, a horribly uncomfortable, unhappy sight to see, "please don't print this. I'll send Mary Lou away, I swear I will. I'll never look at another woman again, I swear it, I'll do whatever you say. Just don't print it and don't divorce me. Why, hell, little gal, I've always loved you, I've never really loved anybody else. I've worshipped—worshipped—the—the gr—ground—you—walk on—and I—always will."

"Don't blubber," she said coldly. "It doesn't become a grown man who is a United States Senator and may

285

be Vice President of the United States. It doesn't become the kind friend of kind Mary Lou. . . . Now I think you had all better go, and let me think about it. I need to be alone, I need to think. Meanwhile, I will thank you to find some other lodging. I don't wish to share the house with you. I've got to think."

"You don't aim to do any thinkin'," he said with a bitter flare of revolt, too late. "Your mind is made up. I know you. You're goin' to crucify me to satisfy your own ego. You're plain goin' to crucify me."

"Get out!" she cried, rising to her feet, pointing at the door and shouting. "Get out, all of you! Get out, get out, *get out!*"

In haste and confusion we did, Gordon, red eyes muffled in his coat, hat pulled down, leading us as we ignored the elevator and hurried as fast as possible down the back stairs, fortunately seeing no one on the way. Tal muttered something and turned off at the newsroom; we hurried on. The presses were rolling, the building shook. Another *Inquirer* was ready for another day.

"Gordon!" I shouted after him as he hurried ahead of us through the storm, compounded now by dusk and lights and clamorous traffic jams. "Do you want to spend the night with me? I've got an extra bedroom."

"No, thank you kindly," he shot back over his shoulder. Then he paused and turned and waited for us to catch up.

"I want you to know," he said solemnly, "that you and Bess have always been true friends to me. You really have. And I've appreciated it. I really have. Thank you both kindly. Thank you kindly."

And gravely he leaned down and kissed Bessie's quivering and suddenly tearstained cheek; shook me firmly by the hand; hunched his coat deeper around his ears, and turned and plowed off through the snow.

"Oh, dear," Bessie said, crying hard now. "Oh, dear, oh, dear, oh, dear, oh, *dear*."

"Yes," I said, feeling like crying myself. " 'Oh, dear' is right."

But the long day wasn't over for us yet, because after we had consumed a couple of hours with drinks and a gloomy dinner at Paul Young's, I drove Bessie home. There was a message for her at the desk. Gordie and Lisa had called and wanted to see us both—"At once," the deskman said. "They said it was *very* urgent, Miss Rovere. You're to call immediately you get in."

We exchanged looks; sighed deeply; and turned without a word to the elevator.

5

My children, apparently considering me worthy of attention now that their father's treachery and their own connivance therein had produced the greatest crisis of our family life, were waiting in the house when I got home. Our talk was bitter, brief and bruising. They attempted to excuse a course of action I could not condone, sought to make me confer a forgiveness undeserved. I think they actually thought they could deflect me from the course my journalistic integrity made inevitable. All they did, as they soon found out, was confirm me in my decision.

—ANNA HASTINGS, *by Anna Hastings*

"SHE WON'T LISTEN TO US," GORDIE SAID THROUGH convulsive sobs, his face, devastated with weeping, looking about six years old. "She *just won't listen.*"

"She's hateful," Lisa said, crying too. "She's absolutely *hateful.*"

"Now, kids," Bessie said, close to tears herself but managing to hang on to a functioning composure, "you really mustn't talk about your mother that way. I'm sure she's crying her heart out right this minute, too—"

"Sure," Gordie said. "Ice cubes."

"Oh, Gordie, stop it! That isn't fair and you know it! Your mother is a very complex human being—"

"Too much for me," Gordie said, and Lisa said, "Me, too."

"—and she always tries to do what she thinks is right. I know that all your lives she's loved you very deeply and has centered all her hopes and dreams in you. I also think she has really loved your father—"

"Aunt *Bessie!*" Lisa said. "You *do?*"

"Yes," Bess said stoutly, "I do. It hasn't been any wild romance, maybe, or any great world-shaking passion, but in her own way, I think she's been very—very—fond of him. In her own way."

"It's a damned funny way," Gordie said bitterly, "when she's about to hang him from the flagpole of the *Inquirer* building for the whole wide world to see."

"No, she isn't," Bessie said desperately. "No, she *isn't.*"

"She says she's going to print the story," Lisa said. "So I guess that's that."

"I don't ever want to see her again if she does," Gordie said.

"Me either," Lisa agreed.

"Ed—" Bessie said helplessly. I pulled myself together and tried my hand at it; not with any better success, I must admit.

"Look, kids," I said, "let's don't anybody take any adamant and irrevocable stands, O.K.?"

"She is," they said in unison.

"Well," I said, "she may sound like it. But your Aunt Bessie and I have known your mother, remember, from 'way back before you came along, and we've known her to sound pretty rock-hard on things sometimes. And then she'll get to thinking it over and before long her sense of fairness comes back and she changes her position."

"She isn't going to change it this time," Gordie said. "She told us."

"She said, 'I am divorcing your father and I am printing his sordid story because he deserves nothing better at my hands,'" Lisa quoted, and began to cry hard again. "Oh, she is just *awful*."

"But I'll bet," I said desperately, "I'll bet you she's home crying right now, too, just as Aunt Bessie says she is. I'll bet you—"

"What good does that do," Gordie inquired, "if she's going to go right ahead and ruin Daddy?"

"But I don't think she *will*," I said. "That's what I mean. I think she'll think it over and decide that she owes him more than that, and then she'll try to forgive him and it will all work out. You'll see."

"Why don't you call her if you're so sure of that?" Gordie suggested. "Call her and find out how forgiving she's going to be!"

"Well—" I said, and they were onto it at once.

"You won't," Lisa said, "because you know what she'll say."

"She probably won't even talk to you, anyway," Gordie said. "She doesn't want to be persuaded to do anything decent."

"You're so unfair yourselves," I said with a sudden anger that startled them temporarily into silence, "that I don't know why Bess and I should bother with you anyway. Your father *did* set up his arrangement with this Mary Lou person—"

"We know her," Gordie said stubbornly. "She isn't a 'person.' She's a nice lady."

"We like her," Lisa said. "She's good for Daddy and we all get along very well."

"And your mother is supposed to take all that without any reaction whatsoever?" I demanded, exasperated. "She isn't to be upset or hurt or resentful or jealous or have any other human reaction? She's just supposed to forgive and forget and let you all get away with this happy little setup and laugh at her behind her back?"

"We haven't laughed at her!" Gordie said, stung out of his youthful righteousness. "We've felt sorry for her."

"Well, then, for Christ's sake *feel sorry for her now!* Stop setting yourself up like two little judges who know everything in the world about everything! You don't, buster, believe me! You don't."

There was silence for a moment while this thought penetrated; but they were not, of course, to be deflected.

"We don't know everything," Gordie said finally, "but we do know that if Mummie had been more understanding and more loving toward Daddy—if she hadn't always tried to run him and us—if she hadn't always been so *superior*—then he never would have looked at Mary Lou at all, probably. He wouldn't have felt any *need* to look at her. He's always loved Mummie so, and been so proud of her, that all she had to do was give him a little love and encouragement in return, and he'd be here yet."

Bess shot me a look, and a cold little wave washed up the back of my scalp.

"What do you mean 'be here yet'?" I asked, trying to sound more casual than I suddenly felt. "Where is he?"

"He's gone to The Dunes," Lisa said. "He said he wanted to think."

"Just like Mummie," Gordie said bitterly. "That's what she's doing too—thinking!"

291

"*I* think," I said carefully, "that perhaps we had better try to reach her, don't you think, Bess?"

"Yes," she agreed, her voice tense for a reason neither of us dared define: but we were convinced it was valid. "You can use the phone in the bedroom."

"Use the one right here," Gordie said, too wrapped up in their resentment to be aware of adult concern. "We want to hear what she says, since you don't believe us and *you* seem to know everything."

"Don't be a smart aleck, Gordie," Bessie said, but her heart wasn't in the reproof. "It doesn't become you. Go ahead, Ed."

"Yes," I said, and dialed the familiar number. It rang three times and LeRoy's polite, cultured and impassive voice came over.

"Mrs. Hastings' residence," he said, with ever so slight an emphasis on the "Mrs."

"It's Mr. Ed, LeRoy. Is Mrs. Hastings there?"

"She's here, Mr. Ed," he said, "but I don't believe she's *about* to come to the telephone."

"Isn't she listening on the upstairs extension? She usually does."

"I wouldn't know, Mr. Ed," LeRoy said blandly. "I'm not upstairs to see."

"True," I said. "Very true, LeRoy. Will you tell her then, that I'm on the phone and that Miss Bessie and I would like very much to speak to her? Tell her that Mr. Gordie and Miss Lisa are here and that *all* of us would like to speak to her."

"I'm afraid, Mr. Ed," LeRoy said, and genuine regret did come openly into his voice despite the fact that we both knew perfectly well she was listening, "that Mrs. Hastings has left word that she doesn't want to receive calls from *anyone,* particularly you and Miss Bessie and Mr. Gordie and Miss Lisa. And especially Senator Hastings, of course."

"Will you tell Mrs. Hastings that Senator Hastings has gone to The Dunes, and ask her what she makes of that?"

"He *has?*" LeRoy said, startled out of his professional dignity. "On a bad night like this?"

"Exactly," I said. "Ask her what she makes of that."

"You can get off the line, LeRoy," she said, and he said, "Yes, *ma'am!*" with alacrity and did so. "What am I supposed to make of it, in your mind?"

"I'm not sure," I said, "but Bess and I, quite frankly, are worried as hell."

"Is that Mummie?" Lisa whispered, and I nodded yes. I could see that Gordie's eyes were beginning to widen as the implication in our conversation began to penetrate.

"Why should you be? It's his home too."

"In a blinding snowstorm?"

Now Lisa too was beginning to look very scared.

"The storm didn't hit down there," Anna said. "It came through about fifteen miles north of Richmond. It's quite all right at The Dunes. A little cold, maybe, but quite all right."

"Why did you check?"

"I had a hunch he might go down there. It's like an animal licking its wounds. It goes to ground in its own hole."

"Since you won't let it go to ground in Patowmack House."

"Why should I? In the name of God, *why should I?*"

"Because that's where he belongs," I said sharply. "He belongs with you!"

"He *does? Now?* After what he's done? He *does?*"

"Anna," I said desperately, "I beg of you, call him as soon as he gets down there and tell him to come home. You can't let him stay all alone at the beach feeling the way he does."

"Why not?" she asked indifferently. "He deserves it."

"No, he doesn't. He deserves to be forgiven and allowed to come home."

"He'll be all right down there. It will do him good to think a little."

"Anna, he *needs* you."

"Poof! That's a laugh."

"He needs you to tell him he's forgiven," I said, staring into Gordie's stricken eyes, aware of Lisa's renewed tears. "He needs you to tell him it's going to be all right, and that the family is going to be back together again."

"And what do *I* need?" she demanded, and for a brief moment the control slipped and her voice sounded ragged with emotion and the shedding of many tears. "Does anybody in this whole wide world ever think of that? What do *I* need, Ed Macomb, tell me that!"

"Anna," I said, reduced at last to the one word that all the tenuous balance of human relationships reduces to, in the end, *"please."*

"I finished my by-lined story half an hour ago," she said, voice again emotionless. "Tal is at the paper supervising the banner headline and the front-page layout. If Gordon calls the paper, as I think he may, Tal is to tell him what is going to happen. . . . And now you'll excuse me, Ed. I'm tired and I'm going to sleep. I hope."

"Anna! For God's sake! Please!"

"We print, Ed. Good night."

"Good night," I said slowly into the dead line. "Yes, indeed, dear Anna, good night."

"I want to go to The Dunes," Lisa said in a scared little voice. "I want to be with Daddy."

"So do I," Gordie said, his face white with worry. "So do I."

"Bessie?" I said.

294

"What else?" she asked, holding out a hand to Gordie, who gave her a helping tug as she struggled to her feet. "Just let me get my coat and hat—"

"Lisa and I can go in my car," Gordie said, his voice young and strained but determined. "We'll meet you down there."

"You will not!" I said sharply. "You'd drive that little bug like a maniac and you know it. We'll go in mine and I'll drive."

"All right, Uncle Ed," he said. "But *hurry*."

This we did, but it still took almost seven hours to get to The Dunes, allowing for weather to Richmond and the exercise of reasonable caution thereafter. It was almost 2 A.M. when we crossed the bridge to the Outer Banks and and turned south toward Ocracoke, and nearly two-thirty when we reached the house. A single lamp was burning in the living room. His car was in the garage but Gordon was nowhere to be found.

It was not until we had searched the house from top to bottom, calling and shouting and feeling more and more desperately upset, that Bessie and I suddenly looked at one another with a single shared thought, and knew.

The kids were still calling to him and to one another around the guest cottages as we stepped quietly out, bundled ourselves against the icy wind whipping inshore, and headed for the beach. There we found what we were looking for, half in and half out of the restless sea. There was a gun, of course, and there perhaps had been some desperate thought that he might be carried away, for there was no note in his pockets. But he was still there; and after a moment I reached down and managed, with some reserve of strength I didn't know I had, to pull him up onto the sand.

"Mrs. Hastings' residence," LeRoy said with drowsy exasperation. "Who in thunder is this at this hour?"

"Mr. Ed, LeRoy. Put me through."

"Yes, sir," he said, brought full awake by my ragged voice. "I'm goin' to listen, if that's all right with you, because I'm mighty worried about Mr. Gordon."

"Do," I said wearily. "Just put me through."

"Yes, sir!"

When I had finished there was a very long silence, broken only by one deep sob from LeRoy which he made no attempt to conceal and which she ignored.

"I didn't think he would," she said at last. "I didn't think he'd have the character."

6

When the story broke next morning in the Inquirer—I had called Tal Farson at once and we were
able to remake the front page for the final edition—
it was considered to be, I believe, the greatest sensa-
tion to hit the capital since Watergate. The minor
Congressional sex scandals of recent months paled
to insignificance beside this episode in which a
United States Senator's infidelity was exposed in his
own newspaper, by his own wife, to be followed almost immediately by his suicide—all appearing, with
full and honest coverage, in the same edition of the
paper. I decided that we would pull no punches, hold
back no slightest fact. I held true to the motto I had
chosen so long ago for my newspaper: "The Truth
—Regardless!" No one could ever again challenge
the integrity of Anna Hastings and her publications.
This was not easy for me but in my heart I knew I
had no choice: the fundamental meaning of my
whole life was at stake. I regret that my children
were not able to understand this though I think for
a brief period they really tried; but I have found my
comfort in the unstinting support of my colleagues

of the media, whose respect, admiration and under-
standing sustain me in all I do.

—ANNA HASTINGS, *by Anna Hastings*

THE FUNERAL, LIKE THE WEDDING, WAS HELD AT THE
National Cathedral; as I said earlier about The Dunes,
Anna likes to tie all the strands of her life together.
Everybody Who Was Anybody once again came out to
see, and be seen by, Everybody Else Who Was Anybody: it was considered by many to have been *the*
funeral of the decade. The President, the First Lady
and most of the Cabinet came: nearly all of the Senate
and most of the House were there; the Chief Justice
opened the service, the Senate Majority Leader read
the eulogy, the dean of the Cathedral gave the concluding prayer. The storm had blown away, the first
bright intimations of spring were in the air. It was a
clear, crisp, lovely day.

The immediate funeral party included Gordon's sister and her husband, two nieces and a nephew, from
Texas; Seab Cooley, looking old and sad and tired;
Bessie, Tal and myself; Mother and Father Kowalczek;
and Anna and the kids. After the other mourners were
seated, the Cathedral full to the doors and overflowing
onto the lawns outside, we entered and took our seats.
At the very end came Anna, pale but composed, looking neither to right nor left, trim, beautiful and indomitable in her simple black dress. On her right she
was flanked by Gordie, on her left by Lisa. They
walked as in a dream and knew us not.

When the service was concluded a small cortege accompanied us to Dulles Airport, from which we flew
(minus Anna's parents, who returned to Punxsutawney, and Seab, who had to stay for Senate business) to

298

accompany Gordon home to the Circle H; and there in the hill country in late afternoon he was buried with military honors and the playing of taps. We then returned to the house for a small meal; the sister and brother-in-law and their children left; and the Old Team, and Gordie and Lisa, were at last alone.

We took our places in the swings and rockers on the porch, watching the waning light slant over the peaceful land, and for a time said nothing at all.

It was Gordie who finally spoke, his voice breaking with emotion suddenly released. "You killed my father," he said, trembling all over. "You *killed him!*"

"Gordie!" I said sharply, but Anna held up a restraining hand and spoke in a tired but steady voice.

"No, let him get it out of his system. And you, too, Lisa. Say anything you like to me. Tell me how awful I am, how much you hate and despise me—anything. I won't stop you and I won't let them stop you. Go ahead."

"Oh, Mummie," Lisa wailed in a lost-little-girl voice, "how could you, how *could* you?"

"It was easy," Gordie said, on the ragged edge of tears. "She isn't human, so it was easy. She just wanted a headline, so it was easy. It was just—just *easy,* for *her.*"

"Was it?" she asked, again sounding infinitely weary but unmoved—and unmovable. "Was it really that easy for me, Gordon?" (Which made us all start, for this was the first time we could ever remember that anyone had called him by his full name; and it finally brought home to us suddenly and irrevocably where we were, and why.) "How little you know your own mother if you think that. But go ahead, as I said, and get it out of your system. I can take it."

"You aren't human," he said, almost in a whisper. "You really aren't."

299

"Why did you hate him so?" Lisa asked through the tears that were at last beginning to flow as freely as they had to for her own sake. "What did he ever do to you—really? Was it really so—so—awful?"

"It was inexcusable," she said quietly. "It hurt me terribly. But I found that as soon as I had written the story and ordered its publication, I had forgiven him. I *did* hate him for a little while but I got rid of it in the only way I know, which was to write about it. And after that it was gone and it no longer mattered to me. I would have told him that if he had come back. But" —and for just a second her face turned bleak before resuming its impassive expression—"he didn't come back."

"You knew he wouldn't," Gordie said, his own unrestrainable tears beginning to come, too. "You knew he'd do what he did. You knew it!"

"I did *not!*" she said sharply. "I did *not!* I never dreamed he would be so weak. I never dreamed he—"

"You made him weak!" Gordie cried, words barely coherent as the full flood of grief hit him. "You made him weak! He didn't start out that way but you made him weak *because that's the way you wanted him!* You want everybody around you weak so that you can dominate them! That's the way you are!"

"Well, if I want everybody around me weak," she said with a bitter humor, "I certainly haven't succeeded with you two, have I? You aren't weak at all. You're as tough as I am, little happy-hippie Gordie and little sweet-as-pie, cold-as-ice Lisa!"

"I'm not a hippie!" Gordon protested; and I'm not as cold as ice!" wailed Lisa. And both began to cry even harder.

"Oh, yes, you are," she said coldly, "so don't try to get my sympathy by pretending you're not and bellowing all over the Circle H. You're as tough as nails, both

300

of you. You've sided with him all your lives, you've never given a damn about me, while I've worked my ass off and done my level best to build up the *Inquirer* and all our other enterprises just for you! *Just for you,* believe it or not! How about that, Mr. Gordon Junior? How about that, Miss Lisa? *Just for you,* and you've never—never—" for just a second her voice began to break with emotion, but she caught it, *"never* appreciated it one damn! How do you think that's made me feel, all these years? Why do you think *you're* the only ones with a grievance? How about me, you selfish, ungrateful, unnatural, *unfriendly* kids! *How about me?"*

"Anna," Bessie said hesitantly into the agonized silence that followed, "don't you think maybe— wouldn't it be a good idea if we all got an early bed? We're all exhausted, physically and emotionally, and we've got to fly back to Washington first thing tomorrow. Maybe this isn't a good time to—"

"It *is* a good time," she said, recovering her composure with an obvious effort—but recovering it. "I want to say something to these two, and I want to say it in the presence of my old friends who know it's true."

She turned and spoke directly to her children, who gradually quieted down and began to listen enthralled as she proceeded.

"I came to Washington an idealistic and enterprising young reporter—and I *was* idealistic, as I think we all were then. I set out to become the best damned reporter on the Hill and I think I almost made it, though I had some mighty good competition. Anyway, I got to the top, which was where I wanted to be. And I began to dream about having my own newspaper, which I remember Ed and Tal and Bessie all telling me I was crazy to even think about. But I kept dreaming and wanting it, meanwhile getting bigger and bigger as a professional name in our business. And then I got the Pulitzer but I still wasn't really where I wanted to go, yet. And I still wanted it, and I still dreamed about it. And one day your father came to the Senate, and I liked him. No, I didn't fall passionately in love with him, but I liked him! And he had money, big money. And I felt I could be a good wife to him and that in return I could use that money to get what I wanted. I'm not going to pretend to you that it was any mad passion, I'm not going to pretend to you that I didn't approach it practically as the way to achieve my ambitions, because I did. I'm not the first person in the world who ever married for reasons like that and I sure as hell won't be the last. But I kept my part of the bargain, I gave as good as I got. . . .

"So we married, and we were happy. He had what he wanted and I had what I wanted. And presently you kids came along, and for a while, until you began to turn against me and against the paper, I thought I had really achieved something beyond even my most ambitious dreams. I thought we had founded a dynasty. I thought we would someday be as big as the Ochses, the Sulzbergers, the McCormicks, the Pattersons, the Meyers, the Cowleses. I thought: *My Gordie!* And, *My Lisa!* And I thought: *We'll show the whole wide world what we can do in this business!* And with your father's help I bought the radio station and the television station and the other papers and the magazines and I kept up my column and got my television program and *I showed them.* And I wanted you to show them too, when you came along. . . .

"But to do this, of course, I had to be tough. It isn't an easy game, the newspaper game, particularly for an ambitious woman who wants to get to the top. I had to be tough; but I think I can honestly say that I have been honest in all my dealings with my employees and

302

with my family and even with the people we've written about. They may not agree with that, and they may feel we've hurt them, *but at least we've been honest about our own point of view and we've been honest about letting them know what it was*. We haven't pulled any punches. We haven't held back. . . .

"Maybe, as you say, Gordie, I like to dominate. Maybe it's my nature to dominate, and maybe I crippled your father and maybe I warped you, by dominating. But I doubt it. I think he was weak to begin with, I think it was inevitable I should dominate him; and I don't think for one minute that I've ever really dominated you two. I think you've done exactly what you wanted to do, and always will. . . .

"But you thought you had a gripe, so you ran wild for a while and then you sided with him. And when he went to somebody else, you tagged along and cried, 'Goodie!' And you thought I wasn't human, so it wouldn't hurt me. Well: it hurt me like hell, let me tell you. But I wasn't going to let that stand in the way of my professional duty. I was going to be a good newspaperwoman to the end. And it was the end, for him. And I'm sorry, but there it is. And I don't really think it could have ended any other way. And while I'll regret bitterly all my life that I miscalculated his weakness, I don't apologize for what I did. It was in me and I had to obey it. I wouldn't have been Anna Hastings, otherwise. . . .

"So here we are at the Circle H, and Gordon lies out there in Texas earth, and you and I—*together*—have the responsibility for deciding where we go from here. I can't demand your help, but I'm going to ask it. Take as much satisfaction as you like from that: your mother is going to ask your help.

"You haven't seen the will yet but I have. He rewrote it about a week ago, so I expect he must have had intimations. He's left you the ranch and the oil wells and increased your trust funds to ten million dollars each. He's also left me a ten-million-dollar trust, all other personal property including Patowmack House and The Dunes—which is already on the market, because I know none of us ever wants to go there again —plus *all* of his stock in Hastings Communications, including the portions he gave you in the new trust. He redrew that last week, too, so that I am sole beneficiary, and you are excluded from the newspaper business as I am excluded from the ranch and the oil wells. He thought that would make us all happy, and bitter though it is for me to acknowledge it, I expect it does.

"*But*. Let me make a deal with you. I won't ever attempt to interfere in the ranch or the wells, because how can I? And you can't interfere with the business, because how can you? So, let me make a deal with you. . . .

"I still want my dynasty. I still want to see 'Gordon B. Hastings, Jr.' on the masthead someday—and someday not too far off, I promise you—as publisher of the *Inquirer* and president of Hastings Communications. I still want Lisa Hastings on the board, maybe as vice president, when I'm emeritus in everything, which will be pretty soon, now, because I'm pushing sixty, and pretty soon it will be sixty-five, and then seventy, and then before you know it, Anna Hastings will join the long parade who have come to Washington, stayed for a while, written big or little on their times and gone on. I'll be lying here beside Gordon, if you'll let me, and the *Inquirer* and all the rest will still be going strong: in your hands, I hope. . . .

"Gordon"—and she reached out and took his hand in hers, and he, like all of us, was so mesmerized that he could not have resisted had he wanted to, and at that moment he didn't—"come and join me on the paper. Give it a try. I'll help you, I'll train you—Lisa will be with us, Aunt Bessie and Uncle Ed and Uncle Tal will be giving advice as they do to me—we'll all be pulling together—it will be fun, it will be like old times—we'll make it an even greater paper than it is now—we'll keep on building and adding all over the country—they won't be able to stop us! The Hastings! That's us! *The Hastings!* Say yes! Say *yes!*"

And after a lingering moment she released his hand and sat back quietly, while all around us the dusk grew heavier and the night came on. We realized suddenly that we were cold, for it was winter in Texas, too. But we had never thought of it while she spoke. Never at all.

Finally Gordie gave a long shuddering sigh.

"Lees?" he asked, using the old childhood nickname.

"I guess so," she said shakily, "if that's what Mummie wants."

And suddenly they were all in each other's arms— and *they* were crying—and *we* were crying—and it *wasn't* cold in Texas—and everything was going to be all right again with the family and the *Inquirer*—and *they* were going to do better—and *Anna* was going to do better—and tomorrow, as Scarlett said, was another day.

7

---

*We returned from Gordon's interment in Texas—
so peaceful and serene, in that restful spot—to begin
our work together upon the* Inquirer *in good spirits
and with stout hearts. But alas for all my dreams!
Young Gordon did not measure up and Lisa was not
really interested. I did my best to help them, but to
no avail. Again life treated me bitterly. Again I had
only my own resources to fall back upon, if I was
to survive . . . I did survive.*

—ANNA HASTINGS, *by Anna Hastings*

THOSE WERE THE DAYS OF GORDIE IN COAT AND TIE,
spruced up and looking very handsome, referred to invariably as "Young Gordon" by his mother in her conversation and in the blue-initialed memos she sent to
the staffs. Those were the days when Lisa, wearing a
dress and looking elfin and pretty, flitted in and out of
the newsroom doing her earnest best to understand
what it was all about. Those were the days when Tal
pretty much ran the paper as he pleased, days when
Anna spent most of her time instructing, encouraging,

supervising, *managing*—and so they were also the days when, inevitably, the emotional dreams at the Circle H faded away and life returned once more to its former unhappy pattern.

Still, it is only fair to say that both she and the kids really tried. They came to the office when she did, an apparently harmonious trio bent upon increasing the power and glory of the *Inquirer* and Hastings Communications. Anna gave them both salaries, which they agreed to accept only if she would in turn accept a percentage of the oil royalties and ranch profits. They were all amused by this and signed an official agreement about it amid friendly joshing. The kids did their best to understand what was going on, she did her best to assist them. Bessie and I were invited over frequently to sit in on staff meetings, participate in editorial conferences, attend board meetings. Anna used us shrewdly to transform the Old Team into the New Team, to bring Gordie and Lisa gradually within the confines of our old friendship and easy working habits, to give them the feeling of being really and truly on the inside.

Many times Bess and I knew that she was deliberately holding back some impatient comment, some biting reminder that *this* was the way to do things, not *that*. She controlled herself sternly, and we admired her for that.

And I think Gordie and Lisa really enjoyed it, for the brief while it lasted. They all stopped circling around each other and began to relax. Their relationship entered upon the most comfortable phase it had known since their early childhood. Somehow they resolved—or appeared to resolve—the bitter memories of Gordon's death, to push into the background and seemingly eradicate their mutual hurts, mistrusts and suspicions. A genuine forgiveness seemed to have been achieved. Bessie and I were very wary of this; but so good was the outer surface and so outwardly determined were they all to make it last that we did not realize how paper-thin it was until two months later, when Anna decided to accept her degrees and Gordie and Lisa, in sudden bitter retaliation for what they regarded as renewed betrayal of their father, left her again—forever, as far as we can tell now.

It so happened that the invitations from Harvard and Stanford arrived on the day we had been asked to come over for an editorial conference. Anna was just beginning negotiations for the television stations in Philadelphia and San Francisco that are scheduled to reach their final stages this year, and we were all supposed to tell her what we thought of this. Tal's advice was terse and to the point:

"You have the money. Go ahead."

Bess and I said much the same, our only caution being to wonder if possibly the corporation might not be spreading itself a little too thinly in view of the economic recession. If not, we agreed, by all means buy.

"What do you think, Gordon?" she asked, giving the impression, as she shrewdly did in those days, that she was genuinely seeking his opinion.

"Well," he said, giving the impression, as he rather touchingly did in those days, that he was delivering it after very earnest and profound thought, "I think, as Uncle Tal says, that you have the funds. I agree a little bit with Aunt Bessie and Uncle Ed, though—aren't we maybe spreading ourselves a little bit thin? Can we really handle it comfortably with all our other enterprises?"

("Whenever either one of them says 'we,' or 'our,'" Anna told me privately one time, "it just thrills me to death." There were genuine tears in her eyes when she said it.)

"What do you think, Lisa?"

"I agree," Lisa said, frowning and looking very cute. "If you're really sure we can keep an eye on everything, then I think we should buy them. But if it's going to be too much for us, Mummie, then I wonder."

"That's something we're going to have to consider very seriously," Anna agreed, "but I think, from the preliminary studies I've had made, that it would be quite feasible. It will pinch a little bit for a couple of years, but I believe we can manage. Against that, we have to balance the advantages of acquiring outlets in those two important centers."

"One of which," Tal said, but not unkindly, "is located in an old stamping ground of the publisher and may even extend its signals as far as Punxsutawney, P.A."

"That's right," Anna said with a smile. "I won't deny that enters in, but of course if it weren't a profitable deal, you know I wouldn't consider it for a minute."

"That's true," Tal agreed. "So, why not have fun with it?"

"That's what I think too, Mother," Gordie said (having begun, with his new dignities, to abandon childhood's "Mummie"). "I think you should do what you think best."

"But I want to be sure you agree, first," she said, which was certainly the New Anna, all right.

"We do, Mummie," Lisa said. "We trust your judgment."

"Good," she said. "Then I guess that's settled and we can begin talking to them. In fact, I might be able to swing by and see them myself, between Harvard and Stanford."

"Are you going to buy them, too?" I inquired, and she hit me gaily on the knee.

"No, silly, I'm not going to buy them, too. They

309

want to give me honorary degrees this year." And quite innocently she picked up two envelopes and tossed them across to the children. "Isn't that nice?"

"That's great, Mother," Gordie said, opening one and handing the other to Lisa. "That's just great."

"It's wonderful," Lisa said. We all watched benignly as they began to read. I think we were as absolutely stunned as Anna when Gordie's face suddenly contorted and he uttered a bitter "No!" to be echoed by Lisa's equally distraught "Oh, *no!*"

"What's the matter?" Anna demanded with a sharp dismay. "What's wrong?"

"Have you read these?" Gordie demanded, his voice choked with emotion, his expression harsh and suspicious.

"No," she said, openly shaken. "No, I haven't. They both called a week or so ago and asked if I would accept a degree. I said yes, I'd be honored. These just came in a few minutes ago and I assumed they were confirmations and you'd be interested to read them. What's the matter?"

"They're attacks on Daddy," Lisa said in a thin little voice. "You can't accept them, Mummie. You just *can't.*"

"But I've already told them—" she began. "What do they *say,* for heaven's sakes? Read them to us!"

"The one from Harvard," Gordie said in a trembling voice, "makes you a Doctor of Letters and Communications, and the citation says—it says"—his face contorted again, but he forced himself to go on—" 'For your courage and integrity in exposing, at great—great cost to yourself, but with an—an inviolate ethical purity, a tragic flaw in your own fam—family—and exposing it to public view, without—fear or favor, thereby upholding the highest tra-traditions of journalistic honor'!"

"And Stanford says," Lisa said, while Bessie and Anna and I looked at one another appalled and even Tal was sobered, "it wants you to be a Doctor of Communications 'for your adherence to the most—most— noble traditions of American journalism in ex—exposing a fatally—flawed—public—servant, even though he was a mem—member of your own—own family, thus displaying the high—highest courage and integrity as be—befits one of America's most re—responsible publishers.' Oh, *Mummie!*"

"Well, I didn't know!" Anna said desperately. "I told you I didn't know! I'll call them, I'll have it changed. I agree with you, they can't say that!"

"*I* think," Gordie said, and his tone was that of a young Jehovah handing down judgment, "that you must refuse them altogether. Don't call: write. Tell them that you find this deeply insulting to you and your family and that you cannot possibly accept such—such awful *crap*."

"I don't know that it's necessary to go that far—" Tal began, but the kids turned on him like tigers: it was the first time we realized how completely they disliked him.

"Why wouldn't you go that far?" Gordie demanded loudly. "Because you despised my father?"

"Yes, is that it?" Lisa cried. "Just because you hated somebody ten times too good for you?"

"I didn't say that," Tal said angrily. "I just think there's a sensible way out for your mother, that's all. You don't have to make a federal case of it."

"*I* do," Gordie said ominously. "If she doesn't write those bastards and say no, then I'll—I'll—"

"So will I," Lisa echoed dutifully. "I'll—I'll—"

"You'll *what?*" Anna demanded, and Bess and I exchanged a look that said, *Oh, no, Anna. Please.* But when the lioness goes after the cubs, innocent by-

311

standers might as well stand back. It tore us apart inside, though, I can tell you.

"Now," she said, breathing hard, her face as grim and adamant as theirs, *"what is this nonsense?* I've told you I'm going to do what I can to get it changed. But I am not going to gratuitously offend institutions whose faculties and students have been most generous and most supportive of me over the years. They have sent me valued employees, they have given me great praise, they have supported me. I am not going to insult them by refusing their degrees. That would be childish and ridiculous!"

"Maybe we are childish and ridiculous," Gordie said in an ominous voice, "but we loved our father and we aren't going to stay around if you won't defend his memory."

"Defend his memory?" Anna cried, while Bess and I shouted futile protests inside. "Why should I? What did he do to me? . . . Listen!" she said, aware then that she might have gone too far but unable to stop. "I said I agreed with you that this language is unsuitable, and I said I would get it changed. I *said* that!"

"You won't refuse the degrees though," Gordie said. "And you didn't say you disagreed with what the language *says."*

"She can't say that," Lisa told him, "because she does agree with it. *We* know that!"

"Yes, Lees," he said, standing up, horribly unfair but not to be stopped in his terrible youthful righteousness, "let's get out of here. It won't work, it can't ever work. We've just been kidding ourselves while she's been sweet as pie to us in these past few months. She didn't like him and she doesn't like us. She's only been nice because it makes us fit into *her* plan for what *she* wants. She doesn't really give a damn about *us.* You can take your newspaper," he said to his mother, suddenly beginning to shout and cry at the same time, "and *shove* it! We've had enough of your bossy ways. Enough! We're getting out of here! *Out!*"

And while everybody shouted at once he reached down, yanked Lisa from her chair, threw the letters back on Anna's desk and rushed his sister out of the room, slamming the door behind them.

That was the third time I saw Anna cry, and it did not last very long: I think she had been expecting this for quite a while, had felt all along that they were living in a dreamworld; that they never had, and never really could, forget Gordon or forgive one another for all the unhappy tangles of the past. But I think she had really tried, and I think she realized, even as they fled, that the kids had really tried; and it was a terribly bitter moment for her. And although our pain could not possibly be as great as hers, it was terribly shattering for Bessie and me, who had desperately hoped, though dubiously, that somehow it would all work out.

Presently she stopped crying and as soon as she did so Tal stood up and said briskly, which was probably best, "I've got to get back to the newsroom. Do you want us to run a story on the degrees?"

"A brief one," she said as she took her purse out of a drawer, found a mirror and began repairing her makeup.

"Shall I let the language stand?"

"No!" Bessie and I said together; but Anna only paused for a second, gave us a quick sad look from unyielding eyes, and said:

"Certainly, why not?"

"O.K.," Tal said. "It will be done."

And so it was, and most of the *Inquirer*'s major colleagues, who had remained deferential and almost completely silent since Gordon's death, used it as a peg on which to hang editorials praising her courage and integrity. Their language was uniformly respectful and low-key, but again her name was everywhere across the country. She received much praise from all branches of the media, her name ran large on page and tube, the rating of her Sunday television show shot sharply up, admiring articles appeared in major magazines. And finally *Time* came out with a cover story: "ANNA HASTINGS: From Fearless Publisher To—?"

All of this, particularly the *Time* article, which apparently appeared at just the right moment, led directly to what she now refers to laughingly as "my last hurrah"—although the Old Team expects that it isn't the last at all, but only the forerunner of similar and perhaps even more exciting possibilities to come.

Whether it is or not, however, one thing is certain: it came at just the right moment for Anna. I really doubt that she would be with us today if it hadn't.

8

I was taken completely by surprise when the flattering offer came; and I will confess that for several weeks I gave it profound and exhaustive thought. There were many reasons why I should accept: for the sake of my publications, for the sake of my country, for the sake of liberated womanhood, a cause to which I have always given allegiance; and, of course, the potential of even greater service to all of these. Equally there were reasons why I should not accept: the inevitable curtailment of my independence, the necessity of divorcing myself, at least for the time being, from the management of my enterprises, which have always been my principal charge and care; the chance that circumstances might make it impossible for me ever to return to them again. The prize was extraordinarily tempting but was the road to it too demanding upon me? It was one of the hardest decisions I have ever had to make.

—ANNA HASTINGS, *by Anna Hastings*

"ED," TAL SAID—I THINK IT WAS THE FIRST TIME HE had called me since the Senate hearing—"can you round up Bess and come over here?"

"What's the matter? You sound a little worried."

"I am worried. Have you two seen Anna since the kids left?"

"I haven't," I said. "I don't know about Bess. But it's only been a month or so, after all."

"Have you talked to her on the phone?"

"No, I've been out of town on some lectures and one thing and another. Why, what's wrong?"

"You'd better come see for yourself."

"O.K.," I said, his tone convincing me. "I'll get Bess and we'll be over as soon as possible."

"Good. I'll try to hold her here for a while."

"Hold her there?" I asked blankly. "When did anybody have to 'hold' Anna at the *Inquirer?*"

"That's what I mean," he said. "Get your butt moving."

"Yes, *sir!* It's out of the chair and on the way."

"Stop by my office first and then we'll go in to see her."

"O.K.," I said, now genuinely alarmed. "Give us half an hour."

It was closer to an hour and a half before we got there, Bessie having been on the Hill doing research for what was to become *The Ups and Downs of Congress: Senate and House Elevator Boys Describe Their Intriguing (and Sometimes Indiscreet) Passengers.* I finally tracked her through the Senate Press Gallery staff, who had seen her in the Dirksen Office Building riding up and down while taking voluminous notes from a flattered and delighted Georgetown law student working his part-time job. Her reaction to Tal's concern was the same as my own. "Oh, dear," she

316

said in a worried voice. "I'll catch a cab right away and meet you at the paper."

We went at once to Tal's office as he had suggested, our arrival causing some stir in the newsroom. He didn't waste time on greetings but just said tersely, "Come on. She's upstairs in the executive suite." When we got there the door was closed and the silence was a little eerie. For more than three decades Anna and the sound of a typewriter had never been far apart. But she wasn't typing today.

Tal rapped three times before he got a response.

"Yes?" she said finally, her voice oddly muffled.

"It's us," Tal said. "Can we come in?"

"Why?"

"Because we want to see you."

"I don't see why."

"Anna," he said, letting a deliberate impatience enter his voice. "Will you open up and stop being mysterious, God damn it?"

There was a silence.

"All right," she said finally in a weary voice. "I'm coming."

And unlocked the door—the sound of the key surprising and alarming us further—and stood aside to let us enter. She had been crying and made no attempt to conceal it.

"Sit down," she said with a sort of wry sadness. "I guess you can find some chairs."

"Anna," Bessie said severely when we were seated and she was looking at us with an almost challenging frankness, wiping her eyes and blowing her nose and trying listlessly to stop the tears that still seemed to be coming, "what are you doing up here by yourself, feeling like this? And why haven't you called us?"

"What good would that do?" she asked, staring out

for a moment into a world that now was lovely with spring.

"What good does it do you to lock yourself in up here?" I asked with equal severity. "Has she been doing this often, Tal?"

"Practically every day," he said. "And going home around three every day, too. Sometimes earlier. Three or four times not even coming in at all. And canceling out on next week's taping for the TV show, too, which has NBC worried as hell. They called me about it a little while ago."

"Oh?" Anna said in the same listless way. "What did you tell them?"

"I told them you weren't feeling very well but would be back next week."

"Will I?"

"You sure as hell will if *we* have anything to say about it."

"That'e *right*," Bessie agreed and I said, "Hear, hear!" trying to be hearty. It didn't help much.

"Well," she said, for a moment making what appeared to be a genuine effort to pull herself together, "you're all very sweet and I appreciate it. . . . The old team! What would I have done without you, all these years! . . . You've really been"—and suddenly the tears renewed themselves in a great burst and she could hardly complete the thought for weeping— "you've really been all I've had, all these years. You've . . . really . . . been . . . all . . . I've . . . had."

"Oh, Anna, dear!" Bessie said, rushing over—if that's the expression for Bess, now pushing 250 pounds —to throw her arms around her. "You mustn't, mustn't, *mustn't* feel that way. We *have* all been your dearest friends, we all *are* your dearest friends, but you've had so much more. *So* much more! Really you have!"

"What?" Anna asked bitterly, disengaging herself

gently but firmly from Bessie's mammoth embrace, sounding bitter but at least a little livelier. "What? A well-meaning oaf of a husband who finally betrayed me? Two kids who've defied me all their lives and now have left me all—all alone and gone off God knows where? What *have* I had, really?"

"In the first place," I said, "God isn't the only one who knows where they are, Bess and I do. They're in Rome with Gordon's sister and they're keeping in touch with us. So don't worry. I expect they're probably crying, too, right now."

"Oh, sure," Anna said bitterly. "I'll bet!"

"I'll bet they are," Bessie said firmly. "They're good kids at heart, and they love you—"

"Hah!"

"Yes, they *do,* Anna! They'll be back. You'll see."

"No, they won't," she said bleakly, and in this she has so far proved to be correct. "They'll never be back. They can't stand me, they told me so, you heard them. Everything I've done for them is just—just"—and the tears welled up again—"just an empty pretense. Just empty, that's all! *My whole life* is just a pretense. Just *empty!*"

And once again, as on those two earlier occasions of family crisis, she suddenly clasped her hands around her knees and rocked back and forth in a kind of primeval animal agony, sobbing loudly and letting the tears fall unchecked.

Which of course sent Bess into a paroxysm, overwhelmed me and even brought Tal a bad case of the sniffles. I must say the Old Team has been through some emotional moments with its leader. This one lasted for about five minutes before the storm began to die down all around. When all that was left was the sound of lovely women quietly sobbing and strong men loudly blowing their noses, it semed to be time for

319

somebody to talk tough. I began it. The others promptly and loyally backed me up.

"Now, Anna," I said, "see here. Stop this maudlin self-pity and snap out of it! It isn't like you to carry on like this. Now, cut it out! Gordon's gone and there's no point in worrying about *that*: you did what you thought you had to do, and it's over. The kids are on the rampage but they'll come back eventually: they're completely independent financially and every other way, you can't force them, all you can do is wait, so put them out of your mind and get on with other things. We're here, the *Inquirer*'s here, the corporation is here and *you're* here. As long as you are, there are a thousand and one things that need your attention. Isn't that right, Tal?"

"That's for damned sure," he said. "I can run this place for a day or two without you, maybe a week or two or a month or two, but I can't run it forever that way. Nobody could. You're so much a part of this place that—why, hell, Anna, you *are* the *Inquirer!* There isn't anybody else! It's just crazy for you to withdraw like this. And it also," he concluded more quietly, "is damned bad for your mental and physical health and we're not going to let it go on any longer."

"Sometimes I wish I were dead," she said, whereupon as one voice we hooted, our nervousness and worry for her prompting us to be even louder and more scornful than we might have been otherwise.

"Oh, Anna," Bessie said, "what nonsense! You sound like some two-bit soap opera! Wish you were dead, indeed! Of all the crap! When so much depends upon you! When you have everything to live for!"

"*What* have I got to live for?"

It was at that moment, as she looked at us from tear-filled, ravaged eyes, not being dramatic at all but genuinely asking the question, that a wild inspiration hit me. Where it came from I'll never know, what conjunction of current events and current crisis brought it into being. But there it was, and I knew, as a veteran Washington correspondent does know when he gets a hunch based on years of immersion in people and politics, that it would work. It would work for Anna, it would work for us, it would work for everybody. (The irony of it also appealed to me, I must confess, as I knew it would appeal to Anna.) And it wouldn't be at all hard to get under way either. A casual remark dropped at the National Press Club bar, a random comment uttered in the Congressional Press Galleries and the White House newsroom, a relaxed and seemingly inadvertent question at four or five of the right cocktail parties and dinners in Georgetown, and it would be well and truly launched as so many things have been in this wonderful, ingrown, incestuous town.

"Anna," I said, and there was a genuine excitement in my voice that riveted the other two and seemed to pull her out of her depression a little, "do you know what I heard about you today?"

"No," she said dully. "What?"

When I told her there was a long silence during which she turned to stare again out the window, her face gradually beginning to come to life again, first with disbelief, then with a growing interest. Behind her back Bess and Tal gave me questioning looks. I winked, light dawned. They nodded with sudden pleased expressions. Once again the Old Team was getting ready to go to town for Anna.

"Do you really think there's anything to it?" she asked finally, her expression not wanting to believe but her voice suddenly eager for confirmation.

"You wait," I said. "You'll see."

And within a week, thanks to my own diligent efforts

and the efficient cooperation of my two partners in the science of news creation, she did.

She was never able to track down, although she employed all the resources of the staffs, and Bess and Tal and I solemnly pitched in to aid in the detective work, where the idea came from. We agreed that we could hardly believe it was simply a spontaneous upwelling of the same inspiration in a number of influential minds, but eventually we were able to assure her that this is what it must have been.

"I guess I'm an idea whose time has come," she said with the first genuine laugh in more than two months. "Now, how do I get out of it?"

Evans and Novak broke the story first, followed within twenty-four hours by Jack Anderson with the *real* inside poop (he thought); Joseph Kraft, relating it to the Big Overall Picture; James Reston, moving it upward to the proper philosophical plane; Mary McGrory, giving it the wry Bostonian double whammy, the knife coming out clean, the victim dripping gore; William Buckley, placing it, with a devastating twinkle of teeth, in its fundamental relationship to the sempiternal infinitudes of the syntagmatic cosmos; William Safire, reporting how it was done when he and Henry Kissinger were in the White House; James Kilpatrick, judiciously appraising the possibilities and warning of the consequences to the vernal Virginia countryside; Betty Beale, shrewdly analyzing what this would mean to capital society and the Arabs on Embassy Row, particularly the Saudis and Kuwaitis; Russell Baker, giving it a delicately weary, Brahmanic what-ho and hi, there; Art Buchwald, knocking himself and everybody else out with a jumping jovial jolly.

When *Time* finally used it a month later as the peg on which to hang its cover story on "ANNA HASTINGS: From Fearless Publisher To—?" Bessie, Tal and I congratulated ourselves that we had it made. And when she received a telephone call from headquarters, we knew it.

At that point both Anna and I also tackled it in our columns. Hers, as was to be expected, was the most widely read piece in the entire country that day and remained the standard reference until the episode ended. Once she was convinced, we were delighted to note, she forgot the kids and everything else and went after it with an all-out enthusiasm and cleverness that were vintage Anna. It may have been "one of the hardest decisions I have ever had to make" but the difficulty was not apparent to the naked eye.

"You will forgive this columnist," she wrote, "if she addresses you in a more direct and personal manner than is customarily found in this space. I know you understand the reasons, and will bear with me while I give you my views on what has suddenly become a paramount interest both in this politics-ridden town and apparently across the country as well.

"The suggestion that I should be the Vice Presidential nominee this year is one which, I assure you, has come as a complete and stunning surprise to me. It has its reminiscent, ironic and unhappy personal overtones, as you all know: on them I shall not dwell. I shall simply give you a little of my thinking as I consider this surprising and unorthodox—yet apparently quite serious—proposal on the part of political leaders whose judgment I respect and whose confidence I deeply appreciate.

"The thought that I, Anna Hastings, should be considered at all for such an exalted post is one which both excites and humbles me. Political preferment is something I have never sought or desired. It has seemed to me that I could serve my country much better through the Washington *Inquirer* and my other publications and enterprises than I could through direct political involvement. Yet perhaps now the time has come to think seriously about this. Certainly others seem to be.

"I am assured, apparently with complete truth, that my name is being very seriously considered by the man who is almost certainly going to be the candidate for President. I am privileged to reveal to you here that he telephoned me two days ago and spent more than half an hour talking to me about it. He has now stated publicly what he told me then: that I am 'very near the top, possibly at the top' of his list of potential choices; and that he wishes me to begin considering very carefully whether I wish to accept a call which he says 'may inevitably, or almost inevitably,' come.

"This I am doing, in an exhaustive review of my present activities and the possibilities of the broader arena in which he believes, or almost believes, that he may be able to use me. I must make up my mind as he has made up, or almost made up, his. We will then know better where we stand. Most importantly, perhaps, since this is the first time this honor has been offered, or may be offered, to a woman, *I* will know where *I* stand. That is why I am now going to make this direct appeal to you, my fellow Americans.

"To all of you who read this column, I say:

"Help both me and our certain, or almost certain, candidate, to make up our minds.

"Give me your advice.

"Express to me your approval or disapproval, as the case may be.

"Pose to yourselves the question: Do I or do I not want Anna Hastings to be Vice President of the United States?

"Think carefully, judge responsibly, decide patriotically.

"Then send your replies either to:

"Anna Hastings, The Washington *Inquirer*, Washington, D.C.

"Or:

"Chairman, The National Committee, Washington, D.C.

"Do this today!

"I need your help, fellow Americans.

"Let me and the National Committee hear from you!"

Which, of course, was a supremely shrewd piece of politics. In one short column she had neatly skewered the equivocations of the gentleman who was "certain, or almost certain," to be the candidate for President; and had, as much as possible, taken the decision out of his hands by appealing directly to the country, knowing full well that, provided the response was what she expected, it would be very difficult for him to set her aside. In that one column, she had taken an enormous and conceivably unstoppable stride toward the nomination.

"I *love* words!" she told me once years ago when we first came to the Senate. "You can make so many things *happen* with them!"

Few things she ever did with them happened so dramatically as the response to that column.

Within forty-eight hours of its appearance in the *Inquirer* and in her 432 client newspapers across the country, she had received some 250,000 replies and the National Committee had received more than 1,000,000. Of the total, more than 750,000 were entirely in her favor; only about 300,000 were negative; and of the remainder, most said they would be willing to give her enthusiastic support if that was the desire of the candidate.

And this was just the first response. As other publications and the rest of the media picked up the column and the story, its repetition brought succeeding waves for many days thereafter. When the flood at last began to slack off, it was found that Anna had a good, solid 10,000,000 backing her for Vice President. And the candidate was busy concealing his annoyance as gracefully as possible in the face of growing demands from delegates to the convention that he announce her selection even before he got there.

This he did not do, being in his homespun, calculating way an extremely shrewd politician himself; but he was unable to stop the flood of publicity on which Anna was floating happily to the top. Her colleagues of the media were delighted with her prospects, both as a news novelty and as the culmination of a career most of them fervently envied and admired; and the candidate was greeted everywhere with polite but annoyingly persistent questions. What did he think of Mrs. Hastings' candidacy? Was she on his list of prospects? Would he confer with her prior to the convention? How was he responding to the growing tide of delegates who wanted her on the ticket? ("It isn't any tide!" he snorted on one rare ruffled occasion. "Down home we'd consider it a little ole dinky creek!"—a response which drew great and open skepticism from his questioners.) Would he give her a Cabinet office if he did not select her as Vice President? Didn't he think it was time a woman got on the ticket, and wasn't she the most logical woman he could see anywhere?

And so on.

Finally, one week before the convention, he issued a formal statement in which he tried carefully to appease Anna, her delegates, the media, women, and anybody else who might be interested, while still leaving himself freedom of choice.

"Mrs. Anna Hastings," he said, "is one of the truly

326

great women of our time—brilliant of brain, beautiful of being, magnificent of personality, powerful of purpose. It is a great honor for her, as it is a great encouragement to me, that she should be receiving such admirable support for the office of Vice President. It guarantees that I will consider her most carefully in making my selection. I wish to thank all, particularly Mrs. Hastings herself, who have made this possible. It gives me an option I find highly appealing. I should feel deprived of much that is precious in the American spirit, much that is noblest in the simple, honest, God-fearing, home-loving, antibureaucratic heart of this great nation, if I did not have this option."

After which candid and unequivocal statement to the public he sent to Anna one of the very brightest of his many very bright young men to convey a private message which said, in effect:

I have the votes to stop you, sister, so knock it off.

"So," she asked us, eyes bright with excitement, determination and the sheer challenge of it—a long way now, thank goodness, from the forlorn figure we had seen a couple of months before—"shall I obey the great man, or shall I go ahead with it? Can I do more for the country by forcing the issue, or can I help it better right here?"

"I think you should do it," Tal said. "You won't be that far away, after all. I can run things here."

This switch of position of course was exactly what worried Bessie and me, now that we had successfully cured Anna of her slump with the therapy of political involvement—but there was no point in a pitched battle on the subject at this late date. It was years after the Senate hearing now; Tal was almost as full of journalistic praise and honors as she was. He had won that one handily and could never be dislodged; he could only be minimized, which Anna still did from time to time when even she felt that he was getting too far over. She was the sole remaining assurance of any kind of balance on the *Inquirer*—when she put her mind to it—and she was beginning to be aided now by the fact that the country seemed to be swinging back to a moderate middle-of-the-road position. Tal was fighting it every step of the way.

"Are you sure," Bessie asked cautiously, "that you really could do very much in that office? Of course it would be marvelous if you were elected and that little man dropped dead—President Anna Hastings, imagine! But if something like that didn't happen, then you'd be stuck for four years or maybe eight without anything to do."

"Yes, but at the end of that I might be able to run in my own right. What about that?"

"But, Anna," I said, trying not to make it sound as rough as it really was for all of us, "do you realize that we'll all be pushing sixty-five by then? That's pretty old to run for President."

"My God!" she said. "I can't believe we're that old! But we are, aren't we, team? We're getting there. Where has it all gone?"

And for several moments we were silent, thinking about this. Far back down the years four bright-eyed, earnest youngsters beckoned to us from the shining new world of Washington. *Hello, there!* they called, and *Hello, there!* we called back: *What happened to you? You were here just yesterday.*

"Well," she said, briskly bringing us out of our reverie, "*I* think probably the sensible thing for me to do is to stay right here. It's great fun, and I'd love to do it, and maybe he will drop dead and I'll always regret the chance I missed to be the first woman President. But on the other hand—even if I can beat his machine, which I doubt—I'd have to divest myself of all my interests here, put them in trust, divorce myself entirely from the *Inquirer* and the others, give up my column and my program, get out of the business entirely—I couldn't do it. It wouldn't be Anna Hastings. It wouldn't be me. Isn't that right, gang?"

"I think you're right," I said, and Bessie nodded fervently; and after a moment Tal said, and meant it, "I agree."

"However, she said, and the light of battle happily flared—our Anna wasn't giving up *all* the fun—"*however,* I think I'll let him sweat a bit. I think I'll just stay in there and let my name go before the convention and *then* I'll withdraw. I think I'll shake him up a little, just for the hell of it. It will be good for him to have *somebody* he feels he has to respect."

And that, as you all know, is exactly what she did.

She picked up the phone, gave us a wink, and called the candidate's brightest of bright young men. She said, smooth as butter, how much she appreciated the candidate's taking the time to give her his candid private opinion concerning her candidacy. She said that with great regret she could not accede to his wish that she withdraw, since that would not be her concept of how democracy worked in America. She said, sadly but firmly, that she didn't really see any way to quit now without greatly disillusioning "the many thousands—or rather, I should say, millions—who believe in me and have expressed their loyal and *unshakable* support." She said the only course she could see, "consistent with my duty to that constituency, and to my concept of what democracy *is* in a free country," would be to let her name go before the convention.

"I really can't see any way to prevent it," she said blandly, "so I guess we'll just have to see what happens. Now, of course, if he wishes to *offend* the many millions who are for me, if he wishes to *antagonize* the hundreds of devoted and dedicated delegates who are supporting my cause—"

"No, Mrs. Hastings," the voice of the brightest young man came over the amplifier, sounding as though he were spitting out acid and wormwood, "I am sure he has no desire to do that."

"Give him my dearest love and cordial best regards," she said cheerfully. "I'll be seeing you all at the convention."

"I'm sure!" said the brightest young man and hung up so fast she burst out laughing, rubbed her ear and said:

"Ouch!"

The rest, as you know, is history.

She went to the convention and we all went with her. Her headquarters was manned by swarms of fiercely eager volunteers who fanned out over that lively scene like a plague of locusts, arguing, cajoling, beseeching, converting—not enough to really affect the outcome, but enough to make the candidate extremely uncomfortable: he was so *earnestly* in search of unity. He tried privately to see her twice, she refused both times; our colleagues of the media picked up the struggle of wills and had a ball. On Thursday night, even though he had already announced his choice, there came the exciting moment (bringing tears to the eyes of the Old Team, even though we knew what was going to happen) when a booming voice said:

"And so, Mr. Chairman, Pennsylvania, the Keystone State, home of Independence Hall, haunt of Washington, Franklin, Jefferson, Adams, Hamilton and the other Founding Fathers, birthplace of liberty, fountainhead of democracy, proudly nominates for the Vice Presidency a great daughter of Pennsylvania, a great figure of her time, a great publisher, *a great woman—ANNA HASTINGS!!!*"

And the crowd, as they say, went wild.

She let it run on for 15 minutes and 18 seconds, according to the television clocks, before she stepped out from behind the backdrop and came forward, head high, arms outstretched, buoyant and happy, all else forgotten, to accept the roaring flood of sound that swelled up to greet her.

Small, blonde, perfectly coifed, perfectly dressed in a long white evening gown, wearing a single red rose and the huge diamond Gordon had given her on their engagement, looking no more than a youthful forty-five or so, she stood there for another seven minutes like a sleek little Miss Liberty, waving and smiling to the front, to the sides, to the back, a small, glistening, fairyland figure, fragile, delicate, ethereal—and, as the candidate and the media knew, as smart as Machiavelli and as tough as nails.

"Mr. Chairman," she said in a strong, clear voice, damping down the loving uproar with grateful gestures, "Mr. President"—and she turned to bow low to him in his box, his face desperately bland as he bowed and waved back—"delegates to this great convention! *Hasn't* it *been* a *great* convention!"

Whoops, roars, huzzahs.

"And in retrospect it's going to look even greater, because in November it will be seen that here in this great city we truly *did* nominate—the next President of the United States!"

Whoops, cheers, hubbub, halloos.

And again she bowed low to him, and again, mentally gritting his teeth, he returned it.

"Delegates!" she said, and the convention quieted abruptly.

"Delegates, first let me express my everlasting gratitude and thanks to those of you—those many, dedicated, loyal, wonderful ones!—who have worked so long and hard to give me this marvelous moment! I shall always be grateful to you for your love and your efforts, as long as I live!"

Yells, screams, shouts, jubilations.

"I only wish"—and abruptly they were quiet again, and the first groans, protests and cries of "No! No!!" began to rise—"I only wish"—firmly—"that it were possible for me to permit my name to remain before you, and to accept your nomination."

Dismay, chagrin, tears, moans (and an unsuppressible start of relief in the would-be Presidential box).

"However—however—I am afraid this cannot be. It is not because I do not appreciate the great, the infinite honor of serving with our great Presidential nominee."

Cheers, disappointed but still loyal.

"It is not because I do not believe in him, or that I will not support him, for that I intend to do, with every bit of strength that is in me, and with every means at my command!"

Knowing those means, more cheers, reconciled, pleased, happy.

"It is simply that I really have no choice. I want you to understand this, so that you will know that Anna Hastings is not insensible of your great honor, is not insensitive to your great cause, but wants only to work —*with you*—*in the ranks*—for inevitable victory in November!"

Great and rising whoops, huzzahs, affectionate cheers; scattered cries of "Good old Anna!" "She's our gal!" etc., etc.

"All my working life," she said solemnly, and now they listened in an intent and respectful silence, "I have been a newspaperwoman—or newspaper*person*, as we say, more fittingly, nowadays. All my working life I have been dedicated to the First Amendment, to freedom of the press, to the strengthening of the media and their preservation as the greatest bulwark of liberty that we have.

"You all know that I have been blessed with some success in these endeavors."

Laughter, warm, affectionate, flattered; renewed cries of "Good old Anna!" "You tell 'em, babe!" etc., etc.

"The newspaper business has been my whole life. It *is* my whole life. I hope it will continue to be my whole life for many years to come."

Cheers, shouts, bombinations, tintinnabulations.

"It seems to me that I can best serve this great, beloved country of ours by remaining right where I am —on the front line in the battle for freedom. On the front line of democracy. Enlisted with all my heart and soul in the cause of freedom.

"This is why I, Anna Hastings, must decline your nomination for Vice President tonight."

Renewed applause, cheers, huzzahs, forgetful, as she intended, that she hadn't received the nomination and didn't really have the votes to get it.

"That is why I, Anna Hastings, must decline this wonderful honor and return to my place in the ranks.

"Because I can do more for our beloved country.

"Because I can do more for this precious dream of liberty we all share.

"Because I can help your great candidate much better this way.

"Because I am *one of you,* and that is how I want it *always* to remain.

"Thank you, my dear, lovely friends! God bless you all, God bless our great candidate, God bless the United States of America!

"And good night."

Again the hall was pandemonium, reaching a wild, ecstatic crescendo when it was perceived that the candidate was leaving his box and preparing to come to the podium. Smiling, waving, perfectly self-possessed and with only the most decorous—or so it seemed to us, standing just below her in the press section—hint of amusement touching the corners of her mouth, Anna awaited him.

When he reached her side on a long, swelling tidal wave of sound, he kissed her with a warmth that minimized but did not entirely conceal a heartfelt relief. She returned it with a bland and gracious air. He seized her hand in his, raised it high above as they waved to the singing, dancing, chanting convention. Then he released her hand, raised both of his for silence. Obediently it came.

"Dearest Anna," he said, and there were approving shouts, "dearest Anna, you are a marvel and an example to us all. I admire your willing sacrifice in the interests of party unity, I deeply appreciate your loyalty and endorsement and I happily welcome your support in the campaign. And after November, I shall look to you to help and guide me in all I do."

He turned to her with a beaming smile, then back to the crowd.

"Thank God America has Anna Hastings!" he cried. "She is, and will always be, the First Lady of Our Hearts!"

(That was the night that Alice Roosevelt Longworth, interviewed in the gallery by CBS, came out with *"E pluribus Anna!"*)

Then they turned, hands linked again, and waved and bowed and laughed while the hall broke apart with sound. Somewhere along the way before it ended, 10 minutes and 29 seconds later, Anna caught our eyes in one of her turns to wave to the gallery above. For just a second she stared at us, off guard and heartbreakingly sad. Then she snapped out of it, gave us a knowing grin, a quick wink and a happy wave.

The leader of the Old Team was still a little shaky, but basically, we realized with grateful relief, she was back on top of her world again.

Epilogue

"THE
FIRST LADY
OF
OUR HEARTS"

———

This last Christmas I went home, as I have on many major anniversaries over the years, to be with my parents in Punxsutawney. They are in their eighties, now, filled with years and the honor given them by a large and close-knit family. There amid my brothers and sisters and their families, I renewed my faith in the simple goodness of America, the strong roots from which I come, the kindness of decent folk toward one another. Essentially, I suppose, I am still little Anna Kowalczek from Punxsutawney, Pa. I sometimes think Anna Hastings lives in some other world, though I know we are the same. A tribute, an homage, a strengthening, a renewal—such have been my visits home. It is good for me to remember the simple sod from which I sprang.

—Anna Hastings, *by Anna Hastings*

"Ed," she said a week before the holiday, her voice sounding oddly nervous and tense over the phone, "where are you going to be for Christmas?"

"I've been planning to go to my sister in Florida," I said. "Why, have you got a better offer?"

"Well, I was thinking," she said carefully. "You went to Florida last year, didn't you?"

"Every year. It's a family ritual. Why?"

"Well, I was just wondering if—if maybe this time you might like to—to come home with me to Punxsutawney. I've talked to Bess and Tal and they're going to come. It would be great to have the team together. LeRoy and Kate are going, too, so we can all ride up in the Continental."

"You haven't heard from the kids," I said quietly, and for just a second her voice broke.

"N-no. So I thought maybe it would be great fun to have you all with me. If," she added with a rare humility that I could tell was genuine, "you would be —be willing to, that is. You know my family, they're nice, you'll enjoy being with them. Do you think maybe—? It would really mean an awful lot to me."

"Why, sure, Anna," I said, wondering how I was going to break the news to my own family, who would not be happy. "If you need us, we'll be there."

"I think I do," she said in a lost-little-girl voice that threatened for just a moment to give way to tears but with great determination did not. "Yes, I think maybe I do."

"O.K. I'll look forward to it."

"Bless you all," she said. "You're my own true friends."

And only, I thought. *And only*.

So early on December 24 we started out to join the long last-minute caravans out of the District to neighboring states and cities. The day was cold, gray, crisp, threatening snow, but the big car was snug and warm as LeRoy piloted us carefully north through the bare-branched countryside. Kate had made up a picnic

340

lunch, the built-in bar Gordon had ordered installed when he got the car three years ago was full of goodies, and before long we were all talking a blue streak and having a great time. Anna's noticeable depression as we pulled away from empty Patowmack House began to lighten as we went along; in a little while she was chatting away as gaily as the rest of us. As she had predicted, more wistful then than convinced, it really *was* great fun to be together again, out for a lark, relaxed and happy, all else forgotten. By the time we reached Punxsutawney in the afternoon Bessie, Tal and I were thoroughly glad we had come. We could see it was doing wonders for Anna, and that was still, in the old loyal way that by now was not only habit but almost instinct, our most important concern.

As we drove into town LeRoy suddenly spoke up in a delighted voice. "Why, Mrs. Hastings! Look at that!"

And there, just beneath "PUNXSUTAWNEY CITY LIMITS," was another sign, obviously new, gleaming white through the gloomy day:

HOME OF ANNA HASTINGS,
JOURNALIST, POLITICAL LEADER,
FINE CITIZEN,
GREAT AMERICAN:
PUBLISHER OF THE WASHINGTON "INQUIRER"

"Isn't that nice," Bessie said softly, "Isn't that nice!"

"Oh, dear," Anna said. "I think I'm going to cry."

And started to for a moment until Tal said in a loud voice, "Now, now, Famous Publisher! Stop that nonsense! It's Christmas Eve and we're all here and everybody's happy! Right? *Right!* And I'm going to have one more quick one before we get to the house. Join me, anybody?"

341

"Sure," I said, against my better judgment but anything to divert Anna. "Bess?"

"Oh *what* the *hell!*" she said, holding out her glass. "Come on, Anna! All we can do is fall at your folks' feet when we come in the door."

"They're Polish," Anna said, brightening up with a chuckle. "They like people who enjoy life. My dad in particular can handle a few. But make mine light if you will, Tal . . . *light,* I said! Somebody has to be dignified when we get there."

"We will defer to our 'stinguished—'stinguished leader," Tal said solemnly. "The Firsh—Firsh Lady of Our Harsh!"

Which struck us all as mightily amusing as we turned into the Kowalczeks' quiet residential street and came finally to the modest house where her folks had lived for more than sixty years. ("I've tried to buy them a bigger one," Anna told me years ago, "but they won't have it. They're happy where they are, so that's fine with me.") Seven or eight cars were already there; from the house came a loud babble of happy talk. The three brothers, two sisters, respective in-laws and kids had obviously already taken over.

It had been probably ten years since we had been to Anna's home. She used to invite us up now and again for family occasions, and about once a year her parents or some brother or sister, and family, would come down to Washington for a few days, stay at Patowmack House to enjoy the exciting and alien life of their glamorous relative; but in recent years as things had grown tenser with Gordon and the children, this had dropped off, though the kids continued to go up to Punxsutawney from time to time. So we knew everybody in a general way, but of course by this time there were older kids, more kids, aging sisters, older brothers, fewer hairs, grayer hairs, more wrinkles, extra pots.

342

Family life: lots of years and lots of changes. We were instantly swept into the warm embrace of the Kowalczeks; hailed by Kowalczeks, kissed by Kowalczeks, hands shaken by Kowalczeks, backs slapped by Kowalczeks, smothered in Kowalczeks. Everybody talked at once, nobody listened, everybody had a marvelous time.

Anna's parents, still a little in awe of their famous daughter and her Washington friends after all these years, greeted us shyly, two little old dried-up people who peered up at us with bright little smiles and bright little eyes that didn't miss a thing. Both of them hugged Anna with a special fierceness that told how glad they were to see her, how much they loved her, how proud of her they were; how sorry they were that she couldn't bring her own family, how much they wanted her to be happy. Again she came close to tears, but with extra hilarity from us and from brothers and sisters who also perceived this, we all managed to keep things light and roaring. Family gossip took over for a while and we became lost in a sea of names and interlocking events that meant little to us but were obviously great for Anna, who became so immersed in questioning that presently she even lapsed into a little rusty Polish, which brought cheers and applause from everybody. By now she was truly home.

Sometime in the early dusk somebody shouted in English, "Evening star!"—and then, *"Wigilia!"* which we guessed meant "Vigil." Mother Kowalczek clapped her hands together solemnly; everybody moved toward the tables that had been set up in the dining room, the living room and the tiny den. There were three, each with twelve place settings—eleven for the family, one of the brothers explained to me, the twelfth for a stranger—in the old country in the old days, it might be left vacant for Christ Himself.

"This time it's you guys," he said with an amiable chuckle. "None of you looks very holy, but we're sure glad to have you." So, one at each table, Bess, Tal and I led the way and the family followed, pausing only for the *opłatek* ceremony before sitting down.

The older kids, who were doing the serving, passed *opłatki,* unleavened flour wafers stamped with figures of Christ and angels. We were instructed to break them into little pieces and pass them around the tables as far as they would go, everybody wishing everybody else health, happiness and prosperity, the loudest of all being Mother and Father Kowalczek, who jointly presented a piece to Anna and in determined little voices cried, "Dear Anna, *happiness!*" Which of course brought on another tight moment. But she managed—a little better, I think, than Bessie, Tal and I did, right then.

Then we sat down, Kate, LeRoy and I at Anna's table, while the kids brought on the nine-course meal, which, since Christmas Eve is traditionally a fast day, contained no meat. We dined on *barszcz,* a soup made from sour oatmeal containing, so the sister on my right explained to me, spoonfuls of *grzyby,* mushrooms, and *ziemiaki,* mashed potatoes.

This was followed by a course of *ryba,* or fish (and plenty of wine, which made things even merrier), and then by platters of *pierogi,* boiled dough turnovers filled with *kapusta,* sauerkraut, and *śliwki,* prunes.

After a couple of hours of this, thoroughly awash in food, wine, harmony and contentment, we sat back while one of Anna's nephews played the piano and everybody sang *kolędy,* Polish carols in which the three of us and Kate and LeRoy joined with some determined humming that won us an amused round of applause at the end. Then suddenly it was eleven and everybody was bustling about stacking dishes, gathering coats, going to the bathroom, making last-minute repairs before leaving for midnight mass.

Anna had long since strayed from the Church; Bessie, Tal and I were Protestants of no particular persuasion; Kate and LeRoy were real, old-fashioned, down-South Southern Baptists; but as Anna said, "It won't hurt any of us to be prayed over, no matter who does it." So in a few minutes the party was walking amicably along toward the local church, which was only six or seven blocks from the elder Kowalczeks' home.

We walked slowly, Anna and two of her brothers in the lead, the rest of us straggling along in no particular order. There came a moment when I was alone. I became aware that I was being overtaken. Mother and Father Kowalczek, trotting along like two determined little bundled-up chipmunks, appeared puffing and twinkling at my side.

"That Anna," her father said presently after catching his breath, voice lowered so the others would not hear. "She is very famous."

"Very," I agreed.

"She has much power in great places."

"Yes, much."

"Is she happy?"

I turned and looked down into their earnest faces, shadowed with worry for this awesome and, I am sure to them (and hell, not only to them, of course), unknowable child, and decided there would be no point in lying.

"I don't know," I said slowly. "I don't think she is, really. But she manages."

"Yes," her father said heavily. "We all manage. But we had hoped for something better for our Anna, when she became so famous."

"She has what she wants," I said.

"She doesn't have what her brothers and sisters have," her mother said. "She doesn't have family."

"No," I agreed. "They've gone away. But they may come back."

"I don't think so," her mother said. "I worry for my Anna."

"Don't you think her old friends do?"

"I know," she said, placing a light little hand on my arm. "I know, I'm sorry. We are very grateful for what you three have done for Anna, all these years. Sometimes we think about her and you are our only hope."

"We try to help her."

"Can anybody?" her father asked heavily. "Is it possible?"

"I don't know," I said soberly, "but I know we three are going to keep right on trying."

And so we have, and so we do, and so we always will, as the years march on for the Old Team and we draw further and further away from those wonderful, bright, untarnished years of the Senate and R Street and youth and idealism and corridor-tramping together for news stories on the Hill. The four brave ghosts are with us still—somewhere. And brightest of them all is Anna's—somewhere.

The kids, to date, have not come back, and there is very little sign that they will. Gordie has dropped college and gone home to run the Circle H: he loves it. Lisa has decided to finish at Smith and then go into decorating: she loves that, too, and she is very good at it. Every couple of months they meet here in Washington, and then Bess and I get a phone call, and we take them out to lunch or dinner. They ask after Anna, though they never go near the house and we never tell her they have been here; and usually they both wind up crying, and we cry too, and nothing resolves itself

346

and we all part with bittersweet farewells and the earnest promise that *maybe next time*—but next time doesn't come. And we see Anna quite often, for she calls us frequently to the paper for advice as in the old days, and on quite frequent occasions we will have a meal with her and a chance to really talk. And she almost—almost—cries too, although the other day at Sans Souci when I accused her of it, she dashed her hand across her eyes, gave me a defiant look and said vigorously:

"Nonsense! I won't cry! Anna Hastings doesn't cry!"

"We've known a few times when you did," Bessie said.

"Yes," she conceded. "But not ever again. For anything or anybody."

And so it goes on, all three unfortunately being possessed more of her iron than of Gordon's placid amicability.

Professionally, the *Inquirer* and Hastings Communications continue to flourish. So does their owner. She remains one of Washington's great hostesses, and in her profession by now she has received so many awards, so many kudos, so many flattering articles, respectful interviews, worshipful references, that there is probably no woman in America, probably in the world, who is better known or better liked by the public than Anna Hastings. She alternates with the Queen for No. 1 on "World's Most Admired Woman" lists and never lacks for praise.

Politically, she is, as she puts it, "in reserve." Her relations with the White House are close again—I think the candidate regrets his burbling convention statement that after November he would "look to you to help and guide me in all I do," because she does, via column, editorial and frequent telephone call. There has been talk from time to time that he would appoint her to something—Ambassador to the Court of Saint James was one firm offer, but she turned him down, much to his secret chagrin. He had thought Grosvenor Square would be far enough away so he couldn't be bothered: she preferred to remain on H Street, next to typewriter and telephone.

"I still may run for something," she says dreamily once in a while. "I still may."

But I don't really think she will. She has too much clout where she is.

Bessie, Tal and I go along about the same. Anna had Bess help her rush out her autobiography immediately after the Vice Presidential caper, "just to lay the groundwork," as she put it to us with a chuckle, and since then Bess has been occupied with more of her inside books on the offbeat side of official Washington. They sell very well (Anna's of course was the best: it's already hit 250,000 in hardback, the paperback has just begun to roll, and the movie is going to give it an extra zap for a while) and Bessie seems quite content. She still tries to diet occasionally, but it's a lost cause and she knows it.

"Damn it, Bess," Tal said impatiently last time we were all together and she was debating a hot fudge sundae, "go ahead and have it. What's a pound to you, for Christ's sake?"

"A girl still has her illusions," she agreed cheerfully as she ordered it, "but I don't let mine stand in the way of my appetite."

Tal is still running the news side of the *Inquirer* pretty much as he pleases, aside from the occasional cautionary interferences from Anna, and probably will until he retires. He has never referred to our conflict at the hearing, nor have I. We still have lunch together from time to time and I suppose there are still colleagues in Washington who are puzzled by this, as I think perhaps some of them have always been puzzled by our rather odd but enduring foursome.

It seems odd to me sometimes, too, but then something will happen such as happened to me the other day when I was on the Hill attending a Senate Foreign Relations Committee hearing on SALT II. It turned out to be dull, without much real column material. I left early and started walking back through the office buildings to the Senate side of the Capitol.

Far down the hall I saw three youngsters, two boys and a girl. (How they would have been insulted by those terms!—they were probably at least twenty-two.) They were carrying pads and ball-point pens, a clutch of press releases, frayed copies of the day's *Inquirer* and *Post*. They possessed an earnest and harried air.

They started toward me, then stopped suddenly to debate something. As I came nearer they looked at each other, walked a few steps, came to a big oaken door, turned abruptly and went in. "MR. BAKER, TENNESSEE," it said. I hope they got the story they were after.

That's why we're still together, I think: that and the general interest and excitement of being around Anna.

As Seab predicted so long ago, bless his heart, it's been quite a skeerazzle.

Yes, sir.

Quite a skeerazzle.

May–August, 1976

THE BEST OF THE BESTSELLERS
FROM WARNER BOOKS!

THE BEST OF THE BESTSELLERS
FROM WARNER BOOKS!

W A Warner Communications Company